"I really enjoyed this book. I wanted to continue reading it because I wanted to know what was happening with each character in the book. Couldn't put it down. Was a great read."

Patricia Demiranda, Co-founder, The William Trippley Youth
Development Foundation and Chester City United

"A captivating read from page one! An awesome page-turner throughout!"

Valeria Ann West, Researcher, Temple University-ISR Field Interviewer

"When I Close My Eyes" is a must read. It is rich and full of detailed research by the author. The book is exceptional in every way. It's a collector's item for young and old alike. It's no exaggeration to say that D.E. as I call her has done a flawless job in her first book. Her enthusiasm, dedication and professionalism shine through on every page. The book is an excellent investment and will provide many hours of enjoyment. It definitely kept my attention. Can't wait for the sequel!!!"

Shavon Tucker, CEO, Barshots by Shay's, Hater Blockers' Boutique

"Curl up in your favorite chair, grab a pillow and blanket and get comfortable. You are about to engage in a page turning adventure that you won't put down until finished. Then, you'll hunger for the sequel. Donna Earl nails the story of intercity; inter family and the effect of external forces on them that deletes the box. A must read, "When I Close My Eyes" is a Nubian soap for the ages."

Dr. Robert A. Benson, Author, Educator, Radio Talk Show Host

WHEN I CLOSE MY EYES

Donna Earl

Library of Congress Control Number:		2015921173
ISBN:	Hardcover	978-1-5144-3734-6
	Softcover	978-1-5144-3733-9
	eBook	978-1-5144-3732-2

Print information available on the last page.

Rev. date: 02/22/2016

To order additional copies of this book, contact:
Xlibris
1-888-795-4274
www.Xlibris.com
Orders@Xlibris.com
732240

FOREWORD

2 Thessalonians 1:6-9
New International Version (NIV)

⁶ God is just: He will pay back trouble to those who trouble you ⁷ and give relief to you who are troubled, and to us as well. This will happen when the Lord Jesus is revealed from heaven in blazing fire with his powerful angels. ⁸ He will punish those who do not know God and do not obey the gospel of our Lord Jesus.

T HIS IS THE last journey for me. I know where I'm going; but, let me tell you where I've been and what I've been through.

Sexual molestation, murder, betrayal, easy money, child out of wedlock. HOPE. It's where you've been; what you know has been. It's life in all its glory: REDEMPTION; GRACE unlimited; LOVE as deep as the oceans and as high as the sky; its FAITH and recognized MERCY. Through it all, we sometimes experience a lack of connection – when we close all our main lines to God to be broken and lose sight of our true purpose. It's forgetting our purpose here on this earth.

When I Close My Eyes. What will you/I remember about me/you?

ACKNOWLEDGEMENTS

FIRST OF ALL, Thank you GOD for making this all possible. I didn't realize I had this in me, but you knew it all the time.

Thank you for the best parents, Jake and Anna Mae Earl with the best parental guidance money can't buy. Thank you for showing me money don't mean everything…that it's all about LOVE. You led with iron fists but hearts filled with so much love that you put your wants and needs aside to make life better for your "biddies." Thank you for the butt whoopings when necessary because you knew I could do better.

Thank you to my brothers and sisters. I love you from the bottom of my heart. Just the thought of you makes me laugh and cry all at the same time. I couldn't ask for a better bunch of people to be related to.

Thank you to my support system, Charlie's Angels plus 1 - Jane, Elyse, Jackie and Roseanne, my girls from way back. Where would I be without you?

Thanks to Robin Blyden of the DC Metropolitan Department. Thanks for answering all my non-stop questions about police work, Robin this and Robin that. Thank you for the "twist" Detective Coleman.

Thank you to Cressie Leona Kearse. Girl, you were my inspiration the whole way thru. I dedicate the title "When I Close my Eyes" to you. You said this daily, giving us fair warning for what was to come. I miss you, your heart and your spirit, straight with no chaser. I told you I was going to do it.

Thank you to Franchette aka "Shavon". My fellow Capricorn born on the same day. Girl, you were always looking out for a sister. You are my "behind the scenes" wall of information. A girl with a definite hustle, Barshots by Shay.

Thank you to my 7th grade English Teacher, Ms. Constance Brown, the "English Ninja." At the time, I didn't realize the importance of the written word, but I do now. Thank you for your "Red Pen."

Thank you to Vickie West, Ms. "Grownie" as I call you. You can verbally rip a person to shreds and smile all at the same time. Thank you for your hard work on this project. I couldn't have done it without you, putting up with my nerve wrecking phone calls. I know I got on your nerves.

Thank you to Teeann Hawkins, a friend since Morgan State University. So sorry you had to leave me but GOD had something else for you to do. If it wasn't for you giving me my first novel to read, I doubt this would be.

Thank you to Dylan, my sunshine. My source of energy when I wanted to give up, my hug when I needed it and my truth always, no matter how brutal. You don't sugar coat nothing. Thanks Sweetie.

Again, I must thank GOD for putting all the pieces together to make this happen. Thank you for each "piece" for bringing out what I had in me all the time.

CHAPTER ONE

WELL, IT'S FINALLY here. It took ten years, but it's finally here. Today is the day it's my funeral. My body is in the casket at the Funeral Home, all decked out. I already checked it out and I am looking fly. Just wait till they see me. Picture it. I am dressed in a slamming outfit, not some nightgown with slippers, but dressed in a beige silk blouse with a brown plaid skirt, a pair of nylons with the seams up the back and a pair of bad, brown sling backs pumps. This outfit is saying something. I brought that outfit months ago, thinking that I would wear it before now, but as you can see....

When I knew it was about that time, I talked to my sister for a long time. As a matter of fact, I made sure that I talked to each one of my brothers and Cece. Barbara and I, we talked about our childhood, about Mom and Daddy and what our childhood could have been if it wasn't for what happened. I told her that I loved her and if there was anything I said or did that hurt her, that I was sorry. I told her what type of casket, flowers and what I wanted to wear at my home going. I wanted to look sharp on that day and baby, I am wearing it. Looking at the arrangements, Barbara followed my wants to the letter.

My body should be here momentarily, all decked out, but as you know, people think that once you're dead, you're dead, but the hell if I am. I am right here, standing in Cletus M. Crockett's' Funeral Home vestibule, looking out the window, waiting for all the people to arrive. Crockett's' Funeral Home is located on the corner of 13th and Kerlin Street, right across the street from Anthony's, a sandwich shop that sells some mean hoagies. Damn, I can almost smell those bad boys. Crockett's has a beautiful landscape, small, but beautiful with a pillar trees and beautiful plants. It looks like a mini mansion with two floors and a driveway. It's a beautiful day, a bit breezy and a little cloudy, but at least it's not raining. It should be a good turn-out, at least I hope…it better be, but you never know.

Oh, what's that I see…I see something coming down Kerlin Street… Oh damn, it's the hearse! The hearse, riding all slow, is all shiny, black and long, and looks like it just got a car wash, rims shining and the tires…wow, I'm shitting in high cotton today, at least my body is. You know Crockett's' Funeral Home sho nuff know how to put it down. The car is at the light and now it's turning the corner. Uh oh, it's stopped, parked and the rear door is opening and they're sliding the casket out. Barbara, I love you!!! It's beautiful!!! Its pearl white with gold trim, I wanted a red casket in the beginning, but as an alternate, I told her white and it's just what I asked. They better not drop it. They didn't. Thank You Jesus!!!

Hmm, now the mourners are arriving, all jazzed up, some parking on Kerlin Street, across from the Funeral Home and others along 13th. I see friends and family. If they could see me now, looking at them… ha!! Now that would be funny. There's my sisters Barbara and Cecelia, Cece for short. That's what she called herself when she was little and couldn't say her name. There's my brothers Rusty (real name Russell) and Reese (real name Maurice). Cece looks nice, but Barbara looks like she's going to the club instead of a funeral with that short-ass dress on. What she trying to do - get a man at a funeral? Rusty's hair is a little gray now, kind of lost its shine.

Will you take a look at Maurice? He looks hung over, face all puffy and eyes red, so red they look orange. Look at the suit he's wearing. That can't be a suit looking like that. Oh, he has on a sweater and slacks. The sweater, from where I'm standing, looks like it's full of lint. Did he just pull it out of the dirty clothes? He needs one of those, what you call them? Yeah, the Miracle Brush. Mom used to have one of them. It really worked. Well, at least they are here. OMG its Francine and Sandy from Juvey!!! They're here!!! Oh, and I see Michael coming and he is walking kind of slow. He's crying!! Oh, baby, don't cry. I hate to see him cry. Wow, he looks like he has aged in 2 weeks and he has the kids with him. Look at my babies, Justin and Julia. I'm so sorry that I had to leave you. Get her hand Justin. Don't let her fall.

Where's Donna? I just knowed she be here. That's my girl. We met when I was coming home from my first job at the water company on 5th street after leaving "Juvey." Aunt Jane got me on. She knew Anthony Games, the Director there. She was my across the street neighbor when I moved to the West side of Chester from the East side of Chester, living

DONNA EARL

behind the Sacred Heart Hospital, in those apartments called Park Terrace on Curran Street. I lived on the East side of Chester, when I first moved from Philly, in my past life (I'll tell you about that later). Just in case you don't know, Chester is a pin drop of a city, located south of Philly and north of Delaware. I would see Donna from time to time, not knowing which building she lived in. We met one Friday evening when I was going home. It was packed outside, people milling around, drinking beer, talking etc. She was standing on the sidewalk with Linda in front of her apartment. Linda lived on the same side of the street I did in the apartments over in the next building. She was married to Keith, with one child and another one on the way. Linda called me, "Hey girl, how you doing? You just getting off?" Crossing the street, walking over to them, I said, "Yeah girl, just getting off after putting in my eight." "I am so damn tired; these people think I am a machine, working me to death. Thank God it's Friday."

See, at the time, I was a receptionist at the water company, guarding the door from them knuckleheads, coming in there complaining about their damn bill. They had no idea that…that ain't none of their business anyway. I didn't know them like that. Michael warned me not to volunteer nothing. I was taking Saturday classes to become a paralegal at the Y annex on 7th and Sproul, right across from the Babyland Clothing Store.

We all laughed and kept talking. As the conversation got good, it took on another subject and we started talking about life and I mentioned that I had diamonds, furs and the like (lying my ass off… trying to sound important) and Donna said, "Well, the only way you could have had all that, you had to have been a mistress or a prostitute." I didn't comment right away, but as I walked away switching, I turned back, smiled and winked, leaving them with their mouths open and a lot on their minds. Wondering. I never had any of these things…there I go trying to sound important.

As weeks and months went by, I would see Donna, exchanging pleasantries, but for some reason, we became more and more friends. We would talk, but I knew she wanted to know more about me, but I would shy away from getting into details since that conversation we had before. So one day, we were having laughs and drinks and so...

Well, it all began…Hold up!!! I have to straighten something out. I want to apologize. I know my language… it may be a little ghetto, but

I've got to tell it my way. Now… Oh wait…how rude of me, I haven't introduced myself…my name is Ruth Louise Walters Campbell. What a name huh? That's an old country name except for Walters. I guess Walters puts a little sophistication on a name like Ruth Louise. Well, that's me. They call me Ruthie for short. I am the third oldest of five. I have two older brothers, Rusty, (real name Russell) he was called Rusty because he has red hair and Reese (real name Maurice). I have two younger sisters, Cecelia and Barbara. I was born on September 20th 19 something…none of your damn business…ha ha!!! Shame on you for trying to guess a woman's age. You never ask a woman that. Well, here goes…

CHAPTER TWO

M Y PARENTS' NAMES were Samuel and Beulah Walters. Both my parents were from Durham, North Carolina. They met as high school sweethearts and wed at an early age. They moved to Philadelphia with promises of good living 'up north' as they call it, from the south by my uncle on my father's side named Louie. Weren't they surprised when they arrived! They took the only jobs they could find - my father a cook and my mother a nurses' aide.

They did pretty good - as good as they could. We lived in Philly, West Philly on Delancey Street, 59th and Delancey, as a matter of fact. Delancey is a little street with row houses, houses on both sides of the street. All the houses had porches, eat-in kitchens and 3 bedrooms. My Mom and Daddy shared one, of course, my sisters and I shared one and my brothers shared the other one. Oh, how I loved sitting on the porch, watching everything going and coming. We didn't live too far from 69th Street in Darby and down the street from Cobbs Creek Park. Our house sat in the middle of the block.

Our neighbour on the left was Mr. Close, who had three sons, Skip, Ernie and Johnnie. All had nappy hair except for Johnnie. He had nice hair, curly and black. I had a crush on him. I use to imagine me running my hands through his hair. I was a fresh little girl early on. Tee hee. Our neighbors on the right were Ms. Mary and Mr. Bill who had a daughter and son, Juanita and Thomas. Our neighbors, immediately across the street were Mr. and Mrs. Collins who had 3 daughters and 2 sons, Rick, Michael, Joanne, Cathy and Brenda. Brenda became one of my best friends until they moved over to New Jersey. I really miss her because we went to Elementary and Junior High School together. We had another neighbor who lived two doors from us named Ms. Etta. She was sweet as pie, but she was so damn nosey. She would sit in her window day and night watching everything. She would know everybody's business, telling who was running with who etc., but when something happened, she did not see nothing. Her favorite saying was,

"Chile, I didn't see a thing, I didn't see a damn thing." She was the one neighbor whose house I ran over to on the fateful night when my life changed forever.

In our neighborhood, we all had small backyards; small backyards where Mom would hang clothes on the line and where my brothers had to put their sneakers because they stank so bad! We had neighbors that stayed in the back of us, Thelma and Buster Holmes. I gotta tell you about these two. They were slinging liquor and kept company day in and day out. Mr. Buster worked on cars and I believe, had a hidden still out back somewhere and Ms. Thelma was an undercover numbers runner. You know, back then you went to her to "put your number in." Like I said, they kept plenty of company, people running in and out of their house all day. They had one daughter named Shirlene, Shirley for short. On more than one occasion, they would play cards, drink and laugh damn near all night. Mr. Buster would plunk that guitar and moan and the others would join in. It's a wonder my brothers ever got any sleep on those nights because their bedroom window faced their backyard. Big Louie, the neighborhood cop, paid a visit there on more than one occasion to silence the noise.

Their backyard was filled with stuff, a picnic table and they even had an old car out there. Let me explain something. Ms. Thelma had a bad habit of coming to the back door and throwing food out in the yard just on GP. That drew rats. With that old car and Ms. Thelma providing food, it was nothing for us to see rats jumping in and out that car because that was their home. The rats were so bad, we would sit on our back step, take a BB gun, pump it about ten times and pick them off like target practice. We had alley cats or street cats, but they were no match for those bad boys. They were as big as they were. They ran that yard and they would not back down. They looked at the cats and seemed to say, "Bring it."

So, one day, my mother and brother were in the kitchen and my Mom says, "Reece, come here." Maurice says, "Yes Mom." She says, "Thelma, just threw some damn food out in the trash can and a rat jumped in there. Go over there and put the lid on the can." See Ms. Thelma kept her trash cans against the fence, so with a smile on his face, he says "Yes ma'am." So he went out the backdoor, walked over to the fence. He picked up a stick and stuck it through a hole in the fence and pushed the lid on the can and snuck back in the house. So those

DONNA EARL

two waited, Mom in the kitchen and Maurice in another part of the house nearby. So when Ms. Thelma came to door, my Mom shouted, "Reece, hurry up. She's coming to put more trash in the can!" Maurice came running and they both watched her. When she took that lid off the trash can, that rat jumped out and Ms. Thelma damn nearly a heart attack. She screamed, dropped the trash she was about to put in the can and ran in the house, skipping the bottom step. My Mom and brother laughed and laughed and laughed! My Mom, said, "I betcha that will teach her ass a damn lesson about throwing trash out in the yard."

Then there was another time Mr. Buster and his friends went to New Jersey and brought back a live pig. Do you hear me, a live pig? They tied that pig up and began drinking and plunking on that guitar. They were partying back. The pig was standing there looking around. In his mind I guess the pig was thinking, "why am I here and what in the hell is going on." We, as kids, had the nerve to play with it. Well, after their bellies were full and everything, you heard a big BAM! The pig squealed and then BAM! BAM! Old Junnie had taken an axe and hit the pig. The pig laid down shivering in pain and he hit the pig once more and it was over. Fresh pig meat was had, pig feet, chitterling etc. Their daughter, Shirlene, refused to eat any of it. My brothers and I watched the whole thing from their bedroom window. As I said before, their window faced their backyard. My Mom was watching too from the back door. What a sight! Blood everywhere!

What a neighborhood I lived in. People just lived. I remember another time; we were in bed. It had to be about 11:30 or midnight. That same house (Mr. Buster and Ms. Thelma) had a party and Mr. Dickie went up the street speeding, high out of his mind made a turn, a dead man's turn and flipped his car on one side. We all heard the noise, including other neighbors and we jumped out of bed and ran outside to see the car on one side. We had a big laugh about that.

We played kid games like softball in Mr. Leroy's field. He lived down the street. He didn't mind. He loved to see us kids play. We played kick the can, red light, green light, hide n go seek, Chinese and regular jump rope, and so much more. I remember Rusty and Maurice were playing in the field across the street from Mr. Leroys'. They called themselves making hotdogs that they stole from the house and set it on fire. The tried to pee on it and everything, but the fire wouldn't go out and got bigger. The next thing you know the fire department was called. This lady that lived near there told my Mom that Rusty and Maurice did it. My Mom and Mrs. Leroy (Mr. Leroy's wife) cussed her out. That was so funny! It took Reese and Rusty to get older to finally confess that the lady was telling the truth.

The best special memory I have of our childhood that tops all memories is, every Christmas morning, we would be waiting on pins and needles for the signal…Daddy would bang on the wall and yell "Merry Xmas!!!" Man oh man we would throw back the covers and dash to the tree. Mommy and Daddy would look at us as we opened up our gifts. They loved to see the excitement in our eyes. One year, we had a race to see who could get to the tree first. Maurice stomped his toe and turned around and got right back in the bed. We laughed so hard!!! We teased him about that for years. Boy, I miss those times. Those were the days of good old fashion fun and laughter.

CHAPTER THREE

I ATTENDED SAVILLE WILLIAMS Elementary School. Elementary school was hard for me as a kid. There were a few good times. One time in particular was when I entered into a talent show with a few of my neighborhood friends. We were called the Psychedelic Kids. The memory of it makes me smile. My parents were big on education. They didn't necessarily finish school so anything short of our best was not accepted. They didn't play. My mother would yell "you must have the "D" disease coming home with all these D's on your report card. You know all the words to the songs that play on the radio even the umphs. Let me see how many umphs you yell out when I'm whooping your ass for bringing home another bad report card."

My parents didn't have a lot of money to buy new clothes all the time, so we had to wear hand-me-downs and our sneakers were brought at the supermarket. I got picked on damn near every day. They would tease me about my clothes, shoes, hair and my looks and I would cry in silence, afraid to fight back. They would often approach me saying, "I heard you was talking about me" or some other childish thing and tell me "I am going to get you after school." I would spend all day at school with butterflies in my stomach, scared to death. Then the school bell would ring and damn, here we go. I would go home and my clothes would be torn and my Mom would say "Girl, what happened to your clothes?" I was afraid to tell so I'd lie. "I fell." It was a nightmare.

I believe that my brothers knew I was teased and they would pick at me, trying to get me to fight. I guess that was their way of teaching me how to fight. That didn't work and it went on and on until junior high and then…Something happened

I was now attending Chesterbrook Academy. The neighborhood kids and I were bussed to this school. We learned to change classes and had different teachers for different subjects. I met different students that lived in other parts of the city and I made new friends. I was teased, but the friends I met seemed to have my back. So the teasing was to a limit, but not gone completely. Remember, the kids from my previous school, went to the same Academy as well. There was a girl name Lydia Brooks and each time she saw me she would grit on me hard. I didn't know her that good and I would look back, looking in wonder, trying to figure out why she didn't like me. Well, one day as I was waiting on the school bus in front of the school, she approached me and said the infamous words, "I heard you were talking about me." And POW! She hit me right in the eye. I wanted to fight her so bad, but I was scared. So I just hung my head down and then she pushed me and some of the kids that were there made her leave me alone. I heard a girl, say, "If that was my sister and she let her punch her like that, I would kick her ass myself." I never forgot that. I made up my mind right then that I would fight back, no matter if I lose, I was not going to let anyone hit on me like that again. Well, my chance to live up to that came maybe a few weeks later.

One day, I was in art class. My teacher's name was Mr. Davis. Mr. Davis was crazy and the students really didn't pay him much mind, laughing, throwing spit balls and just talking. I went to his desk and asked could I go and get a drink of water. The water fountains were in the hall. He said, "Yes, and come right back." I went out to the hall and as I was going, a girl name Janet, tall and big, came up to me and pushed me. I guess the word got around the school that I was an easy mark. I was, but that was about to change. Something came over me. I grabbed that girl and I knocked her ass into that water fountain and commenced to punching the hell out of her. She was screaming and Mr. Davis and the whole class came out into the hall to see what happened. Mr. Davis grabbed me and I was huffing and puffing and ready to get her yellow ass because I wanted to make an example out of her to leave me the fuck alone. He took me to the principal's office. The principal asked me what happened and I told him. He gave me a warning and sent me back to class. He did call my Mom though and told her she had to bring me back to school the next day. That same day, I saw Ms. Lydia, the one who punched and pushed me a few weeks earlier, in the stairwell and she broke her neck to speak. I guess she heard what happened. That fight broke that shit up of picking on me. I didn't have any problems after that. Life went on and the school year ended and I passed my subjects and that summer all hell broke loose and it changed my life… FOR THE BAD…real BAD!

CHAPTER FOUR

HOME LIFE WAS simple from the outside, but what people don't know, the inside was slowly coming apart at the seam. Mom and Daddy had this love/hate relationship and could be somewhat funny at times. We had simple things. As I mentioned before, Mom was a nurse's aide, working the day shift, sometimes working doubles. She would come home tired as hell, but she would make time for us. While cooking dinner, she would help us with our homework or tell us funny stories. Daddy, on the other hand, was a cook and would bring us some good desserts to have after dinner. He'd come home every day with a white bag that had Danish or cake in it for us. Our parents were good to us and good to each other most times. We did church and Sunday school every damn Sunday the Lord sent. I sort of enjoyed it, especially around Easter and Christmas. We had Sunday school programs and we were given a "piece" as they called it and had to recite it in the program. After the program, we would get a chocolate Easter egg or a box of Christmas candy.

We also managed to get a dog that we named Trixy. My brother brought him home and we built a dog house out back for him. He had his dog friends that he played with in the neighborhood and he even had a girlfriend, if you could call it that. She was a smut all the time, it seems, carrying a load of puppies from some other dog she'd been with. When I say she is a smut, I mean a smut. For some reason, she would hang out with him. I guess because he had a dog house and food. Even as a dog, she did have sense enough to hang with one who could keep her warm and feed her. Well, one day, Mom found out. Mom went out to hang clothes. He and the smut princess were laid back chilling in the dog house. He must have heard Mom and poked his head out and so did she. Mom got to hollering, "Trixy, get that goddamn dog out here right now." Trixy had good sense. He and the smut princess trotted out of the yard and she never came back. Later on, as time passed, Mom went to the dog house to clean Trixy's blanket and found a dead puppy in there. Mom was cussing.

I remember one time; we had heard a song called "Signifying Monkey" by Rudy Ray Moore. How we heard it, I can't remember, but we were singing, "signifying monkey, stay up in your tree, you just always lying and signifying and you better not monkey with me." We would sniggle and laugh. Daddy tolerated us singing that song for about a minute. When he had enough, he said "All right now, that's enough, stop singing that song and go to bed." We went to bed, but kept singing real low. Daddy heard us and said, "Come in here, I got a surprise." I said, "Ooh, surprise." We all went in the room where he was and Daddy jumped up and started hitting us, "Go to bed!" We flew in that bed. That was the surprise. Hee hee!

CHAPTER FIVE

LIKE I SAID, Mom and Daddy had this love/hate relationship. For the most part they got along, but would argue something fierce especially when they drank that ignorant oil. When we were younger, their drinking and partying were to a minimum and when they did drink it was mostly on the weekends. During the week, they would be lovey dovey, talking nice, but on Fridays, after a couple of drinks, it was "party over here." Beer and liquor bottles and cigarette filled ashtrays were everywhere when the party was over. I would complain to my sister, "I am so tired of cleaning up their mess every week." I had got to the place that I hated to see Fridays come because I knew it would be loud music, cussing, smoke and fights. Rusty and Maurice were grown and somewhat on their own. They had practically moved out, had jobs and moved in with girlfriends. We hardly saw them because of their work or "adult" life. As we got older, the parties seem to happen more frequently and so did the arguments. By this time, Mom and especially Daddy started to drink more heavily.

Well, this particular Friday evening, the party was in full swing. Daddy and Mom had the usual people over Mr. Ben, The Colonel (that's what they called him), Junebug, and Ms. Ida Mae, just to name a few. We were upstairs, listening to all that noise. The record player was playing the song "Misty Blue." I'll never forget it. All of a sudden a loud argument started. Mom and Daddy were going for it. Mom was accusing Daddy of feeling on Ms. Ida Mae. See, Ms. Ida Mae was known to have slept with a few of the good men in the neighborhood and Mom wasn't having Daddy to be next (not that he hadn't been there already). Daddy was denying it saying, "Beulah, I didn't do nothing, we just dancing." Mom said, "You's a damn lie Samuel, I saw you." "Aww woman, you just drunk," he replied. "I only had one glass of wine so I know what I saw Samuel." It went back and forth until Mom ended up putting Ms. Ida Mae out, screaming and cussing as she went. Mom and Daddy kept arguing, and then all of a sudden, I heard running footsteps on the stairs and the door opening. It was Mom. My sister and I looked at each other with fear. Then we heard Mom go tearing back down the stairs and then BOOM and then another BOOM. My sister and I grabbed each other and then I snatched away and ran to the door. My sister said, "Where are you going?" "Come back." I said, Ssh! I gotta go see."

As I descended down the stairs, there was Daddy, lying in the middle of the floor, in a pool of blood, not moving. Mom was just standing there looking dazed and tipsy. She had just knocked the living shit out Daddy with a billy club she kept hidden in their room. I screamed, "Daddy!" I ran over to him and turned to Mom and said "OMG! Mom what happened?" She just stood there, looking all stupid and dumbfounded. I said it again, "What happened Mom?" She started blubbering and moving her mouth, making no sense at all. I wanted to shake the shit out her. By this this time, both of my sisters had ran down the stairs. When they saw Daddy and the blood, Cece started crying and Barbara was screaming. Mom was still standing there moving her mouth but nothing was coming out. Can you believe that none of the other stupid asses (Mr. Ben, the Colonel and Junebug) ever thought to turn off the music? By this time, I think I heard Jerry Butler singing an "Understanding Mellow." What's so damn mellow about this shit?

I thought, "we need to call the ambulance," but wouldn't you know it? Our phone was disconnected. So I ran to Ms. Etta's house, leaving the door wide open. Thank God she lived two doors down. When I got to the door, I started banging, banging and hollering for Ms. Etta to open the door. As I was banging, I can hear her saying, "Who in the hell is that banging on my door like that?" "Ms. Etta, I screamed" "it's me, Ruth. It's an emergency!!" She swung that door open with her ratty housecoat on, cigarette hanging from her mouth and her hair in rollers. I was a mess, crying and slobbering and all I could say was "Daddy."

"Ruthie!!! she said, Ruthie, what happened?" I was able to tell her "Mommy killed Daddy" before I collapsed in her arms. She broke free and said "Ruthie, we need to call the ambulance and the police and report what happened. She left me standing in her living room while she placed the call. She dialed the number and when it was answered she said "My name is Etta Wiggins and I would like to report an accident." The dispatcher asked her some questions and she told the dispatcher

her location and said, "Please hurry." Within minutes, the police and ambulance were in route.

After a few minutes passed you could hear the sirens wailing, oooweeeoooh! Ooooh! oooweeeoooh! ooooh! (The sound from the Wizard of Oz.) Crazy ain't it? I know. That's the only way I can describe it) and the lights flashing. Help is on the way. Ms. Etta and I rushed back to the house and went in. Wouldn't you know it; the music is STILL playing. "Mr. Big Stuff" by now. Ms. Etta came in behind me and yelled, "What the hell is wrong with y'all? Turn that goddamn music off." Scratchhhhh! The sound of the needle, skating across the record. The music is off. My Mom was sitting in the living room with her head in her hands, my sisters were standing next to her with dried tears on their face. The police and ambulance came in and started their job. I went over to my Mom and sisters and glanced out of the window. Wow, news travels fast. The neighbors started gathering outside looking and whispering. I guess with all the noise and lights flashing, the neighbors were doing what they do best, being nosey.

The ambulance attendants rolled in with the stretcher and checked my Daddy. His heart was beating, but it was weak. They put him on the stretcher and whisked him off to Pennsylvania Hospital. Seeing my Daddy like that brought out more crying and moaning from my sisters and my Mom. She puzzled me...she was just looking. The Police Officer pulled out his trusty notepad and pen and started talking to all that were there. If it had of been me, I would have gotten ghost, but the Colonial, Mr. Ben and Junebug stayed around. They told their side of the story and the police came in the room where my Mom, my sisters and I were standing. Ms. Etta was in there too. You could hear a pin drop. We weren't saying anything. The police approached my Mom and said, "Mrs. Walters, can you tell me what happened?" I wanted to see if she would do them like she did me, just stand there like a knot on Fido's pecker, but she looked at the Officer and said. "I don't know."

The police Officer then radios for backup and a Detective. He says, "This is Officer Coleman White, I have a possible assault." The Officer then says to my Mom, "Mrs. Walters, I need you to say put until the Detective arrives." By this time, Ms. Etta starts to leave the room and heads towards the door. The Officer says to Ms. Etta, "Ma'am, I need you to take a seat. The Detective is on the way and he may need to speak with you." Ms. Etta starts to get smart, but from the look on the

Police Officer's face, she thinks better of it and takes a seat. "So, Mrs. Walters, the police Officer said, "tell me what happened again." She took a breath and looked at him like he was getting on her nerves and said a bit nonchalant, "My husband and I had some friends over and we were drinking. He was dancing with this woman and I saw him feel on her, he denied it and we went back and forth. I told him he was a damn liar and he told me I was a lying ass bitch and I didn't see shit. I told him, "that's alright I'll be your bitch" and left the room. I came back and went in the kitchen and the next thing I know he was on the floor."

"Well, the Officer said, Mrs. Walters, your husband is hurt badly and something had to happen to him and I need you to tell me what really happened." The conversation was interrupted by a knock at the door and the Police Officer gets up to go answer it. Uh oh, the Detective is here!!! Detective Blake Coleman comes in and speaks with the Officer. The Officer tells the Detective what my Mom said. The Detective then directs the Officer to secure the crime scene and calls for the Mobile Crime Forensic Team. He also tells the Officer to call for additional units to transport the witnesses. The Officer goes to his squad car and gets the yellow tape that says in bold black letters, **Police, Do Not Cross**. You can hear the walkie-talkie squawking. Shortly there was another knock and the Mobile Crime Forensic Unit is here!!! The unit gets busy in collecting fingerprints, takings pictures of the room, where the weapon was found, glasses used by everybody, what they were drinking, and drawing diagrams on the floor were my daddy's body was, etc. The Detective talks with the Officer while awaiting the additional squad cars. Moments later, about four squad cars came with lights flashing. They stop in front of our house and all the police officers storm in. The Detective then informs them that everybody is going down to the station for questioning. The Officer asks my Mom to stand up. He tells her, Mrs. Walters, "I am afraid I am going to have to take you down to the station for your statement." Cece ran over and grabbed my Mom and screamed, "Mommie, please don't go, please!!!" Ms. Etta asks the Detective, "Sir, may I go now?" He says, "Yes you may go." She says, "thank you" and switched her old self on to the door. I followed her and asked if she would call Rusty and Maurice because as I said before our phone was disconnected. She asked for the numbers. I wrote them down and she said to me, "It's going to be okay Ruth." I'll go and call the boys and have them to come right away." I said, "thank you Ms. Etta." Closing the door, my mind was racing, replaying what went on, wondering about my Daddy and if worst comes to worst, what is going to happen to us. I went back in the room with my Mom and sisters and from the looks on Cece and Barbara's faces, they were scared.

Just as my Mom, Mr. Ben, Junebug and the Colonel were being escorted out, Maurice and Rusty barged in asking, "What's going on here and where are you taking my Mom?" Cece cried, "They're taking Mommie away!" The Detective says, "An assault has taken place here and we are taking your Mom and her friends down to the precinct for questioning." Barbara was standing there, stoic, but tears were just flowing out of her eyes.

The Officer took Mom out of the door and into the car she went. The neighbors were still standing there looking. The police cruiser pulls off, lights flashing and sirens blaring oooweeeoooh! Ooooh! oooweeeooh! ooooh! Don't laugh. I couldn't think of nothing else. Barbara, Cece, Maurice, Rusty and I gathered in the kitchen, and discussed what happened. I pieced together what happened. Then I asked, "Maurice how did you get here so fast?" He says, "Mike-n-Ike called me." He told me, "Man, you better get to your Mom's house." The police are everywhere." I asked him what happened and he said he didn't know. He said "I'm here visiting Mom and we saw the police and ambulance fly by and stop at your house." You remember him? Mike-n-Ike is Ms. Collins' son Michael. He grew up on the same block we live. He's the same one that his Mom would chase him around the tree in the front yard and down the street." Barbara quietly says, "I want to go and see Daddy." "Me too" chimed Cece. As for me, I was scared to see him, but I third it. Rusty says, "Ok." So my sisters and I change clothes. We go out to the car. Rusty had some piece of car, a brown Nova. We got in and he turned the key. The thing acted as if it didn't want to start. Rusty talks to it and says, "Come on hully, come on baby." The car must have liked how he said it because she cranked right up. So off to the Pennsylvania Hospital we go. Pennsylvania Hospital is located on 8th and Spruce Streets between Locust and Pine. The ride was short since we live right on Delancey Street, about 10 miles.

We got there and Rusty looks at the parking bulletin board and cursed to himself when he finds out how much it cost to park. He puts the car in reverse and we ride around the block and find parking on

Eighth Street, which is where the main entrance is. We get out and go inside. Wow, this hospital is huge I think to myself. We located the Patient and Guest Service desk and asked for Samuel Walters and what room he's in. The greeter tells us he is Room 511 in the Schiedt Bldg. which is the blue building located where the critical patients are housed and the main entrance is located on Spruce Street. So we had to walk back outside and around the corner to the building.

Suddenly, Rusty decided, "Y'all go ahead to see Daddy. I'm going to go to the precinct and see about Mom. Maurice you take them to see Daddy and I'm going to meet y'all back at the house."

Reluctantly, we go inside and enter the elevator to the 5th floor. You know how it is in most elevators, everybody looking all around except at each other, looking at the ceiling, the floor etc., We did just that. The elevator arrives at the 5th floor and we all take a breath not knowing what we will see when we arrive at my father's room. There's a policeman standing outside Daddy's door. We walk past him and we gasp. There's my father with IV'S, his head is bandaged and a monitor is beeping. There's a nurse in his room. She asked us were we his family?" Maurice says. "Yes."

"You can stay, but not long. He needs his rest."

Maurice then asks, "How is he?"

From the look on her face, it told it all.

She says, "I'll let the doctor know you have arrived. He should be here shortly."

We all walk over to his bed. I was the first one there. He is just lying there with his eyes closed. I hold his hand and call him.

"Daddy, I say. It's me Ruth. We're here Barbara, Cece, and Maurice. "Rusty will be here later. Everything will be okay and you'll be home soon." I choked back tears.

Each one of us took turns talking to him.

We wanted to let him know that we were there. The doctor walks in.

"Hello, my name is Doctor Bobbit and I am the doctor on his case."

Nice looking man, older with white hair and glasses. He looks like he knows a thing or two. He says, "Do you have any questions for me?" My brother Maurice, with tears in his eyes says, "How's my Daddy? Will he be alright? The doctor did not shuck or jive us in anyway. He put it all down front. He said, "Your father has suffered a blunt force trauma to the head and has slipped into a coma. We all gasp. " We do not know how long this coma will last, but we are giving him the best care possible in this situation." "We are at your disposal if there is anything you need." "Here's my card with my phone number. Call me if you have any other questions." He shakes my brothers' hand and leaves the room. Almost, all at once, my sisters and I burst into tears, with Barbara almost becoming uncontrollable. My brother is crying too!!! It was so sad. We just embraced each other and held each other for support.

CHAPTER SIX

MEANWHILE RUSTY IS driving towards the 18th precinct on Pine Street. Being ever so careful to not get stopped, he is driving with extra care because his tags have expired by one day and he is driving on a suspended licence. As he's traveling down Walnut, questions of what happened are rushing through his brain; questions like, "What the hell happened? Did Mom do this? I better not find out that Junebug and them rushed my Daddy." He turns left on 55th and turns right on Pine. The station is on the left hand side. The ride takes about 15 minutes, but to Rusty it seemed endless.

He finds a parking space and goes in the station. All of a sudden, he gets to sweating as if he is about to faint. He has NEVER been in a police station before and it gives him the worst feeling. His palms are sweating and he starts to see double. He pauses to get a hold of himself and silently prays to GOD, "GOD please help me." Wiping his brow and straightening his clothes, he goes in and is greeted by a police cadet, Shirley Calhoun, at least that is what her name plate says. She says" Hello and how may I help you?" He squeaks, "My name is Rusty, I mean Russell Walters and I am here to see my Mom."

"What is your mother's name?"

"Her name is Beulah Walters."

The cadet checks her clipboard carefully and lifts up her eyes and studies him and says, "Your Mom was just brought in for questioning." The Detective is in with her now." Please take a seat."

Rusty takes a seat on the bench. He notices how hard the bench is and the dull grayish paint on the wall. He says to himself, "Man, I'll be glad when this is over so I can get the hell out of here. "They sure make this place as uncomfortable as shit." He didn't realize just how uncomfortable this place would become, but he was sure as hell to find out shortly.

Back at the hospital, Maurice, Ruth, Barbara and Cece are still visiting their Dad and then decide it was time to leave. Maurice steps back and releases his grip on us. He wipes his face with his hands and says in the strongest voice he can muster "Stop crying y'all. Daddy's gonna be alright. We need to be strong for him until he can be strong for himself. Let's go home so he can rest". "We need to be there to wait for Rusty to hear about Mom. So, let go."

We settled ourselves and opened the door to leave Daddy's room. As we are walking down the corridor, Cece says. "Daddy don't look too good."

"Yeah, I know" Maurice says, but that's because of all the stuff they have on him. He'll look better tomorrow, you'll see."

Well, tomorrow never came. Daddy goes into cardiac arrest and passes away and we don't know, but the police does!!!

CHAPTER SEVEN

A T THE STATION, Rusty is getting frustrated and short-tempered, but he knows where he is and holds his peace. It's late now and he is wondering what is going on and why is it taking so long. He's thinking "Where is my mother and why is it taking so long? I have read this magazine I know every bit of ten times and she is still not here."

Detective David "Day Day" Brown and Lead Detective Blake Coleman have Junebug, The Colonel, Mr. Ben and Mrs. Walters in separate interrogation room. They know Mrs. Walters had something to do with what went wrong at the house, so they save her for last. They talk to Junebug first. Boy, Junebug is light-skinned, but by the time the detectives got to him he was pale. He is shaking like a leaf!!

They come in the room and sat down. Junebug's eyes are big as quarters. Detective Coleman is the first in the room and introduces himself and his partner. "Hello Junebug, my name is Detective Blake Coleman and this is Detective David Brown". Detective Brown says, "Junebug, is that your real name?"

"No" Junebug says, my real name is Crown Royal."

"Seriously?"

"Yes sir." "That is my given name."

"Well, Mr. Royal, we need to ask you a few questions."

"Yes sir," Junebug says.

"So tell me what happened."

Junebug says nervous as hell, "Sir, we were over to Samuel and Beulah's house and we were having some drinks. We were all sitting in the dining room at the table, myself, Beulah, Colonel and Ben, and Samuel was up dancing with Ida Mae and all of a sudden they, Beulah and Samuel, got to arguing about him feeling on her. "They got to cussing at each other. We was kind of tore up so we was just looking and Beulah took off running up the stairs. We didn't think anything of it and thought it was over because they fought like this before and then kissed and made up. Next thing you know, she came running down those stairs and hit Samuel over the head with the stick. That's all I know."

Detective Coleman says "Okay, Junebug, I mean Mr. Royal, what else did you see?"

"Beulah hit him twice and then just stood there. Then the kids came running down the stairs."

"Okay, Mr. Royal, you may go."

Detective David Brown and Detective Blake Coleman interrogated the Colonial and Mr. Ben the same way and the stories varied just a little, but they said the same thing. Detectives David Brown and Blake Coleman talk amongst themselves after they are gone and let Mrs. Walters stew a little while longer. They go to where she is and watch her. She is in there cussing up a storm and pacing the floor.

"Is somebody coming the fuck in here to talk to me?" I wish they would come the hell on so I can get the fuck outta here."

Detective Coleman sighs and says, "I got this." He opens the doors and goes in. "Hello ma'am, sorry this is taking too long." "My name is Detective Coleman." Please have a seat." Beulah sits down.

"Would you care to have something to drink, water, coffee maybe?"

"No thank you."

"Long day isn't it?"

She just stares.

He starts, "Listen, the little we know is that something happened at your home that led to your husband being hospitalized. Can you tell me what happened?"

"Nothing happened, sir."

"Nothing? Come on Mrs. Walters, talk to me. I can only help you if you help me".

"Help me?" I didn't do a damn thing."

"Calm down Mrs. Walters. I'm just trying to find out the facts."

"The fact is I didn't do nothing and I want to go home."

"Mrs. Walters," Detective Coleman calmly says, "from what we learned from the witnesses" …

She jumps up, the chair falls back, "witnesses, who?" "What the fuck did they say?"

"They said you hit your husband over the head with a stick and now he's in the hospital."

"Those drunks know they lying. I didn't do shit!"

A knock came at the door and opens. Detective Brown gestures Detective Coleman to meet with him in the hallway. He leaves the room and now Mrs. Walters is nervous, she is up pacing and ringing her hands. She has a look in her eyes of defeat. She can't sit down. The Detective returns and sits down. He looks at her.

"What?"

He looks at her....

"Is he okay?" ...

He looks at her....

"Is he?" "OMG!!!! OMG!!" She howls. Then she breaks down...

"You didn't mean to hurt him did you?"

She just lays her head down on the table and cries a blood curdling cry.

"Ma'am, this is formality, but I need to read you your rights. You have the right to remain silent, anything you say can and will be used against you in a court of law. You have the right to have an attorney present. Do you understand?"

"Yes", she says through tears.

"Will you talk to me without an attorney?"

She doesn't answer the question, she just start talking. Through tears she says, "Samuel is a good man." "We had our ups and downs, but I loved him with all my heart." "There was nothing that man wouldn't do for me. His heart was good, but his hands were a horse of a different color. He was a notorious flirt and at first, I would take it even though it would bother me. Things just got outta hand. He was dancing with this woman named Ida Mae. Ida Mae is one of those "everybody's friend" type of woman and I sat there watching them just a going at it. He was grinding and a feeling and she was just a giggling, ole stinking thing. "I just couldn't stand it no mo so I said something and we got to arguing. I had to put that thing Ida Mae, out! Samuel knowed how I felt about his ways. He denied what I saw and just hearing his lies made me madder and madder. Then he called me a lying ass bitch and hearing him saying that sent a charge through my body I never felt before. I thought about last Christmas, how he was doing the same thing right in front of me and I had to slap his face. I thought about how he was always disrespecting me, acting like I wasn't his wife and this time it stung harder than all the times before. I swear Sir, I didn't mean to do it" she cried.

DONNA EARL

"Did your anger make you want to hurt him?"

"No sir, I just…Oh God, He can't be dead." I can't believe I hit him that hard!" "Mrs. Walters, the forensic evidence we have, we know that there was drinking going on." "Were you drinking?"

"Yes sir there was drinking, but I only had one glass of wine."

"Okay Mrs. Walters, I understand." The Detective stands up and approaches her saying, "Mrs. Walters, please stand and place your hands behind your back. We are placing you under arrest for 2nd degree assault"

"Oh God please sir don't do this! She cries. I didn't mean to hurt him" she says as tears flow down her face.

He don't wait for her to stand on her on, he grasps a hold of her arm and tries to pull her out of the chair. She rears back, making it a little hard for him. He tugs harder, pulling her up and he turns her around, placing her hands behind her back and handcuffs her. They walk towards the door and she is mumbling, "Please God, I didn't mean it!"

He opens the door of the interrogation room and walks her down the hall to receiving. Once down to the jail area, she is given over to a police woman by the name of Lillie Manchester.

"Officer Manchester, Mrs. Walters is placed under arrest."

CHAPTER EIGHT

R USTY IS STILL sitting in the police station waiting room, waiting to hear about his mother. He walks up to the front desk and asks the police cadet what is going on and who does he need to speak to about his mother.

"Ms. Calhoun, I've been here for at least an hour I know waiting for Mrs. Walters. Can you please tell me what the holdup is?"

"Sir, I am not sure. "I believe she is still in with the Detective." "Let me check and have someone come and talk to you."

"Ok", but looks puzzled as he turns back around to go and sit down. "Talk with me?" he thought, "what would they have to talk with me about?" "What's going on?" "I just want to know when my mother will be coming out so we can go home." "I know Maurice and them are home by now." Rusty hears the Cadet on the phone.

"Hello this is Cadet Calhoun and I have a Russell Walters here for Mrs. Beulah Walters." She hangs up and announces "Someone will be with you shortly." Detective Coleman appears after about ten minutes. He approaches the desk and the Cadet Calhoun points him in the direction of Rusty. He approaches Rusty and calls his name.

"Russell Walters?" Rusty stands up says, "Yes that's me."

Detective extends his hand and says, "Hello my name is Detective Coleman Green. Cadet Calhoun says you are here for Mrs. Walters."

Rusty shakes his hand and says" Yes" and asks in the same breath, "Where is my Mom?"

"I would like to speak with you in private."

Rusty, looked at him like he was crazy, but he followed him down the hall.

They arrive at Detective Coleman's office and they go in. In his office, there's a desk with a wing leather chair behind it and two chairs sitting in the front. There's some pictures and awards on the wall, and two file cabinets. On his desk, sits his name plate, Lead Detective Coleman and in plain view is a manila folder. Detective Coleman pulls out his chair and sits down.

"Have a seat Mr. Walters."

Rusty sits down and glances around taking notice of everything. He glances at the desk and notices a manila folder and he thought he saw his mothers' name. The Detective takes notice and moves the folder and ever so slightly turns it over.

"Mr. Walters, or can I call you Russell?"

"Sure, Russell is fine."

"Would you care for something to drink, water, soda, coffee?

Russell in his mind says "Let's get this show on the road so I can get out of here", but outwardly, says "No, thank you." Russell's mind is racing now. "What the hell is he about to tell me?"

"Well Russell, as you may or may not know, I am handling the case involving your father and I am afraid I have some bad news. Your father has died and your mother is being held for 2nd degree assault."

"Say what?!" Russell is up out of his seat now. "What the fuck are you talking about man? Oh hell no!!"

"Calm down, Mr. Russell."

"Calm down my ass!" "Man you got to be joking."

"Russell, I'm afraid not".

"Do you know what you're saying to me man? Do you?" "Ain't no way my Mom did this. Hell no!"

The Detective is out of his seat now, ready for whatever Russell does next. Then Russell puts his hands up to his face and burst into tears and mutters OMG!!! OMG!!!

Detective "Day Day" Brown hears all the shouting and comes to the door, knocks one time and enters with his hand on his holster. "Is everything alright?" he asks looking from Russell to Detective Coleman. Russell forgets where he is, looks at Detective Brown and says, "Hell no, everything ain't alright. This motherfucker just told me my Mom killed my Dad!"

Detective Coleman says calmly, "Everything is alright. I had to inform him about his Dad and Mom. I got this. It's okay, he's upset. Detective says "okay" and turns around slowly then turns back around to make sure and then leaves the room.

"OMG! OMG! OMG!!!!" Russell cries and spins around with his head in his head. He plops down in the chair and sits there looking stunned.

Detective Coleman says, "I know this is a lot to swallow right now." If there aren't any questions…."

Russell holds his hand up like a stop sign and asks "Can I see her?"

"Right now son, she is not allowed visitors. You will be allowed to see her when she appears in court on tomorrow which is Saturday."

"Saturday?"

"Yes. Under normal circumstances arraignments are Monday through Friday but in such cases as this, they are done immediately. She will be assigned a public defender unless you have an attorney. You may sit here in my office, if you need some time to get your thoughts together."

"I 'm okay. I need to get home and talk to my family."

"Okay Mr. Walters. Here's my card with my phone number on it if you have any other questions. Please feel free to call me."

"Thank you, sir" and gets up.

The Detective then comes from around the desk and shakes his hand. Russell sighs and turns walking slowly to the door, walking like he aged 20 years in 30 minutes. He walks down the corridor with his head hung low, thinking, "how am I going to explain this to them?" He passes the front desk and sees Cadet Calhoun. She is looking at him, but says nothing. He reaches the front door to the station, pushes it open and goes down the steps, damn near falling because he wasn't paying attention. His mind is elsewhere. He reaches his car, unlocks the door, gets in and shuts the door. He just sits there. His eyes start to fill up and he starts to sniff. The sniffles lead to sobs and then an all-out howl escapes his throat. He bangs on the steering wheel and screams, "Noooooooooo!" He hasn't cried like this since he was a little boy. Daddy! Daddy! Daddy! He cries. He cries until he could cry no more and then he settles himself. He looks in the glove compartment and finds a dried up tissue and wipes his eyes. He starts the car, puts it in drive and head home.

At home, Maurice, Ruth, Barbara and Cece are sitting in the kitchen, hardly saying anything. They had just eaten dinner, if you call tuna fish sandwiches, potato chips and Kool-Aid, dinner. That's all they could find to eat in a flash, plus that's all Maurice knew how to fix. He looks at his watch and says out loud, "Where is Rusty?" He should be home by now. It's almost 11 o'clock. We need to talk about Daddy and he needs to tell us about Mom."

They hear car brakes screech and a car door slam. Cece runs to look out the window and sees Rusty coming up the walk. She's young, but she senses trouble and runs in the kitchen, saying in a little timid voice, "Rusty's home." Rusty walks in the house and closes the door. He hears voices coming from the kitchen and walks down the hall.

Maurice says, "Hey man, where you…before he can finish, he sees the look on Rusty's face. "What wrong Russ man?"

Rusty just stands there.

"Y'all, I just left the police station."

Rusty stops talking.

"What man?!! What?!!!" By that time, we were all staring in Rusty's face, eyes bucked.

He repeats, "I just left the police station and Mom has been arrested and charged with 2nd degree assault for Daddy."

Maurice is heated. "What are you talking about man?!! Mom didn't do that? Who the hell said that?"

"They have witnesses…Mr. Ben, Colonel and Junebug."

Maurice is pacing the floor, "Russ, fuck that man. They probably did it and trying to blame Mom. "You just wait until" …. Rusty stops Maurice dead in his tracks when he hollered, "She confessed Reece!!! Man, she confessed!!!"

"Damn."

Rusty continues. "The Detective says she confessed and they have it all on tape." With tears flowing down his face, he says "we can't see her or nothing." "We can see her tomorrow morning when she appears in court."

"Tomorrow is Saturday."

"I know. She's being arraigned. We gonna need an attorney."

"Oh shit Rusty, what we gonna do?"

"There's something else I need to tell y'all."

"What's that" I said.

He wouldn't say at first. Then he blurted out, "Daddy died!!!"

When he said that, Barbara took off running and ran right out the house. "Barbara!" Rusty hollered, "Barbara!" then he took off running after her. You can hear her hollering as she ran down the street. Me, I was numb, didn't know whether to cry, scream and all of a sudden the room started spinning and then it went black. I don't remember what anybody else did because I was out like a light. When I came to, I was laying on the couch with a cold rag on my head.

"What happened?"

"You fainted after Rusty told us that Daddy died."

The living room has become the meeting room and Cece was sitting on the floor in front of the couch, watching me. She was looking so scared. I wanted to hug her, but when I tried to sit up I still felt dizzy so I laid back down. Rusty had returned with Barbara by this time and she was sitting in the arm chair snivelling with her arms folded hugging herself. Her face was ashy with traces of dried tears. Maurice was sitting on the bottom step of the stairs and Rusty was leaning against the wall.

Rusty started, "Y'all we need to talk about what happened and where do we go from here."

"We sure as hell do," shouted Barbara. She knowed better than to cuss and it was a shock to hear her say the word hell. "Why did she do that to Daddy? Her voice trembling" "I hate her, I hate her, I HATE HER!!" and burst out crying. That started Cece to crying. Emotions were raw that evening.

"Yeah man, Maurice said shaking his head, why did she have to do that to him?" Rusty, trying to keep from crying himself, said quietly, "Y'all I don't know. I am as lost as you all are. That's why I asked the Detective could I see her. I wanted to know what she would say. What reason did she have to hurt Daddy? I will never understand. What I do know is, we have to figure some things out. We need to call the family and let them know what happened. Since the phone here is disconnected, I will call the family from my place. Ruthie, do you know where Mom keeps the address book? I need Uncle Louie's number as well as Uncle Clements, Aunt Louise's and Aunt Lena's in Carolina."

"Yeah. Her red phone book is over by her bed on the nightstand." "I'll get it" Maurice said while getting up from the step. "I need to go use the bathroom anyway."

Rusty asked, "Are Aunt Bunchie and Aunt Jane's numbers in there too?

"Yeah."

"Okay.' We need to call the Funeral Home to make arrangements after talking with Uncle Louie. I want him to go with me."

We hear the toilet flush and footsteps moving around upstairs. Then Maurice comes running down the stairs with the red book in hand. Barbara starts whining again.

Maurice, shouts, "Barbara, don't start that!" He then went over and hugged her and said, "I'm sorry baby girl, I shouldn't have hollered at you like that, but we need to get through this."

"Yeah, Barbara," Rusty says. "I'm sad too, we all are, but we need to stay calm and strong." She looks at the both of them and rolls her eyes. Rusty, says, "Okay, bro, between the two us, we ain't got no money so we need to find insurance papers, policies of any kind. We need to contact Daddy's job as well as Mom's. Ruth, what's the name of Daddy's job?"

"It's the Bellevue Stratford Hotel located downtown on Walnut Street and Mom she works at the Philadelphia General Hospital."

"Okay," Rusty says, "that's a start. Well, it's getting late. Let's go to bed and we'll start working on things tomorrow."

Cece looks up at Maurice with her pretty little eyes filled with fear and tears asks, "Maurice, are you and Rusty going to stay with us tonight?"

"Of course shorty," he pinches her cheeks and smiles, trying to lighten up the mood.

At the police station, the shit is about to hit the fan.

CHAPTER NINE

EVEN THOUGH ITS' late, Detective Blake Coleman, Officer White and Detective Brown are having a round table discussion about the Walter's case. Detective Blake Coleman is leaning back in his wing chair behind his desk, Detective Brown is sitting on the corner of the desk and Officer White is sitting in one of the chairs in front of the desk. They are reviewing the case and making sure that they have dotted all I's and crossed all T's.

"Guys," Detective Coleman says, "what we have here is a case that's emotionally charged. The suspect truly is the cause of the injury that resulted in her husbands' death. At first, she didn't confess, but after some gentle prodding she spilled her guts."

Detective Brown butts in, "Yes, she did and the evidence supports it."

Officer White chimes in, "How do you think the prosecutor will handle it?!"

"Well, I filed the form PD163 with all the vital information on it and sent a copy down to central cell block with her. Now all I need to do is to walk the original form down to the District Attorney's office to the Assistant Prosecutor, Andrew Dunlap. It could be 2nd degree assault, but since he died, it could be murder."

Officer White felt sorry for her. "I don't think she meant to do it."

"Yeah, I know, Detective Coleman says, but you know fellas, what is going to mess her up is when she went upstairs and got the weapon. It was a split second decision for her, but she had the time to calm herself and go another route. It can go either way, whether it's pre-mediated or deliberate. She allowed her emotions to run the train and now it's derailed. As for me, I am leaving well enough alone and let the prosecutor decide."

"So am I", says, Detective Brown and Officer White third it.

It could have been different they all silently thought. Officer White and Detective White left the office.

He then picked up the phone to call his wife, then hung the phone up, thinking I better get over to the DA's office. He glanced at his watch. "Shit, its almost 12 midnight. Let me get going since she will be going in front of the magistrate so I can go the hell home." He got up, grabbed his jacket, walked to the door, opened it, turned off the light, walked out and closed the door. Night Night.

We had all gone to bed and were calling the hogs when we heard a banging on the door. Bang, Bang, Bang! Rusty woke up first and said to himself "who is that banging on that damn door like that?" Bang Bang Bang! Rusty came out of the room and turned on the hall light. He went stomping down the hall and down the stairs. "Who is it?" he shouted.

"It's Uncle Louie and Aunt Evy!! Open the door!"

By this time, I'm up and so is Maurice. Barbara and Cece were still sleep. Gosh! It's Uncle Louie and his witchy poo of a wife Evelyn. None of us are big fans of Aunt Evelyn. She treats Uncle Louie like a henpecked husband, more or less her child, always telling him what to do. Rusty turns on the lamplight and unlocks the door.

"Hey Uncle Louie, Aunt Evelyn, come on in."

Uncle Louie pushed his way in, turns around and said, "What the hell happened here tonight? It's all over the news, Channel 6, Channel 10 and Channel 3."

"Mom and Daddy got into an argument and Mom hit Daddy in the head."

"Why didn't somebody call?"

"The phone is disconnected Unc."

"So how is he?" "How's my nephew?" asks Uncle Louie.

"Uncle Louie, Rusty said, Daddy died!

"Oh God No!!" Witchie poo screamed. "What they say happened to him?"

Maurice spoke up, "They said Daddy went into cardiac arrest and died as a result of the head injury."

"Unc, Rusty says, I was going to call you in the morning after we got some rest. Mom will be appearing in court tomorrow and we need to go there to see what she is charged with. The Detective said she could be charged with 2nd degree assault, but since Daddy died, she could be brought up on charges of murder."

"Oh God", Uncle Louie said, "Well, we will spend the night here to save time."

In her cell, Beulah is pacing, like a caged animal. She's a wreck. She don't smoke, but she could sure use a cigarette, a joint, a drink, anything to calm her nerves right now. "Lord, she starts praying, if you hear my prayer, I knowed what I done was wrong, but I didn't mean to hurt him." I loved Samuel. I remember when we first met back in high school, 11th grade, ole shy thing. She smiles slightly. We were in the same math class. He sat in the row next to me, but in the seat over in the corner in the last row. He wouldn't say anything, but would look and when I catch him looking he would turn his head. My girlfriend, Shirley Mae, who sat in front of me, nudged me, "I think he like you Beulah" she would say. She would sing "Beulah and Samuel in a tree, KISSING…Shut up Shirley." I told her and play punched her in the arm. So to break the ice, I went over to him after school and said, "My name is Beulah, asked him his name and if he could help me with a few of the hard math questions. He said, "My name is Samuel Walters and sure." So he walked me home and we sat on the stoop. We went over the usual questions, but before you know it, we were talking as if were knew each other for a long time. We talked about everything, our future, etc. This went on for several months then we started going steady, going to the movies and long walks. We quietly fell in love. After playing coy, we went beyond the normal petting and made love. Since we both were virgins, the first time was a disaster. I brought him home to study and nobody was home. We started kissing and he put his hand down my…you know and it was on. I think it was over before it began, but after several times, "Man, whoo!!" Then one day, I started feeling blue, really funny and I got dizzy. The feeling would pass, but then I noticed I hadn't come on my period and hadn't for about two months. I talked to Shirley Mae about it.

"Are you pregnant?"

"I don't know."

"Well, you better be finding out."

"I'm going to make an appointment and sneak over to the Dr. Logan's."

"I started crying." "My mother is going to kill me if I'm pregnant." I threatened to kill Shirley if she told anybody. I went to Samuel and told him what I'd been thinking. He didn't get mad or nothing. Actually, he was over the moon.

"I'm going to be a Daddy!"

"You're going to be a dead man when my father find out."

"Beulah, I love you and if you're going to have a baby, I want to get married, do things right."

"Samuel, I am too young, we're too young."

"Beulah, I've never felt this way about no one else. Let's go see and then we'll know what to do."

So we snuck over to Dr. Logan's office the next day and took a test. A short time later, he comes out into the waiting room and calls me into his office. Samuel jumped up out of his seat and went in there with me. We sat down and Dr. Logan's said, "Beulah, congratulations, you are pregnant." I don't remember anything else after that because I fainted.

The doctor revived me and Samuel and I left his office. How am I going to tell my parents? (How can I tell my mom and dad that I've been bad? Remember that song...hee hee). That's was the longest ride I ever took. My knees where knocking by the time we got to my house. It wasn't easy, but we told my parents. I opened the door and my father and sisters, Bunchie and Jane were sitting down in the living room watching TV, I think cartoons. Daddy was reading the newspaper and Mom was in the kitchen sitting at the kitchen table, shelling peas.

"Hi Daddy."

"Hey Bee," he called me that for short.

Samuel spoke, "Sir." Daddy said, "Son."

"Where's Mom?"

"In the kitchen, where else?"

I told Samuel to sit down. "I'll be right back. I'm going to go and talk to Mom."

I sat down and said "hey Mom"

"Hey girl."

"Mom, I got something to tell you".

Not looking up, she said, "What is it?" still shelling peas.

"I'm pregnant."

"What?!!!"

The bowl and the shelled peas went all over the floor.

"I'm pregnant Mom and Samuel and I want to get married."

"Lee, come in here right now" Mom yelled.

Here come Daddy, stomping. "What is it Dot?"

"Lee, this girl just come in here and told me she was pregnant and she and Samuel want to get married." Daddy didn't say a thing, He turned and around and went straight to Samuel.

You could hear him yelling, "Boy, what the hell you mean getting my girl pregnant?" He grabbed Samuel in the collar.

"Daddy!" I yelled while running in the living room, Mom right behind me. Bunchie and Jane were sitting right there on the floor in the middle of everything.

Mom was yelling, "Beulah, you're too young!!! You can't do this!! I will not let you."

To make a long story short, we ended up eloping, leaving Durham and having our first son Russell born months later in Philadelphia.

The mist of the daydream drifted away and reality set in. "OMG!!! What have I done? I killed my husband!!!" She laid on her bunk and stares at the ceiling and finally fell asleep.

SATURDAY, the day of reckoning is here!!!

CHAPTER TEN

U NCLE LOUIE AND Aunt Evelyn are the first to get up. Rusty and Maurice are up too. I hear a soft knock at my bedroom door and Maurice peeked his head in. Barbara, Cece and I are still in bed. "Ruth, y'all get up. We get things to do today." He closed the door. We start to get up, wiping sleep out of our eyes. I rushed out the door first to the bathroom for my morning pee, nearly knocking Barbara down. As I was going in the bathroom, I see a man looking like Uncle Louie going down the hall. I finished my business, washed my hands and left the bathroom, passing Barbara going in after me and head downstairs. As I got downstairs and went in the kitchen, I see Uncle Louie, Aunt Evelyn, Rusty and Maurice sitting at the table drinking coffee in their nightclothes.

I say, "Hey Uncle Louie and Aunt Evelyn. I thought that was you."

"Evy and I came last night after we heard on the news what went on here. We came to see for ourselves."

Cece and Barbara came in the kitchen and Cece asks, "What's for breakfast? I want bacon and eggs."

"Can't you speak?" Reese chastised them.

"Sorry. Good Morning Uncle Louie and Aunt Evy."

"That's better."

"Now, ain't no cooking this morning Cece, Rusty says. You can have cereal and milk."

Cece stuck her lip out. I get the cereal, milk, bowls and spoons for everybody. "Hurry up and eat too," Rusty bellows. "We got to go to court and see Mom and go to the Funeral Home after that."

We sat down and began to eat. As we were eating, a knock came to the door. Maurice gets up from the table and walks down the hall to the front door. As he gets closer, he asks, "Who is it?"

"It's your aunts, Bunchie and Jane," they answer.

When Maurice opens the door, Aunt Bunchie and Aunt Jane were standing there along with Ms. Etta. Our Aunts Bunchie and Jane,

Mom's sisters, drove up from Chester. "Good morning nephew," Aunt Jane says as they were coming in. Hey boy", Aunt Bunchie says and Ms. Etta just says, "Morning."

The door closes and you can hear their heels clicking as they were coming down the hall to the kitchen. They sound like they were marching. When they got to the kitchen, "Good morning, everybody," they say all together. We all say "good morning."

Aunt Evelyn asks, "Y'all want some coffee?"

"None for me," Ms. Etta says. "I done had about 2 cups already."

Both Aunt Bunchie and Aunt Jane say "Yes."

Aunt Bunchie and Aunt Jane are as different as day and night. Aunt Bunchie had on these tight jeans and huge hoop earrings and so much makeup that it looked as if she had cake on her face and Aunt Jane had on a pair of pants and a smock like blouse. She was plain, but pretty.

Rusty says, "Ruthie, if y'all are done, go and get washed up and dressed so we can be ready to leave soon."

We push our chairs from the table, put our bowls and spoons in the sink and head upstairs. Aunt Bunchie, Aunt Jane sat down and Ms. Etta just stood against the wall.

Aunt Bunchie spoke first. "What the hell happened here last night? I was watching the TV and the newscaster got on there talking all this bullshit about a woman and man fighting and they mentioned this address. I missed part of it and the newsman said more on News @ 11. I called first and the telephone woman got on there talking her shit, the number you have reached 215-437-0000 is not in service, please check the number and try again." "I told that hussy that this is the right number than I realized it was a recording and that the phone was disconnected." She sorta giggled at herself for being so silly. "Jane called me and asked had I heard about it. I told her I heard bits and pieces and that I would call up here to find out. That's when I got the operator. So we decided to come up here to find out."

She kept talking. "So, tell me Reece, what happened here? I mean, I don't understand. What did Beulah do?"

"Aunt Bunchie, I don't know what happened either. All I know is that Mom is in jail for hitting Daddy. They had an argument, she hit Daddy and sent him to the hospital and he died. I think they are charging her with 2nd degree assault. I'm not sure."

Aunt Jane had a shocked look on her face and covered her mouth with her hand.

Aunt Jane took her hand down from her mouth and asks, "So what happens now? What do we do?"

Well, Reece says, "Well we have to be in court at 10 this morning for the arraignment and then we have to go to the Funeral Home to make arrangements."

"Have y'all called Sam's family yet?"

"No, not yet." "The phone is disconnected, as you know, so we have to do that after we make the arrangement."

"After we do that, Rusty chimed in, Uncle Louie will call the family from my house."

"Oh Shit", Aunt Bunchie says. Were you able to see your mom?"

Rusty says, "No, we will not see her until today when she appears in court."

"Well, we are going with you to court. I need to see her."

Rusty says, "Ok, that's fine. We all need to get dressed now because it's almost 9 now."

Ms. Etta, with tears in her eyes, finally spoke. "Kids, I had to come by to see how things are. Y'all know Beulah is like a sister to me and I am here for you if you need me. Stop by after you take care of things and let me know."

Rusty hugs her and says, "Ms. Etta thanks for all your help. We will let you know how things are later on."

Ms. Etta says, "Y'all take care." All at once, everybody says, "Thank you."

She walks out of the kitchen and down the hall. Rusty is following behind her to let her out. The front door opens and closes and Rusty comes back in the kitchen and says, "Well, it's show time."

CHAPTER ELEVEN

B EULAH IS UP early…matter of fact she never slept really…
maybe a few winks. She got up and sat on the side of her bunk.
She looked around at the gray walls and saw the bars. She closes her
eyes, hoping they'd go away. She opens her eyes and still, they were
there. She started scratching. "I think something bit me…spider bites
or maybe roaches. Hope it wasn't…," … a mouse ran across the floor.
"Oh hell no!!!" She put her feet up on her bunk, scared!!

"Oh Lord! she says, what is going to happen to me?" She hears
voices from the other cells.

Then she hears, "Rise and shine Ms. Walters!" The Correctional
Officer is at her cell. "Come with me. You are due in court to see Judge
Clifton Long."

"Today is Saturday," Beulah says.

"All day long," the Officer says.

"Smartass," Beulah thinks to herself. Beulah shuffles to her feet,
brushes her orange jumpsuit and smooths out her hair. "I can sure use
a comb," Beulah calls out to the Officer.

"Run your fingers through it," she says. Beulah gritted on her hard.

"Bitch" she says under her breath. Even under her circumstances
she was still a firecracker.

"Hands behind your back!"

"Is this really necessary?"

"Hands behind your back."

Beulah turns around while the Officer cuffs her. The Officer
unlocks the cell door and Beulah walks out. The Officer slammed the
door and grabs Beulah's arm. Into the Department of Corrections van
I go. I'm helped on the van for the short ride and she had the nerve
to feel me on my butt. I wanted to slap the shit out of her, but under
the circumstances…. I did let her know I don't play that by the look I
gave her.

At the courthouse, Beulah tries to snatch away, but the Officer grabs her arms tighter and walks her down the hall, where they were greeted by another Officer, Officer Michael Wilson. Both Officers escort Beulah to the elevator that led to the courtroom. Beulah was sweating now. Beads of sweat formed on her brow. Officer Wilson pushes the elevator button and the elevator doors open. They walk in and push the button with the number 5 on it. The number lights up and the elevator door closes. Beulah feels the elevator go up and then it stops on the fifth floor. The elevator doors open and she and the Officers walk out. The sign on the wall read Courtroom A, B and C to the left. She and the Officers make the left and walk down the hall to the left to Courtroom B. They reach the brown doors and the Officer grabs the handle and pulls the door open and they step in. There inside was the Public Defender, Sheila Mathis as well as the Prosecutor. Beulah stood still and looked around the courtroom and her eyes got BIG!!! She saw the witness stand, the jury box and the Judges' stand, the clock, the flag and all these people! The other defendants and their families were there too. "Damn, she thought, do we have to do this in front of everybody?" By the time she got to her seat, she was shaking like a leaf. The Officers unlocked the handcuffs and she is sat down with a thud. The public defender started talking to her, introducing herself and explaining what to expect. Beulah sat there in her own thoughts as the time for the judges' appearance drew near.

CHAPTER TWELVE

W E LEFT FOR the courthouse. Uncle Louie and Aunt Evy rode in their car. Aunt Jane and Aunt Bunchie rode in Aunt Jane's car and we in ours, Rusty's, that is. The courthouse is located on Filbert Street, in south Philadelphia. The ride took 20 minutes, but it was the longest 20 minutes I ever experienced. I sat in the back with Cece and Barbara. Cece was half sleep and Barbara was just quiet, looking around. I was checking out the scenery as we rode the streets. We rode through DOWNTOWN PHILLY!!! I saw the stores, galleries, street vendors and food stores. By the time we made it to the courthouse my stomach was growling because all I had was cold cereal and milk. My mouth was watering looking at the food stores.

We have arrived!! There we were in front of the Philadelphia Municipal Court. Wow!!! Look at that building. It looks so scary. We found parking right in front. I took it as a good sign. We got out and walked up to the doors and were met by security. Security was tight, Officers all over the place. We had to be searched and Aunt Evy, Aunt Jane and Aunt Bunchie's purses were checked. Rusty, Maurice and Uncle Louie had to take everything out of their pockets. We were clean as a whistle. Rusty told the guard where we were going and he told us to take the elevator to the fifth floor.

Before the Judge came, Beulah looked to the back of the courtroom and saw her kids, her sisters, Uncle Louie and Aunt Evelyn. Her eyes filled with tears and she smiled briefly before hearing, "ALL RISE!!!"

She jerked her head around and stands as the bailiff bellowed. The Honorable Judge Clifton Long is presiding. Everybody is standing. The Judge in his black robe appears and climbs the stairs to his podium. When he is seated he tells us, "You may be seated." Cece cries out, "Mommy!!!" and tries to run up to Mom and I held her down.

The Judge puts on his glasses and takes sips of water. Defendant after defendant is called. By the time her case was called, she felt dizzy.

"Case B12764, Pennsylvania vs. Mrs. Beulah Walters. Will the defendant please stand and state your name?"

"My name is Beulah Walters".

"Mrs. Walters, you are charged with 2nd degree assault, how do you plead?"

The public defender opens her mouth and says, "Your Honor my client pleads... "Not guilty god dammit," Beulah hollered, cutting her off.

The Judge looks over his glasses at Beulah like she was crazy. The public defender touches Beulah arm to quiet her and she snatches it away. The Judge warns the public defender, "Quiet your client." The bailiff steps close to the defendant's table with his hand on his gun.

The judges' eyebrows are raised and his eyes were blinking fast. He mouth is slightly parted as he stares at Beulah as he repeats, "How do you plead?

"Didn't you hear what I said? "I'm not pleading to shit, but not guilty."

The bailiff stepped in my Mom's face and told her to sit down. She sits down slowly, gritting on the Judge hard. Running out of patience, the Judge questions the public defender. "Counsel, have you spoken with your client on how to behave in a court room?"

Again, the public defender starts to speak "Your Honor, I..."

Beulah, cutting her off again, says, "Behave? Who the hell is she to tell me how to behave?! I'm a grown ass woman!!

By this time, the bailiff was on my Mom like a dog. He snatched her out of her seat and spins her ass around like a top ending with both hands behind her back. He began to handcuff her and throw her out of the courtroom. Rusty got so excited seeing the way the bailiff was treating my Mom that he jumped up out of his seat and yelled, "Hey man, take your hands off my Mom like that!!" Aunt Bunchie was on her feet too, yelling and screaming.

The Judge yelled, "Order!! Control yourselves or I will clear this courtroom here and now!!!"

Aunt Bunchie sat down, breathing all hard and Rusty sat down mumbling under his breath, "He didn't have to treat her like that."

Uncle Louie, sitting next to him, patting his arm, says, "Son, I know." "Hang in there and let's see how this goes."

Before the bailiff could escort Mom out, he stopped him. "Mrs. Walters, I am going to give you one last chance to control yourself and sit down." She looked in the back of the courtroom and saw her family looking at her in horror and total shock and acting right ignorant, so she sat down.

The Judge spoke, "Understand this!! Mrs. Walters, you are facing some serious charges and it would be wise for you to act like you have some sense. One more outburst like that from you and I will have you forcibly removed from these proceedings. Do you understand?!!! Do I make myself clear?!!!"

"Yes, Your Honor," hanging her head.

"Now, the Judge says, counsel we may proceed. "How does your client plead?"

"Your Honor, my client pleads not guilty."

"Since your client pleads not guilty the next phase is to set bail."

The prosecutor stands and says, "Your Honor, based on the seriousness of the crime and the evidence I have presented to the court, the state motions that bail should be denied. The defendant could be a flight risk and should be held until her court date."

The public defender stands up, "Your Honor, my client understands the seriousness of said charges. I motion that my client is not a flight risk and should be allowed to be free until her court date."

The Judge says, "I have heard your arguments and have read the docket pertaining to this case. At this time, bail is denied and the defendant shall be reprimanded in custody until such time. Looking at my calendar, the available date is June 30th for the preliminary hearing. That is ten days from now. Do either of you have any objections?"

"Your Honor, with the courts approval, I am asking for additional time to gather more evidence to solidify my case."

"Do you object, Counsel?"

"No, Your Honor."

"Good then, the hearing is set for July 11th."

"Yes, Your Honor" they both answered almost together.

"Court's adjourned," the Judge bellowed and banged his desk.

I looked to Aunt Evelyn when he did that and she told me he was banging his gavel. I said, "That's so loud!!" She just smiled.

"All Rise," the bailiff shouted and we all stood up. The Judge left in a puff of smoke. We didn't get a chance to speak with my Mom.

DONNA EARL

As soon as the Judge left the room, the Officer had my Mom up, cuffed and on her way out of the courtroom. She tried to look back, but the Officer was too quick. She whispered something to the Officer. She turns to us, smiles and slightly waves. She mouths "I love you" and then she turns around and he takes her out.

"I want Mommy!!!" Cece cried. 'I want Mommy!!!'

We left the courtroom and started walking down the hall.

Maurice sighed and said, "Well y'all, Mom is going back to jail until her court date. She don't look so good."

Aunt Jane said, "Yeah, I'm scared for her. I wish I could talk to her or at least give her a hug."

Aunt Bunchie didn't say a word…a first for her. She always had something to say.

Rusty said out loud, "I wonder if we can visit with her before then?"

Uncle Louie said, "I don't know, but I am going to find out and that's for sure."

"Well," Rusty said, "Me, Maurice and Unc are going to the Funeral Home from here. No need for all us going. Aunt Evy, would you please take the girls back home and we will meet you there."

"No problem Rusty," Aunt Evy said and hugged him. "Come on girls" and she shooed us out.

"Bye," I said.

Uncle Louie, Maurice and Rusty left the courtroom for the Lars Funeral Home on 17th and Ritner. When they got in the car, Rusty unlocks the door and crawls over to the passenger side and unlocks that door as well as the back door. Rusty starts the car and turns on the radio to WDAE 104.7 to hear some "clear your head" music. EWF comes on and "Happy Feeling "is playing. "Feeling! Happy Feeling, Happy Feeling!" Perfect!!! My jam!! Rusty bops his head a little, just to shake loose the thoughts of what just happened. He sees from the corner of his eye that even Uncle Louis is tapping his toes.

"Russ, man, Maurice says, turn that down some. I got a headache."

Rusty turns down the music just enough to get a whiff of the song. Rusty puts the car in gear and pulls off.

As they drove off, the conversation started.

"Mom really showed her ass today at her arraignment." Maurice says. What is wrong with her"?

Rusty thought out loud. "She is just scared."

Uncle Louie replied, "I would be too if I was facing 2nd degree assault. That may not be as serious as murder, but it's still serious."

"2nd degree assault!" Maurice shouts. "Damn, what are we going to do? And now, we're planning Daddy's funeral. "Shit!!!"

CHAPTER THIRTEEN

THEY ARRIVE AT the Funeral Home and park across the street. Lars Funeral Home looks pretty decent from the outside, they all thought. They are greeted at the door by the Funeral Homes' henchmen, I mean associates. Uncle Louis goes in first and introduces himself to the receptionist, Stella Lewis.

"Hello. My name is Louis Walters and we are here to make funeral arrangements for my nephews, their father."

"I'm pleased to meet you, sir. If you'd take a seat Mrs. Lars, she will be with you shortly."

Minutes later, Mrs. Lars comes out of the office and extends her hand, "Hello, I'm Mrs. Lars. How may I help you?"

Uncle Louie tells her why they were there and she escorts them to the slumber chamber. Mrs. Lars was about 5'7 with a pretty decent shape. She wore a two-piece brown pantsuit that brought out her cocoa complexion. Uncle Louie was definitely checking her out. Rusty and Maurice had smirks on their faces, checking out Uncle Louie in action.

They were both thinking, "Look at Uncle Louie trying to get his Mack on." Maurice was also thinking, "Mack on Uncle Louie because we sho nuff ain't got no money."

"Mr. Walters, this is our slumber chamber."

They look around and see all those caskets. They see a beautiful black casket that looks affordable.

"Do you have a dollar figure in mind?" she asks

"Well, Mrs. Lars, smiling, showing off his pearly whites, we are bereaving on limited funds, so what can you do for us?"

After going over the numbers, they came up with an affordable home going. The grand total, including the extras, totalled $6,500. The funeral was set for next Friday.

Leaving the Funeral Home on the ride home, Rusty says, "How in the world are we going to pay for this?"

"Nephew, I will give you at least half so $3,250 is all that is left."

"We need to find out if Daddy had any insurance papers."

Maurice says, "Come to think of it, when I was looking for the address book, I think I saw all kinds of papers and I think I saw a brown envelope with Lincoln Insurance on it. That might be it."

Well, let's check when we get back home." Rusty says. "But first, we need to stop by my house to call Daddy's folks and let them know what happened."

Oh Boy!! Maurice sighs.

Aunt Evy drove us home as slow as she could. She was chattering about this and that, but I wasn't even listening. I don't think any of us was listening. I kept replaying the courthouse thing in my head. I turned my head to the backseat and Barbara and Cece were both sleep. Aunt Jane and Aunt Bunchie were right behind us in their car, having a conversation of their own.

Aunt Bunchie says to Aunt Jane, "Can we drive any slower?" They both laughed. Jane took her que. She had been brainstorming about the girls ever since the arraignment.

"You know Bunch, all jokes aside, Beulah's going to get some time, point blank, how much, only God knows, but quiet as it's kept, Rusty and Maurice are going to want to raise these girls. In the beginning, things may go smooth, but men are men, boys are boys and they gonna want to run the street. These girls need guidance and I suggest they come home with either you or me or both. I mean, it wouldn't sit right with me to leave these girls up here with little or no supervision."

Aunt Bunchie agreed with her with all her heart, but her mind didn't. "I don't want to take care of the kids I got. Hell, I want to run the streets too! To take on more responsibility…I ain't feeling it she thought, but…"

"Well, push comes to shove she says out loud, I'll take in Ruth and you take in Cece and Barbara."

"Okay, when we get back to the house, let's run it by Rusty and Maurice, but not in front of the girls."

Rusty, Maurice and Uncle Louie arrive at Rusty's apartment on Walnut Street. They pull up to the curve and get out. They walk to the front door and Rusty pulls out his key and opens the door. Just inside the door is the living room. Rusty says "Make yourself at home.

"Water for me," Uncle Louie says as he sits down on the sofa. Maurice roams around trying to see what he can get into.

"Got any of the hard stuff Russ?"

"Reese, right now, I have only beer." Maurice walks over to the refrigerator and gets the beer and then he gets a glass out of the cupboard and gets the water out the spigot and brings both the water and beer to the living room and hands the glass to Uncle Louie. Uncle Louis nearly downs the full glass. He then sits the glass on the table.

"Alright, who do we call first?" Rusty asks.

"We need to call your Daddy's sister Julia first and then we need to call Uncle Clements and Aunt Louise. Reece, you got the phone book?"

"Yeah, here it is."

"Okay, now where is the phone?"

"It's on the wall in kitchen."

Uncle Louie gets up and goes in the kitchen. He leafs through the phone book and finds Aunt Julia's number. He dials.

"Hey Julia!! It's Uncle Louie."

"Hey Uncle!! How are you doing?"

"I'm alright Julia."

"How's Aunt Evy?"

"She's good."

"Look Julia, the reason I'm calling…" Silence.

"Uncle!! Uncle!! What's going on?!"

"Well, Julia there's been an accident."

"Accident? What accident?!! Talk to me Uncle!!!"

"Julia, Sam is dead!"

She drops the phone and a loud scream is heard. "OMG!!! OMG!!!"

"Julia!! Julia! Uncle Louie is screaming. "Julia!!"

She comes back on the phone and she is crying. "What happened?!!!"

"Well, Julia, he takes a deep breath and says, Sam and Beulah got into an argument and….!!!"

"What did she do to him?!!!"

"Julia, she hit Sam in the head and he ended up in the hospital and he went into cardiac arrest."

"That Bitch!!!!" She was hollering now. "I knew she was trouble from the time I met her. I told Sam not to fool with her!!! Now look!!! Where is she now?" Julia asks.

"She is being held in jail on 2nd degree assault charges."

"I hope the bitch fries."

"Take it easy Julia."

"No Uncle, she killed my brother. He was all I had in this world with Mom and Daddy gone. I ain't got nobody now on account of that woman."

"Calm down, Julia. I know its hurts, but all this foolishness is not going to bring Sam back."

She is quiets down.

"Now, the funeral is Friday here in Philly at Lars Funeral Home on 17th and Ritner at 10:00 a.m. "I'll call Squeak, Uncle Clements and Aunt Louise."

"No, Uncle, speaking calmly now, I'll call them and the rest of the family. How's the kids doing?"

"They are doing okay. Aunt Evy and I and Beulah's sisters are looking after them."

"Well that's good to hear."

"Julia, are you okay?"

"Yeah, Unc."

"Well, Uncle Louie says, the phone at Sam's is disconnected and I'm calling you from Rusty's." I'll call you back with more details. If you need to get in touch with me call me at home or here and leave a message."

"Okay Unc."

"Love you Julia."

"Love you too Unc."

"Bye."

Uncle Louie, Rusty and Maurice are back. They came in one by one and sat wherever they could because we had taken all of the available seats around the kitchen table. The coffee's brewing and Aunt Evy offers them some. Maurice and Rusty turn her down, only Uncle Louie accepts. Aunt Bunchie and Aunt Jane where already drinking some. Aunt Evy gets a cup and saucer from the cupboard and pours him some. She sits it in front of him and asks, "Well, how did it go"?

"Well, the funeral is Friday and it cost $6,500. Since it's my nephew, I'd thought we'd help. We are going to give half."

"What?!"

"Now Evy don't fight me on this. I offered half to help them out. He's family and I know these boys do not have any money and their Daddy needs to be buried. It's the least I could do."

"Louie, I don't think…"

"Who's paying you to think Evy? We doing it and that's that!!!"

"Ni.." she stopped short. Embarrassed, she said, "Okay", but the look on her face said something else. It said "How dare he talk to me like that in front of all these people? I don't care if they are family. How he gonna offer that kind of money without talking to me first?"

"Hey Reece, didn't you say something earlier about an envelope from Lincoln Insurance?"

"Oh yeah, that's right. Let me go get it." Maurice gets up from the table and goes upstairs, taking two steps at a time.

"Did you phone the family?" Aunt Jane asks.

"Yeah, I called Julia. She didn't take it well." He deliberately left out the part of her bad mouthing Beulah. "She's okay now, he continued. She's going to tell the rest of the family. I told her the funeral was Friday at 10 a.m. They'll probably be here early."

Everybody got quiet knowing how bad this is going to be. There will be hell to pay and payday is on Friday.

CHAPTER FOURTEEN

EVERYBODY'S HUNGRY SO Aunt Evy, Aunt Bunchie and Aunt Jane talked about what to fix. They decided on fried chicken, cream potatoes, string beans and cornbread. Aunt Evy and Uncle Louie offered to go the ACME market to get the food. Barbara, Cece and I went with them.

When the door closed, Aunt Jane started in. "Rusty and Maurice sit down. I want to talk to you."

"Talk about what?"

"Your Aunt Bunchie and I were talking on the way here about Ruthie, Barbara and Cece."

"What about them?"

"Well, we were thinking that after the smoke clears with the funeral and everything that the girls come and live with us."

"NO!! NO!!" Maurice blurts out. "No Aunt Jane."

"Why the hell not?" Aunt Bunchie jumps in.

"I don't think that's a good idea," Maurice answers.

Rusty says, "I agree. They have gone through too much right now. They'll think we don't want them, that we are leaving them."

"Think about it Rusty. You guys are young and three girls are a lot of work. These girls are still young and need proper supervision. You guys think you can do this, but…."

"But what?" Maurice was offended. We can take care of them, Aunt Jane."

"No you can't!" Aunt Bunchie stepped in. No you can't! These girls are young yet and so are you. You are still wet behind the ears and you think you can raise three girls? Child please, you are still raising yourselves. Running the streets, partying and women are what you're into now. Not raising your sisters. Think about it guys. We love them just like you do. We just want what we feel is best for them."

"Well, we will think about and run it by Mom. We are going to try and see her. I made a call from the house to the public defender and left a message."

Aunt Jane brings her point home, "Okay, you know we love you and we wouldn't even talk like this, but considering the situation..."

"I understand where you're coming from Aunt Jane," Maurice says, sounding so sad.

"I do too," Rusty seconds it.

"We're back!!!" Cece yelled as we came in the door with the groceries.

"I can't wait to eat" Uncle Louie says. Aunt Evy teasing him says, "You always hungry, Louie." Aunt Evy is still pissed, but she plays it off. She churned him or pinched him for lack of a better word in the car to let him know, "This is not over. Ow Evy" is all he would say. He knew he was in for it later. We giggled.

They tried to hide it, but something went on while we were gone. Barbara hunched me, "Something ain't right."

"Why you say that?"

"Look at them, they look crazy."

"You are seeing things."

"Okay Ruthie, say what you want. Something is going on and I have a feeling we aren't going to like it."

My uncle and brothers went in the living room while the women prepared dinner. Soon, they had that kitchen stinking...I mean that in a good way. They chattered back and forth as they floured, seasoned and fried. Barbara and I peeled potatoes. Little Cece stirred the Kool-Aid. After all that, it's finally done.

"Ruthie and Barbara, wash your hands and set the table" Aunt Jane told us. Then, "Dinner!!!" My uncle and brothers rushed the table and sat down. We sat down and held hands while Aunt Evy blessed the table. "Lord, bless the food we are about to receive for the nourishment of our bodies. Amen"

Everybody said "Amen."

We all dug in like the food was going to run away. All you heard was forks clanging the plates, slurping of the Kool-Aid and an occasional 'pass this' and 'pass that.' It was the best dinner ever, but a feeling of dread seems to linger... like this was one of the last dinners we would have together.

After dinner and dessert, Barbara and I began to clean the table. Everyone else was sitting there all stuffed, suffering from the "itis." Cece, said quietly, "I miss Mommy!! I want to see Mommy" and she starts to cry a little. Rusty pulls her from her chair and sits her on his lap.

"Cece, we all miss Mommy and we will see her real soon." I put in a call to the public defender and we should know soon."

"You promise?"

"I promise." He hugs her. With the kitchen cleaned, we went into the living room and watched TV. It was getting a little late----Tomorrow is Sunday and everyone agreed to go to church. We stayed together as a family that night and that feeling stayed with us the next day before and after church, even when Aunt Evy, Uncle Louie, Aunt Jane and Bunchie left for their homes Sunday evening. It was a good comforting feeling that I had.

Everything is set, but.........

It's Monday. At the District Attorney's office, Assistant Prosecutor Andrew Dunlap was reading over his notes about the Walters case. He read the witnesses account of what happened as well as Beulah's confession. It was a difficult case, even if she confessed. He thought "was she coerced; did she really do it or? He needed to see the tape. He phoned the detective and asked to meet with him. He buzzed his secretary, Janis Jim. "Janis, would you get Detective Blake Coleman, at the Philadelphia Police Department on the line." "Yes sir." She buzzed him to let him know Detective Coleman was on line. "Detective, this is Assistant Prosecutor Andrew Dunlap."

"Yes Andrew, how may I help you?"

"I need a favor. I need to see the tape of Mrs. Walters' confession."

"Sure. When? "I am here until 3."

"I'm on my way."

She is sitting at her desk and reading over the transcript from court. She has the confession as well as the witnesses account. "Something just don't read right." She decides to make a surprise visit to see Beulah. She gathers her keys, briefcase and heads to her office door. She is on her way out the door and calls to her secretary, Carolyn Bates. "Carolyn, I am leaving for the jail to see a client."

"Okay, but before you go, a Maurice Walters left a message for you on the night operator's switchboard.

"Did he leave a number?"

"Yes, I wrote it down. She hands her the message."

"Thanks. If he calls back, tell him I got his message and that I will phone him when I return."

Before she could get out the door good, the phone rings.

"Sheila Mathis's office."

"This is the Andrew Dunlap from District Attorney's office. May I speak with Shelia?"

"One moment please." Carolyn puts him on hold and gets up from her desk to try and catch her.

"Wait!! Ms. Mathis. It's the Asst. Prosecutor on the phone. He says it's important."

Sheila turns around and head back in the door. "Okay, I'll take it in my office."

She walks back to her office and closes the door. She drops her purse and briefcase on the visitor chair as she goes behind her desk. She sits down and picks up the receiver. "Hello Andrew."

"Hello Sheila, I need to meet with you to discuss Mrs. Walter's case. It's called discovery, you know."

"Look Andrew I know my job and I don't need to hear your crap this early in the day. As a matter of fact, I was on my way to see her."

"Ha, Ha, Ha." You're still the uptight lawyer that never seems to have a good day."

"Well, I was having one until you called."

"Yeah, sure. When can we meet?" "I am free to see you later this afternoon."

"See me? Look, Andrew don't even try it. We can meet to discuss the case and that's it."

"OK OK OK Sheila." "I have an appointment at 2 and should be back around 4."

"No good Andrew. I have a previous engagement."

"Previous engagement? With who?"

"That ceases to be none of your business anymore. Let's try for tomorrow around 9:30."

Silence.

"Andrew!!"

"Sheila, I…"

"Andrew!!!"

"Okay Sheila 9:30 is fine."

CLICK!! She smiles," Serves you right." She again leaves her office and this time she makes it to the elevator just when it was about to the close. "I made it." Now to see Mrs. Walters.

CHAPTER FIFTEEN

R USTY LEFT FOR work early and Maurice left us alone for a minute while he went to Ms. Etta's to use her phone to call his job to let them know he would be needing time off for his Daddy's funeral. Rusty said he would tell his job when he got there.

After he came back from Ms. Etta's, Maurice hung out with us all day. We went through the day talking playing etc. We were on the porch when Rusty came home. Barbara and I was playing jacks, Maurice was reading the Daily News and Cece was combing her doll's hair. He pulled up to the curb in front of the house and parked. He crossed over the front seat and came out on the passenger side.

He yelled to us as he climbed the steps, "Hey, what y'all doing?"

"Hey Russ" we all said together.

Maurice asked "Russ, have you spoke with the lawyer about seeing Mom?"

"Nah!" "I stopped by my apartment and there were no messages. So I called her office and her secretary said she was out, but that she got my message. She supposed to call me back later. I left her Ms. Etta's phone number, just in case she couldn't reach me. So, what's for dinner?"

"Your guess is as good as mine. Let's go out."

"You got money?"

"No, you do."

"Yay!!!" Cece yelled.

We had a ball. We went to Creole Creations on 69th Street in Upper Darby. Everybody ordered fish, except Cece and me. Rusty ordered her the children's spaghetti, but me, I had to have fried chicken. By the time the food came, Maurice's lips were white from hunger. When I ordered the chicken, he fussed. "Ruthie, why couldn't you order fish? You know chicken is going to make our order longer to come."

"I want what I want," I answered.

Well, it was well worth the wait. The chicken was finger licking good. When dinner was over, Rusty called the waiter over for the check and asked for hand wipes. We cleaned ourselves and left the restaurant not before stopping at the counter grabbing a handful of mints. We ended the night with ice cream cones from the Dairy Queen. We went home stuffed and enjoyed the memory of the evening, not realizing this was one of the last dinners we'd have as FAMILY...

CHAPTER SIXTEEN

S HEILA IS ON her way to her office to prepare to meet with the Asst. Prosecutor the next day. She's recounting her visit with Beulah in jail yesterday and the visit left her drained. She sits in her car and relives the entire day, starting with the jail visit. She arrived at the jail. She had called ahead, letting them know she was coming to see her client. She went through the procedures; the search of her belongings, etc. Each time she felt violated. That's was the one part she hated about being a servant of the court. She was led into a room by the CO where the only thing visible was a table and two chairs, one on either side. Also inside the room, sat Mrs. Walters in her orange jumpsuit, looking depressed, withdrawn with black circles under her eyes and her hair was wild. Before she could start talking, as soon as she saw her, she looked her straight in the eye and said, "I want this over."

I'm sorry I don't understand. What do you mean by that?"

"I have no fight left in me and I want to plead guilty."

I said, "Wait a minute."

She held up her hand. "No, you wait a minute. I did it. I killed my husband and there's no question about it. I didn't mean to do it, but why drag this on."

"Do you understand what you're saying? You're giving up your rights to a trial."

"I don't want a trial."

"You're playing with your life."

"I understand everything I am saying to you. Either you go to the Judge or I'll get somebody else."

"So you want to plead guilty?"

"Yes."

"Okay, I'll set up a meeting with the Asst. Prosecutor and see about settling for a lesser charge thru a plea agreement."

"What's that?"

"It's an agreement that is between you and the prosecutor, agreeing to guilt.

"I am guilty."

"So you say, but by signing the agreement, you are giving up your constitutional rights?"

"Look, Ms. Mathis, I killed him, okay? Draw up the papers and I'll sign."

"Mrs. Walters…"

"Bring the damn papers!!!" She scoots her chair back and gets up. She walks to the door and yells "Guard." She then she turns around and says, "Oh, by the way, I want to see my kids."

The guard appears and she says "I'm ready." I hear the key being inserted into the lock and the guard opens up the door and leads her out. I just sat there, not believing what just happened.

DONNA EARL

CHAPTER SEVENTEEN

T HE DAY WAS moving along really slow. Today is just Tuesday. I kept expecting my Mom and Daddy to come home, to come in saying "I'm home" but... We basically went through each day, playing, eating etc. just normal stuff. Uncle Louie and Aunt Evy were over talking about family stuff such as the funeral.

"Maurice, did you find out about the insurance?"

"Well, Unc, the insurance company said Daddy had a small policy and I think, from what the agent says, it was worth about ten grand."

"That's good. So you can pay the remaining balance and have some left over."

"Yeah, we can pay you back."

"That's alright nephew, keep it, because you'll need it."

Aunt Evy's eyes got big. Her eyes were saying, "What's he talking about? We need too!!"

CHAPTER EIGHTEEN

S HEILA ARRIVES AT her office early, around 8:00 a.m. She is meeting with the Asst. Prosecutor, Andrew Dunlap at 9:30. She speaks just above a whisper, "I need to speak with Mrs. Walter's son." She looks in her purse to find the number. She can't find it. "Where the hell is that number?" She's tearing through her purse. She dumps her pocketbook out on her desk. She keeps looking. "Oh, here it is!" She dials the number and it rings two times.

"Hello." Ms. Etta answers.

"Hello, may I speak with Russell Walters?"

"Who is this?"

"This is Sheila Mathis."

"I'm sorry he isn't here right now. May I take a message?"

"Please tell him to call me."

"Does he have your number?"

"Yes, but let me give it to you. Do you have a pen?"

"Hold on a minute" Ms. Etta tells her.

She lays the phone down on the table. She searches the desk drawer for a pen and paper. When she finds them, she comes back to the phone. She picks up the receiver and says, "Okay I have it now."

"My number is 215-872-0876."

"I'll give him the message."

"Please tell him it's important."

"I sure will."

"Thank you." Click!

Ms. Etta stood looking at the receiver and questioned out loud "Now, what was that all about?" "Well, there's only one way to find out." She stumps out her cigarette and puts on her slippers. She heads out the door towards the Walter's house.

'Rusty, have you heard from..." The conversation was interrupted by knock, knock, knock.

"I wonder who that is." A question asked by Rusty to no one in particular. He gets up from the table and heads towards the door. He gets closer and yells "Who is it?"

"It's Ms. Etta," she answers. He opens the door.

"Hey Ms. Etta. Come on in."

She comes in and he closes the door. She follows him down the hall to where we were, in the kitchen as usual. "How's everybody?" she asks.

"Hey Ms. Etta" we all say at once.

"Rusty. Here." She hands him the note. "You got a message from a Sheila Mathis."

"Well, it's about time."

"Who's that?"

"Oh, that's Mom's lawyer. From the message, she wants me to call her. I hope it's some news about seeing Mom.

"When you gonna call her back?"

"Her office is probably closed now. I'll call her tomorrow."

CHAPTER NINETEEN

S HEILA IS MEETING with Andrew at the D. A's office. She arrives about a half an hour early and is sitting in the outer office. Her mind is cloudy. She is reliving the conversation she had with Beulah. "I'm pleading guilty. I killed my husband." The door to the office opens and in comes Andrew. "Hello Sheila." The sound of his voice brings her out her daydream. "You're here early."

"Hello Andrew", she answers sorta rough.

"My, my, my, somebody woke up on the wrong side of the bed. Date didn't go well I take it."

"Look Andrew, I'm not in the mood for your bullshit this morning. Can we just get this over with?"

"Fine!! We are meeting in the conference room. Do you want some coffee or something?"

"No."

"Suit yourself."

Sheila gets up from the couch to follow him down the hall. She is walking a little slow. Her mind is trying to figure out the best deal she can get for her client. She thought to herself "even if she pleads guilty, she still deserves…"

"We're here" Andrew announces.

In attendance were herself, Andrew, Andrews' boss, the Lead Prosecutor Byron Duncan, and Blake Coleman, the Lead Detective from the Police Department. In the conference room, at the roundtable, Sheila sat across from the Detective and Andrew sat across from his boss.

"May we begin? Andrew begins. "Case B12764 PA vs. Beulah Walters. Mrs. Walters is accused of 2nd degree assault. We have forensic evidence, witnesses and the tape of confession. After review of the tape, the defendant was not coerced in anyway."

"I haven't seen the tape."

"Sheila, you had plenty of time to see the tape. I tried to meet with you yesterday afternoon, but what did you say? I have a previous engagement."

"Andrew, my availability to meet with you yesterday has nothing to do with me not seeing the tape."

Byron Dunlap and Detective Coleman were looking at each other, wondering what was going on.

She continues. "As a matter of fact, I met with my client yesterday and…."

"And what Sheila?" Andrew asks.

"Nevermind."

"Nevermind? Did you hear that? What kind of answer is that?" Andrew's boss spoke up. "Ms. Mathis, if you have any information important to this case, I suggest you spill it".

"Well, I spoke with her and she wants to change her plea to guilty."

"What?!!!"

Everybody in the room had a shocked look on their faces.

"Yes, she wants to plead guilty."

"And that's it?" yells Andrew. Sheila ignores Andrew and continues.

"I propose a plea of voluntary manslaughter, serving 5 years with a chance of parole."

"Fat chance Sheila. You know the law as well as I do. In this state, Pennsylvania does not allow a defendant a voluntary manslaughter charge if the defendant had enough time to cool off or calm down between the act of provocation and the homicide."

"Andrew, Ms. Walter admits she was upset because of the argument she was having with her husband."

"Sheila" he says sarcastically, "she left the room and came back and hit the man in the head."

Sheila is pleading with him now. "Andrew, this happened in the heat of passion."

Andrew rolls his eyes and kept on talking. "If this happened right when the argument happened, I can see that, but she left the room, got the weapon, came back and BAM!! You better be glad I am not seeking murder."

Sheila was beside herself now. She had it with him. "Andrew, you're just being a jackass!!"

"Stop it right now!!!" Byron Duncan jumps in. "This bickering back and forth is not getting us anywhere. Let's take a break and meet here in about 15 minutes."

Sheila got up and left the room in a huff. She was pissed. The Detective left to make a phone call, leaving Andrew sitting there, breathing hard and his boss, staring at him so hard, he could have burned a hole in his head. He got up and closed the door.

He starts in on Andrew. "What the hell is going on here? Instead of a meeting of the minds, this looks like a spat between lovers. What, did you screw her before?"

"Sir, I'm sorry."

"Sorry for what?"

"We use to date -- about a year and a half."

"What?!!

"I thought I could keep my feelings…."

"Do you know what could have happened if this was found out? We could have lost before we began. What, did you forget who she was and what went on between you two when you saw her in court? You should have excused yourself from this case right then. That's alright, I am excusing you right now. As of now, you are off this case." "I should fire you for this shit. Does anyone else know about this?"

"No sir. We were discreet. I was involved with someone else at the time."

"Well, I'll be taking over as of now. You are on thin ice for this Andrew. Leave this room right now!!! As a matter of fact, take the rest of the day off. I need time to think."

Sheila returns to the conference room. The only person present was the prosecutor.

"Where's Andrew?" she asked.

"I know about you and Andrew, Sheila."

"Sir I…"

"Sir my ass Sheila!!! No need to try and bullshit me with some lame as excuse. Andrew told me everything. I knew something was up. I sensed it before now and after seeing what I seen today, I was right. I can't believe the both of you thought this was not going to come out."

"Sir…"

"I don't want to hear it. So, with that said, I am now in charge of this case and the charge is this…based on the evidence given, the charge is involuntary manslaughter, serving 7-10 years with no chance of parole. No, let me change that, with a chance of parole after 7. I do have a heart. I will draw up the paperwork and have it messengered to your office this afternoon and I expect a signed copy in my office by close of business tomorrow."

"How am I supposed to do that?"

"I don't know Sheila." I guess this time you'll have to use your mind instead of your body."

He stands up, walks to the door and cracks it. He turned around, smiles, winks and says, "meeting is adjourned and have a good day" and walks out.

Sheila sits there staring at the door as it closes with tears in her eyes. She knew what his smile meant. It meant GOTCHA!!! She also knows she screwed up…. she screwed up big time.

CHAPTER TWENTY

LATER THAT AFTERNOON, Sheila is back at her office. She has a glass of water and some aspirin on her desk. She is rubbing her temples because she has a migraine. Just as she puts the aspirin her mouth takes a swallow of the water, her secretary buzzes her.

"Ms. Mathis, Russell Walters is on line two."

Sheila takes a deep breath and pushes the blinking button. "Sheila Mathis."

"Hello Ms. Mathis, this is Russell Walters."

"Hello Russell, how are you?"

"I'm good, but I'd be better if you have good news about seeing my Mom."

"Well, Russell your Mom is being housed at the Philadelphia Detention Center and there are procedures in visiting her."

"Procedures?"

"Yes, let me explain. Visiting hours are 10 am to 6 p.m., Monday through Friday." "Defendants visiting days are according to their last name and since her last name begins with a W, most likely Friday will be the earliest for a visit."

"Friday?!!!" He shouts. Friday is the day of my Daddy's funeral. I thought we could see her before then. We haven't been able to see her and talk to her in days."

"Russell, I am not sure there is anything I can do. The best I can do is to call and find out if an exception can be made."

"Have you had a chance to see her?"

"Yes, I have and frankly the visit did not go as well as I wanted."

"What do you mean?"

"Your Mom changed her plea from not guilty to guilty."

"What?!!"

"Before I could talk to her about the case, she blurted out that she was tired and she didn't want to drag this out. I explained to her what she was giving up. I asked her did she understand and she said yes."

"What does that mean for her changing her plea?"

"I met with them yesterday and the prosecutor is charging her with involuntary manslaughter, which is a class 2 felony, serving 7-10 years with a chance of parole after seven."

"OMG!!! OMG!!! Is there anything you can do?"

"I'm afraid not Russell. I wish I could. She is so dead set on pleading guilty. The evidence is overwhelming, plus, she confessed."

"So what happens next?"

"Since she is pleading guilty, the next step is a plea agreement."

"Plea agreement? What is that?"

"It's an agreement between your mother and the prosecutor, whereby she agrees to plead guilty. What's on the table now is involuntary manslaughter serving 7-10 years with parole. Before it was without parole."

"Has she signed it?"

"No, she hasn't seen it yet. The papers just arrived today."

"I want to see her before she signs."

"The only thing, Russell, the prosecutor wants a signed copy by tomorrow.

"Oh No!! Please Ms. Mathis!!! Please, try and get us in to see her before she signs the damn thing!!!"

Lying through her teeth, she says, "Okay, Russell, I'll call the Prosecutor's office, when we hang up, to see if I can get an extension."

"Thanks for your help Ms. Mathis." I'll look forward to hearing from you soon."

"No problem."

"Goodbye." Click! She hung the phone up knowing full well she didn't have a chance in hell to get an extension. She starts to cry.

"I'm so sorry Mrs. Walters" she says to no one. How could I be so stupid?" She grabs a tissue out of the tissue box on the desk and wipes her eyes. She got out of the chair, grabbed her purse and keys and heads out the office door leaving a note for Carolyn of her destination.

After talking to Ms. Mathis, Rusty goes back to the family with the latest. When he got home, he was greeted by Cece. "Rusty" she screams!!!

"Hey shorty!!! Where's everybody?"

"They are in the kitchen." Aunt Bunchie, Aunt Jane, Uncle Louie and Aunt Evy are here too!"

"They are?"

"Yeah." They hold hands as they go down the hall.

"Hey Rusty" we all say at once.

"Hey everybody."

"Where you been?" Maurice asks.

"I stopped by my place for a change of clothes and you know, to call Mom's lawyer."

"So, what she'd say?" asked Uncle Louie.

Rusty pulls out a chair to sit at the table. He folds his hand together and starts talking.

"Well, since the arraignment, Mom has been taken to the Philadelphia Detention Center."

"Cool, that's right down the street," Maurice perks up. "We can go see her, like tomorrow!!"

"We can't, not just yet."

"Why the hell not?"

"According to her lawyer, at the Center, defendants only can receive visitors on certain days."

"Certain days? That doesn't sound right" Uncle Louie cuts in.

"Well, that's what she said. She also said that visits are assigned according to their last names and since her name starts with a W, her visit day is Friday.

"Friday!!! Oh hell no.!!! That's the same day as Daddy's funeral."

"I said the same thing, man, but that's not the best part. Mom changed her plea from not guilty to guilty."

"What?!!" "No she didn't!" Aunt Jane says.

"Yes, she did."

"Are you serious?!! You've got to be kidding."

"What does that mean?" I asked.

"That means sugar, Aunt Evy butted it, that your Mom is saying that she did it."

"We all know that!!!" Barbara screams...

"Barbara!!!" Rusty yells.

"Well, she did!!"

"What the hell you say girl?" Aunt Bunchie hollers as she stood up out of her chair, inching over to her, daring her to keep talking.

Not letting Aunt Bunchie's approach scare her, she kept talking. "We were there remember Ruthie," pointing her finger in my direction.

I was looking at her like "don't even try it."

"Girl, you better shut your goddamn mouth and shut it right now before I slap the piss out of you!!!" Aunt Bunchie says to her. She was right in Barbara's face now. Barbara was scared now with her breath right in her face. She just rolls her eyes and sucks her teeth.

"Git somewhere and sit down before I knock you down, running your damn mouth." Aunt Bunchie was breathing hard.

Aunt Jane jumped in. "Alright Bunchie, that's enough." Aunt Jane had to get in between them before anything happened. She knew how short tempered Aunt Bunchie was and she didn't want her to haul off and hit Barbara. It was quiet for a few minutes after that, everybody taking a deep breath.

"What else did she say, Rusty?"

"Well, with Mom changing her plea, she could be serving 7-10 years. She also has to sign a plea agreement."

"What's that?"

"It's an agreement that she signs admitting her guilt and agreeing to the terms. Once it's signed by her, it's reviewed by the Judge and if he agrees to it, then the sentence is handed down at the sentencing phase."

"What's going to happen to us?" I asked.

"Ruthie, we'll have to talk about that later. Right now, we have to worry about the funeral in two days. By the way, when are Aunt Julia and the rest of the family getting here?"

"Well Rusty, Uncle Louie spoke, the last I talked to them, it was Friday morning."

"I hope they come before so we could have time together. Speaking of that, we need to visit the funeral parlor to make a payment and to make sure Daddy is ready."

Maurice added, "I took Daddy's suit over there yesterday."

"Good, so all we have to do is make sure he's together. Aunt Julia will have a fit if he's looking raggedy. What time is the viewing?"

"It's at 9:00, one hour before the funeral."

"You know," Uncle Louie says shaking his head, "I can't get that visitation crap out of my mind. It just don't sound right. I have a friend whose family member jailed before and he never said anything about that bullshit that lawyer girl is talking."

"I haven't either, come to think of it, Aunt Bunchie seconds it. That's news to me. What is the name of that place again?"

"It's called The Detention Center of Philadelphia."

"Well, I'm calling to find out."

CHAPTER TWENTY-ONE

SHEILA WAS BACK at her office from visiting Beulah. Having time to think, Beulah was rethinking her guilty plea.

"You sure I'm doing the right thing signing this? I really didn't mean to kill him."

"Mrs. Walters, like I told you, the evidence is overwhelming...they have witnesses and don't forget, you confessed."

"I know, but I was upset at the time."

"The last time I was here, you were so set on pleading guilty."

"Well, I've had a change heart."

Sheila's heart was beating fast now. She was scared this was going to blow up in her face. She had to do some fast talking. "Mrs. Walters, if you don't sign the agreement, the D.A. may change the charge to murder. If you go to trial, you may get life." Laying it on thick, she kept talking. "No matter how many tears you shed or how many times you say I didn't mean to do it, if you're found guilty, you may serve the rest of your life in prison. If you sign, you do seven and you're out."

Beulah sat there, not saying anything. When she did, she said "Where do I sign?" On the inside, Sheila was grinning!!

He who laughs last gets to cry first and Sheila was going to be doing a lot of crying.

CHAPTER TWENTY-TWO

RUSTY AND I went to the funeral parlor to make sure Daddy was sharp on his day. Maurice, Cece and Barbara stayed home.

"Hello Mrs. Lars. My name is Russell Walter and this is my sister, Ruth." We just stopped by to make a payment and to check out our Daddy."

"Sure, right this way."

As we are walking, Rusty grabs my hand and I grab his hand tighter. She explains the details about tomorrow.

"Everything is in place for your family tomorrow. The family car will be to pick you up around 9:15 a.m."

"We aren't there for the viewing?"

"No. That is the time for all the well-wishers to have their moment and to pay their respect."

We walk into the sleeping chamber and there he is…go on slick!!! Daddy is sharp as a tack. He is dressed in a black suit, stripped black and white shirt and a red tie…hot damn!! He even has on red socks and his shoes are shinning. He looks as if he's sleeping.

I touch him, but pull my hand back fast. He is stiff. "Rusty, why does Daddy feel like that?

"Ruthie, they filled his body with stuff to preserve this body until burial."

"Oh."

"That's how all dead bodies feel."

We view his body a little longer, adjusting this and that. When satisfied, we go to leave. We find Mrs. Lars. She is in her office.

"Mrs. Lars, Daddy looks good. Thanks for all your help."

"You are quite welcome." She smiles.

"We'll see you tomorrow. Ok Ruthie, time…." He looks at me and notices that I am quiet. "What's' wrong?"

"I'm just sad."

He hugs me real tight and kisses me on the top of my head. "It will be ok, Ruthie." We walk out.

"Since we're out here, I need to stop home and pick up my suit and shoes."

"Okay."

"That's right, you haven't been to my place in a while have you? I got it all jazzed up now."

"No. I can't wait to see it."

We arrived at Rusty's. We get out the car and walk up to his front door with me right on his heels. Rusty opens the door and we walk in.

"Sit down baby girl and get comfortable. I'll only be a minute."

Rusty walks through the living room and into the kitchen.

"Ruthie, do you want something to drink?"

"Can I have a glass of juice?"

"Sure."

He walks in the kitchen. While in there he notices the light blinking on his answering machine. He pushes play and hears Aunt Julia's voice. "Rusty, it's Aunt Julia. Me and your Uncle Book are coming tonight instead of tomorrow. We should be there by 8:00. Smoot is coming tomorrow early with Uncle Clements and Aunt Lena. We'll see you soon. Bye." Click.

Coming back into the living room with the glass of juice in his hand he tells me, "Ruthie, Aunt Julia left a message. She and Uncle Book are coming tonight." Uh oh!!

Sheila had to meet with the Byron Duncan, Lead Prosecutor. She sat out in the outer office, waiting with her head down in thought. She wanted this over as soon as possible. She feels like shit, knowing she hoodwinked Mrs. Walters into signing the plea agreement. She really didn't trick her, she just didn't or couldn't fight harder. She put herself in this mess. If only...

"Hello Sheila." He comes out and greets her. She stands up and shakes his hand.

"Hello Byron."

"Please come in."

She walks in. His office is painted a light tangerine. His carpet is plush, light cream with faint tangerine specks. He has a big oak desk with a leather chair behind it and a leather sofa on the left wall. He has plants galore. And look at that view!!

"Please have a seat."

She sits down and looks around. "This office is nice," she thinks to herself.

"Want some coffee, water?"

"No, thank you."

"Do you have the agreement?"

"Yes, I do."

"Signed, I take it?"

"Yes, she signed it." She takes it out of her briefcase and handed it to him.

"Look Sheila, I know you feel bad and if it was me I would too, but, in reality, the evidence is the evidence. She may have not deliberately killed her husband, but her actions led to his demise, plus, she confessed. I saw the tape and she was not under duress nor did the detective force her hand. She willingly did all that talking. I know if it was under different circumstances, it could have been a dog fight in court. I've seen you action, but at the end of the day, Mrs. Walters nailed her coffin shut by confessing. I am not trying to make you feel better, I am just stating facts."

"I understand, sir. This is a road I will not travel again."

"Well," standing up and coming from around his desk, I hate to cut this short, but I must file this agreement with the court. You know the Judge will have the final say. Thanks for coming and under better circumstances, next time okay?"

"Most definitely."

He extends his hand and she shakes it. She leaves his office - not before turning around and smiling.

That smile lasted while she ran a couple of errands, it lasted until….

After seeing her so call lawyer, Beulah was feeling depressed. "I want to see my kids" she said to no one in a voice, just above a whisper. She was sitting in the dayroom at the Detention Center. The dayroom was a spacious room with many tables and cut off stool-like chairs and a TV. It was decorated with freshly painted off white walls and blue doors. If you didn't know any better you, it would seem you were in a cafeteria, except for the surveillance cameras, security and the two person rooms.

Normally, despite everything, Beulah was trying to be herself. She would cut up, crack jokes etc., with the other women, especially with a woman she befriended named Annette. Annette was an around the way girl, that caught a robbery charge. After her visit with Sheila, she was sitting by herself with her head down, looking at the floor. Annette walked in the dayroom and noticed her mood. She approached her, "Hey girl, what's wrong?"

"Oh, nothing really."

"Don't give me that Beulah, something's wrong. What is it?"

"Well if you must know, I miss my kids!"

"When's the last time you seen them?"

"It's been about a week."

"A week? Is that all? I haven't seen my kids in at least a year."

"I'm sorry to hear that, Annette. You don't understand. I am here waiting to see what's going to happen to me. When I first came, here, they explained to me that I needed to give them a list of visitors. When I did, they said seeing my kids could take up to thirty (30) days. Thirty days, Annette!! My children are young and they have no idea what's going on with me. I need to explain some things, make arrangements for them. I can't call them because my house phone is disconnected and to talk to them on my neighbor's phone will not do. I need to see them in person."

"Well, Annette began, there are such things as 'special visits'."

"Special visits?"

"Yeah girl! The visits are done on non-visiting days and are approved by the Captain."

"You think they will approve one for me?"

"Yeah, I think so. Just tell the CO that you need to talk to the unit manager about a special visit. Look, there is the CO, right there. Go on and talk to him." Beulah hesitates getting up. Annette pulls her up and pushes her, "Hurry up girl."

CHAPTER TWENTY-THREE

UNCLE LOUIE CALLED the Detention Center of Philadelphia several days later to inquire about the visiting hours. That mumbo jumbo he heard did not sit right with him. It was the first thing on his mind when he got up this morning. He called information and the operator gave him the number. He couldn't dial that number fast enough.

"Detention Center of Philadelphia, how may I help you?" the clerk answered.

"Hello, I need some information. I would like to know how families can visit inmates."

"Well, sir, first of all, visiting hours are Wednesday through Friday from 6:15 a.m. until 2:30 p.m. You must be on the inmates' visitors' list and inmates will not be allowed no more than five visitors at a time. Children under the age of 16 may not visit unless with an adult. Visitations last for one hour."

"Is there some way to find out if your name is on the list?"

"Sir, normally we don't give that type of information over the phone. I've told you as much as I can."

"Please, ma'am"

"Sir, are you trying to get me fired?"

"No, but please, it's important."

"What is the inmates' name?"

"Beulah Walters."

"One moment. Sir, she has her children on the list and it looks like a special visit request was made for the children and approved."

"Thank you Miss. You have been very helpful."

When Uncle Louie hung the phone up he shouted "I knew it!" Aunt Evy came running in the living room.

"What's wrong, Louie?"

"Ain't nothing wrong Evy, but the bullshit the lawyer had been telling them kids didn't have any truth in it nowhere. They could have seen their mother days ago. Normally, it takes thirty days for the background check and everything, but there such things are special visits. Their visits could have been an exception, if the lawyer spoke with the authorities."

"You've got to be kidding me."

"No babe, I'm not."

Rusty and Ruthie get back home. She comes in the house and runs and dives on the couch. Ruthie is dog tired because Rusty had her going here and there. "Can't hang, can you girl?" He laughs. He heads to the kitchen. Maurice was in there by himself, drinking a glass of water.

"Hey bro!"

"What's up kid?"

"Ain't nothing bro."

"Uncle Louie and Aunt Evy were over."

"Oh yeah?"

"Yeah. They'll be back later."

"Ok. Did they say what time?"

"No, why?"

"I stopped by the house and Aunt Julia left a message about her and Uncle Book coming tonight."

"Oh hell, we better start cleaning up."

"By the way, Unc said he called that Detention Center today."

"He did?"

"Yeah."

"He said that silly lawyer of Mom's didn't tell the full truth. He said that in order for us to visit Mom, we have to be put on her visitor list. We are. He also said in certain instances, they grant special visits. Mom must have explained her situation and requested one. It was approved. He also said that the lawyer could have done the same thing if she wanted."

"Well I'll be damn!!! I wonder why Ms. Mathis didn't tell us that."

"Rusty, you better get that thing on the phone right now! Tell her we want to see Mom and see her now."

Before Maurice could count to three, Rusty was out the door and on his way to Ms. Etta's house.

"You just wait until…she'd better have some answers."

When Rusty arrived at Ms. Etta's door, he was mad as hell. You could see it on his face. His nose was flaring and he was sweating on the top of his nose. When that happens business is about to pick up. We found that out the hard way. One day he and Reese were having words, back and forth. Reese was jumping up in Rusty's face and he was just looking at him. All of a sudden, Rusty grabbed Reese by the throat and lifted his ass up in the sky and looked him dead in the eyes. Then he put him down. Reese went somewhere, anywhere to get out of Rusty's sight. "We've been had by this woman." He knocked on her door. When Ms. Etta was taking too long, he banged. She came to door with a look that said, "What… Oh it's you Rusty. Come on in."

"Ms. Etta, may I use your phone?"

"Sure, Rusty."

"I need to call Ms. Mathis."

"Who?"

"You know, Mom's lawyer."

"What's wrong?"

"I just found out the lawyers' been lying to us."

"Boy, hush."

"Yeah, Ms. Etta."

"Well go on and call her. You know where the phone is."

Rusty goes in the kitchen and uses the phone. Ms. Etta pretended to go back and watch TV, but she had the sound down. "I got to hear this," she thought.

It was 2:00 and Sheila was still smiling inside when Carolyn buzzed her. "Ms. Mathis, its Russell Waters on line 2." She pushes the flashing light. "Sheila Mathis." Rusty didn't even say hello.

"I don't know what kind of game you are playing, but I'm not the one to be played with." Russell was yelling in the phone. She could feel the steam coming through the receiver.

"I beg your pardon."

"I'll beg your pardon alright."

"Ms. Mathis, I just found out that we could have seen our mother long before and you knew it."

"I'm afraid I don't know what you are talking about."

"Cut the bull lady. Don't act like you don't know Ms. Mathis. We did some checking and found out that our mother has us on her visitors list and that a special visit request was made and approved."

"Oh no," she thinks to herself. "Russell, I did not know that." He cuts her off. "You know the system a hellava lot better than I do. The

DONNA EARL

same damn information that we now know is the same information you knew all the time." Ms. Etta was eavesdropping the whole time. "Get her Rusty."

"All this time you were skinning and grinning, knowing full well what our options were, but what I do know is that if you don't have some visit information to me before the day is out, I am going to pay a visit to the courthouse myself. Is that clear Ms. Mathis?" Slam!!! The smile was off her face now.

He left Ms. Etta's house. If possible, you could see steam coming from his ears. He hadn't given her a chance to answer. He just hung up. He could have gone buck wild and threatened to come to her office and get that ass, but his message was loud and clear.

CHAPTER TWENTY-FOUR

WE CLEANED THE house from top to bottom, making sure everything was in place. We had the music blasting, listening to *WDAE*, that song "Say You Love Me Girl" was playing by the group Breakwater. It seems playing music made cleaning house more fun and faster. Cece dusted, I vacuumed and Barbara cleaned the bathroom upstairs and the small powder room downstairs. Maurice helped with the mopping of the floors while Rusty mowed the lawn. We changed the linen on the beds and cleaned the windows. When we were almost done, we all sat back and were proud of how good things were looking.

Rusty had just finished putting the lawnmower away. He was coming back around to the front just in time to see Aunt Julia and Uncle Book pulling up in front of the house in a silver Buick. He stood there waiting on the sidewalk as they both got out the car with Julia having a big smile on her face.

"Hey nephew!!," she yelled as she grabbed Rusty.

"Aunt Julia!!!" They hugged each other real right.

"Hey Boy!!," Uncle Book said as they greeted each other with a strong handshake.

"So glad y'all made it safely."

"Yeah boy, it was a long drive, but we're here."

"Come on in."

"Ok, but first let me get the bags."

"Let me help you." Uncle Book and Rusty go around to the back of the car and open the trunk. Aunt Julia made her way to the front door. She wasn't hardly helping carrying bags. Uncle Book says, looking at her, "typical woman."

"You better not let her hear you."

"I know." They both laugh. Uncle Book asks "Who's here?"

"Aunt Evy and Uncle Louie are here." Rusty answers.

"Where's the rest of the family?"

"They'll be here. Lena and Clements should be here in the morning. Noonsie and all who else are coming gonna meet at their house and will come together."

As Julia was making her way to the front door, Uncle Louie saw her coming through the front window curtains. He swung the door open and cried "Julia!!"

"Uncle!!!" They hug.

"How you?"

"I'm good.

I'm so glad to see you."

"Come on in here and sit down." By this time, Rusty and Uncle Book came in the door struggling with the suitcases.

"Hey Book!"

"Hey Uncle." They hug.

"How was the drive?"

"Long!!!" They laugh.

"Julia, Uncle Book said with smiling eyes, you could have helped us with the bags, woman." She looked at Uncle Book, rolled her eyes and said "Hmphf."

"Are Clem and Lena coming?"

"Yeah. I told Rusty, they'll be here in the morning with Noonsie and them."

"Good."

"Y'all hungry?"

"No. Julia made me stop on the way. She claimed she was hungry."

"You were hungry too Book so don't be putting it all on me."

We laughed at those two. They are the same crazy couple I remember, always jonning on each other, but they loved each other to pieces. They make a cute, but funny couple. Aunt Julia is a squirt of a woman. She is the splitting image of Daddy. Uncle Book is a black, tall giant with specks of grey in his hair. It was so nice to see them. It has been about a year and a half since we've seen them. I believe it was at the family reunion in Durham. I remember Daddy putting us in the car in the wee hours of the morning. It was still dark. The drive was for, it seems, forever. The reunion, a two-day event starting with the picnic on Saturday, was at Eno River Park. We met the family there. When we arrived, it was boo coo people everywhere. We got out the car and you could smell the grill and see the smoke. The music was blazing. We had a ball!! We ate, played, ate and played. The food was endless. We played volleyball and horseshoes. We played card games like tonk, pittypat and we played pokeno, while the adults played poker and drank liquor. My Mom and Daddy had an old tymey ice cream maker. I remember it looked like a bucket. It was blue and had a crank you put on top. You added salt, a custard, some ice and cranked it real hard. My Daddy put us kids to work. All the kids took turn in cranking. The faster you cranked, the smoother the ice cream. We had a good time. The memory of it is making my mouth water. The reunion was the best and we didn't want it to end. We stayed at Uncle Woodrat and his girlfriend, Suzy May's house overnight and went to church the next day. Boy, what a memorable time.

Despite the reason for their visit, they were in good spirits, especially Aunt Julia. The rest of the evening was uneventful, just sitting around talking. The adults, Uncle Louie, Uncle Book, Rusty and Maurice stayed up while us kids, Barbara, Cece and I, went to bed. Daddy's funeral is tomorrow. RIP... I don't think so.

CHAPTER TWENTY-FIVE

SHEILA SAT IN her office. She is looking out the window in her office. She just got off the phone, leaving the message on Rusty's answering machine that their visit will be on Monday. His threat is still lingering in the air. "He's right to be angry. If Judge Tucker finds out ......! Oh Jesus, I would be screwed. Well what's done is done. He and his family are going to see their Mom on Monday. Carolyn buzzes her.

"Ms. Mathis, its Byron Dunlap on the line."

"Oh shit" a voice went on in her mind. "Thanks." "Sheila Mathis."

"Hello Sheila, this is Byron Dunlap."

"Hello Byron."

"This will be brief." The Judge accepted the plea agreement and the sentencing hearing will be next Friday at 9:30. Please make your client aware of these proceeding and what to expect. Have a good weekend. Goodbye." Click. She looked at the receiver and said, "Dag, he wasn't lying. That was quick."

CHAPTER TWENTY-SIX

I T'S 7:30 A.M. The day of the funeral is here. My stomach is in knots. I laid awake just about all night. I'm so nervous, lying here looking at the ceiling. Did I sleep? I know I have to hurry up and get dressed, but I have no idea what to wear. I've never been to a funeral before. Maurice warned us that the car was coming at 9:15. So, I tell myself, "Get up Ruthie." So I get up, so I can beat the rush for the bathroom, with all the company we have. Aunt Julia and Uncle Book were here. Other relatives were due anytime.

I hurried to the bathroom just in time, because I see Aunt Julia coming down the hall.

"Good Morning, Aunt Julia."

"Hey Ruthie."

"You wanna go first?"

"No child, you go. I can wait. I'll just go in and visit with your sisters."

I go in the bathroom and clean up, but when I started to wash my face, it hit me! Today, we are burying Daddy and Mommy's not here! I started crying. As I looked in the mirror, tears were flowing down my face. Knock, knock, knock. "Ruthie!" She must have heard me sobbing. Aunt Julia peeped in.

"Ruthie are you...?" She could see that I was crying. "Ruthie, aw child, come here." She hugged me, soothing me with her touch. "Shush, now, its' okay baby," patting me on my back. She held me in her arms rocking me back and forth. She held me until I felt better. She said, "Ruthie, I miss him too!" I look up and see tears flowing down her face. She was crying too. "Okay, Ruthie, wiping my tears, go and get dressed."

"Love you, Aunt Julia."

"Love you too, Ruthie."

I left her in the bathroom. In my closet, I found a dark blue dress to wear. Barbara and Cece were up now. I said, "Barbara, Aunt Julia is in the bathroom right now, so when she is finished, please help Cece get washed and dressed."

To my surprise, Rusty and Maurice were already dressed and had coffee brewing.

"Good Morning Ruthie."

"Morning," I say as I made my way to the refrigerator.

Rusty walks over to me and says in a hushed voice, "Ruthie I want to tell you something."

"What?"

"I got some news about Mom."

"What is it", I asked nervously?

"Well, we will be going to see her on Monday."

"How?"

"Well, I went home this morning to check on my place and she left a message on the answering machine. Don't say anything to Barbara and Cece yet. We'll talk about it later after everything. Okay?"

"Okay."

Around 8:30, two carloads of other relatives arrive. Uncle Clements, Aunt Lena, cousins Noosie, Smoot and Sandra were in one car and Cousins Clara, Robert, Sylvia, Charlotte and crazy Willie in the other. They knock on the door. Bang, Bang, Bang! Maurice says, "What the hell…!" He walks to the door and the leader of the pack banging was crazy Willie. Maurice swung that door open and said, "Man, why in the hell are you banging on that door like that?"

"Aww cousin, you know me."

"Not today!!!" Maurice says and turns away leaving the door open so they can come in.

"Hey everybody!"

"Hey," we all shout.

Everybody is mingling, exchanging pleasantries when the car arrives from the funeral parlor. Showtime!!!

We pile in our cars and make the journey to the funeral. We arrived at the parlor and the street is lined on both sides with cars. Knowing a lot of people were here made me nervous. We walk in and it's packed. We were escorted to the front row and right in front of us is the casket and it's open. Before we sit, we viewed the body. Daddy looks so good!!! Once we were done, then the rest of the viewers are allowed. When they were done, the casket was closed. We were greeted by Daddy's co-workers, his friends, our friends and neighbors. It was a great turn out. Aunt Julia held up real well and we kids, we cried, but we did good. I thought for sure that Barbara would faint, but we all did alright. People spoke well of my Daddy. It was good to hear.

Aunt Bunchie and Aunt Jane had arrived at the funeral parlor just about the same time we did. They sat in the car talking, watching everyone, including us, go in.

Bunchie started in - "I don't know…should we go in? I don't want any shit from Sam's family."

"Bunchie, don't worry. We just paying our respect, plus we're here for the kids."

"Well…"

"Well nothing, let's go."

We buried Daddy. That was the hardest thing to do and see. Maurice, Barbara, Cece and I held hands as Daddy's casket was lowered down in the ground. Uncle Book had to hold Aunt Julia up. I noticed Aunt Bunchie and Aunt Jane there. They were in the back. Aunt Julia noticed they were there too and gritted on them hard.

The repast went on without no problems… Everybody mingled and ate and after a while, people started leaving. We said our goodbyes, shook hands, and hugged all who were there. My relatives, who drove up this morning, decided to drive back home to Durham. After everybody left, we went home. We, including Aunt Jane and Aunt Bunchie, drove back to the house. We all were drained from the day so when we got home we just we sat around in our own thoughts.

We started talking about Daddy, trading funny stories, trying to lighten up the mood. The adults started "tasting" and the kids had soda. After a few drinks, Aunt Julia started acting real simple. She talked about Daddy and mentioned my Mom and how they got married and left town.

"I never could stand that woman."

Aunt Jane and Aunt Bunchie eyebrows raised and bodies stiffened, but they kept their lips clamped.

Uncle Book says, "Now Julia, I think you've said enough."

"No, I haven't. If it wasn't for that stinking thing, we wouldn't be here at Sam's funeral." "The only good thing about her was…"

"Hold up Julia, Aunt Bunchie said. That's our sister you're talking about." Drunkenly, Julia kept talking.

"I don't give a fuck if she is your sister. She killed my brother and she was nothing but a whore."

"Julia shut up!!" Uncle Louie roared.

Julia stood up.

"Don't tell me what to do. I do as I please." She walked over to Aunt Bunchie and Aunt Jane stepped in front of her.

"Normally, I don't act a fool, but I know how to, Aunt Jane warned her. We didn't come here for this. We're here for the kids, so back it up."

"What you gonna do?"

Uncle Book grabbed her arm, but she snatched it away.

"Julia, you don't want none of this." Aunt Julia came closer and Aunt Jane quickly reached in her purse and brought out her 'running partner;' a straight razor.

"Now, I done told you. You bring your ass any closer and I'll cut you too short to shit!!"

Everybody's eyes were bucked.

"Aunt Jane!!" Maurice called her name.

She shushed him with her hand, but kept her eyes on Julia. Aunt Jane was upset so her voice was a little raised when she said, "Look Julia, my sister done a bad thing and she's gonna pay for it. You know as well, as I do it was a mistake. She didn't mean to do it, but don't think we're going to sit here and let you talk about our sister like that."

Aunt Julia just stood there. Then she put her hands up to her face and started crying. "I miss him!!!"

Aunt Jane put her razor down and walked over to her and the two of them just stood there in the middle of the floor, hugging and crying. Through her tears and sobs, Aunt Julia says "I'm sorry Jane. Please forgive me."

"I'm sorry too, Julia."

Aunt Julia was crying for her brother and Aunt Jane was crying for her sister. Everybody just watched with eyes full of tears.

Time to go to bed!!!

CHAPTER TWENTY-SEVEN

SUNDAY MORNING WAS beautiful. After last night's episode, everybody was in good spirits. All my aunties made a spread to die for. We had fried apples, potatoes, grits, biscuits and eggs. It was GOOD!!! After breakfast, we cleaned the kitchen and sat around with full bellies.

"Well, Uncle Book says, I guess it's time to get on the road."

"Oh No! We hate to see you go."

"Yeah, but you know you can always come down."

"We will soon," Rusty added. Rusty, Uncle Book, Uncle Louie and Maurice grabbed the suitcases that were by the front door and walked out to pack the car. Aunt Evy and Aunt Julia hugged each other and said their goodbyes. Then it was Aunt Julia, Aunt Bunchie and Aunt Jane's turn. They hugged, but there was still a little tension left. Julia cut through the tension and said, "It's not your fault ladies and I have nothing against you. Please forgive me."

"We do Julia. It was something that happened and I know in my heart she didn't mean it."

"It was a tragic accident and I'm aware of that."

"Take care of yourself Julia and have a safe trip," Aunt Bunchie adds. They walk her to the door. She walks out to the car and Rusty and Maurice hugged her and shook Uncle Books' hand. They piled in their car and with waves, they drove down the street, on their way back home.

The rest of the day was quiet. A little later, Uncle Louie and Aunt Evy went home. Aunt Bunchie and Aunt Jane stayed back.

"Rusty, what's going on with you all seeing your Mom?"

"I didn't tell you, but we are going to see Mom tomorrow."

"We are?", Barbara asked.

"Yes, we are Barbara. All of us." She was about to say more, but Aunt Bunchie had a bead on her.

"How'd that happen?"

"Well, you remember when Mom's lawyer was talking all that ying yang about the visiting hours and visiting days?"

"Yeah, I remember."

"Well, Uncle Louie checked it out. We found out that Mom has all of us, including you, on her visitors list and that a special visit request was made and approved."

"You're kidding?"

"No. So I blasted that lawyer and told her that she'd better fix this or I was going to the courthouse myself."

"Good for you Rusty."

"I went by the house yesterday morning and she left the info on my answering machine."

"Well, now that we know we can go see her, we want to go with you."

"Auntie, do you mind if we go first?"

"Not a problem, that's probably a good idea, but let us know how she's doing. Tell her we'll probably come Wednesday."

"Okay."

Getting up from the couch, "Well we'd best be getting on."

"We'll keep in touch."

"Do that."

We said our goodbyes and they were off.

Everybody's gone now. We kids were left to face tomorrow and who knows what tomorrow brings…SHOCK!!!

CHAPTER TWENTY-EIGHT

RUSTY OPENS OUR bedroom door and turn on the light. He yells, "Ruthie, Barbara and Cece, y'all get up and get dressed!!"

I sat and looked at the clock. Its 6:30 a.m.!!! Cece wakes up, but just lies there. Barbara sleepily says "Why?"

"We're going to see Mom."

Cece cries "Ooh Mommy!! I wanna go." She jumped out of bed. She got so excited.

Barbara says "I don't want to go and turns back over."

"Get up Barbara and get up now!!"

"No!!" she hollers back.

He walks over to her bed and snatches the covers back. "Barbara, don't make me hurt you!!! She got up and stomped across the floor to the bathroom. We all watched her go. Slam!!! He turned to Cece and me, "Get dressed."

After getting dressed, we made our way downstairs. Barbara was still mad so she slumped down in the chair.

Rusty says, "I'm sorry Barbara for yelling. This is important. We've haven't seen Mom and I thought you'd want to see her." She didn't say a word. She just sat there with her lips poked out.

"Come on Barbara. Don't be like that," and pokes her. She slaps his hand, but smiles a little, very little.

"What time is our visit?" I asked

"Well, we got to be there early to get checked in. Visiting hours start at 6:15 and end at 2:00. Our visit time is 9:30. We only get an hour. I want to get there by 9:00. Ruthie, please fix breakfast so we can go."

I get the cereal, milk and bowls. I poured the cereal in the bowls and gave Barbara and Cece each a bowl. We ate in silence.

For a young girl, I was learning more and more about getting around in Philly. While riding, I always paid attention to the signs. We drove down 60th Street and turned right on Chestnut. Then we turned left on Schuylkill Avenue. We drove until we got on Vine Street expressway towards 1-676 to Central Philadelphia. I saw a sign saying I-95N/Trenton.

"We're going to Trenton?"

"No Ruthie."

"Oh."

We got off at Cottman Avenue exit. We rode Cottman Avenue and then Rusty made a right on State Road. OMG!! We are here.

State Road is a long road. It was so spooky going down there, but when we saw the building, it looked like a school with a lot of windows or several apartment buildings built into one.

"Whew!!!" "That's not so bad." We walk in the building and there are badges everywhere!!! I've never seen so many lawmen in one place in my life. I grabbed Maurice's hand so tight that he had to pat my hand for me to let up a little. We are processed at the front entrance. We were questioned, we showed ID, birth certificates and we were all scanned and searched. It took like forever. After it was over, we were given a table number and escorted to this big room, with tables and chairs and told to be seated until our Mom was brought in.

About 15 minutes later, MOM!!! OMG MOM! She was walked in the room by a CO and was brought over to our table. We grabbed each other all at once! We knew the deal about hugging her, so it was brief, but long enough. We all were crying!!!

While Beulah is having family time with her kids at the Detention Center, Sheila Mathis is making her way there to let Beulah know of her pending sentencing hearing on Friday. "How can I look her in the face? The woman is looking at 7 years because of me." Honk! She almost has an accident. "Get it together girl," she says to herself. Sheila is looking bad. She hasn't slept well since her conversation with Rusty. She has bags under her eyes yay long. She is talking to herself. "If it comes out that I took this case knowing that Andrew and I had a thing, Judge Tucker is... "I mean I couldn't change things because she confessed and there were witnesses. The Judge is not going to see it like that. Just like before, "You should have excused yourself from the case knowing you two had history." He warned me. "The next time..." Beads of sweat formed on her brow. "He can't find out...He can't."

Public display of affection is limited in there, so we sit.

"Mom, we miss you!!!"

"I miss you too." Surprisingly Barbara was in on the missing too.

"So guys what's been happening? How are you?"

"Well Mom, we are doing okay but …"

"But what?"

"We buried Daddy Friday."

Beulah just stared. She was speechless. She hung her head down.

Rusty chimes in, "Mom, we had to tell you now because we didn't know how to tell you earlier. You see, your lawyer bullshitted us into thinking that we couldn't see you before now until we learned better. She knew of the funeral and everything. I guess she could have told you."

"Rusty, I haven't seen or heard from her."

"Well, we buried Daddy and it was beautiful. We made sure that he was laid to rest properly."

"How did y'all get the money?"

"Well, Uncle Louie helped us. Aunt Julia and Uncle Book came, as well as Uncle Clements and Aunt Lena."

"I know Julia dogged me out."

"She tried, but your sisters, especially Aunt Jane, weren't having it. They almost had it out, but they squashed it."

Barbara spoke up. "Mom, what happened that night? Why did you kill Daddy?"

Maurice pinches her.

"Ouch!" She hollers and punches him.

"You guys, I didn't mean for this to happen. It was an accident. I loved your father with all my heart. Your Daddy and I, well we got into an argument and it got out of control. One thing led into another and the next thing you know…please understand, I didn't mean for any of this to happen. You've got to believe me. I am really sorry."

"We know, Mom." Barbara didn't say a thing. She just stared.

"Listen you guys, we don't have much time left on this visit and I need to tell you something. I need you to understand something. In a matter of time I will learn my fate. I'm still waiting to hear from the Judge about the plea agreement."

"Yeah, the infamous plea agreement," Maurice says.

"If he accepts it, I will be sentenced and will be away for some time."

Maurice asks, "Mom, why did you sign the agreement?"

"Maurice, what I did, I need to pay. As I was saying, I've given this a lot of thought and I decided that Ruthie, Barbara and Cece should go to Chester to stay with my sisters."

"Noooo! Noooo!" I shouted.

Beulah cut her eyes over to the Correctional Officer who was looking at us hard. "Ssh! Be quiet!"

"No Mom, please!"

Cece cries, "I wanna stay with Rusty and Maurice."

"This is for the best. These girls are going to Chester as soon as I talk with my sisters."

"Mom, they suggested this same thing, but I told them we could take care of them."

"Rusty, Maurice, you are young men, young men who need to live your lives and not be tied down like this."

"Mom, we don't see it like that. We are their family. We are all they got."

"I know this, but they'd be better off."

"No Mom," Maurice cuts her off.

"Look, it's settled so don't fight me on this."

"Mom…"

"What the fuck did I say?!!! Boy, don't argue with me." Her nostrils were flaring and her eyes were blazing. "Do as I say!!!" She was loud and wrong, but we knew she meant business. The CO's were on their way over to us.

Visit over.

CHAPTER TWENTY-NINE

S HEILA VISITED BEULAH in the Detention Center on the
same day. She pulled in the parking lot and found a slot three
cars from the Rusty. She didn't know that until she saw them coming
toward their car. She slid down in her car and laid on the seat making
sure they couldn't see her. She waited until they pulled off to get out.
Once she knew the coast was clear, she went in to see Beulah. She went
through the necessary Center procedures and was led to the visiting
room. About 10 minutes later, Beulah was brought out.

"Hello Mrs. Walters."

"Ms. Mathis."

"Mrs. Walters, I'll make this brief. I was informed that your plea
agreement has been accepted and the sentencing phase is Friday at
9:30." The Warden has already been made aware and he'll make the
necessary preparations.

"What's going to happen to me?"

"At the time of the hearing, you will be brought up to the Judge and
asked your side of the story." He will then sentence you. "Do you have
any other concerns or questions?"

"No."

"Well with that said, I will see you Friday."

Beulah returns to her cell. She is upset by the days' events. She is so
upset she didn't want to talk to Annette or anyone for that matter. She
needs time to think with her sentencing coming on Friday.

"I had to do it this way. I can't let them find out. Not now. It's better
this way." She sits on her bed and then turns over on her side. She sheds
a tear as she drifts off to sleep.

It was good to see Mom, but the bomb she dropped on us left me
with knots so big that I thought I was dying. How can she do that to
us? To snatch us from the only home we know? Maurice and Rusty can
take care of us.

We left the detention Center feeling let down. The ride home was quiet.

That night in bed, Barbara and I were talking.

"I knew it," Barbara said looking up at the ceiling. I was lying on my side listening to her.

"You knew what, Barbara?"

"I knew something was up since the day we came back from the grocery store with Aunt Evy and Uncle Louis. Remember that Ruthie? When we got back, they were looking all goofy. I told you then something was going on."

"Yeah, I remember you said that, but I didn't think it was about us moving to Chester."

"Well, you know now."

Moving to Chester!!! Aww man. Lying in bed, I couldn't sleep. The thought of it makes me sick. The only time we went to Chester was on Mother's Day to see the Mothers' Day parade. We would go every year until Daddy got sick and tired of taking us. It was like a major thing. We would meet up at Aunt Jane's house, go to church and then stand on 7th and Tilghman Street and watch all the acts, the cars, floats, fire truck etc. march down the street. The Chester High School Marching Band was the highlight of the whole thing. In all their orange and black finery, they would jam, having the crowd dancing in the street. They would all march, ending up on 3rd Street in front of the Elks Lounge for the final judging. The only other times we visited Chester were very few and far in between. Then, we would hang out with Calvin and Penny and go skating at the Leopold skating rink on 5th and Penn. Now to live there.........

CHAPTER THIRTY

NOW THAT THE funeral was over and the first visit from Hell with Mom was over, we went through the days as normal as possible. Maurice and Rusty stayed home from work one more week to stay with us and to figure things out. My aunts and uncle made sure they stayed in touch. As a matter of fact, Aunt Bunchie is going to see Mom tomorrow and she promised she would stop by to let us know about her visit.

Aunt Bunchie is cussing all the way to the Detention Center. She got lost twice and almost turned around and went back home.

"Where in the hell is this place?" She finally finds it and parks her car. We told her of the clothing regulations and she made sure she was dressed to the nine. The guards stop talking when she walked in. She was looking good! She had on a tasteful white pantsuit that hit her curves just right. One of the guards had the nerve to try and crack on her. When it came time to scan her, he went down her body real slow. He said only loud enough for her to hear, "Hey snow white, can I be one of your dwarfs?" She tried to play it off, but she was already scheming. Mental note: "He looks like he got money. Get the digits on the way out."

Aunt Bunchie is seated in the visiting room and in comes Beulah. "Sister! Sister!" When they saw each other, they couldn't help but cry. They hugged and held each other real tight. Beulah had to break free before they got in trouble.

"Hey girl! How the hell you living?"

"How the hell do you think I'm living being up in here?"

"I'm sorry Beulah I was just trying to be cheerful."

"That's okay Bunch. How's Jane?"

"She's doing. She couldn't come this time, but she will the next time. So what's going on with your case?"

"Girl, don't you know...you will not believe...!" They leaned in towards each other ever so slightly so it's not noticed and they whispered and talked in a language to each other like they did when they were kids. If you passed by you can see their mouths moving, but you couldn't hear a word or understand what they were saying.

After visiting with Beulah and getting the CO's number on the slip tip, Bunchie left the Center. She was on fire! "I can't believe it… she could have done more. Getting in her car, she thought "I'm going to visit that trick right now!" She went straight to Sheila Mathis' office.

She arrived expecting be played off, but THANK GOD the outer office is empty. The door to Sheila's office was slightly cracked and she hears voices talking so instead of barging in she stopped to listen. She overhears Sheila and Andrew on the phone.

"I went to see your boss and he said he knew about us. Andrew, he made me get Mrs. Walters to sign the plea agreement."

Bunchie thinks to herself, "Andrew? Now where did I hear that name? Oh yeah, that's the Assistant Prosecutor."

"I wanted to do more, but I had no other choice but to lie to her to get it signed. I made her think there was no other way. Even though she confessed I believe I could have done more. I told him no one knew. I know Andrew. No one can know about us…hold on a minute. I think I hear something."

She put the receiver down and goes out to Carolyn's desk and OMG! There stands Bunchie with her hands on her hips and the look of death on her face. Sheila had a look like a deer caught in the headlights.

"May I help you?" she asks with a shaking in her voice.

"No child, I don't think so."

"Who are you?"

"I'm Beulah Walters' sister and I heard every damn word you said. So you set my sister up? You were screwing the assistant prosecutor and he has the nerve to be white, huh? You trifling Bitch!"

"Please! You've got it all wrong!"

"How's that Ms. Mathis? You had my sister's future in the palm of your hands and you let it slip through your fingers for some dick?! I should kick your ass." Sheila was shaking like a leaf. "It's not like that. Let me explain."

"Explain!"

"Andrew and I were in a relationship long before I met your sister. When I took this case I didn't know he…"

"Yes, you did! Listen, don't try and play me. I'm old school and I got game too!"

"Please, Ms. Caldwell, let me finish. His boss figured it out. He threatened to tell the Judge we had an affair unless I got her to sign the plea agreement. I didn't have a choice, but if you want to be honest about the whole thing, your sister sealed her own fate when she hit her husband. I tried to convince Andrew this was done in the heat of the moment, but my fault was I knew Andrew was on this case and I should, or we should have excused ourselves because of conflict of interest."

Bunchie was half listening to this song and dance. She was trying to figure out how to get paid for her silence. There was this matter of a $5,000 debt that she had hanging over her head.

"Well, that sound real good Ms. Mathis, but my sister was had, misled. I need to see the Judge. Maybe I can talk to him."

"You can't do that!"

"I can do any damn thing I want."

"Please, what can I do to keep your silence?"

A smile appeared on her face. Silence is expensive. "I need you to grease my palm."

"Grease your palm?"

"I want $10,000."

Bunchie ain't shit!

Sheila almost cursed Bunchie out, but she just stares. She remembers the last time and the firm warning she was given. Her eyes filled with tears as she went to the file cabinet in her office. There in the bottom drawer, she found her pocketbook and her check book. With tears falling from her eyes, she wrote the check and handed to Bunchie.

Bunchie grabbed the check. As she stuffs the check in her bra, she turns to walk out, she tells Sheila, "Enjoy the rest of your day."

With her new found fortune, she left Sheila's office with a smile on her face. Today was a good day after all!

After depositing the check in the bank, Bunchie made her way to let the kids know about her visit. "I ain't got no shame in my game," she says to no one. She pulled up in front of the house and walked up to the door. She knocked on the door. Rusty says, "Who is it?"

"It's your Auntie, open up." She goes in and walks through the house. "How's everybody?"

"Good." We were sitting at the table eating peanut butter and jelly sandwiches.

"Want one?"

"No."

"How was your visit?"

"It went well. She looks a little crazy, but she's alright. She told me the agreement was accepted by the court and she will be sentenced on Friday."

"What? When did she find that out?"

"She said her lawyer came to see her on Monday."

"What time is the sentencing?"

"9:30 a.m."

"Well, we'll be there."

"For sure. Well, I'm going home now and call your Aunt Jane."

Rusty walks her to the door and she tells him, "I'll be here on Friday early so we can go together."

"Okay, Aunt Bunchie thanks for coming by."

CHAPTER THIRTY-ONE

"WELL. GOD, IT'S me and you. Go with me as I enter this courtroom. "Give me the peace I'll need to accept what's to come. Look over my kids…watch over them. In the name of Jesus, I pray, Amen."

Beulah gets off her knees saying "Thank you GOD." She is sitting on her bed when the CO came for her. She stands and turns around to be handcuffed. Click! She turns around and the door is opened and she walks out. The CO is right behind her and they leave for court.

Oh Well! Here was go again. I'm beginning to not like Fridays. We buried Daddy last Friday and here Mom's gonna be buried in court. Aunties Jane and Bunchie were here bright and early. We gather in our cars and head to court. Like in the Wizard of OZ, they were off to see the wizard, we're off to see the Judge.

Judge Tucker looks so big sitting up there. Mom is sitting there with her fake ass public defender Sheila Mathis looking. I can't find the words to describe her. All I know is - this will not be me. Nope I don't ever plan to be in any court of law. (I had to eat those words. Later, okay?)

"Would the defendant please rise?"

"Mrs. Walter, I have had an opportunity to review the Plea Agreement, I have listened to the sentencing arguments from both your attorney and the state's attorney. Having pled guilty, it is now up to me to sentence you. The plea agreement recommends a sentence of 7-10 years with parole. In this state, that would mean that you would have to serve a minimum of 7 years before you would be eligible for parole. This Court has the ability to accept this recommendation or reject it and impose a different sentence. In making the recommendation, the Prosecutor noted that your crime was particularly viscous. Your behavior during and after the crime strikes me as cold, calculating and without remorse. Although you are crying right now, I do not believe that your tears are for the victim, but are tears for yourself as you now face the possibility of spending at least 7 years of your life in prison. I accept the recommendation of the Probation Department and sentence you to custody of the Pennsylvania Department of Corrections for a term of 7 - 10 years after which you will become eligible for parole after serving 7 of those 10 years. You have the right to appeal this sentence, but your rights are limited and you must file a notice of your intent to appeal within 60 days after sentencing. Your attorney can help you with this filing. Ladies and Gentlemen, the court is now adjourned." BANG!

Well, it's done. Mom is officially sentenced.

Before she was led to start her journey, she turned to us, smiled as tears flowed down her face and mouthed "I love you." Mom is gone. We couldn't help, but cry. My heart is officially broken. I grabbed Maurice and hugged him real tight. Rusty grabbed us all in a group hug. We stood there in that huddle until…

Trouble never rests!

Rusty and Maurice had to go back to work. It has been two weeks since they've been off. It was their first day back and our first day of having Ms. Etta as our official babysitter. I told Rusty when he approached us with the idea. "We don't need a babysitter. I'm 14."

"That may be so, he said, but you're still going over there."

So every day, Barbara, Cece and I stayed at Ms. Etta's cigarette smoke filled house until they came home. All we did at her house was watch TV, play cards or go to Bob Wilson's corner store a half a dozen times. Barbara would ask, "Why don't she write everything down so we can make one trip?" "Dag, I'm getting tired of going to the store fifty eleven dozen times."

I would laugh.

"It's not funny Ruthie."

"Yes it is."

We learned to play hearts, 500 Rummy and Spades. Today is Friday and we were playing Tonk. We heard a knock on the door.

Ms. Etta asked out loud, "I wonder who that is?"

"Cece, look and see who it is." Cece ran to the window and pulled back the curtain.

"It's Maurice."

"Ok baby. You can open the door."

Cece opens the door and Maurice walks in. As he closes the door, he speaks to us.

"Hey."

"Hey."

We noticed from the clock on the wall that it was well before the normal pick up time.

"Hey Maurice, you are little early today. What you doing here?"

"Well, Ms. Etta, I got some bad news. I just got laid off."

Friday…oh no not again.

CHAPTER THIRTY-TWO

AN ENVELOPE ADDRESSED to the Judge marked confidential and without a return address was sitting on the desk of the Judge's secretary, Ms. Alma Hall. Ms. Hall is about 65, but she looks younger than her age. She dresses in the now, but age appropriate. She just returned from getting coffee and noticed the envelope on her desk.

"What's this? Hmm, a letter for Judge Jake Tucker marked confidential. "Who left this?" she wondered out loud. She picked up the letter and looked at it. She turned it over to see if any information was on the back. She put it up to the light to see it contents. Nothing. She put it down and went about her normal duties, sorting the other mail, but the envelope kept calling her, "Open me." She picked it up and started to tear at it. "Maybe I can open it just a little. No, I better not. I don't feel like hearing his mouth. I'll find out soon enough." She took the envelope and the rest of mail and put it on his desk, making sure this mysterious envelope was on top. "He'll be in shortly and I'll be right here, waiting." Several hours later and its quitting time. To wait for him would mean staying late and that is against her religion. "I want to know, but I don't want to know that badly. I'm going home." She gets her pocketbook out of her bottom desk drawer and sits it on her desk. She puts the phone on "night" and closes the blinds. Before walking out the door, she grabs her purse. It'll have to keep until tomorrow. Goodnight.

CHAPTER THIRTY-THREE

BY THE TIME Rusty came home from work, Barbara, Cece and I were sitting in the living room watching TV. Maurice was in the kitchen.

"What's up my people?" Rusty asks as he comes in the door.

"Hey Rusty." He was in a good mood. Well, that was about to change. "Where's Maurice?"

"He's in the kitchen." Rusty strolls down the hall and greets Maurice.

"Hey man."

"Hey."

"Damn man, what's wrong with you?"

"I got bad news."

"What's up?"

"Well, today they laid me off."

"What?!"

"Yeah man. Things are slow right now so they gave me a two-week severance package and sent me on my way."

"Oh no."

"That's not all." We got a shut off notice from the electric bill and the rent is due."

"Well, we may be able to buy some time on the bills and rent."

"Naw man. Mom and Daddy were already behind on the bills and rent when things went down. According to this notice left on the door, I think they were about to get evicted before everything went crazy. With me being laid off now and you still responsible for your crib, Russ, man let's face it, we can't make it."

"What do you suggest we do?"

"Well, I can always stay at my girl's house. As for Ruthie and them, I think it's time for them to go to Chester."

"That's it?!! That's your suggestion?!"

"Yeah, I think we have to do it. There's no other way."

"Maurice, I hate to do that. Maybe I can talk to the electric company and the rental office."

"Russ, the electric is two months behind and the rent is three. Where are you going to get the money?"

"Maybe we can ask Uncle Louie."

"Russ, it's over…It's all over."

"Well, I guess I better tell them."

"Ain't no sense in us dragging our feet."

"Ruthie, Barbara and Cece turn the TV off and come in here. We have to talk."

CHAPTER THIRTY-FOUR

I T WAS AROUND 5:30. The office blinds were closed making the room seem dark. That let him know Ms. Hall Had left for the day. He goes into his office and turns on his desk lamp and notices all the mail on top of his desk. He sifts through the mail and stumbles across the envelope marked confidential. "Who is this from?" He picks it up and turns it over and sees it's not properly addressed. Just his name. He grabs the letter opener and tears open the envelope. He takes the letter out of the envelope and starts to read. "What the hell?!!"

We turned off the TV and head to kitchen. When we got there, Rusty told us, "Sit down. We need to talk."

From the look on his face, I knew this wasn't going to be good. We sit down with scared looks on our faces.

"Well, we got some bad news. We found out that Mom and Daddy had not been taking care of this house as they should. They are three months behind in the rent and have not paid the electric bill in several months. We got an eviction notice, several as a matter of fact and a shut off notice for Tuesday from the electric company."

"What has that got to do with us?" Barbara asked with her arms folded across her chest.

"Well, smart ass, Maurice says, it means we are being put out. It also means that we don't have the money to stay here and that we all have to find another place to stay. So the only other choice is to send y'all to Chester to stay with Aunt Bunchie and Aunt Jane."

"We can stay with you Rusty," Cece chimed in.

"No, you can't baby girl. It's not enough room. I only have a one-bedroom apartment."

"I want to stay with you!!" She is crying now and stumping her feet. "I don't want to go to Chester and I'm not!"

Barbara says, with tears are running down her face. "I want to stay here."

"I know, but with everything that has gone on, Daddy's funeral and Mom being sent to jail, we weren't paying attention to the house bills. We just don't have the money."

My heart sank and I start to cry. "I don't want to go Chester!!! I don't want to go!!"

Maurice hugs me. "Ruthie, I know baby, but we don't have any other place for you to stay."

No matter how much we cried and pleaded with Maurice and Rusty to stay in Philly, Chester PA, here we come.

The next day, Saturday, Rusty left to work overtime at his job and Maurice was left to babysit us. Bad news travels fast because Aunt Bunchie and Aunt Jane were at our house by early afternoon to get us.

Aunt Jane starts, "Girls, Rusty called us this morning and told us what was going on, so we're here to pack up your things. Ruthie you're going to live with your Aunt Bunchie and Barbara and Cece, you are coming to live with me."

Aunt Jane was glad, but Aunt Bunchie had an attitude. She seemed to be in another world. In her mind, a little voice was speaking. "I didn't want any part of these girls coming to Chester, let alone living with me. Why can't they stay with their Uncle Louie? Better yet, they can all stay with Jane. I don't want any more mouths to feed."

She snapped out of it when Aunt Jane called her name. "Bunchie, come on now. We need to get these girls packed."

In a matter of three or four weeks, our lives changed. I'm going to live with Aunt Bunchie and Barbara and Cece are going to live with Aunt Jane in Chester, PA of all places. How will we see each other? I got a sinking feeling our family will be broken for good.

CHAPTER THIRTY-FIVE

SATURDAY MORNING AND the Judge is home, sitting in his study. The letter he received yesterday got under his skin. He couldn't get it out of his mind. "I warned her. If she involved herself in anymore of these side bar antics again, I would nail her to the wall. Enough!!! Sheila, you've torn your clothes this time." He remembered his Daddy telling him that when he was young and in BIG trouble. He used it from time to time. He picked up the phone and dialled her office.

The answering machine answered. "You have reached the office of Sheila Mathis. Please leave a message after the beep and I'll return your call promptly."

He hung up. He decided against leaving a message. "I will talk with her face to face, but I got to do something else first." He placed another call. While dialling the phone, he was shaking his head. "Sheila, Sheila, Sheila."

We're all packed and it is time to leave. We didn't even get a chance to say goodbye to any of our friends or neighbors. We were crying the whole time we packed. Aunt Jane tried to soothe us. "It'll be okay girls. You will make new friends and everything."

We took our things downstairs to the living room, where Maurice was waiting. asked, "Can't we wait until Rusty comes home to leave? I want to say goodbye."

"Ruthie, he wanted to be here, but this was the only free time I had to come. I got church tomorrow and work on Monday."

"This seems so quick," Barbara says.

"Well, Barbara, we could wait until next week, but the electric will be off on Tuesday. Do you want to sit in the dark?"

"No."

"So that's why we are here now. Let's go."

We cried as we hugged each other. I mean we CRIED!!! We didn't want to let each other go. We were holding on for dear life. "I don't want go Reese, please!"

"I know Ruthie, kissing the top of my head. Don't worry; I'll be down to see you soon. Both Rusty and I will come and see y'all soon. Barbara, Cece, be good girls."

"We love you, Reese!" we all said.

"I love you too!"

Soon never came. I was a long time before I saw either one of my brothers. A long time!!

Rusty couldn't stand to see his sisters go. That's why he stayed away. He wasn't at work. He was in his apartment feeling sorry. He felt like a failure. He was talking to himself, "I wish I could have done more. I just couldn't. We just don't have the money. Maurice is not working now, the landlord wants three months of back rent and the electric will be off in just three days."

Rusty called Uncle Louie, but he was tapped out. He felt shame in asking.

"What happened to the money from Sam's insurance?" he asked.

"We thought we would have some money left over from the Daddy's Insurance, but his funeral costs took all, but $500 dollars and we used that to eat."

"Russ, man if I could I would. You know that."

"I know Uncle Louie, but thanks anyway." He hung up the phone and sat there feeling depressed. The phone rang and interrupted his pity party. "Hello."

"Hello, may I speak with Russell Walters."

"This is he."

"Mr. Walters, this is Judge Jake Tucker calling."

"Yes." Rusty's heart is beating fast.

"The reason I am calling is, I have reason to believe your Mom's lawyer, Ms. Sheila Mathis, acted in an unprofessional manner that may have affected your mother's case. Is it possible to speak with you?"

"Now?"

"No." Is it possible to meet with you at the Longshore Restaurant on Monday?"

"Sir, I have to work."

"What time do you get off?"

"I get off around 4 p.m. I can meet with you around 5."

"That's perfect, Mr. Walters."

"See you then." Rusty was beside himself when he hung up. "Maybe Mom can get out soon."

CHAPTER THIRTY-SIX

"WHAT'S THE NAME of this street? I can't see the sign. Does it say Baltimore Pike? Yeah. Hmphf. I never been this way before." Baltimore Pike is like an outside mall that stretches for miles. Stores of all kind, clothing stores, car dealers, places to eat etc. are on this stretch of highway. Only place I recognized was the Strawbridge and Clothier store. Mom took us there one time. Not this one, but the one in downtown Philly. We got into the left hand turning lane at the light. I saw this big mall. The sign reads Springfield Mall. There's John Wanamakers. We made our turn and found ourselves on Sproul Road. Sproul Road is a tree-lined street that has huge houses on both sides. We continue on and what's this I see?" The sign reads Swarthmore College! I heard about this school. "Wow, it's huge." We continue on until we came to a fork in the road. We bear left and now were are on Providence Avenue. We climb the hill and at the light, there's a sign big as day says "Welcome to Chester." The other sign says E. 24th Street. So far so good. We continued down Providence and I see a sign that reads Widener University. After that, we did so many turns off of Providence that I couldn't keep up, but we ended up on Melrose Avenue. We made a right on Morton Avenue and rode past this brick building and it was playing some loud music. I believe the name said The Livewire Bar. We made a left on E. 8th Street. We're here. We stop in front of this house. OMG! This can't be it. This place is run down and I'm going to live here?! No way. We've been to Aunt Bunchie's where she used to live before and they were okay, but this one...Ugh!!! I wanted to cry sooo bad. I mean break down and hoop, but I put on a brave face. The house looked as if nobody lived there. I could tell those were bed sheets up to the window where curtains should be. There was no yard and two steps led you right into the house. We got out the car and went in the house. I wanted to turn around and run but...

"Welcome home," Aunt Bunchie had the nerve to say. It's not much, but it'll do."

"You're telling me," I thought in my mind. The furniture was plaid and one of the cushions had a rip in it. The walls were painted, but it looked as if they stopped painting in the middle.

"Penny, we're here," Aunt Bunchie yelled. "Make yourself at home." Penny came running down the stairs with a pair of shorts so short I thought they were panties.

"Hey Mom! Hey cuz!!" She hugged me. "You're staying with us now?"

"Yeah."

"That's good."

"Where's Calvin?"

"I don't know Mom. I ain't his keeper."

"Don't sass me, heifer." She put her hand up like she was about to slap the hell out of Penny. Penny put her hands up to block the shot. "Where the hell is Calvin?" Aunt Bunchie asked again.

"I think he's with Chocks, Sylvester and Weasel," She took two steps back and turned my way and said, "You can take your stuff upstairs to my room. You'll be sharing a room with me. It's the room in the back."

My sisters and I take my bags upstairs. I know Aunt Bunchie could tell from the look on my face that I didn't want to be here. She wasn't proud of her place, but with her working as a barmaid, what else could she afford? She has lived in several places in Chester, but she's always been evicted - I think twice. I overheard Mom and Aunt Jane on the phone talking about it before. We walk down the hall to the room and I swear I saw a mouse running in the same direction we were going as if he was showing us the way.

I stopped dead in my track. "Eek!!! I screamed. Running in the back of me, Barbara said, "What?!!"

"I think I saw a mouse." Dropping the bags, all of us ran back down the hall, almost knocking each other down. When we got back downstairs, we were breathing hard.

"What's wrong?" Aunt Bunchie asked.

"I saw a mouse."

"Girl, you ain't see no mouse."

"Yes I did." Ignoring her, I asked "Aunt Jane, can I stay with you?" Aunt Bunchie's face lit up with hope.

"I'm sorry Ruthie, with my kids, Frankie Jr. and Linda, we don't have the room. We hardly have room for Barbara and Cece."

Both Aunt Bunchie and I, our faces hit the floor with disappointment. So Barbara and I start back upstairs. Barbara turned and asked, "Cece, aren't you coming?" "No, she answered, I'm staying here." After helping me unpack, Barbara and I came back downstairs and Aunt Jane announced that she had to leave so that meant Barbara and Cece were leaving me here in this hellhole. We hugged and said our goodbyes. Barbara whispered in my ear, "I love you and it'll be okay." She could tell I wanted to cry. We promised to see each other soon and then they walked out the door. I walked them to the car. Everybody piled in. Barbara gets in the front and Cece sat in the back.

Aunt Jane rolls down the window starts the car. "Ruthie, I love you. Come and see me you hear?"

"Yes ma'am." Cece and I lock eyes. Those little eyes. Aunt Jane drove down the street a little and makes a u turn in the middle of the street. They drove back past the house to the stop sign. I never stopped looking and neither did Cece. Cece turned all the way around in her seat so she could see me and I her. They get to the stop sign and waited until the traffic cleared. We never stopped looking at each other. Watching the traffic Barbara yelled, "Clear" and they made a right onto Morton Avenue. We're still looking. They're gone now and I never stopped looking.....

CHAPTER THIRTY-SEVEN

RUSTY AND THE Judge met at the Longhorn Restaurant. The Judge arrived first and was already seated. Rusty walks in the restaurant and was greeted by the hostess.

"Hello and welcome to the Longhorn Restaurant."

"I'm here to meet Judge Jake Tucker."

"He's here and is anticipating your arrival. Please, let me show you to the table." Rusty follows the hostess to the table. When he arrives at the table the Judge stands up and shakes his hands.

"Hello Mr. Walters. Thanks for coming."

He gestures to Rusty to take a seat. Rusty sits down.

"I hope you don't mind, but to save time, I took the liberty of ordering the special, crab cakes for the both us. Hope that's okay."

"That fine." Well damn." I guess I'd be short if I didn't Rusty thought to himself.

Soon after the food arrives. They ate while they talked. "So, Mr. Walters, the Judge started, let me get to the subject of this meeting. I received an anonymous envelope informing me of the lack of professionalism shown you and your family by your mother's legal counsel, Ms. Sheila Mathis."

"Really?"

"Yes."

"May I ask your opinion of the service you received by Ms. Mathis?"

"Well, Rusty answered, Sir, in the beginning she was on the up and up. She seemed concerned, but towards the end she started making up shit."

"How?"

"For instance, she started acting funny when we asked about seeing our mother, especially round the time of signing the plea agreement." The Judge just listened.

"See, we wanted to see her before she signed, but Ms. Mathis started giving us this long and drawn out story about visitation."

"Oh?"

"Yeah."

"She said defendants only can receive visitors on certain days. She said visits were assigned according to their last names and since her name starts with a W, her visit day fell on the Friday, the same day our Daddy was buried."

"Mr. Walters, the Judge answered, that does happen in certain prisons, but not where your mother is housed."

"We found that out," Rusty continues.

"How?"

"My Uncle Louie did some checking and found out that all we needed was to be on her visitor's list and she was approved for a special visit."

"Did you get to see your Mom?"

"Yes, but after the plea agreement was signed. It took me to threaten to go to the authorities for her to see things our way."

"I see."

Rusty could tell from the look on the Judge's face that he was angry, but he was cool about his.

"Mr. Walters, let me be the first to apologize to you for your experience with the judicial system. I assure you that I will definitely get to the bottom of this."

"Don't be too hard on her." They both smiled.

"However, let me remind you, even though your experience with Ms. Mathis was truly unprofessional, this, by no means, plays any part in reducing your mothers' sentence. Let me make that clear. Your mother…."

"I know sir," Rusty cuts him off, you need not say anymore."

"Good."

"Well sir, Rusty stands up, I am going to head out now." They both get up and shake hands.

"Thank you for coming."

"Thank you for the invitation."

"Take care of yourself, Mr. Walters."

"You too, sir."

The Judge sat back down as Rusty turns to leave. As the Judge watches Rusty disappear out of sight, he takes a sip of his drink. He thinks one thing…Sheila!!!

CHAPTER THIRTY-EIGHT

L IVING WITH AUNT Bunchie was horrible from start. It always smelled of cigarettes and it was not the cleanest place. The bathroom was not just dirty, it was filthy. The first week, I went to take a shower and there was something brown in there. I didn't know what it was, but from then on, I made sure I had shoes on. Dishes in the kitchen sink were the norm. I don't know how. Wasn't anybody really cooking anything and the cupboard was a semi-bare, "old Mother Hubbard." I ate dumb stuff all the time and not eating the right things, I became so constipated that I had to...I tell you it was rough. I learned how to put something together mighty quick. I didn't take to the neighborhood right away. I stayed to myself because I was scared. This was new to me. We lived around the corner from the Livewire Bar and it was noisy all the time. People were standing outside all hours either cussing at each other or cussing at their kids. Sharing a room with Penny was no picnic either. I was given one drawer of a rinky dink dresser, the bottom one at that and a half of closet. Even though we were cousins, in the beginning, Penny treated me like a complete stranger, completely ignoring me, hanging with her friends. I wasn't too much of a stranger when I found out one day she was wearing my things, my underwear at that. We didn't have a washer so we had to go to the laundromat. The laundromat was located a couple of doors down from Shags. Well, in the closet in a pillowcase, is where I kept my dirty clothes until it was time to wash. I kinda' noticed that what little bit of underwear I had was coming up missing. Well, when I gathered my clothes for washing I found them stuffed in the back of the closet on the floor. They were 'stained.' "That trifling...!!! I hit the roof.

"Penny!!!"

"What?"

"What the hell is this?" I asked with the evidence in my hand. "You've been wearing my panties?!!!"

"So what." "I needed them." "I ran out," she answered. Before I knew it, I slapped the living daylights out of her and we got to fighting. Aunt Bunchie is what stopped us.

She rushed in our room. "What is going on in here?"

"Penny's been wearing my underwear."

"Well, she must have needed them."

I couldn't believe what I just heard. That's all she had to say? From that moment, anything I had in my drawers, I took them out and locked them in my suitcase. We didn't speak for at least 2 weeks. To make up with me, she would try and get me to hang out with her, but I would say no. Her friends thought I was stuck up, but I didn't care. I was still mad at everything and everybody. Eventually, I had to make a choice... let it beat me or make the best of it. I chose the latter.

I started hanging out with her, walking with her to Shags' store and other little places. I even went as far as to go to a dance with her one Friday at the Y on S. Eyre Drive. I was sitting on the couch watching TV and Penny came and plopped down next to me. I knew she was up to something from the look on her face.

"Ruthie, come and go to the Y with me?"

"No."

"Aww, come on. You haven't done nothing since you been here."

"What Y Penny?"

"The Y over on S. Eyre Drive. It's a dance from 8:00 to 12:00."

"Aunt Bunchie's not going to let me go."

"We'll sneak." She's at the bar and not coming home till it closes. We'll be home before that.

"I don't have anything to wear."

"You can borrow something from me." I thought for a second and then agreed to go. We went upstairs and took our showers and got dressed. I borrowed a blue denim skirt that was way too short, a red t-strap shirt, with a red sweater and a pair of red sandals. I must say, I looked cute!

"We're not going by ourselves are we?" I asked

"No, Karen, April and Carla is gonna meet us here and we going to walk there," she answered while combing her hair. By the time we were finished primping in the mirror, they were here. Party over here!

To get in the dance, it cost $5.00. Calvin, Penny's brother just happened to be standing outside and got us in for free. We walked in and they were jamming! I couldn't help, but get into it. I realized something about me…I love to dance. I stayed on the dance floor for every fast song except that song called, mmm, I think it's called "The Meditation." They did a certain dance, like a line dance. They would move side to side. When I saw what they did when the man said "Jump call, Meditate" and then all that grinding… Nah, that's not for me. I thought. I would just stand there and watch. Even when the slow songs came on, I found myself standing on the wall. The D.J. is playing the song "In the Rain" by the Dramatics and I was swaying to the song when this guy walked up to me and asked, "Wanna dance?" He took my hand and said "I don't bite." At first, I hesitated, but when I looked into his eyes, I said "Yes." I had no idea what I was doing. This was my first dance. I just followed his movements. For the first time slow dancing, I was doing alright. All of a sudden, I felt him!!! I stop dancing and started to walk away. I knew what it was. I'm no dummy. My Mom had the birds and the bees talk with me when I was about 11. The song was still playing.

"I'm sorry" he said. "Can we try again?"

"Okay."

We started slow dancing again. Again, I felt him and backed up a little. He grabbed me tighter and was grinding his heart out. He was sweating and singing in my ear. He didn't have a bad voice. *"I wanna go outside in the rain…it may sound crazy…,"* so I kept dancing. When the song went off, he released me and disappeared. I spent the rest of the night looking for him, but he was gone. So I thought.

When the dance was almost over, they played this song "It's Time to Go Now." That song told you the party was over. You ain't got to go home, but you got to get the hell out here. The lights came on and I found my cousin Penny and her girls and we walked outside. We got outside and bam! He was there. I got a good look at him and he was FINE!!! He had a copper complexion with a small fro and the prettiest teeth. He walked up to me and smiled. My cousin and her girls started giggling and walked away. He asked me my name. I told him Ruthie - his name was Ira.

"You live around here?"

I said "No, I live on 8th Street."

"Where on 8th Street?"

"8th and Congress."

"Oh, by the Livewire Bar?"

"Yes."

"Where do you live?" I asked.

"I live on the west side near the Wards Grill."

"Where's that?"

"You don't know?"

"No, I just moved here from Philly. I live with my Aunt."

"Ok. Can I get your number?"

"Like I said, I live with my Aunt and I'm not sure I can give it out."

"Well, here's my number. Call me."

"Okay." He walked away and I caught up my cousin.

"Girl, he's cute! What's his name?"

"He said his name is Ira."

"Did you get his number?"

"Yeah."

"You gonna call him?"

"Yeah, I guess."

"Well, if you don't, I will," Penny, my cousin added.

I looked at her thinking, "I can't believe she just said that."

The next night we snuck in the Livewire Bar...OMG!!! Aunt Bunchie is sitting at the bar with her back facing the door. She doesn't notice us because she was so busy grinning in some man's face. I guess we'll see him at the breakfast table tomorrow morning. That's how she rolled, a different man all the time. I guess that's how she made her ends. I believe she's an undercover escort...a broke one at that. Her "area" has got to be stretched like a big rubber band because of all the "traffic." We snuck out before we could be seen. Aunt Bunchie may not have noticed them, but Ruthie is unaware she was noticed by a man named, "Mr. Blue", real name is Theodore Brooks. "Hmmm.... that's a pretty girl." He checked her out from head to toe. She's young, but I wonder....."

Monday morning, the Judge was in his office, bright and early. He was there before Ms. Hall arrived. He had already left a message on Sheila's answering machine letting her know that he needed to meet with her today. Around 9 a.m., Ms. Hall arrived at work. She comes in the office and notices that the office lights are on and the blinds are open.

"Oh he's in, but his office door is closed." She hurries to put her pocketbook in her desk drawer. She knocks on his door and peeks her head in.

"Good Morning, Jake."

"Good Morning, Alma."

"You're here early."

"I know I need to catch up on some things."

"Hot case?"

"Not a hot case, but there's an urgent matter I need to address."

"Does it have something to do with that anonymous envelope?"

Smiling, "Something like that." She sat down, prepared for some gossip. "Do you know who sent it?"

"Alma…."

"Come on Jake, you know you can tell me."

"The letter contained some unflattering information about one of the public defenders who engaged in an unprofessional matter that could have tainted this office."

"Honey hush! Who?"

"Sheila Mathis."

"OMG, not again."

"Yes."

"What she do this time?"

"I can't go into detail, but lets' just say I have had enough. I need to end this bullshit once for all."

"What time are you seeing her?"

"Around 2 p.m." Playfully he said, "Okay Alma, you got the lowdown so go do some work."

She laughed, "Yes Sir."

Aunt Jane was off from work so she brought Barbara and Cece by the house. "Barbara! Cece!" "Ruthie!" We all screamed. We ran to one another and hugged and hugged.

"I'm so glad to see you!"

We couldn't get enough of each other. While Aunt Jane and Aunt Bunchie went into the kitchen and talked, I took Barbara and Cece on a small tour of the neighborhood. Cece walked ahead of us so I filled Barbara in on what's been going on.

"Guess what Barbara? "I went to a dance and met a boy."

DONNA EARL

"You did? Oooh!"

"Shut up! Aunt Bunchie doesn't know and you know Cece got big ears." "She might tell."

"Yeah, I know."

"So what happened?"

"Nothing, really. Penny and I snuck out and went to the dance. I had big fun. I slowed danced."

"You did?!"

"What was it like?"

"Well, we were slow dancing and I felt his thing."

"His what?"

"You know what I'm talking about."

"Oooh!!"

"Shut up, I said. I pushed him away. He said he was sorry and we tried it again. It wasn't so bad the second time."

Barbara started laughing real loud. Cece eased up behind us trying to hear what we were saying.

"What were y'all laughing about?" Cece asked.

"Nothing!" We both said it at the same time. We changed the subject. "Have you heard from Rusty and Maurice?"

"Nope."

"We haven't either."

"Aunt Jane said she was going to find the hell out why they haven't been to see us."

"I sure miss them."

"Me too."

"When you coming to see us?"

"Maybe the weekend; maybe I'll spend the night."

"That'll be nice just like old times. We better get back before. Aunt Bunchie comes out the door hollering."

"Yeah, that sounds like something she'll do."

"Come on Cece, we going back."

We laughed and giggled all the way back. Just like old times. Ruthie was not aware, but a pair of eyes were watching her again. He watched her from across the street as she made her way in the house. "Nice!!! One day...."

CHAPTER THIRTY-NINE

WHILE THE JUDGE was on his way to meet with her, Sheila's in her office a nervous wreck. She replayed the messages he left on her voice mail over and over. Her office door was closed and she had the volume down so that Carolyn couldn't hear.

"Sheila, this is Judge Jake Tucker. I need to speak with you about an important matter. I should be arriving around 2 p.m. so please clear your calendar of any afternoon appointments."

"Clear your calendar? I wonder what's so important. "2 p.m.?"

He is prompt. The Honorable Jake Tucker is in the house!!! Can he stay? He is some kind of fine. He strolled his 6'3 nicely built frame in her office and Carolyn's mouth dropped open. Good Gosh!! She's seen him dressed before, but not like that. He's looking GOOD! He's looking sharper than a mosquito's "peter." He is dressed in this Brooks Brother black suit with an extremely bright white shirt with a polka dot tie. Yummy!! It looks good against his mocha complexion. His lips are thin, but just big enough to suck on and I bet he carries a "weapon" most women would enjoy, she thought. His salt and pepper hair is neatly cut as if he just left the barbershop. He noticed how she was looking at him and smiled, mostly with his eyes.

"Good Afternoon. I have a 2 p.m. meeting with Ms. Mathis. Is she available? If she's not…"

"Sure sir, let me buzz her. Ms. Mathis, Judge Jake Tucker is here to see you."

"Thank you Carolyn, show him in."

"You may go in." She thought, "Can I go?"

"Thank you," he spoke as he left her desk leaving a hint of Aramis in the air as he breezed by.

"Hello Sheila."

"Hello Your Honor. Please, have a seat."

"Thank you."

"How are you today?"

"I'm good sir."

"Good to hear. Listen, I wanted to talk to you about some information dropped in my lap about the Beulah Walter's case."

"Sir?"

"I received some troubling information about your unprofessionalism in handling her case."

"Sir, I'm not sure I follow."

"Well, follow this. I warned you about your after hour relationships with your colleagues."

"Wait"

"No, you wait. You thought by waving your panties in Andrews' face, that you could worm things your way. I must say, the information I received, it was rattling, but I wanted to dig a little bit deeper before I brought this to your attention. So, I contacted her family and spoke with them about the service they received. It was said that at first they felt comfortable, but when the subject of visitation and the plea agreement came into play, you went left field on them. You started them on a wild goose chase. They informed you of their desire to see their mother before she signed."

"She wanted to sign it, sir."

"Be that as it may, Sheila, but you didn't' play fair. From what I understand, you painted this horrible picture about trial and what not and forced her hand. You and Andrew both knew that it was in the best interest of the defendant and the court, that you should have excused yourselves. This is not a game Sheila. I cannot, in good conscience, excuse this behavior any longer. I warned you."

"You don't understand!" She was blubbering now.

"I understand everything so save it Sheila. Just so you know, before coming here, I had no other choice but to submit my recommendation to have both your license as well as Andrew's, suspended indefinitely and it will be such until further review. You can't play both sides against the middle."

"Please!!!"

"Clear your desk…you are through!!"

Little did they know, Carolyn had the intercom bottom pushed down so that she was able to hear the conversation. "That's just what the hell you get."

CHAPTER FORTY

T HE END OF the summer is fast approaching and the school year is about to start and I am finally enrolled in school and I will be 15 on the 20th of September. If it wasn't for Aunt Jane requesting my sisters' and I permanent records from our old schools, we, at least me, wouldn't be going anywhere. I will be attending Chester High School with Penny. She is going in the 10th grade and I'll be in the 9th.

"Home of the Clippers, she boasted. Chester High has the baddest b-ball team. They have won championships back to back for years." She did this cheer, "CHS, the baddest school from east to west." Chester High School is located on 9th and Barclay Streets. From the outside, it looks like a prison, but I can't wait till school starts so I can see what it looks like on the inside.

What a summer it's been. My Daddy dies, my Mom is in prison and I am now living in Chester. So far, it hasn't been that bad. I went to my first dance and I met Ira. I phoned him about a week or so after meeting him. I waited until I had the house to myself to call. I dialled his number and then hung up before anybody answered. I dialled again. This time I let it ring. He answered after 2 rings.

"Hello?"

"Hello, may I speak to Ira?"

"This is he."

"Hi Ira, this is Ruthie."

"Who?"

This is the girl you were grinding on at the Y last week." Remember?" We both laughed and that broke the ice.

"Yeah, I remember. What's up girl?"

"Nothing."

"I didn't think you would call."

"Why is that?"

"Because I thought maybe you was scared of it."

Silence.

"Anyway, I was calling to talk. What have you been doing?"

"Aw nothing too much…just chilling. I've been thinking about you. When can I come see you?"

"I told you I live with my Aunt and she don't …"

"Look, I know where you live and I want to see you. I'm coming over there."

"Wait!!" Click! OMG!! He didn't come that day, but 2 days later, I was sitting on the stoop with Penny…he shows up!!

Penny says, "Ooh Ruthie, look who's here."

"Hey y'all."

"Hey Ira."

"Well, I'm going in the house." Penny giggles and gets up and walks in the house. Ira took her place on the stoop. Little did I know, Aunt Bunchie was watching the whole time from the sheet covered living room window. She asks Penny when she comes in, "who's that?"

"His name is Ira."

"How she meet him?"

Penny lies and says, "We were at Shags store and he happen to come in."

"I've never like no shit colored men."

"Mom, he's not here for you."

"Well, I'm keeping my eye on her. She ain't gonna be no fast ass like you."

Penny replied as she was going upstairs, "I got it honest."

The other eyes on Ruthie had turned blood red. "Who's that she sitting with?" "I don't like it." "Real soon." EXTRA - Soon!!

School!!! I was excited and scared at the same time. I felt funny because I didn't have any new clothes, so the clothes I had would have to do. I remember every year when school started, Mom would buy us new clothes. I miss my Mommy. Penny was all decked out in her finery, new clothes and new shoes. he had gone shopping on Friday. Getting out of this gray Lincoln with some man, she came home from the Granite Run Mall, loaded down with bags.

"Who's that Penny?"

"Mind yours."

"Well, excuse me" I thought.

She went straight upstairs and hid the bags in the back of the closet in our room. I saw them later that day when she went to Ms. Sally's to get her hair done. When I asked Aunt Bunchie for school clothes and things, she said, "I ain't got no money for that. Wear what you got."

It looks like I'm going to have to find a job or something to buy the things I need.

We walked to school and you know Penny, Ms. Butterfly, was flapping her wings as well as her tongue, trying to be seen. Her girls Karen, Carla and April met us at the corner and we walked to school. Before the school bell rang, everybody was milling around talking and laughing. Ring!!! There goes the bell. Penny knew I was nervous, so she walked me through the first day of school jitters. We went inside and there were tables set up with alphabets taped to the front of them. We walked over to the table marked W-Z.

"Your name?"

"Ruthie Walters."

The lady handed me my homeroom assignment, my lunch card, my schedule and locker number.

Penny was right there to help me understand it.

"Ok Ruthie, see right here? This is your homeroom number, Room 212, and your locker number is 227. Come on so we can find it."

"Aren't you going to be late?"

"Don't worry about that."

We walked down the flight of stairs to the 2nd floor. We found my locker and my homeroom was right around the corner. She walked me to my homeroom door. I noticed the room was empty except for a few students.

She hugged me and said "Ok Ruthie, I gotta go. Don't be nervous. You'll be fine. I'm here if you need me." She ran down the hall before she was too late for own homeroom roll call. I sat in the back of the room and before you knew it, the room was packed. My homeroom teacher's name is Ms. Byrd. She's nice. She called the roll and with each name called you heard "present" or "here." After that, she decided to put us in alphabetical order. We had a little homeroom time left before the first bell. "Ring." Uh oh class time. I was completely lost. I knew I looked like a tourist, looking all around and asking a whole lot of questions like "can you help me find" or "do you know where? but surprisingly, I made it to my first class just in the nick of time.

My first day of school was not as bad I thought it would be. I made a new friend name Felicia Myers. She was a little on the heavy side, but she was friendly. We had several classes together, so I learned she lived in the Fairground Projects on Tolston Street, had two brothers and was raised only by her Mom. Her father was in her life, but lived elsewhere with his new girlfriend. She was "Street" but I could tell she was book smart.

"Tell me about you."

I told her I had just moved from Philly and lived with my aunt and two cousins and I had two brothers and two sisters.

"What made you move here?"

I lied and told her my Mom was sick and my Daddy left."

"Oh, I'm sorry to hear that. What time is your lunch?"

"11:30."

"So is mine."

"Let's meet for lunch."

"Ok. I'll meet you in the caf around that time."

"Okay." As I walked away for my next class, I thought "Lunch. I don't have any money. What am I going to do? I gotta find Penny." GOD is good because I ran smack into her in the hall talking to some boy. She had her back to me so she didn't see me coming. I walked up to her calling her name "Penny." She turned her head around with a disturbed look on her face, but when she saw it was me, it softened.

"Hey Ruth." She introduced me to her friend. "Ruth, this is Michael. Michael Campbell, this is my cousin Ruth. We both said hi at the same time. His 'hi' was more like a nod. In my head, I thought "He's cute."

"Penny, can I talk to you?

She turned back to Michael, "Okay Michael, I'll see you later."

"Who's that?"

"Nevermind him Ruthie, what's wrong?" Her voice was tight.

"It's almost time for lunch and I don't have any money."

"What happen to the lunch card they gave you?"

"I don't know plus I don't want anybody to know I get free lunch."

"Girl, you better get over it."

"Please, Penny."

"Okay, here's ten dollars, but either you brown bag it or use your card. Ain't nobody got time to be giving you money every day."

"Thanks Penny. I'm making my lunch from now on," I thought. After lunch and my afternoon classes, I met up with Penny and her girls and we walked home chatting about the days' event.

By the time we made it to 9th and Avenue of the States, that same gray Lincoln I saw Penny get out of the other week, pulled up beside us. Penny and her friends recognized the driver. He rolled the passenger side window down and said "Want a ride home?" "Hell yeah" they all screamed. "Come on."

I didn't know him so I said "no."

"Come on Ruth. It a long walk home and it's hot."

"I don't know him."

"I do and I promise he's safe." I hesitated, but I too was hot and to get home quick would be nice, so I agreed and got in, but in the backseat. We pulled off from the curb and rode down 9th Street and he asks "Who's your friend?"

"This not my friend, this is my cousin Ruth. Ruth, this is Mr. Blue."

"Hi."

"He works with Mom at the Livewire." "Like that's supposed to make me feel better," I thought. He asked Penny and her girls, how was school. They were chattering back and forth, filling him in on their day, but I was quiet. For some reason, he put me on edge. I felt his eyes on me the whole way home. I caught him looking at me through the rear-view mirror. It seem like it was taking forever to get in front of the house and when we did, I damn near pushed Carla out the car without the door being open. She felt it because when we did get out, she pushed me. I stood there with my fist balled up and gritted on her HARD! The look on my face said, "You don't know who you messing with." She got the message because she looked away.

Several weeks went by and my new found school is not so bad after all. I joined the FBLA (Future Business Leaders of America) club, Pep Club and Dance Movement. I still remember the steps to the dance move we were taught to the song, "Don't you worry 'bout a thing" by Stevie Wonder. My favorite class was Black Studies taught by a spitfire of a teacher name Julia Warren. She was well liked by all her students, but especially by the guys. She was strong, sassy, and she knew her stuff. She demanded full class participation by all her students. What a class, learning about our people. I was also having a ball learning typing and shorthand too. I became quite good at it.

Wouldn't you know it, as the season changed so did my life! Not again!!

My friend Felicia and I became really tight. I would visit her, (when Aunt Bunchie allowed it). She would give me the third degree, "Where you going? What time you coming back?" She didn't really care. She just wanted me around to clean up behind her and her nasty kids. That was my payback for having to live with her. I would walk home with Felicia to hang in the "Field." The Field was located in the center of the Fairground Projects. We would sit on the seesaws and merry-go-rounds by the basketball court and watch the guys - Hump, Bobwire, Cody and others play ball. Hump was a runt but he could ball!!! There were girl b-ball players too, like Debbie D, Karen and Denise. Those girls could get down!!! The field was packed with people all the time and everybody seemed to get along with everybody. There was an occasional "fair one", but for the most part it was easy. I was up there so much that Felicia told me her Mom missed seeing me when I couldn't come. So when I saw her crying, I wanted to know why.

"What's wrong Licia?" She wouldn't tell me at first, but I kept pushing her. "I'm sick of people making fun of me." That statement took me back to my elementary days when I was picked on so I knew how she felt. Who's making fun of you?"

"Don't worry about it." I grabbed her arm and turned her so we were facing each other. "Who?" The tone in my voice told her I meant business.

"Mary Scott."

"I knew who Mary Scott was. I had a minor run in with her about her man Michael. Michael is the boy I met one day when he was talking to Penny. He was also the same boy, after that, tried to talk to me. At the time I met him, I didn't know about Mary.

I had left my Black Studies book in my locker so before class, I ran to get it and I saw him. He was coming out the boys' bathroom and we literally bumped into one another. I said "hey" and he did the same. I walked to my locker, worked the combination and it opened. I reached in, grabbed my book and when I closed the door, he was standing there checking me out. He stepped to me, a little too close. I backed up.

WHEN I CLOSE MY EYES   ~131~

"Aren't you Penny's cousin?"

"Yeah."

I stepped around him, at least I tried, but he blocked my way.

"Excuse me."

"Hey, I just want to talk to you." "Is it possible that I can get your number or come see you?" "I'd like to get to know you better."

"I don't think so."

"Why?"

"Aren't you dating my cousin?"

"Oh no, me and Penny, we just friends."

I thought for a minute or so then I told him, "Give me yours."

"Bet!"

He snatched my book away from me and wrote his number on the cover. I was a little embarrassed because my book cover was homemade. I made it from a brown paper bag since Aunt Bunchie wouldn't give me any money for a real one.

"Call me."

Smiling, I said "okay." Little did I know, he was dating Mary and her girlfriend, Yvette was at her locker the whole time watching and listening to the entire conversation. She couldn't wait to go back and tell Mary.

Mary caught me later in the hall the same day. "Hey Ruth, can I talk to you?" She had her girls, Yvette and Lisa with her. I can tell she was a little nervous about approaching me.

"About what?"

"Michael."

"What about him?"

"That's my man!"

I waved my hand at her and said "Girl go head somewhere with that," and I started walking away and she said, "You better watch yourself."

"I didn't know you had some words with her."

"Yeah, but I squashed that real quick. I'm from Philly."

"You may be from Philly, but you in Chester now and it's a WHOLE different thing going on here. You got the girls from the LV, the McCaf, The Gardens, The Penn and not to mention the Eastside and don't sleep on the Fairground either. Just because you hang up there sometimes don't mean everybody up there like you. They're already step to me asking me who you are. You betta be careful about all the Philly shit."

"I didn't mean nothing by it."

"I'm just saying."

"I was really talking about Mary and her girls. Look Felicia, don't pay them no mind. She just jealous."

"Jealous of what? I'm all fat."

"Look, don't let me hear you say that anymore. You are not fat… you're beautiful. You have something she don't."

"What's that?"

"Brains."

We both fell out laughing and went on our way.

Quiet as it's kept, Michael and I started sneaking around a little bit. I didn't even tell Felicia. I'd hook school and he would come over when nobody was there. He was my first kiss. I didn't let him go any farther than that. I don't know why. He didn't try to make me either. I guess he was getting it from Mary. Fine with me. I wasn't ready for that.

I don't know how, but Mary found out about me and Michael. It was Thursday after school and I was coming out of the building to meet up with Penny and her girls to go home. Next thing you know, Mary came running up to me yelling, "You bitch, you messing with man. I told you."

Her hair was in plats and she had grease all over her face. She must have told people she was going to get me because I hear yelling and cheering. She swung and punch me right in my face, near my ear and I heard ringing. For some reason her punched didn't hurt, but it caught me off guard. Honey, we got to fighting right there on the sidewalk. I grabbed that hussy by her blouse and ripped it off with one sweep. The guys were out of their minds by then, hooting and cat calling, "Ooh titties." That didn't faze her one bit. She kept swinging and so did I. We were on the ground going back and forth. She was on top of me trying to gouge my eyes out. I grabbed the skin on her face and tried to pull it off. She screamed. I managed to get on top of her. I put my knee in her windpipe, cutting off her air and beat her all in her face. They finally broke us up and she ended up with a lot of scratches and a black eye and I had a nasty scratch on the side of my face. Penny was there the whole time watching to make sure I didn't get jumped.

The school's staff came out and took us in the principal's office. He yelled and screamed at us for fighting, telling us we should know better. "Before I let either one of you back in school, I want to see your parents, looking at Mary and your Aunt in this office tomorrow at 9:00 a.m." After listening to him for another half hour, he told us we were dismissed. Mary practically ran out of the office and I was dragging, thinking, "Dag, I gotta go tell Aunt Bunchie, I've been suspended."

Penny was standing right there when I came out. She asked, "What happened?"

"They told me that I couldn't come back unless Aunt Bunchie comes back with me."

"Mom is going to be pissed."

"I know."

It was hell to pay that night. She screamed at the both of us. At Penny for being late and me, for being late and getting suspended. Aunt Bunchie slow walked up and down on me that night.

It's Friday and we sat in the principal's office. It wasn't enough that she cussed me out last night but she continued her madness again this morning. She is going off.

"Your stinking ass made me miss a day at work to bring your stupid behind back to school."

The secretary was shaking her head listening to how she was talking to me. I was embarrassed as hell. To make matters worse, Mary's in here with her mother listening to everything. I looked at her and she had a smirk on her face. I just listened to her rant and thought, "I've got to do something to get out her house." I knew she was common, but this takes the cake.

"You are on punishment young lady. That means no going out and no phone calls. You were supposed to spend the weekend over your Aunt Jane's with your sisters, but that's out. You hear me?"

"Yes Ma'am." I said it real low.

"I don't hear you."

"Yes, Ma'am," I screamed.

That night, Penny and I were sitting on that raggedy couch in the living room looking at Fuzzy the TV. That's what I called it because most of the time the picture is snowy. Watching Fuzzy gave me a headache, so I turned it off. Aunt Bunchie had gone out. Calvin and his three friends, Chocks, Sylvester and Weasel came in the house all highed up. Eyes all red.

"Hey, what y'all doing?

"Nothing." His friend Chocks hugged Penny.

"Boy, get off me with your stinking self. You smell just like reefer."

She hurt his feelings so he let go and went and stood on the wall.

"Mommy gonna get you coming in here all high. She told you about that."

He waved his hand. "I'm not hardly worried about that."

"You got some more?"

"Why you worried?"

"Gimme a joint."

"I'm not giving you nothing, but I'll smoke one with you."

You down Ruthie?"

"No."

"Aww come on. It ain't gonna hurt you."

Weasel found one of Aunt Bunchie's albums and poured the reefer out on it to sort out the seeds. After it was clean, he rolled up a fat joint.

"We better go outside so the smell will not be in here" Penny warned. We went outside and stood by Chocks car. He was the old head of the bunch. He unlocked the door and we all climbed in. Calvin in the front while Penny, Weasel and I got in the back. Calvin lit the joint. He coughed a little and held the smoke in.

"This is some good shit!"

They all took a hit and passed it to me. I don't know anything about smoking, so when I took a puff, I damn near cough myself to death.

"Take your time Ruthie," Penny coached me.

I took another puff and passed it. Man, after that I was floating. Then I got the giggles and couldn't stop. We were all laughing after a minute, laughing at stupid stuff.

"I'm hungry."

"Me too."

We all had the munchies so Weasel suggested "Let's ride to Stackys' and get some hoagies." Chocks started up the car and off we went. I knew I wasn't supposed to leave the house, but at the moment, I didn't care. I was high and feeling good. We got to Stackys' and ordered two hoagies and two cheesesteaks. Sylvester pulled out a twenty and paid for them. We killed those bad boys right in the car.

With our highs coming down Penny said, "I hope we get home before Mom."

"Don't worry, we'll get back before she do."

Wrong!!! When we got in front of the house, Penny and I got of the car and started walking to the front door. Calvin got out telling his boys, "Alright y'all. I'll get back later."

When we opened the door, there was Aunt Bunchie sitting on the couch waiting. "Where y'all been?"

"Mom…"

"Mom my ass!!! Look at you, coming in here all fucked up on that shit." She turned to me, "Ruthie, I thought I told you not to leave this house."

"We went for a ride."

"Well, ride this!!" She jumped up and whipped out her extension cord and started swinging. We started running through the house like roaches and she was right behind us. Calvin ran right out of the house. "Come back here, you black bear."

He kept running. She chased Penny and me around the living room. We ran around the couch, round and round we went. You could hear the wind of the cord as she swung. She chased us in the kitchen and around the kitchen table. We then ran up the stairs with her right behind me. It felt like my whole body was on fire with every lick. The only reason she quit hitting us because she was out of breath. Thank God. When she was done, we inspected ourselves. Penny had a few welts here and there because she was in the front, but I had welts on my arms, legs and back. This was no regular spanking. This was a WHOOPING!!! All I could do was lay down and cry. I cried, cried and CRIED!!! As I laid there on the bed, Penny held and rocked me. I cried like I never cried before. I want my Mommy!!!!

The next day was Saturday. It was early so everybody was still sleep, except me. I was up, just looking out the bedroom window. I was thinking about my brothers, sisters, Daddy and Mom. I missed them and Philly. I'm going to ask Aunt Jane to take me to see Mom when she gets a chance. The thought of the whipping crossed my mind because my arms, legs and back where still stinging.

Knock, Knock Knock.

"Who's at the door this early," I thought. I went downstairs and looked out the peep hole. It was Aunt Jane.

"I see you peeping, so let me in."

I opened the door, forgetting how my scars looked. All I had on was a sleeveless nightgown. I should have put on a robe.

"Hi Aunt Jane!"

"Hi Ruthie!"

We hugged and I winced in pain. "Bunchie told me you were on punishment. She didn't say why, so since I was out, I'd thought I would stop by to see you."

"Where's Barbara and Cece?"

"That's why I am early. I dropped them off at the church. They had choir rehearsal."

"They sing?"

"Yeah girl and they sound good."

"I miss them."

"They miss you too. They were disappointed when I told them you weren't coming. Where's everybody, still sleep?"

"Yes." I was rubbing my arm, frowning in pain.

"What's wrong?"

"Nothing."

"Why you rubbing your arm like that?" She peered a little closer and saw the marks on my arms and then on my legs.

"What happen to you?"

I just looked at her. "Bunchie!! "Bunchie!! Get your rotten self down here right now!" We could hear rustling and cussing and then we heard footsteps stomping down the hall and now on the steps.

"Look at this girl! What happen to her?"

"I whipped her behind."

"For what?!"

"First of all, she got suspended for fighting."

Aunt Jane looked at me. "That's no reason for this," grabbing my arm.

"Plus, she came in this house with Penny and Calvin all highed up from smoking reefer."

She looked at me, "Ruthie!!" I hung my head.

"You smoke drugs now?"

"No, Aunt Jane. I just tried it. I took one puff."

"Ruthie, one puff is more than enough!"

"Yes, ma'am."

"Back to you, Bunchie. I don't care what this girl did. There's no reason to whip this girl like that. Beulah trusts us to take care of her kids and this is how you do?"

"Well, take her home with you if you think I'm not doing a good job."

"Bunchie, I would take her in a heartbeat if I could."

"Well."

Aunt Jane step to Aunt Bunchie. "Look, don't get smart. You know me and you know me well. You may think you bad, but you know how I get down. I turned that life off a long time ago, but I know how to flip the switch. Now, if I come back here and see this girl looking wrong, I'm gonna want to talk to you up close. I'm not playing!"

Aunt Bunchie didn't say a word. She didn't make a sound. She just glared at her. Aunt Jane was the only one that could put Aunt Bunchie in check.

CHAPTER FORTY-ONE

DESPITE MY FOUL living conditions, I still flourished in school. I kept my grade average at B and I still kept seeing Michael. For some reason, Ira and I didn't click, but we remained friends. The reason for that, I found out, was when my back was turned, Penny got a hold of Ira and did some things to him that blew his hair back. Michael and I were a couple now so we didn't have to sneak. Mary had to bow down. She didn't want it with me after our fight.

That Monday, after leaving the Principal's office, Aunt Bunchie left and I went to class. Felicia saw me at school and was out of breath telling me all she knew. She told me people were taking about how Mary wanted to fight me again and that her friends teased her something terrible. The day of the fight she wasn't there. We normally met just as school let out, but that day she had an early dismissal for a doctor's apt. She missed the whole thing.

"Ruthie, I overhead some people talking that she was going to come after you."

"How she gonna do that? She can't hardly see after the black eye I gave her." Felicia sniggled but she was concerned. "I'm not worried," I told her. It was all talk because when I did see her, she had nothing to say. As a matter of fact, she'd turn and go the other way.

There was a big game Thursday at the "high", Chester High vs. Interboro. The gym was packed; it was electric. I was in the Pep Club so I stayed after school so I wouldn't have to walk back. I was sitting in the bleachers waiting for the game and in comes Michael. He told me he might make it to the game. He sat in the bleachers with me to help cheer on the team. Our cheerleading Squad was great in their orange, black and white outfits. I thought to join the squad or the band. I just wanted to make the best of my time here. During halftime, Michael asked, "What you doing tomorrow after school?"

"I don't have any plans."

"It's Friday, lets' go to the movies."

"What you wanna see?"

"I don't care."

"Okay, it's a date. Around 6:00 okay."

"Yeah."

After I got home from the game, I ask Aunt Bunchie could I go. I know she'd say yes just to get me out of her hair, but out of respect I asked. She's been mellow towards me since her talk with Aunt Jane.

"Aunt Bunchie, Michael asked me to go to the movies tomorrow. Can I go?"

"Well, I..."

"I promise I'll be home before it gets late."

"What time is the movie?"

"The matinee starts at 6:45."

"I guess it will be okay."

"Thanks, Aunt Bunchie."

Friday went on without any problems except the teachers piled all this homework on me. That same day, I officially found out that Ira and Penny was dating and it had been going on for some time. I was preparing for my movie date when she walked in the bedroom.

"What you doing?"

"Getting ready to go out with Michael. Why?"

She blurted out, "You know I've been dating Ira?"

"No, I didn't know!" I thought, you slimy.... How long has this been going on."

"It started right after he stop seeing you."

"Seeing me? I only saw him one time! No wonder we didn't click. You were giving up the panties."

Penny is light skinned so she turned beet red. "I wanted to tell you before he came over. He's coming tonight."

"Dag, Penny. You don't waste no time"

She couldn't say nothing, but look at me with shame written all over her face.

That night Michael and I went to the State Theatre on 7th Street. The theatre was across the street from the Town Bar. We saw some stupid movie. I don't even remember what the name was. When the movie let out it was still early so he took me to his house. Michael lived in Apartment 3B with his Mom in the Crosby Square Apts. on

Crosby Street. We went inside and there on the couch was his Mom, watching TV.

"Hey Mom."

"Hey Michael."

"Mom this is Ruthie."

"Hi Ruthie. Sit down and make yourself at home. That's an old name for a pretty girl."

"Thank you. My name is really Ruth, but most people call me Ruthie. I don't know what my parents was thinking when they named me that." We both laughed.

"Where do you live?"

"I live with my Aunt on E. 8th Street."

"Where about on 8th Street?"

"Near the Livewire Bar. You heard of it?"

She laughed. "Heard of it!? Child…., she waved her hand. I could tell you some stories." She got off couch. "I'll let y'all have some privacy. It was nice meeting you."

"Nice meeting you too."

"Now Michael, don't have that girl out too late."

"Yes Mom." She went down the hall to her room and closed the door.

Michael and I sat on the couch. We were supposed to be watching TV, but Michael's hands were roaming all over my body. Playfully I said "Stop!" pushing them away, playing hard to get. For the most part, all Michael and I did was kiss and a lot of talking about school, the future, things like that, but tonight I felt I was ready, but I wasn't ready right this minute. Believe me, before tonight, he had been hounding me to drop my drawers, but I kept him at bay. I'm only 15. We started kissing and then he started picking with my banjo with his fingers. The music he played with my banjo was something I never heard before. I had my eyes closed listening and he kept playing and then …and then and he stopped.

My eyes sprung open. "What?!"

He looked into my eyes. "Ruthie, I want to be with you. I wanted you the first time we met." He kissed me real soft.

"You were with Mary."

"True, but Mary's not you. "It's just something about you."

I was so young and dumb, I fed right into that bullshit. He kissed me again. He started feeling on my breasts. "Ruthie, I want you so bad." He started playing with my banjo again. He was so fine and the words he spoke dripped off his lips like chocolate. I had to taste them, so I gave in.

As we were tip toeing to his bedroom, I whispered, "How we gonna do this with your Mom home?"

All he said was "Ssh." We made our way to his bedroom. It was in the opposite end of the apartment. He started to kiss and undress me slowly. He then undressed. When I saw his…"no way." He laid me down on the bed. He knew I was virgin and that I was scared.

"I promise I won't hurt you" he said. He started playing my banjo again and it felt good. He then climbed on me and started….my eyes got BIG and my breath came in spurts. I almost stopped breathing. OMG!!! This really hurts. I tried to push him off, but he wasn't having it. He went a little further.

"Just Relax Ruthie."

OMG!!! I was clawing at his back because it hurt so badly. I felt like screaming, but I bit my bottom lip. My whole body felt as if it was going to rip any moment. He saw that this was killing me, so he started moving slow and coaching me.

"Just relax baby. Relax."

As I relaxed, it started to feel better.

"That's it baby." We got it going and then he yelled, "Yeah!"

I guess the newness of it made him… After all of that banjo playing, I laid there and thought "Is that it?" I thought I would feel WOW!!!, but I didn't. It was over before it began. He rolled off me. He saw that I was disappointed and he apologized.

"Sorry Ruthie. You just felt so good."

"Yeah right." Quickdraw!!!

His Mom must have been dead to the world. I thought for sure she would come to his bedroom door, but she didn't. You know, he had the nerve to fall asleep. I laid there with my banjo strings broken and it STUNG!! I went to the bathroom to pee and almost jumped off the toilet. It was burning!!! I thought, "This is not the way I wanted my first time to be." Hindsight is twenty-twenty. I always pictured my first time to be romantic. Michael and I would run off to Atlantic City walk along the boardwalk hand in hand. There would be people all around, but all we would see is each other. He would hold me in his arms and kiss me softly on the lips. We would stay in one of those high class suites. We would have dinner and champagne. We would slow dance to smooth music playing and make love in one of those lace draped queen size bed and...... ZZZZZ!!! His snoring woke me from my fantasy to find that I am in a small four corner room in a twin size bed. I hunched him.

"Wake your ass up. I want to go home." It was 11 o'clock. He got up. We didn't have much to say as we both dressed. My hair was all over my head. I borrowed his brush and fixed my hair. We left the apartment to take that long walk to my house. We started walking, talking. We talked about everything else, even the stupid movie neither one of us can remember the name of it, but we didn't discuss what just happened. I think he was embarrassed. We got down to Edgemont Avenue and Thank God we saw a cab. It's quite a dip from Crosby Square to Morton Avenue. Michael hailed the cab. The cab stopped and pulled to the curb. We got in.

Michael told the driver the address and the cabbie turned on the fare box and pull away from the curb. As we rode down the street, Michael held my hand, kissed my cheek and told me he would make it up to me. I think he was afraid I would break up with him and tell everybody what a dud he was in bed. It took about 10 minutes before we were pulling up in front my door. The house was dark except for the light in the living room. He told the cab driver to wait for him while he walked me to the door. We got to the door and he hugged me real tight, kissed me and said goodnight. He waited until I was in the house before he turned and walked back to the cab. I stayed in the door and watched him get in the cab. He blew me a kiss as the cab pulled off. I closed the door. From the clock on the wall, it was 11:30 and nobody was home. Thank God for that!

Ruthie did not notice, but a grey Lincoln has been following them. It parked on the corner out of sight when the cab pulled up in front of the door. "She's home. It's about time."

I went upstairs, took a shower and got dressed for bed. "What a wild night. Thank GOD we used a rubber," I thought. I got in bed and pulled the covers over my head. I don't know what time everybody else came in because I fell asleep.

CHAPTER FORTY-TWO

PENNY IS UP. She's going to the bathroom. Knock Knock Knock. She hears the knocks, but first she finishes her business. She flushed the toilet, washes her hands and runs downstairs to see who it is. She peeks out the door and finds Aunt Jane, Barbara and Cece on the stoop. She opens the door and lets them in.

"Hey Aunt Jane! Hey Cuzzins!"

"Hey, Penny! We just stopped by after choir rehearsal. Where's Ruthie?"

"Upstairs."

Penny comes to the bottom of the stairs and yells, "Ruthie! Ruthie!"

"What?"

"Aunt Jane and your sisters are here!"

I jumped out the bed and ran downstairs. "Sisters!" I yelled. We hug. "I'm so glad to see you. How are y'all doing?

"Good. We just finished choir rehearsal."

"Aunt Jane told me you were singing."

"We are good too!" They were both smiling.

"I want to hear you sing."

"That why we are here. We want you to come to church and hear us sing."

"Yeah, I wanna come. What church?"

"It's Trinity Memorial on 4th and Mary Street."

"Okay." Aunt Jane was all smiles.

"We'll come and get you around 9:00 to go to Sunday school and church is 11:00."

"I'll be ready."

The rest of the day went smooth. Michael called and asks if he could come by. At first, I hesitated, but after some smooth talking, I let him come over. He just knew he was coming to get some, but Aunt Bunchie was not working at the bar tonight, so it was not happening. Eventually, she did go out, but by that time Michael had left. Good for you!

Sunday morning and Aunt Jane and my sisters came to take me to church. I was excited to go. We arrived at church in enough time for Sunday school. I was put in the immediate class taught by Patricia Harris. It was fun. We learned about Jesus. She handed out *Sunday Pix* magazines. *Sunday Pix* is a study guide that puts the bible in pictures. I really enjoyed reading it. It helped me to understand the scriptures better. After Sunday school, we attended the church service. The choir was rip roaring and the pianist, Carol, played the piano so good it almost talked. The choir, including my sisters, marched in singing, "We Come This Far by Faith." I was up clapping my hands. The pastor's name was Theodore Summers. His voice was strong and his sermon was clear. Church let out at around 1:00 p.m. I had a good time!!

On the way home, Aunt Jane asks me "Did you enjoy the service?"

"Yes, I did! Aunt Jane. Is it like that all the time?"

"Yes indeed child. We Praise the Lord!!"

"I'd like to go again."

"Anytime."

"Aunt Jane?"

"Yes, baby?"

"Can you take us to see Mom?"

"Sure sugar. Thanksgiving is Thursday. How about next Saturday? I would take you this Saturday, but I got plans already."

"Yay!" We all screamed.

"Okay, I'll set it up and pick you up."

"Thanks Aunt Jane."

Thanksgiving!!! Can you believe Aunt Bunchie volunteered to have it at her house? That suggestion was turned down immediately.

Aunt Jane said "We can have it at my house."

"What's wrong with my house, Jane?"

"Nothing girl. I just think everybody would be more comfortable at my house because I have more room."

"I think you're trying to be funny."

"Don't be like that Bunch."

I thought to myself. "Fo' sho. Who wants to eat at the roach motel?" So, we had Thanksgiving dinner and all the family came together except Rusty and Maurice. I don't know why we haven't seen them by now. It's been since July. Uncle Frank, Frank Jr. and Linda. It was good to see them because I didn't get to see them much before. Even Uncle Louie and Aunt Evy came. Aunt Jane had called and invited them. Dinner was off the chain. We had turkey, ham, rolls, candied yams, greens…the works. I invited Michael, but he's having dinner with his Mom and said he would be by later. We filled our bellies with good food and sweet potato pie for dessert. After so long, you know how people do, eat and run. Before too long it was back to the regulars…the crew. After so long, we headed home.

Michael finally came by the house and we went to the movies. I didn't know, but Michael got this cousin to rent him a room at the Howard Johnsons hotel. After the movies, Michael hailed a cab.
"Where we going?"
"You'll see."
We pulled up to the Howard Johnson's Hotel.
"What we doing here?"
He had this sneaky look on his face. We walk in.
"Here Ruthie, sit in the lobby while I get the key."
Michael looks older than 17 so he didn't have any problems getting the key. So he motions to me to come and follow him. We find our Room, 117. We get in the room and make ourselves at home. There in the mini bar is some snacks and liquor. Michael mixes us some drinks. We drink our drink and relax and talk. Then we start to fool around a little. Instead of jumping right in we took a shower together. It was beautiful…sudsing each other, kissing etc. After that, we made our way to the bed and girl, he made up for all those few times we had sex…this time we made love! It was slow, and deliberate. He touched and kissed me from head to toe. Oooh!!! I will never forget that night. I think that was the night I fell in love and…..OMG!!!

DONNA EARL

CHAPTER FORTY-THREE

SCHOOL IS STILL on point as well as my relationship with Michael. After our special night, we made love, but it was not that often. We didn't have that much privacy, plus I had joined the Student Government at school so that took up a lot of my time. I also started going to church on the regular and started feeling funny about having sex with Michael like I was, but I couldn't help it. I fell hard for him. I was in love.

I was up on Saturday getting dressed. Aunt Bunchie asks "where you going? Aunt Jane is coming to take me and my sisters to see Mom."

"Oh yeah?! Well, I'll go too." "I haven't seen her in a while."

I really didn't want her to go, but who am I to tell her she couldn't? Aunt Jane pulls up and Aunt Bunchie and I come out to get in the car. Aunt Jane had a look of surprise on her face when she saw Aunt Bunchie.

"Where are you going Bunchie?"

"I'm going with y'all. I hope you don't mind."

"No, but..." You could hear the disappointment in her voice when she answered. We're off on the road to see Mom and we sang songs to make the trip fun. We arrive at the Detention Center and park the car. We get out and made out way to the door. We went through the usual procedure to get in and then we wait. Mom comes in.

"Mommy!" we scream.

She hugs us real quick. We know she is not allowed to touch us, but for a quick moment. We all sit down.

"Hey, Bunch."

"Hey, Jane."

"Hey, Beulah."

"How you doing?"

"Girl, it's rough, but I'm doing."

Mom turns to us and asks how we were doing. We fill her in on our comings and goings. She seemed happy to hear we are doing okay. We ask her had she heard from Reese and Rusty.

"Yes. They were here to see me not long ago."

We told her that we had not seen them.

"I'll make sure I get with them about that."

Mom was really glad to see us, but she noticed something different about me that I didn't know.

"Ruthie, are you pregnant?"

Both Aunt Jane and Aunt Bunchie jerked their heads my way so hard they could have caught whiplash.

"No," I said. Why you ask that?"

"You look pregnant. You got a boyfriend?"

Aunt Bunchie jumps in "Yeah, she got some little boy smelling behind her."

"Have you had sex?"

"Mom!!"

"Answer her," yells Aunt Bunchie.

"Bunchie!!"

"Answer her Ruthie!!"

I put my head down "Yes."

Aunt Bunchie said, "God damn!!!"

Barbara and Cece were sitting there, **eyes wide open**. Aunt Jane calmly spoke. "We'll take about later."

"No, we gonna talk about it right now!!!"

Aunt Bunchie's outburst almost had us put out. There wasn't too much to say after that, so we left. The ride home was hell. I was crying and Barbara held my hand. Aunt Bunchie screamed all the way home.

"If we find out you're pregnant, you're getting the hell out my house!!"

Aunt Jane was pissed. She was through. She felt Beulah could have done that better. With her in a place like that she didn't know how, but she knew Beulah shouldn't have done that. If she had it her way, she would have slapped Beulah right across her face to put her daughter on the spot like that.

After they left, Beulah returned to her cell. She felt bad that she did that to her daughter. "Maybe I could have called her on the phone. I don't know. Oh Lord, what I have done to my daughter?" Looking at the reaction from Aunt Bunchie, she was now a little afraid for Ruthie.

We got home. Aunt Jane told us girls to go in the house while she talked to Aunt Bunchie. We got out the car and ran in the house.

Aunt Bunchie held her hands out in front of her, palms up. "Jane I don't want to hear it. I don't want to hear it."

"Bunchie wait."

"Jane, I love my niece. Lord knows I do, but I can't do this. As hard as it is with my own kids and now a possible baby?"

"I know Bunch, but what can we do?"

"This girl moved here not even a year and now look. How she gonna take care of it?"

"Bunch, the girl made a mistake."

"She gonna get rid of it."

"That's not for you to decide. It's up to her and the father. Bunch, until we find out for sure, we're getting upset for nothing."

She looked at Jane as if to say, "Get a grip Jane. She's pregnant."

They got out the car and walked in the house. Aunt Bunchie was so upset that she went straight upstairs to her room and slammed the door.

"Please don't leave me here."

"Don't worry baby, you'll be okay. I'll call my doctor on Monday and set up an appointment. Don't go running your mouth to anybody until we know something."

"Yes ma'am."

"Please…"

She pats my hand "It'll be okay." I say goodbye to my sisters.

"Are you going to church with us tomorrow?"

"No."

"Okay." Both Barbara and Cece hug me like….

Bunchie thought about that thing all night. "If that girl is pregnant, she has got to go. I am not trying to hear no screaming babies. I want to go in there and beat…I can't do that. I remember when that daughter of mine, Penny, comes to me talking that pregnant crap. I jumped on that girl and beat her to an inch of her life. Calvin called the cops on me. I spent the night in jail and had to go to court. Scared me so bad… I know, I'll call Reese and Rusty and tell them what's been going on. Maybe they will talk some sense into her. With a slight smile on her face she thought, maybe they will take her home with them.

All day off and on, I thought about the possibility of me being pregnant. I was walking around in a daze. Penny kept asking me, "What wrong with you girl?" "It's nothing Penny." Inside I was screaming. My head was spinning, "What if I am?" I caught myself crying. "How will I tell Michael? How could I be so stupid?"

I went to school on Monday like nothing happened. I met up with Felicia for our normal girl talk. I wanted to tell her so bad, but… I was good at pretending. No one would guess the hell hole I lived in and the ogre of an Aunt I lived with. I'm sure they had an idea looking at Penny and Calvin. There was no shame in their game. They looked good on the outside, but…just because the package is nicely decorated doesn't mean the contents are any good. I'm not saying they live foul, but you would think they did because of how they act. Penny is an average student, but could be as trifling as her Mom, my Aunt. She's a beautiful person, but she carries herself like a common trick, always grinning up in some guy's face. I don't know what kind of booty she got, but there's no shortage of admirers. I got to give it to her. If she is a trick, there were no free rides. Ira showered her with all kinds of stuff and she talked to him like a dog. She had her own hustle going on. Something, I will find out about soon enough. Now Calvin, he didn't care. He was a free spirit, always laughing, cracking jokes. His only downfall was he always was getting high. I can't believe how he manages to get good grades. I was surprised to find him studying and going to class. He admitted to me, "Ruthie, I may play around, but for real, I want better. Don't judge me by what you see. There is nothing stupid about me."

The day flew by. When I got home, Aunt Bunchie was waiting for me. I don't know how I beat Penny and Calvin home. I saw them as I was leaving.

"Where's Penny and Calvin?"

"I don't know Aunt Bunchie."

"Well, your Aunt Jane called. Your appointment is Thursday at 10:00. She is coming around 9:00-9:30 to pick us up."

"Us?" OMG!

With my doctors' appointment on Thursday, I couldn't help but wonder what Michael would say. He noticed I was being a little distant.

"What's wrong Ruthie? Are you still mad with me about…you know?"

"No," I lied and kissed him on the lips. "Just got a lot on my mind with my Mom being sick."

"Is she getting better?"

"Oh yeah. Day by day."

"That's good." He asked could he come over. I know if he came within 10 feet of the house, Aunt Bunchie would hit the roof. She would let the cat out the bag before I knew anything. I told him I would come and visit him.

I have no idea what it's like to be pregnant. None whatsoever. All I know is my stomach is always doing flip flops and I feel dizzy. I would lay down and when I would try and lift my head up the room would spin. Penny knew something was up ever since Saturday when she saw me crying. I felt her watching me. One night we were in our bedroom and she just came out with it.

"Ruthie, are you pregnant?"

"No girl. What are you talking about?"

"You just look funny to me."

"Funny how?"

"I know you are Ruthie."

Silence.

She lowered her voice. "I was pregnant before."

My eyes got big and my mouth flew open. "What happened?"

"I miscarried."

"Oh Penny!"

"I was about a few weeks to a month pregnant by this guy name… that don't matter now. Anyway, I told Mom and she went OFF!!! She was sitting on the couch when I told her. She jumped up and started beating the living shit out of me. I tried to talk to her, but she wasn't having it. She pushed me and knocked me on the floor. While I was down there, she kept kicking me in my stomach. I did whatever I could to get up, but she kept kicking me. It was like she was a different person. If it wasn't for Calvin coming home when he did, I don't know what would have happened. He called the cops."

"Wow, I didn't know."

"Nobody knows about this not even Aunt Jane or your Mom. She was smart to leave marks where people couldn't see. Calvin left and went and got Chocks and they took me to Crozer. I stayed overnight. They examined me, but it was too late for the baby. You will not believe some of the crap we've gone through with that woman. "Aunt Jane knows some of what life has been for us, but not all."

"I'm so sorry."

She sat there with a faraway look. I guess reliving what happened in her mind. I brought her back when I called her name.

"Penny, my eyes were pleading, please don't tell anybody. I will not know for sure until Thursday."

"Don't worry Ruthie, I promise. Just promise me you'll keep my secret. I have never told my girlfriends and Calvin threatened to kill his friends if they told. They took that to heart. Calvin may play around, but once he is turned on, it's hard to turn him off."

"Okay, I promise."

DONNA EARL

CHAPTER FORTY-FOUR

A T SCHOOL, FELICIA was looking for me. She ran into Penny in the hall. "Penny, where's Ruthie? I didn't see her today."

"Oh, she had a doctor's appointment this morning."

"She didn't tell me. Is she okay?"

"Yeah sure. She just went for a check-up."

Felicia had a sinking feeling something wasn't right.

Well, it's Thursday and Aunt Jane, Aunt Bunchie and I head to Aunt Jane's doctors' office. The doctor's name is Dr. Estella Trimble. The office is located next to Crozer Chester Medical Center in the Professional Building. I smile to myself thinking despite everything, I bet Aunt Bunchie haven't had hers looked at in years. It'll probably talk to you. We walk in the office and Aunt Jane lets the nurse know her 10 o'clock is here. She signs my name and takes a sit next to me.

This is my first time at a coochie doctor. I was so nervous. The nurse calls my name, "Ruth Walters." I walk to meet the nurse and both Aunts were right behind me.

"There's no need for all you."

"Yes it is!" Aunt Bunchie roars.

I thought to myself, "She make me sick."

She weighs me and takes my blood pressure. She hands me a plastic cup and asks that I take it the bathroom and pee in it and bring it back. When I was done, I handed the cup to the nurse. We were then put in a room. She puts my new chart in the holder on the outside of the door. She hands me a gown, the kind that ties in the back and tells me, "Please get undressed from your waist down and the doctor will be with you shortly."

I start to get undressed.

"Come on Bunch, let's give her some privacy."

They gave me a few minutes. When they thought I was dressed they came back.

Dr. Trimble made her appearance. "Hello ladies, how are we doing today?

"Fine."

"Let's see, from the looks on your chart, you're here for a pregnancy test."

"Yes ma'am."

"Well, since this is your first time, I need to explain some things. Ladies, will you please step outside?"

Aunt Jane was glad to go, but Aunt Bunchie act as if she wanted to stay. I guess it been a long time for her.

After they left, Dr. Trimble starts in. "Ruthie, I need you to climb on the table and I will begin the examination."

She picks up this thing that looks like shoehorn or a spatula. "This is a speculum. I will use this instrument to open your vagina. Now I want you to lie back and put your feet in the stir-ups. Good." She took her seat at the bottom of the table. "Now scoot your bottom all the way to the edge. That's it." She turned on the lamp at the edge of the table. "Now Ruth, I'm inserting the speculum and I want you to relax." I feel her put that thing in and I squeezed my eyes shut. "Relax Ruthie. Relax." When she said that it reminded me of Michael. "Almost done." She showed me this long Q-tip. "I'm using this to gather cells from your cervix."

Oh, this is sooo uncomfortable.

"Okay Ruth, you're all done."

When she finally took that thing out, I was so glad. My coochie was too. I think it gasped.

"You may sit up and get dressed. When you are finished, please return to the waiting room. I'll get the results of your test and call you when I am ready."

"Yes ma'am."

She left. When I got off that table I felt like my insides were going to fall out any minute. I got dressed and joined my aunts in the waiting room. Soon as she saw me, Aunt Jane ask me, "Are you okay?"

"Yes."

About 10 minutes passed when I heard my name. "Ruth Walters." Again, we all got up and followed the nurse to the doctor's private office.

"Please be seated." I already had tears in my yes.

"Well Ms. Walters, you are about 2 ½ weeks pregnant. You will probably deliver around September 11th."

"Oh No!! Oh No!!"

Tears rushed out my eyes. Aunt Jane didn't do anything, but hold me. I couldn't have hugged her any tighter. Aunt Bunchie didn't say a word. "Plan B," she thought!

I went back to school the next day. Felicia was waiting for me when I got there.

"Ruthie, are you okay?"

"Yeah, why?"

"Penny says you went for a check-up."

"Yeah girl, I did."

"Oh okay. Girl, Ruth, Felicia squealed, I can't wait. Two more weeks until the Christmas holiday!"

Silence.

"Hello?!!" Felicia snapped her fingers Snap!! Snap!! .

"What's wrong Ruthie?" Her eyebrows rose suspiciously, she asked, "Ruthie, are you pregnant?"

"What?"

"Are you pregnant? Come on now…we girls. You can tell me."

Tears well up in my eyes.

"Oh God Ruthie! Tell me it isn't so. Come on and let's go to the bathroom."

She grabbed my hand and practically dragged me to the bathroom. We go in and the first thing we did was check the stalls to make sure we were alone. We bent over looking under the doors to see if we see feet. None.

"Okay Ruthie, talk."

"Ok. I just found out that I am about 2 ½ week pregnant."

"What?!!"

"Yes."

The eyes of the person that is standing on the toilet got BIG!

"It's my own fault. We weren't thinking about nothing, but getting busy. I love him Felicia."

"Have you told him?"

"Not yet, but I have to soon."

"What are you going to do?"

"What do you mean Felicia? I'm keeping my baby!"

"What if he doesn't want it? What about school?"

"Felicia, I don't know anything right now. It's all new. The first thing I need to do is tell Michael. Come on. Let's go before we are late for homeroom."

We left the bathroom, but little did we know Mary heard the whole conversation. She was in the bathroom primping in the mirror when she heard our voices outside the door. Running into Ruthie was the last thing she wanted to do so she hurried up and stood on the toilet. "Don't worry boo-boo. Just wait…I'll tell him for you."

Mary looked for Michael throughout the day. She saw him several times, but there were people around. She wanted to bust him out, but she still had feelings for him and she wanted to play this right. She wanted him back so to embarrass him she thought better of it. "No, I'll wait". She finally caught him at his locker. He had his back turned so he didn't see her coming. She walked up behind him and put her arms around his waist. He thought it was Ruthie. He grabbed her hands, pulling her closer. He even had his eyes closed. When he turned around to see who it was he was disappointed to find out it was Mary.

His smile disappeared. He pushed her away.

"Get off me girl."

"Oh, it's like that now? You weren't saying that last night."

"Come on, Mary."

She said, "I'm coming" and started walking towards him with a slick smile on her face.

He didn't respond the way she wanted so she turned cold.

"Where's your girl, Ruthie?"

"Why are you asking about her? You jealous?"

"Why would I be jealous of someone stupid enough to get pregnant?"

He looked at her like she was crazy. "What?"

"You heard me! The stupid tramp is pregnant!"

"Shut up, Mary!!!"

He was so mad and shocked that he pushed her hard with both hands into the locker. He wanted to punch her in her mouth. Instead he just stormed off to find Ruthie. Mary didn't care. "Na Na Na Na Na, Ruthie is pregnant!" She sang it like it was a childhood rhyme.

She straightened her clothes. That was her payback. "That's just what she get."

School let out and there's a knock on the door. I peeped out the door and saw it was Michael. He looks disturbed. I hadn't seen him around school all day. I felt like he was hiding from me. I let him in.

"Hey Michael!"

"Hey Ruthie!"

I went to hug him and he half accepted it.

"Where were you yesterday?"

"I had a doctor's appointment."

"Oh really? Doctor's appointment, huh?"

"Yeah."

"When were you going to tell me?"

"Tell you? It was a doctor's appointment."

"Tell me you're pregnant!" he hollered.

I couldn't say a thing.

"Yeah Ruthie, I know!"

"Michael I…"

"I had to find out from somewhere else!"

My mind went…who told him?

"Ruthie!"

"Michael I was going to tell you. I just didn't know how."

"How long have you known?"

"I just found out for sure yesterday."

"So what we going to do?"

"What we going to do? What do we do Michael? Both of us are in school. We don't have jobs, plus…"

"Plus what?"

"My Aunt is pissed. She's going around the house mumbling, cussing me out under her breath. I don't know how long I'll be staying here."

"Well, I haven't had a lot of time to think about it, but I don't want you to kill my baby."

"I haven't had a lot of time to think about it either, Michael. I want to keep the baby, but we have no way of taking care of it. Maybe we can give it up for adoption."

"Nooo!!" That is not an option. I don't want my kid calling nobody Mom and Daddy, but us."

"Michael, we…"

He grabbed me off the couch and in his arms. "It'll be alright. We'll think of something."

CHAPTER FORTY-FIVE

EARLY SATURDAY MORNING, Penny and I got up and headed over town (downtown Chester) to catch the 109 Septa bus to the Springfield Mall. She wanted me to go with her to shop, have a girls' day. We've become closer since we had our heart to heart. We went to John Wanamaker's and Bambergers and several other stores. We had a good day. By the time we got home, we were dog tired. We walked in the house and... Rusty and Maurice!!!

"OMG!!!" I screamed. My whole face lit up when I saw them. I ran to them and hugged them real tight. "Where have you been?"

"Oh, we've been busy, working."

"Why haven't you been to see us?"

"We've been busy tying up loose ends."

"What's been going on?"

'Well, you know, Mom's lawyer, Ms. Mathis?"

"Yeah, I remember her."

"Well, after Moms' case, she had her license temporarily suspended."

"Why?"

"I don't know. Speaking of Mom, have you been to see her?"

"Yeah. We saw her last week. Aunt Jane took us. We were going the Saturday after Thanksgiving, but Aunt Jane said she had something to do. I told Mom we would try to come again around Christmas. Barbara and Cece are going to be mad they missed y'all."

"No, we're going to see them when we leave here. We called Aunt Jane and told her we were stopping here first then we would stop by her house."

Maurice tried to contain himself, listening to all this crap. He shifted around in the chair until he couldn't stand it any longer. He waited until Rusty put a period at the end of his sentence then he dove in.

"Ruthie, what's this stupid shit we hear that you are pregnant by some dude name Michael? What you think you're grown now? You leave Philly young and dumb and you still young and dumb! The difference now is your carrying a baby. I know you ain't thinking of keeping the baby."

"Yes, I am!"

"How stupid is that Ruthie? What about money, shelter, clothes? Does Mom know?"

"She told me!"

"What?!"

"She told me when we went to see her. She said I looked pregnant so she asked me. So I went to the doctor and found out."

"That's what I'm talking about Ruthie! You are too young."

Rusty cuts in… "Ruthie what about school? From what I hear, you are excelling in school. Why would you want to ruin that with this big of a responsibility?"

Maurice kept on. "Where is…what 's his name? Michael? Where is he so I congratulate him with my foot up his ass for screwing my 15-year-old sister?"

"He said he would help me."

"How Ruthie? Where's he working?"

"We are going to work it out."

"Well, you better figure out something because Aunt Bunchie made it clear, THIS IS YOUR BABY!!!"

We were screaming at one another so hard we ran out of breath.
Silence.

"Well, alright then, we are going to go to Aunt Jane's house." Both Maurice and Rusty stood up.

"You want to go?"

"No."

"Okay, give me a hug."

I hugged Rusty, but didn't want to hug Maurice. Reese pulled me to him.

"Come here girl and give me a hug. I know you mad. I am too. I love you and I just didn't want this for you right now. Take care of yourself. We'll be checking on you. Think long and hard about your decision Ruthie."

They say their goodbyes, hugs and kisses. I walked them outside.

"What's the best way to get to Aunt Jane's?"

I stood on the stoop and directed them. "Make a right at this corner. Keep straight until you get to 9ᵗʰ Street. Make a left. Follow 9ᵗʰ Street all the way until you get to Wilson and make a left. It's easy. You'll know you're at Wilson because it's a light right there and Sacred Heart Hospital will be on your right."

"Okay lil' sis. See you later."

"Bye."

Aunt Bunchie was upstairs on the top step listening. "Hmphf, so my plan didn't work. They are mad, but not mad enough to take her black ass back with them. That's alright. She's on her own as far as I'm concerned."

Rusty and Maurice drove to Aunt Jane's house. They follow Ruthie's directions and make the left on 9ᵗʰ Street. They stop at the light in front of King Chevrolet. They see the sign "Chester High."

Isn't that the school Ruthie goes to?"

"Yeah."

"Not bad, but it looks like a prison."

They continue on to the big intersection of 9ᵗʰ and Kerlin.

"Are we going right?"

"Yeah, we're still on 9ᵗʰ.

They ride pass the Bennett Homes, go under the Commodore Barry Bridge underpass and stop at light, 9ᵗʰ and Engle.

"Where is Wilson Street?"

"Just keep straight, Rusty. We're bound to run into it."

"Okay, this is Townsend Street and look there's a park. The sign says, 'Memorial Park.' Nice."

At the light, they see the Wilson Street sign.

"Make this left Rusty."

Rusty makes a left at the light on Wilson Street. Maurice was still pissed at the idea of Ruthie being pregnant. He was fussing, hands waving in the air, blocking Rusty's view. He had to push his hands away a few times so he can see. Rusty was sympathetic.

"How can you feel sorry for her Rusty?"

"How you going to call somebody stupid Reece? Remember, you got Carolyn pregnant. She was young."

"Yeah, and she had an abortion."

That settled him down a little, thinking about it.

"I'm not too happy about that, man. Remember Mom had you young too. She was only 17 and look how hard she struggled. I don't want that same life for her Rusty, not finishing school. She'll have it hard without at least a high school diploma."

"Well Reese, if she is dead set on having this baby, we will have to support her, but one thing for sure, we will make sure she finishes school."

They arrived in front of Aunt Jane's house. She has a Christmas wreath on the door and you can see her Christmas tree through the window. Merry Christmas everybody.

DONNA EARL

CHAPTER FORTY-SIX

MY PREGNANCY WAS like hot news at school. For the first three months, everybody was talking about me like a dog. I would meet Felicia every morning like usual and she would fill me in on what was being said. It got to the point that I told Felicia, "Don't tell me nothing else." I held my head up, but school was becoming a nightmare. I was called everything, but a child of GOD behind my back. They didn't dare say it to my face. They knew better than that. Baby or no baby I wasn't having it, but like I said, school was becoming harder and harder to take. If it wasn't for Mary letting the cat out the bag (Michael told me she told him) to the whole school no one would have guessed at least for the first three months because I could still fit my clothes. My face just got fuller. Note to self: "Kick Mary's behind when I drop this load." My home life was already hard, but Aunt Bunchie had become almost impossible to live with. She wouldn't lift a finger to help me. A few times at school, I went to the main office and called Aunt Jane telling her how cruel she had become. She told me she would talk to her. When I had doctor appointments, it was either Aunt Jane or Michael's mother that took me or I had to get the bus. His mother was not too happy at first about our decision to keep the baby, but as time went on she became overly excited because this would be her first grandchild.

The phone rings…" Hello."

"Hello Bunch, this is Jane."

"Hey Jane, what's up?"

"Look, I'm at work so I can only stay on this phone for a few minutes. I just got a call from Ruthie and she was crying. She says you are slurring her and treating her bad. Now, I thought we talked about this."

"Jane…"

"Bunch I asked you nicely. Please don't have that girl calling me not another time about you over there mistreating her. She needs your support. Does she have it?"

Aunt Bunch says yes so low Aunt Jane couldn't hear her.

"What you say?"

"YES!!"

"Okay Bunch. I'll talk to you later." Click.

SLAM!!!

"Who does she think she is? I'm not scared of her."

You should be!

By my fourth month, I started to show and the kids at school really started to ride me. Sometimes I would hide in the bathroom and just cry. Felicia would try and defend me, but they threatened to jump her. They actually tried and she had to come out of her bag on them. Even Penny got into a few shouting matches defending me. One day I told myself, "I've had it." I started to go to school less and less then I stopped going all together. When Michael found out he was pissed, but he understood my frustration. He didn't argue with me too much because my hormones were out of whack and I had become meaner and meaner, so he left me alone. My family, Aunt Jane, my sisters, etc. were not too happy about me dropping out of school. I told them it was temporary. I told them "I'll go back when I have the baby."

Time flew by. It was getting close to "drop that load" time. I was about 7 or 8 months along when Penny planned a surprise baby shower. Felicia, Carla, Renee, Aunt Jane, Michael's mother, my sisters and some other people came to the shower. We had a good time. Even Aunt Bunchie came, but I knew she was seething inside. She was on her best behavior. Aunt Jane didn't make it obvious, but she was watching her. My gifts: clothes, bottles, blankets, diapers, a small crib, undershirts, you name it. I was so moved that I was brought to tears. I received a special card from my mother. She sent it to Aunt Jane and she gave it to me after the shower was over. "Don't open it until later." It read:

"Dear daughter, I love you with all my heart. I may not be there in flesh, but I am there in spirit. I'm so proud of you. You know where I am if you need me. Love Mom."

Tears flowed freely. "I love you too Mom…I miss you."

OMG this hurts…The pains woke me up out of my sleep. "Oooh! Oooh!" Penny woke up.

"What's wrong Ruthie?"

"My stomach is killing me."

"I think you're in labor."

My stomach was squeezing as if I had to crap. "Penny, it hurts!!"

"Okay, let's get you to the hospital."

She ran down the hall to get Aunt Bunchie. She bust in her room. Wouldn't you know it, there's a man in there. I think they had just finished, you know… They were just lying there with Aunt Bunchie smoking a cigarette. Penny didn't care.

"Mom, Ruthie is in labor!"

"What the hell you telling…" she caught herself.

"Mom, come on."

"I'm coming." She lifted up, things hanging and sagging. What a sight! Penny ran back and helped me get dressed. Once we made it downstairs, she called the doctor, Aunt Jane and Michael.

"Ruthie's in labor…meet us at the hospital!"

By the time we got to the hospital, I was all, but howling. Those pains were kicking! Everybody was there, but my sisters.

"Where's my sisters?"

"They home. I left them with my kids, Frank Jr and Linda."

Dr. Trimble enters the room and told me she needed to check me. "Check me?" She lefts up the covers around by my feet and checked me by inserting her hand in my 'area.'

"Goddamn, that hurt."

"Yes, I know Ruthie, hang in there. I have to check you to see how far you are."

I wanted to kick her. She was really patient with me.

"It will not be long. You are about 4 centimeters."

Michael tried to comfort me.

"Get off me."

Hours later, an eternity, Dr. Trimble comes for the last time. She checked me again.

"Okay Ruthie, you're ten centimeters. It's time to push."

"Okay."

"Only two people are allowed in the room."

Michael and Penny stayed. They had me put my feet in the stirrups.

"Okay Ruthie, when you feel a contraction, I want you to put your chin to your chest and bear down. Okay push."

"Grunt."

"Come on, don't you want the baby out?"

"Yes."

"Ok then, push!!"

Grunt!!!!

"Good Ruthie. Rest. This baby will be born in no time. Push!! Here it comes. That's it, keep pushing!"

I hear the baby crying. "Wah, Wah!"

"Congratulations, it's a boy!!!"

Justin Michael Walters, born September 11 at 6:06 weighing 6lbs and 6 oz. Michael was a little disappointed that I didn't give him his first and last name, but he was happy.

After two days, I was allowed to take Justin home. Aunt Jane took me home to get me settled in. Surprise! The room I shared with Penny was set up like a nursery. What a welcome home gift. I had no idea how to take care of a baby so everything was trial and error. With a little help from Michael's mother and Aunt Jane, I learned quickly how to care for him. Aunt Bunchie stuck to her word. She did very little to help. When Justin cried, she would yell "can't you shut that baby up?" Michael's mother knew I did not have a way to care for the baby financially so she told me I needed to apply for aid at the welfare office. The welfare office was located on 12th and Avenue of the states. I walked in the door and young girls for miles were seated in there. I was given a number, number 58. My care worker's name was Annabelle Reynolds. She was hateful. She acted as if she was giving me money out of her pocket. She screamed all these instructions and questions, like "Who's the father? etc." She told me that I had to go out Media and sue the father and all this stuff.

I was given an emergency check that I had to pick up the next day. My total welfare package was $200 dollars in greenies, $300 in food stamps, WIC and a medical card. Aunt Bunchie, the thief, would steal my food stamps or demand I give them to her.

"You need to pay your way here somehow."

I had this stupid grin on my face thinking $200 was a lot of money, that I was paid, but I soon found out that $200 didn't last a minute with the cost of pampers, baby clothes, etc. I complained to Michael and he helped as best as he could. With him still in school, he was only able to get a part time job.

One day I was down to my last $5.00 dollars and Justin needed some pampers. He had a few left, but I knew before the day was out I would need more. I could have gotten the money from Calvin or Penny, but they had left for school. Speaking of school, I missed it. I had 3 more weeks before I could go back. So anyway, I thought I may have a few dollars somewhere around here. Maybe I left some money in my pants pockets.

While the baby slept, I went searching. I searched all my jeans, turned my pocketbook inside out. No luck. got an idea. "I know… maybe Aunt Bunchie has some money laying around."

She was always searching through my things so one good turn deserves another.

"Hmphf, she ain't home. I'll search her room."

I was careful not to disturb anything, gently lifting things, etc. I first looked on her nightstand. Ewww! A condom wrapper. I dropped that and wiped my hands on my pants. I then went in her top drawer, looking around and stumbled across a check stub. The stub had her name, date and dollar amount: $10,000. $10,000! There was another name in the corner at the top. Sheila Mathis. Sheila Mathis? That's Mom's lawyer. What? Who? My head was spinning. I hurried up and closed the drawer.

Justin started crying, so I hurried to him and started dealing with his complaining. He was wet and his greedy butt was hungry. So I changed him and fed him a bottle. While I was feeding him, my mind drifted to the $10,000. First of all, what is she doing getting money from Sheila Mathis? Secondly, the date. The date was right around the time my Mom was sentenced and right before we moved here. "Did Aunt Bunchie have anything to do with my Mom's case?" Is this some kind of payoff?" Setting Justin down in his crib, an idea he wasn't too crazy, he instantly started fussing. "Ssh!!!" I pat his back a few times and he finally got quiet and fell off to sleep. I crept downstairs and grabbed the phone and called Aunt Jane. Thank God Aunt Jane was home.

"Hello."

"Hey Aunt Jane, this is Ruthie."

"Hey Ruthie. Becoming alarmed she asked, "Is everything okay?"

"Yes everything is cool. I just need to talk to you."

You can hear her voice relax. "I'm all ears."

"I found something. I don't know what it means."

"What did you find?"

"I found...," I peeped out the window and saw Aunt Bunchie pulling up. I whispered, "Aunt Bunchie is coming. I can't say now. Can you come and get me?"

"I'll be there as soon as I can."

Just as I hung up, Penny and Calvin walked in the back door.

"Who was that?"

"Aunt Jane. She said she was coming by."

"My Mom home yet?"

"I think she just pulled up."

They both immediately disappeared upstairs. Aunt Bunchie finally makes it in the front door.

"Hey Aunt Bunchie."

"Hey Ruthie."

"Any calls?"

"Just Aunt Jane. She's coming by to take me to the store."

"Hmmm, that's good. Y'all go out, bring me something back."

"Okay."

"Where's the baby?"

"He's upstairs sleeping."

"Calvin and Penny home?"

"Yeah upstairs."

A half hour later, Knock Knock.

"Hey Aunt Jane."

"Hey Ruthie."

"What's going on?"

"Nothing. Where's Cece and Barbara?"

"Home doing homework. Big Frank got them covered. He is really enjoying them, especially Cece. She got him playing Candyland. Bunch home?"

"Yeah, she just got here."

"Hey Bunch!!"

Aunt Bunchie heard her voice and same downstairs. "Hey." They talked their sister talk and after so long Ira and Michael stopped by. Michael to spoil Justin and Ira to see Penny.

"So, Ruthie, let's go to the store before it gets too late. What you gotta get?"

"Some pampers and formula." I went to Michael and put my hand out. He greased my palm with $20 dollars. I said "Thank you, baby" and kissed him on the lips.

"That's enough of that…that's how you got the first one." Aunt Bunchie chastised.

"Anybody else want to go?"

"Naw, I'm good Aunt Jane" Calvin answered.

Penny and Ira had gone in the kitchen for privacy and Michael said, holding the baby, "I'll be right here when you get back waiting for my change."

I looked at him and said, "Yeah, right." We both smiled.

Aunt Jane and I left out and got in the car. We drove to the Pathmark in Brookhaven. While driving, Aunt Jane started in, "So, what going on?

"Aunt Jane, I found something in Aunt Bunchie's drawer."

"Now Ruthie, it's not good to go snooping thru people's stuff."

"I wasn't really snooping. I was looking for a few dollars for pampers when I found a check stub in the amount of $10,000."

"A what?"

"I found a check stub in the amount of $10,000."

"You lying?"

"No and guess who it's from?"

"Who?"

"Sheila Mathis."

"Sheila Mathis? Who the hell is that?"

"Oooh, Aunt Jane you cussed!"

"Forget that. Who is she?"

"That's Mom's lawyer."

"Why in the world would she be getting money from her?"

"I don't know."

"Well, I'm sure as hell going to find out."

"Do you know where she is?"

"No, but Rusty may know and I'm going to call him TONIGHT!
"Don't say nothing for now okay? Act as if nothing's changed. Okay?"

"Okay."

Let me find out.......

WHEN I CLOSE MY EYES

Aunt Jane meets with Rusty and Maurice about two days later. They met at a halfway point in Springfield at the Southern Cooking Restaurant.

"Why would Ms. Mathis pay Aunt Bunchie $10,000?" They talked low because the place was packed.

"I have no idea."

"We need to meet with Ms. Mathis to find out."

After some searching, they found that she was working at a legal counsel office in Darby. She found the job through her old boss, Mark Stiles from the Public Defender's office. He found out what happened to her and felt sorry. He called in a favor from a friend and asked could he give her a job. Her license has been temporarily suspended for one year, so for now, she refers clients to lawyers.

They pulled the glass doors open and were greeted by the receptionist. "Hello, may I help you?"

"Yes, we'd like to see Sheila Mathis."

"May I ask your name?"

"Tell her it's Russell Walters."

She buzzed her. "Ms. Mathis, you have a Russell Walters here to see you."

When Sheila heard that name. "What? Can't be..."

"Ms. Mathis?"

"Ok, send him in."

When they walked in her office, she immediately recognized Rusty, but didn't let on.

"Hello Ms. Mathis. Do you remember me?" Rusty asked.

Taking off her glasses, she squinted her eyes. "I'm trying to place you."

"Don't even try it Ms. Mathis."

"Yeah, I remember. You are Mrs. Walter's son, right?"

"Don't play dumb. You know exactly who I am."

"What are you doing here?"

"We need to talk to you."

"About what? I'm no longer your mothers' lawyer."

"We know that, but what we want to know is why you paid her sister $10,000."

She stiffened. By this time, Sheila could care less. She'd been tried and convicted by her peers so she blurted it out. "She blackmailed me."

"What? How?"

"Let me explain. when I took your mother's case, I wasn't forthcoming that I had a relationship with the Asst. Prosecutor. In the eyes of the law, that is considered a conflict of interest. I should have excused myself from the case, but I thought with our past, I could get Andrew to bring lessor charges, but the outcome resulted in..."

Maurice chimed in, "We know...our Mom is spending 7 years in the clink because of you."

"No, that is not true. Your mother CHOSE to sign that plea agreement."

"Sure she did Ms. Mathis, but after you convinced her there was no other way."

"I tried to convince her otherwise, but the ultimate decision was hers."

"Yeah right. Back to the $10,000."

Sheila recalls the entire conversation. "So, she overhead me having a conversation with him about the case. So that's how it happened."

"So, you paid her?"

"Yes, I gave her the money."

"Ms. Mathis, you are a servant of the law. You could have had her locked up for blackmail."

"I know, but at the time, I was trying not to be found out. I was thinking about my license and career. At that time, I would have done anything, but as you can see, it didn't work. It was found out anyhow and that's how I ended up here."

"Well, Ms. Mathis, I can't say I feel sorry for you."

"I'm not expecting you to feel sorry. You asked me, so I told you. It's out now and I can move on. I've considered bringing charges against her for blackmail, but I didn't want to damage myself for the future, but trust me, it's not off the table."

"Well, thank you for filling us in on what happened."

"Let ME ask you a question? How did you find out the money?"

They didn't answer.

"We'll take our leave now. Thanks again."

They walked out of her office and out of her life for good.

So they thought.

As Sheila was leaving for the day, sitting in her car, she thought seeing them brought about feelings she tried to squash. After being called on the carpet and having her license suspended, she started drinking heavily. "If it wasn't for this job I don't know…if it wasn't for…I'm going to get you Ms. Bunchie, as they call you." It's not over."

Riding home, they discussed their new found information.

"What are we gonna do now?" Silence. Each one was in their own thought.

They drove back to their meeting point and Aunt Jane got out and climbed in her car. Before closing the door, she told Rusty and Maurice, "Follow me."

I knew of the meeting and I was expecting a blowout. I didn't let on to Calvin and Penny that hell was about to break loose. I had no idea it would happen like it did. It was Friday about 6:30 and Penny, Calvin and I were sitting around, watching Fuzzy, the TV. Penny was waiting for Ira and Michael had to work. He told me he would stop by when he clocked out. Aunt Bunchie was upstairs resting. She had to be at the bar around 8.

There was a knock at the door and Penny went running.

"Ira?"

"No, it's your Aunt Jane and your cousins Maurice and Rusty."

She opens the door and let them in.

"Hey!"

"What y'all doing here?"

"We were in the neighborhood, so we thought we stop by. What y'all doing?"

"Getting cranked up!! Its' Friday night," Calvin said, dancing around. He was kicking it out.

"Boy, you silly," Maurice chirped. "Where's your mom?"

"She's upstairs."

Aunt Jane walks to the bottom of the stairs.

"Bunchie!!"

"Hey!!"

"Come on down."

"Okay, be down in a minute."

She comes down all decked out in this red pantsuit. Only thing missing was her earrings. She was putting them on while coming down the stairs.

"Where you going?"

"I gotta go to work girl. I need to be there by 8. Hey Russ and Reece."

"Hey there, Aunt Bunchie."

"Hey Bunch, before you go, I want to ask you something."

"What's that?"

"You remember Sheila Mathis?"

"Yeah, what about her?"

"Well, we just left her office."

"Oh."

"She said she paid you $10,000."

"What?!!!"

Calvin clicked Fuzzy off so he can hear.

"What did you say?"

"You heard me Bunch. Sheila Mathis says she paid you $10,000 in hush money."

"Who's Sheila Mathis," Penny asked?

"She's your Aunt Beulah's attorney." Aunt Jane answered without taking her eyes off Bunchie. She had taken steps toward Bunchie getting closer and closer. Bunchie was scared now and backed up some. Maurice & Rusty said "oh shit" under their breath. Penny and Calvin mouths were hanging open and I was just standing there, looking.

"Don't lie Bunch. We got proof. We saw a copy of the check."

Silence.

"Then yeah, I did it! So what?!!"

"So what?!"

"Is that your answer, Penny questioned? Mom, I can't believe you did that?"

"Oh you a smart Bitch!" Aunt Jane said as she got within grabbing distance. Aunt Jane was coming out of her bag. "I can't believe you are that slimy. It's bad enough that you would stoop that low for money, but you took from the kids. You knew how desperate they were to stay together and you took that from them. You don't give a damn about nobody but yourself. I've had enough of your trifling bullshit."

Before we knew it, Aunt Jane went off. She grabbed Aunt Bunchie by the throat and started choking her. Aunt Bunchie was clawing at Aunt Jane's hands trying to get her off, but Aunt Jane didn't let up. While choking her, thoughts of all the lies, the SECRETS and the backbiting from over the years came back in a flash. She thought about the fact that her own sister screwed her husband, something Bunchie didn't think she knew about and squeezed tighter. Rusty and Maurice tried to break it up, but she was too strong. When she flipped the switch, she flipped the switch.

Calvin jumped off the couch and ran to them "Get off my mom."

Penny was screaming, "Stop! Stop!"

Aunt Jane had turned into another person. Aunt Bunchie was running out of air and was swinging wildly.

I ran over, "Aunt Jane stop," I cried. Please stop!!"

Hearing Ruthie screams through the fog, she let go and Aunt Bunchie fell to the floor gasping for air. We were standing there. What could we do? Aunt Bunchie got herself together and stood up, hair all over the place. Maurice and Rusty had Aunt Jane boxed in.

Holding her throat with mascara running looking like a racoon, "I want you out of my house!!!!" screamed Aunt Bunchie.

"Make me get out! I'm not going anywhere until you explain to these kids why you did it and I want the truth."

Breathing hard and fixing her clothes, "Look, I needed the money, okay."

"For what?"

"It's hard to make ends meet on a barmaid's salary. "These bills, these kids…"

"Don't forget your men," Penny added.

"Shut up Penny!!" Aunt Bunch screamed. "So, when opportunity knocks…"

"You'd do anything for money won't you Mom," Calvin asks?

"That's no excuse, Bunch. These kids had just lost their Daddy and their Mom goes to jail. They needed the money more."

Maurice jumped in, "Let's see how slick you are when she brings charges against you."

"What?"

"Yes, indeed Aunty. Sheila Mathis's closet is clean and wide open. Can you say the same? I know about some of the dirty low down things you have done over the years, but this takes the cake. To think you just knew you were getting away with something. You blackmail a lawyer who knows the law. How stupid is that? If only you could see the look on your face now. Don't feel so smart now do you? I'm outta here. You coming Russ?"

DONNA EARL

"Yeah, I've seen and heard enough. Aunt Jane?"

"Yeah, I'm coming."

There's a knock at the door. It's Michael. He comes in and the look on his face says, 'What went on in here?'

"Bunchie, I have nothing else to say to you."

"Well, since it's like that, take Ruthie with you."

I got bold. "I have one question. With the money you stole, what did you do with the money?"

Aunt Bunchie looked at me, staring.

"Well, you can look at me funny all you want. I'm not going anywhere, Aunt Bunchie. You owe me. You owe my family. You stole from us."

"Goodbye Bunchie" Aunt Jane says. "Remember payback is a mother...."

Lurking in the dark, he sees all these people coming out the house. "I haven't seen her for some time now. "She's not with them. Damn."

CHAPTER FORTY-SEVEN

WITH EVERYTHING GOING on, I almost forgot I have a birthday coming up in 2 days. I'll be 16 years old on September 20th!

It was Indian summer so it was still kind of warm so people were still cooking out. Penny and Calvin went to barbeques, but I stayed home with Justin. We had our own barbeque. Menu: Depression and low self-esteem. Michael's family had a picnic and he asked if I wanted to go. I turned him because I didn't feel presentable. I still had baby fat and the clothes I had were tight and faded. I never had money to buy anything new. I've been in Chester for 1 year and in that time I didn't do nothing, but give birth. At 15 going on 16, I'm a mother. A mother!!! I started to cry. It's gotta get better. It did for a short period of time. On my birthday, as a matter of fact.

My Aunt Jane and sisters surprised me by coming to get Justin and I, taking us to dinner. "Happy Birthday, Ruthie!"

"You guys...!" We went to Flagstaffs for dinner and the waiters at the restaurant sang "Happy Birthday" to me. I also got a chance to spend the night away from Hell's hotel. It was so nice to smell a different smell, lie down on a comfortable bed and watch a better TV. Watching Fuzzy, my eyes are starting to play tricks on me. If this continues, I'll need glasses. Oh, Paradise!!!

Maurice and Rusty visited Beulah in the Detention Center. From the moment she sees them, her mother instincts kick in. Something's wrong. They greet her and the minute she sits down, she asks, "What's wrong?" They never could lie to her.

"Mom, you will not believe what's been going." They began to tell her and Beulah is done...

"You've got to be kidding me."

"Yeah Mom, it was like that."

Meanwhile, in another part of town, Sheila is speaking with her colleague, plotting her strategy. "Are you sure, Sheila?" "Yes, I'm very sure."

CHAPTER FORTY-EIGHT

ONCE A WEEK, for a while now, Penny and I have heart to heart conversations. I'd bathe, powdered and feed Justin. After his greedy butt fall asleep, I'd lay down. Looking up at the ceiling, I thought about my money situation. Penny had just come in from her date with Ira and was rolling her hair.

"The baby sleep?"

"Finally."

"Penny, I need to talk."

"Talk."

"Penny, I'm so broke. This welfare don't last no time before it's all gone."

She just stared at me.

"Penny, are you listening?"

"Yeah, I'm listening. I'm just thinking."

"About what?"

"A way you can make some money. Well, I don't know...you may not like it."

"How?"

"Coming to work for Mr. Blue."

I looked at her cross-eyed. "Mr. Blue?"

"Yeah, Mr. Blue."

"Doing what?"

"I don't know Ruthie. I don't know if I should tell you."

"Tell me what?"

"You can't tell anybody."

"Tell anybody what?"

"About, you know, working for Mr. Blue."

"I promise. Cross my heart." I crossed my heart when I said this.

"Listen, ever since before you came...No, I'm not going to tell you." I'm scared!"

"Come on Penny! I swear I'm not going to tell. I crossed my heart, didn't I?"

"Okay." "I've been working for Mr. Blue."

"Doing what?"

"I deliver packages."

"What kind of packages?"

"You know."

"No, I don't."

"I deliver drugs to different drop houses."

"Penny, you're doing what?!" Are you crazy?"

"Ssh! It's real easy. At first, I was scared, but as time went on I stop being scared."

"Oh, so that's how you make your money? I thought you were…"

"What? Tricking? Child please! Ain't nothing happening."

"I don't know Penny." It sounds risky."

"Think about it and I'll talk with Mr. Blue. I'm going downstairs to get a snack. Want something?"

"No."

Penny left the room.

I thought about it, while pulling the covers up on the bed, "Penny is crazy!!! I'm not doing that. I don't need money that bad."

Downstairs, Penny got a glass of milk and some cookies. She pulled a chair out from under the kitchen table and sat down. She took a bite of the cookie. As she chewed, she thought of what she told Ruthie. She is second guessing getting Ruthie involved. "Now that I think about it, I'm not doing that. Something happen to her, I'd never forgive myself." She thought about how she first came across Mr. Blue. Mr. Blue is darker than night. He is so dark he looks blue black. You would think that was why he was called that. No, it is because he wears blue all the time. He had a wife name Minnie, but she passed away. He is a low level hustler at least from the outside, but anyone who knew him was well aware of his dealings. He has a record yay long. Word on the street everybody knows he dabbles in "oil." Even his wife, but her problem with him she couldn't stand his "catting" around. His operation is done out of the abandoned storefront next to "Shag's" formally owned by this lady name Mattie Mae with her two sons name Barry and Willie. To look at it you wouldn't know because the normal store dealings are done in the front of the store, but towards the back where the meat case is there's a door with a combination hid by a tall freezer.

"He knew I was a minor when he first tried to talk to me. Old dirty dog."

It wasn't so long ago. It was just last year or maybe, I'm 16 now going on 17, so yeah, it was two years ago. I was 14, but built like an 18 year old…. ass, hips, and BREASTS. "I'm killing them." I had old and young men drooling. Just like Mom said, I was hot in the butt, smelling myself. Well, he was standing outside the Livewire bar. I gotta admit he was one fine older man. I'd walk pass to go to Shags store and he'd watch me, making me feel self-conscious. So I got grown one day and asked, what you looking at?

"You."

"You like what you see?"

"Yeah!!!"

I know I didn't have any business talking to that grown man like that.

"Well, you better keep your eyes to yourself before I tell my Mom."

"Who's your Mom?"

"Bunchie."

"Bunchie? Oh, I know her."

"Look little girl, I'm just playing with you. I'm a grown man passing the time away talking to you. "You better be careful how you step to grown people, men anyway."

"I better be careful nothing. Ain't nobody going to do nothing to me."

"Okay, little girl."

"Shut up, old man."

He just laughed. He must have taken a liking to me because every time he saw me, he would smile and wave.

"Hi Penny."

"Hi Mr. Blue."

This went on for weeks, but one day he wasn't paying me any attention. This got to me. The doors to the bar was open, because it was hot and I know I walked pass that bar about ten or fifteen times. He was looking, but played it off. So that last time I passed, he was sitting on the stool, looking outside and called me. "Penny!!!" I didn't have any business in there, but since it was in the daytime, I don't think anybody paid it any attention. I stood there and talked to him for a long time, then I would leave because it started getting dark. So for a while, when we'd see each other in passing, we would talk. He'd ask me about me, what I wanted in life, about school, home etc. He was paying me the attention I craved from my father, whom I hadn't seen in a long time. My father is some man, that's right, I said it, some man named Winston Barclay. They call him Winter. At least that's who my Mom says he is. Calvin has his father and this man is mine. He would come and visit, give me money and sometimes take me around, but it was more as something to do, not as a daughter. I think that's why I flocked to Mr. Blue's attention. He would talk to me and make me feel comfortable around him, but it was all a set-up. His attention led me to give up my virginity to him. The first time, OMIGOSH! It felt like hell leaving my coosinany stinging, but he was a grown man so he knew how "to get down." Yeah, I liked it so we did it a few times. He taught me what it took to please a man. When I told him I missed my period, we snuck to this back alley doctor name Dr. Evans that confirmed I was pregnant. He felt shame in what he had done. He knew I trusted him and he took advantage. He didn't rape me or nothing. I willingly gave it up, but he felt bad just the same. He asked that I meet him so he could take me to get the abortion, but me and my big mouth I went and told my Mom about my pregnancy, leaving out the fact that Mr. Blue was the father. All Hell broke loose. When I told her, she beat me screaming the whole time, "Who's the father?" She thought it was my teenage puppy love boyfriend nicknamed 'Eyes.' Bruce Jackson is his real name. In his dreams. He never was within smelling distance of it. Calvin knew though. He had the nerve to get on me about hanging around Mr. Blue. So after Mr. Blue found out about my Mom almost killing me, he never touched me again. We never stop talking, but that jumping up and down stopped. Eventually, I started working for him undercover, dropping off packages. Tears running down her cheeks, Penny shook her head to erase the memory. "I can't do that to her. I can't."

CHAPTER FORTY-NINE

MAYBE IT'S ME, but for some reason, Michael is slacking. I'm seeing him, but not as frequently. He used to come by just about every day, but now I barely see him, maybe two or three time out of the week. I guess the newness of Justin coming has worn off. When I see him, He's not all there. It's like he's in another world. When I'd ask him where you been? His answer would be working.

"Get out of here! Working huh?! Then where is the money Michael?"

"Ruthie, I'm doing the best I can. School has started! You know this is my senior year. I don't have a lot of time."

I thought "Whatever." Something else is going on. School has never been a problem before. He is trying to sell me sugar knowing its shit. Well, I'm not buying it. The truth is about to raise its ugly head.

Felicia called me, filling me in on what's going on at school.

"When you coming back?"

"I'll be back in about two more weeks."

"Well, that's not soon enough. I miss you."

"I miss you too. I got a question for you?"

"What's that?"

"Have you been seeing Michael in school?"

"Now, Ruthie, I don't go around following Michael. I got my own thing going on."

"Just answer the question."

"Yeah, why?"

"Nothing, just asking."

Two weeks later, I was back to school. Michael's mother volunteered to watch the baby for me for now. She was on 2nd shift at her job, so I was able to go back to school. It was just like I never left. I had to repeat a few classes and then they allowed me to take a test to get me current, you know, in my right grade, the 10th. Can you believe Penny is in the 11th and Calvin is graduating? Miracles do happen.

Anyhow, like I said things were running smoothly, still had Ms. Mary googling at me, but I paid that trick no mind. One Friday night, Michael stopped over the house and invited me to hang out with him for a while. He was looking and acting goofy and I started not to go.

"Go ahead Ruthie. I'll stay with Justin. Beside Ira is coming over."

It was right around the middle of October. So I grabbed my jacket and Michael and I went out. We didn't have a car so we walked around and ended up by the Ethel Waters Park. We did some serious walking. I was tired so we sat on the bench and I jumped up.

"What's wrong," Michael asked?

"I'm not sitting on that."

"Why not?"

"It's too COLD!!! I might get the piles."

"The piles?"

"Yeah, my Mom used to say that when I would sit on my old stoop when it was cold."

"I got something that will warm you up."

"You are so nasty."

"Not that." He pulled a plastic pouch that had some white powder in it.

"What's that?"

"Cocaine."

He offered me some.

"No Michael, I don't want any."

"Come on Ruthie?"

"No!!! Is that what you're into now?"

"Ruthie, I got a lot on my mind, school, etc."

"Kill that noise! That's just an excuse. How long have you been using Michael?"

"Not long."

"Liar! I've noticed you stop coming as much and when you do you're looking crazy. Now I know why and where your money is going. Does your Mom know about your 'new' girlfriend?"

"No and you better not tell her."

The look on his face told me he wasn't playing with me on that and he scared me. Not letting on, I kept talking. "Well, I tell you what. Keep using that crap and Justin and I will be ghost. I stormed off towards home.

He stood after a minute, watching me storm off. He put it away and ran to catch up with me. When he caught up to me he grabbed my arm and turned me around to face him.

"Ruthie, I'm sorry. I promise I will stop."

"If you ever come around me all highed up on that stuff, it's over."

"Baby I'm sorry. I'll stop."

"Yeah right."

As we walked back to my house, I knew in my heart that he was not going to stop, but I wanted to believe him so I dropped it. I didn't mention a word about it as we walked. I'll just keep an eye out, keep my guard up until I see changes.

Michael was slowly becoming a junkie. He would spend a lot of time in his room 'tooting.' His Mom wasn't any the wiser because she worked shift work. After his fight with Ruthie, when he went around her, he made sure he was straight, but the threat of losing her and his son wasn't enough to straighten him out until...

Before going out with his friend Lynell, he was in his room. "Before I go out, let me get a toot going." 'Toot Toot.' One hit and the 'caine' had him going. He dances around, almost spilling it. "Whoa Jack!" Instead of putting the caine in its usual hiding place, he slid it under the corner of TV.

At least that's what he thought he did. He was so 'on' that he didn't realize that he left it in full view. His Mom, home by now, watched him walk out of the door. She has noticed for weeks the change in Michael.

"Something wrong with that boy."

Saturday is usually wash day, but she wasn't doing anything at the moment so she decided to do it now. She went in his room to gather clothes for washing. She started looking around and saw the bag on his dresser. She looked...what? She had an idea, so she tasted it. "Oh hell no!" She checked his pants pockets and found more. "You just wait 'til he gets his narrow self in here."

Later that evening, he came home almost out his mind from snorting caine with his boy, Lynell. The minute his toenail crossed the threshold, she was on him.

"What is this Michael?"

She was holding a plastic bag in her hands, holding up it so close to his eyes he had to step back.

He was all highed up. "I don't know."

"Well, I do."

She started beating him about the head. He was holding both his hands up trying to block her blows.

"Are you on this shit?!"

"No."

"Yes, you are! Get out!!!"

"Mom, please!!!"

"Mom, my ass! Get out Michael!"

"Mom! Please don't put me out. I don't have any place to go."

"You should have thought about that."

He was now crying and blubbering all at the same time.

"Michael, let me tell you something. I put up with this dumb shit from your Daddy, the lies, the stealing, the staying gone half the time. His drug of choice was horse, you know boy, heroin. I'm not having this in my house. I'm giving you a fair warning. If you bring your narrow behind in here all high or with this crap in your pocket again, not only will I kick your behind, but you're getting the hell out! You understand me, boy?"

He was too busy crying to answer.

"Do you understand?!"

"Yes ma'am."

CHAPTER FIFTY

S HEILA DIDN'T KNOW if she had a leg to stand on, but she
was moving on with it anyway. Her only hope was that Andrew
overheard the whole conversation.

"Sheila what the hell was that? What's going on?"

"That was Beulah Walters' sister Beatrice."

"Did you hear her?"

"Yeah, I did. She wanted money for her silence. Don't tell me you
paid her?"

Silence.

"Sheila, No!"

The mist of her daydream went away. She was setting the wheels
in motion to get even with 'Ms. Bunchie' for scamming $10,000 from
her. She wanted to get even. So when she went to her old boss with her
complaint, she wasn't sure he would do it. He told her he would take a
look at the motion, but he has yet to contact her.

"I want her head on a platter."

CHAPTER FIFTY-ONE

LULA MAE CAMPBELL aka "Trixy," Michael's mother, loved taking care her grandson. She kept Justin while his parents, Michael and Ruthie, went to school. He was a joy to keep. The babysitting setup was sweet. Michael would come home early. Since he was senior he left school about 1:30. He would either take her to work or she would drop him and the baby off at Ruthie's, then pick him up on the way home. Most of the time, he would drive her to work. All that was about to change.

Just as she was about to start her shift, she was met by her supervisor Rick Weathers.

"Ms. Campbell, may I speak with you."

She thought, "Oh Lord, what's wrong now?"

He could tell from the look on her face she was thinking the worse.

"There's nothing wrong, Lula Mae. I just want to talk to you about a position we have that I know you would be a perfect fit. The position, Dayshift Supervisor, comes with a pay raise and more responsibility." He explained to her that with her attitude and experience, she would be a better help to their company to work the day shift permanently.

"You are an asset, he told her, and I really need you on the day shift."

"Mr. Weathers, I need to think about it."

She explained to him about taking care of her grandson.

He understood, but he needed her.

"That's fine. Take the time to think about, but let me know as soon as possible. It starts in two weeks."

After dropping the baby off and spending time with Ruthie, Michael left to pick up his Mom. He waited in the parking lot right in front of the building of her job. He sees her coming out and flashes the headlights. She sees him and walks toward the car. The bounce in her step was missing. Uh oh!

She gets in the car. She's not cheery. From her attitude, something's wrong.

"Hey Mom."

"Hey baby."

"Bad night?"

"Not really."

As they drove towards home, she started in.

"Michael, we have problem."

"Good or bad?"

"Good and bad. My supervisor stopped me today and offered me a new position, more money and responsibility."

"Mom, its sounds like a sweet deal. I can't see how you can turn it down. Okay, so what's the bad?"

"Michael, its day shift and it starts in two weeks. That means I can't watch the baby no mo."

"Damn."

"I know, baby. What y'all going to do?"

"I don't know Mom, but we'll figure something out."

After their knock down, Aunt Jane and Aunt Bunchie were half speaking, but they still talked. I would hear them talking on the phone. The conversations were short, but at least they were communicating. Aunt Jane surprised me by bringing my sisters to see me. She wasn't sure Aunt Bunchie would let her in, but she took her chances.

"Hey Ruthie!"

"Sisters!"

"Hey, Ruthie."

Cece asks, "Where's Justin?"

"Sleep."

"Oh."

"Ruthie, where's your Aunt Bunchie?"

"Here I am."

She heard Aunt Jane and my sisters come in so she came downstairs.

"What do you want?"

"Bunchie, I'm not here to fight. I just came by because the girls wanted to see their sister, plus Beulah called."

"Oh, yeah?"

"Yeah."

"She wants us to come and see her."

"Ooh, can we go?"

"No baby, not this time." Cece lowered her head and stuck out her bottom lip. "Just the two of us will be going."

"I don't want to go," Bunchie answered.

"Why not?"

"I don't feel like going, that's all."

"Come on Bunchie, it's been a while."

Bunchie was slow to agree. She had a feeling Rusty and Maurice filled her in on what's been going on and she did not feel like hearing any ying yang from Beulah. To be honest, after the fight, she had time to think. She was ashamed of what she did. She understood the damages she caused by her greed. She wants to make it right, but she didn't know where to start. As a matter of fact, she was up most night pacing the floor because it was worrying her to death. She thought, "I'm a big girl. Okay, let's do this. Whenever you're ready, Jane."

Michael went to see Ruthie. He had no idea how to break the news that his Mom couldn't watch Justin anymore because of her new job. He talked to his Mom asking her if she knew of anybody, but she was fresh out of ideas. She said she'd check around and get back to him. As he reached her door, he thought "Ruthie's gonna be mad." He knocks on the door and she answers.

"Hey babe!"

They hug.

"Hey Michael. You hungry?"

"Nah, Ruthie not right now. "Where's Justin?"

"Penny got him. I'll go get him."

"Wait, before you go, I gotta tell you something."

"Okay."

"Ruthie, we got a problem. Mom got offered a new job on day shift and will not be able to watch the baby."

"What?"

"Yeah."

"The job starts in two weeks."

"What are we going to do?"

"I don't know baby. Mom said she would check around for us."

"Well, Michael until we find somebody I'll have to stay home."

"No Ruthie!!"

"Michael we don't have a choice. Penny and Calvin are in school, Aunt Jane works and I will not feel comfortable with just anybody watching him."

"You think your Aunt Bunchie will want to watch him?"

She looked at him like he was crazy.

"Okay, Ruthie, I get it."

"Don't worry Michael, it'll work out."

Well, it never did. They couldn't find anyone willing to watch the baby they felt comfortable with let alone for free. I'm out of school. This time for good.

Both sisters took the drive to go and see Beulah. The ride was quiet with both of them in their own thoughts. Neither knew what to expect from Beulah, but they had an idea. Bunchie was nervous, butterflies flying around in her stomach. Aunt Jane had gospel music playing on the car radio trying to ease the tension. It wasn't working for Bunchie. She was actually scared. They arrived at the Center and Aunt Jane parked and got out. Aunt Bunchie didn't get out right away.

"Come on Bunchie!"

"I'm coming."

She was gathering her thoughts. She finally got out, but as she walked her legs felt like jelly. She didn't have that "swish swish" walk she normally had. He was walking stiff. The Correctional Officer remembered cracking on Bunchie from her previous visits and tried to get her attention, but she wasn't in the mood.

They went through the normal Center visiting procedures to see Beulah and waited at the table for her. The Correctional Officers brought her in. They hated seeing her in chains. She'd grown thin and her hair was long with streaks of gray. It's only been one year, but she seemed to have aged. They unchained her so they could hug. It was quick. They sat down.

"Hey ladies."

"Hey, Beulah" Aunt Jane answered.

"How you?"

"Good." Aunt Bunchie didn't open her mouth.

"How's my kids?" Aunt Jane kept talking.

"Everybody is doing. Ruthie is good and her little boy is getting big. He's about three months. Cece and Barbara are in the choir."

"They sing?"

"Yeah girl and they are good. We are getting ready for Christmas."

"Yeah, it's right around the corner." Beulah hands Aunt Jane a present.

"For me?"

"You wish."

"What is it?"

"It's a scarf. I made it for my grandson. Give it to Ruthie for me."

"Okay, I'll make sure she gets it."

Beulah turns her attention to Bunchie. "Hey, Bunch you all quiet over there. What's going on with ya?"

"Nothing girl, I'm just listening to you two talk."

"Listening huh? You ain't got nothing to say?"

Aunt Bunchie shook her head no.

"Well, I do, Beulah said sarcastically. I heard about you."

"Me?"

"Yeah you. I heard you got $10,000."

Aunt Jane stiffened, while Aunt Bunchie stared.

"Reece and Rusty told me all about the $10,000 you sweet talked my lawyer out of. Is it true?"

Aunt Bunchie spoke real low, "Yeah."

Beulah asked, "What you say? I can't hear you."

"Yeah," she replied just a little louder.

Beulah kept talking, "You know I'm not saying what you did was wrong. No, I'm not. To tell you the truth, I probably would have done the same thing with the slimy way she hooded me, but what bothers me the most is you didn't bother to share it with my kids. You could have helped with rent, lights or something."

"It wasn't like that Beulah."

"Oh no? Tell me how it was?"

"Well…" Aunt Bunchie started.

Beulah held up her hands stopping her. "You know what, it doesn't matter. It's probably a lie anyway."

Quiet as it's kept, the reason why Bunchie did what she did is because of Calvin, at least partially. Calvin was side hustling for Mr. Blue until he started using the product. He owed Mr. Blue money and Mr. Blue threatened to kill him. She did it for her son.

"If it wasn't for you my kids would be together. No, I take that back. I'm the blame for my kids being split up, but you added gas to the fire. That money could have allowed them to stay in the only home they knew. For how long, I don't know, but at least it would have been a help. You kept it all to yourself and now my family is split up; with my 15, now 16-year-old daughter with a two/three month old son. In truth, if I could put my hands on you….forget that. You are not worth it."

Bunch was listening to her with tears running down her face. Aunt Jane was just looking sad.

Beulah continued. "Bunch, I know you are not over there crying. You better not be because I don't want to see them. It's too late for that. I hope you enjoyed every penny of that money. I hope it was worth it. Just know one day what you did is going to come back and bite you. One more thing…Bunch, please don't come back. I'm not trying to hear you or see you after this."

"Beulah!" Aunt Jane called her name.

"Jane, I don't want to hear nothing. Bunchie, you hurt me."

"Beulah, please don't shut me out. I'm sorry for what I did. I've thought of nothing since my fight with Jane."

"You should have thought about it while you were doing it. You are only sorry because you got caught. If it wasn't for that you wouldn't be sorry about a damn thing. Like I said, don't come back Bunch!"

"Beulah!" Aunt Jane hollered.

"Guard!" Beulah yelled. The guard appeared. "I want to go back."

The guard put her back in chains and walked her back to her cell, Beulah never looked back. Aunt Bunchie is beside herself with sorrow. She laid her head down on the table and cried while Aunt Jane just stood back and looked, shaking her head.

CHAPTER FIFTY-TWO

AFTER SEVERAL WEEKS of not being in school, it's starting to get under her skin. She thinks, the same thing every day. "I'm just sitting here going blind watching Fuzzy the TV, watching game shows, soap operas and talk shows. If this keeps up, I'll need glasses. Christmas is right around the corner and I have no money for gifts. I can't even buy a mosquito overcoat and if you can't buy a mosquito overcoat, as small as they are, then you are pitiful." Tears start falling from her eyes. Then an all-out howl came from her. She cried until she couldn't cry anymore. By that time, Justin is awake and needed her. He is the brightest point of her life. She wiped her eyes and went to take care of him.

Sheila received good news. Her old boss agreed to take her case against Bunchie for extorting money from her. It was just a matter of time before his office served the papers.

Michael was still getting high despite the threat of being put out and having his son out of his life. He was just a little more careful. He didn't go around Ruthie high and he made sure he was together before he went home and faced his Mom. As a matter of fact, Lynell had introduced him to freebasing. Freebasing, he learned, was a high he never experienced before. However, he was rookie and it had not captured him like it did Lynell. One day he went over to his boy's house. He knocked and knocked and it took him forever and a day to open the bad boy. When he finally did, what Michael saw made him jump. Lynell's eyes were so wide and big it looked like they were about to jump out his head.

"What's going on man?"
"Nothing man, just you know."
Lynell was nervous and couldn't keep still. He was 'wired.'
"You got anything?"

"Naw, man just what's in here, showing Michael the pipe and I got a little on the mirror."

"Gimme that."

"No, that's all I got and I want to smoke it."

"That's alright then."

"Come on Michael and try it man. The high is almost better than a nut." Michael smirked a little at what Lynell just said. "Come on man."

"Alright Nelly." Like a dummy, Michael tried it. Lynell, working like a mad scientist, cooked up the cocaine turning it into a watery paste. He added a little and a little of that, stirred, cooled it, dried and then it was done. He then cut it into pieces. He then took a piece and put it in the pipe. He took a match and burned the stem to make the cocaine melt down. He took the pipe and turned it over and took a match and kept burning the stem. As he burned the stem, he pulled on it real slow. The slower he pulled the more smoke filled the pipe.

"Damn."

Michael was amazed to see the smoke fill up in the pipe. He inhaled on the stem, took in the smoke in and held it. He looked as if he was about to pass out. He then passed the pipe to Michael and instructed him. Man, Michael puffed on that thing and after a few tries, he got a rush out of this world. It was a mean high, but afterward his head hurt for hours. He told himself, "This is not for me." "Lynell got that. "No more of that shit for me."

So from then on, he stuck with what worked for him and that was "tooting." Even that was now getting old. It was becoming an every now and then thing for him.

Christmas had come and gone. Very little gift giving was done. Ruthie's sisters gave Justin gifts and Aunt Jane gave Ruthie a winter coat. Michael came over bearing gifts, a watch for her and some clothes and toys for Justin. In a nutshell, Christmas was just another day. New Years' eve started out as another day as well. Everybody was doing their own thing. Ruthie, Michael, Ira and Penny were celebrating together, toasting and laughing. Bunchie was at the bar and you know Aunt Jane and the girls were in church. Calvin was out with his friends and Beulah brought the New Year in on her knees, asking the LORD for forgiveness.

Ruthie, Michael, Ira and Penny were having fun. Ruthie did indulge in reefer smoking every now and then. So while they were toasting, the joint was being passed around. They were all highed up when Michael pulled out his trusty plastic bag.

Ruthie got an instant attitude. "Michael, what did I tell you about that?"

"Aw come on Ruthie."

"We're celebrating the New Year," Penny chirped. Her eyes were big and she unconscientiously licked her lips. She wanted some. Ira did too. Again, she was easily swayed into it.

"Where's the mirror?" Michael asked. Greedy Penny ran and got the mirror and handed it to him. Michael put 4 lines out and rolled up a dollar bill for a makeshift straw.

"Ruthie, are you ok with this?"

Reluctantly, I agreed.

"Who's first?"

"Me!" Penny chirped. She grabbed the dollar bill and she hungrily snorted hers up. Ira went second and Michael went third.

"Your turn Ruthie." I hesitated, not sure.

"Go ahead," Penny coached.

I took the rolled dollar bill and tooted it. My eyes watered. At first, I didn't feel anything then all of a sudden, I started tingling. I felt like the peppermint patty commercial, "I feel the sensation of a cool breeze running through my...y'all know the rest." Only I felt like my brain was freezing. My nose felt like a faucet with a constant drip. I kept sniffing, but it felt good. Y'all done gone and started something.

Sheila just knew she had Bunchie by her wig when her old boss Mark Stiles, decided to take her case. Little did she know before he proceeded, he met with Judge Jake Tucker. They exchanged war stories about her. The Judge didn't think she deserved anything.

"Her client, Mr. Walters did the crime, yes, but if Sheila had kept her legs closed... Her handling of the case left a sour taste in my mouth," the Judge said. How she pulled a fast one on her client's family, I feel she shouldn't get anything back. She could have handled herself properly."

"Jake, I agree. I truly hesitated about getting involved, but her sister had no right to bribe her. She's out $10,000. My only question is, did anyone other than Ms. Caldwell know about this?"

"I asked Sheila and she said no, but I get the feeling the air was let out of Sheila's tire by someone else."

The Judge sat there silently. He knew who it was…it was Carolyn, Sheila's secretary, who dropped a dime on her.

"I am not sure, but, you're right. At the end of the day, a law was broken and the person responsible should be punished. I'm not giving my approval, but…"

Bunchie will be served, but when?!!

Since her last experience with cocaine on New Years' she couldn't let the feeling go. After all the complaining about Michael's habit, she found herself becoming a fiend. Every time she got her welfare check, she secretly bought a dime or a twenty piece and had herself a ball. She had one person she dealt with, a guy name Gregory "Dibbles" Pierce that lived on McIlvain Street. He was a street corner pharmacist that kept his pharmacy open well after banking hours. During the day he was a Redline bus driver, but on his off hours you could find his "open" sign flashing. "I got that," he yelled to her one day when he saw her trying to comp from his rival. He had an eye for customers and he sensed she was new to the game.

When she walked toward him, he thought, "I know her from somewhere. Aw man, ain't that Mike's girl? As she came closer, Yeah it's her. What she doing out here?" She still pretty and all, but he could see the subtle tell-tell signs of drug use.

"Hey Ruthie." She seen him around too, but she was shocked he knew her name. "You know you shouldn't be out here."

She kept the conversation short and never would look him in the eye.

"Look, don't worry about me. What you do is what you do." He thought, 'I'm not telling him his girl is out here. I'm not getting in the middle that. "I'm just here to serve the people."

Seasons come and go and it was approaching spring again. Prom time!! The school prom was April 23rd and Michael asked Ruthie to be his date. She was so glad to go, so she excitedly accepted his invitation. Yeah, Michael! Their colors were Pool blue and Brown. Aunt Jane sprung for her prom dress and Ms. Sally was to do her hair. No one was wise to her drug use yet, but they had noticed she was losing weight. One day Michael hugged her and noticed he could feel her bones.

"You getting skinny Ruthie. What you doing?"

"Nothing. I'm exercising and watching what I eat. I want to look good for you when we go to the prom."

He gave her a sideway look out the corner of his eye, thinking "Yeah right." "Let me find out."

Days before the prom, Aunt Jane stopped by to make sure she was ready for her big day.

"Try on the dress Ruthie so we can make sure if we have to hem it we'd have enough time and get it cleaned."

Ruthie was hesitant, but she did it anyway. When she showed her, Aunt Jane had the raised eyebrow expression what the hell look on her face. In Aunt Jane's mind she thought, "Now I know when I brought that dress for her it fit fine now it looks like it falling off of her." She wasn't one to bite her tongue so she asked.

"What's going on with you? You look so skinny child."

Ruthie put on the performance of her life. She sat on the bed and started fake crying.

"Aunt Jane I'm stressed out. I dropped out of school, no job, no money and I'm with the baby 24 hours. I have no help. "Michael is trying, but I'm worrying about my future and the way it look." Aunt Jane hugged her and dried her fake tears. She then looked her in the eyes.

"Baby, don't worry so much or you'll disappear." They both smiled.

Prom night. The baby stayed with Aunt Jane so Ruthie and Michael were free to let their hair down. They had a ball. They danced all night and the thought of cocaine didn't enter Ruthie's mind. It was there, but she was too busy partying. She was a shining star that night.

She was jonsing now and didn't have a dime. She had a little bit in her stash, but she knew it was not enough to quiet her demon. By this time, she had it bad, but was able to keep it under wrap except from Calvin. He peeped her hold card from the first glance.

"Ruthie's what's going on with you. Look at you. You're getting skinny as shit. You on that candy cane?"

"No."

"Stop lying. Look I have my own issues with that stuff."

"You're not going to tell, are you Calvin? I'm trying to stop, but I be thirsty. It be calling me."

"How long?"

"I tried it New Years and I liked it ever since, so I bought my own from time to time as casual use, but now…as you can see."

"You got some now?"

She shook her head yeah.

"How much?"

"Why?"

Calvin had a monkey on his own back and he was looking to comp, but the drug gods shined on him through Ruthie.

"I got a little bit."

"Well, let's smoke it."

"Smoke?"

"Yeah. Go get it."

She didn't want to, but she was afraid he would tell. So she went upstairs and got her stash. Calvin was rubbing his hand together. He smiled as he thought, "We going to get on!"

She brought her stash back down and Calvin went to work cooking it. After he finished doing his thing, he cut it up and pulled a homemade pipe out of his pocket. He had it all fixed up with a screen and everything.

"What do you do with that?"

"Just watch."

He took a piece of the 'caine and put in the pipe. He warmed the stem. The cocaine melted and he pulled on it slow while he held a match to it. She was looking in amazement.

After he had his hit, he passed the pipe to Ruthie.

"Now it's your turn."

She took the pipe.

"Now, while I light it pull on it like you pulling on a joint, but slow." He lit the match and held it to the pipe. She started pulling…

"That's right Ruthie, slow." Now let up and hold the smoke in."

She did as he instructed and Ruthie was gone!!! She took one hit from the crack pipe and from then on she became a slave to the rhythm.

OMG!!! Ruthie is gone. She started stealing small items she thought wouldn't go missing and take them over to the pawn shop with Justin in tow. You would see her, pushing the stroller like ninety going north. She be on a mission. She went so many times the sales person knew her by face. She would get $20-$30 dollars or whatever they felt like giving her and she was happy. It got so bad she pawned the night and day pearl ring Michael gave her. With no money and no prospects, she started hanging out with Twinkle, a known piper and a so called drug dealer. Little did Ruthie know, Twinkle was being watched all of the time by 5-0. "The man" had been trying to get at her for some time, but she always managed to get over. With this new plan up their sleeve they were sure it would work. Anyway, Ruthie was over to Twinkles' house and they were getting high. They had just smoked a joint when the police came banging at her door.

Bang Bang Bang. "Who is it?"

"It's the police. Open up!"

"Oh my God!" Ruthie screamed and jumped up. She hid while Twinkle started spraying, she went to the door.

"Yes?"

"Hello my name is Officer Gates and this is my partner Officer Mims. We received a 911 call at the station coming from this address."

"911 call? Nobody here called."

"Are you sure?"

"Officer, I would know. "I live here."

"Do you mind if we look around?"

'I already told you nobody called."

"We just want to make sure."

"Do you have search warrant?"

"No."

"Well, Officer, then I decline."

"We could get one."

"Well, I guess that's what you'll have to do."

"Watch your tongue young lady."

"Hmphf" was Twinkie's response.

"What's that I smell?"

"What is you talking about?"

Silence…

"Well, we will not take up anymore of your time". As they turned to leave Officer Mims said, "One of these days."

"What you mean by that Officer?"

He just smirked and tipped his hat. "Good day, ma'am."

Twinkle shut the door and Ruthie came out from hiding.

"I'm getting out of here."

"Where you going?"

"I got to go!!!" Ruthie haul assed. That was the last time she went around there.

With her last five dollars and without anything else she could pawn, she thought she could get over on Dibbles, thinking he would give her some on credit until her next check. Wrong!!!

She made sure Justin was asleep before she went on her mission. She locked the door and made her way to Dibbles. She knocked on his door and it took a minute before he answered. He peeked out the door and saw it was Ruthie. "Perfect timing," he thought. He was in an 'I need to get fucked mood' and she was right on time. He let her in.

"Hey Ruthie."

"Hey Dibs. You got that?"

"Yeah, what you need? You got money?"

"I got 5 dollars, but I thought you may let me hold something until I get my check to give you the rest."

Rubbing his chin, "Oh really now?"

She was standing there grinning with her ashy lips and scratching. She just knew he was going to give it to her.

"Well, I don't do credit, but if you give my "Johnny" a bath," holding himself, I'll forgive the rest."

He wanted her to be his private dancer, all for 'caine. Tears formed in her eyes because that was something she did not want to do.

"Come on Ruthie. It'll only take a minute." He took her hand and led her to nearest armchair. As he sat down in the chair, he was rubbing himself in anticipation. He unzipped his pants and pulled out his "tool" and waved it at her. He wanted it, ashy lips and all. He didn't want her 'box.' Ruthie just stood there.

Becoming impatient, "Are you going to do it or what?"

Ruthie got on her knees and grabbed his "Jimmy" in her hand. He laid back and closed his eyes, waiting for her lips. Just as she was about to perform, something hit her.

"OMG!! What am I doing?" she jumped up and hollered, "No" and took off running to the front door. She swung it open and kept running until she was almost home.

Just as she rounded the corner, Mr. Blue was sitting there in his car. He rolled down the car window and called her name. "Ruthie!!" She stopped, with tears in her eyes and some running down her face, turned to see who was calling her. When she saw his face, she knew just who it was. Mr. Blue!!!

"Ruthie, come here."

She went over to his car.

"What's happening with you?" Don't tell me… Oh No!!! Look, I've been watching you for some time now, watching you the whole time going in and out, hanging with that skunk Twinkle. She's bad news. I hate to see you go down that road."

"You don't understand."

"Sure I do."

"Look at what's happening to you. You're skinny as a rail and your skin has taken on an ashy look. You're better than this." "Your son needs you. I need you. I need to be able to see that pretty face from time to time."

Ruthie smiled though her crusty lips. She licked them.

"Get yourself together. I got something I want you to do."

"Do what?"

"Don't worry about that now."

"Just clean yourself up and I'll help you."

Several nights later, Ruthie was asleep. Penny got ready for bed, but she needed to talk to her. She shook her awake.

"Ruthie wake up."

Ruthie didn't budge.

Shaking her, "Ruthie wake up!!! I need to talk to you."

Ruthie opened her eyes. "Hey Penny."

"I know," is all Penny said.

She sat up in bed, wiping sleep from her eyes, "Know what?"

"Don't play stupid with me, girl. You on that glass dick. Ruthie, you don't have to say nothing. You can't deny it with how you looking, all skinny and shit. I cannot sit back and watch this no longer I've known for some time now and I want to help you. As a matter of fact, Michael knows too."

"He do?"

"Yeah."

"He pulled me aside in school and we talked for a long time. "He really loves you Ruthie and he is sorry he even introduced you to any of it. He feels it's his fault. He told me he found out from Dibbles. (Dibbles told because Ruthie refused to dance for him.) "He threated to take

Justin If you don't get yourself together. I told him I would talk to you and try to help you or get you help."

Ruthie burst out crying. "I'm so ashamed of myself."

Through her tears she told Penny, "Mr. Blue stopped me today and told me if I got myself together he would give me a job."

"Oh, he did?"

"Yeah. Help me Penny!!! Please!!!"

"I'll help you, but you got to want to help yourself."

"I do Penny. Please!"

"Ok."

They hugged and Penny climbed in bed with Ruthie until she fell asleep.

CHAPTER FIFTY-THREE

G RADUATION DAY WAS here. The graduates, Michael and Calvin were preparing themselves separately to walk across the stage at Sun Center in Chester Township. The graduation ceremony was at 6:00 p.m. Calvin was tooting and Michael was chilling and primping. Ruthie and Justin, nine months old now, along with his mother were at the graduation. The thought of losing her baby put the fear of GOD in her heart. Trust, it hadn't been easy for her. She slipped and fell a few times. Her ex-get high partner Twinkle, stopped over with a little something trying to coax her.

"You know I got that. Want some?"

"Nah, you go 'head. I don't do that no mo."

"Since when?"

"Since now. Look, I don't mind you stopping by, but don't bring that in here." It took everything Ruthie had in her to turn it down. She was determined. After getting a real good look at herself, she saw her ribs and collarbones and she was horrified. The monkey on her back was damn near on the top of her head, but she prayed to GOD to take the desire from her. "Lord, I thank you for your healing power in releasing the chain that has had me by the stranglehold. Forgive me for my sins, Father and bless me coming in and going out. In the name of JESUS, AMEN."

Every day she did not use, she got down on her knees at night and thanked Him. By now, everybody knew of her struggle and prayed with her. She was so proud to see her baby, Michael, walking across the stage when they called his name.

To keep herself busy, she was now, against her better judgement, working with Mr. Blue. She was only 16 and had not got her working papers so she couldn't get a real job. She had to wait a few more months until she turned 17. She worked with Penny on the weekends taking small day trips to pick up money. Penny did all the transactions. She just went along as company. Her sister Barbara or Michael's Mom kept Justin when she took her trips. The particular trip was a local yokel to a guy named Nolan that lives on Diamond Avenue in North Philly. Penny was teaching Ruthie the ropes. They caught the ticky-tock train towards downtown Philly at the Chester Train station. Temple University subway station was their stop. It took almost an hour to get there. They walked out the station and walked the blocks until they reached 9th Street. Penny looked at the piece of paper given to her earlier.

"Okay Ruthie, Diamond should be a few blocks down this way according to Mr. Blue's direction."

"What's the address?"

"Um…it says, 900 Diamond Avenue."

Nolan "Nobs" McCall, their contact, is a two-bit hood who made a name for himself in Philly. He did a 15 year bid in the Federal Pen, but since then he pretended he was a model citizen, but the Drug Task force knew better. They already had some inside info that he was "dabbling in oil." Nolan didn't know his boy, Beetle, from around the way was the spy amongst his camp. He's been spoon feeding 5-0 every time something went down, but they needed more. They wanted to catch him red-handed. So, they watched him constantly, but he was too slick. If he knew they were on to him, he didn't care. His attitude was "business as usual. Their normal "bird watching" netted two young ladies visiting him. They seemed out of place no matter how normal they acted. Penny was cool about hers, but Ruthie gave off a scent that only the DRUG TASK FORCE could smell. I think it was the "I'm a tourist look." She was looking all around, unsure of herself; her whereabouts. They knocked and after a few minutes, Nolan himself answered the door. They went in…stayed maybe 10 minutes and came out and headed to the subway. Dead giveaway!! The DRUG TASK FORCE thought, "Whoever sent them should have taught them better than that." SNAP goes the camera.

On the way home from the Chester Station, with the job completed, Ruthie was relieved.

"That was easy Penny."

"I told you. Piece of cake."

"We still need to keep it between you and me."

"Okay."

With the pictures taken at Nolan's, the police needed to know who these young ladies were. They did some checking and found out some good information. They lived outside their jurisdiction, so their hands were tied. They decided to call the Chester Police Bureau and put them on the case. Bernard AKA "Bennie" McKnight placed a call to Chester to speak with Officer Alan Mitchell. They go way back.

"Hey Al."

"Hey Bernard. How you be?"

"I be good. What do I owe the pleasure of this call? You must want something. That's the only time I hear from you."

"Naw, man it's not like that."

"Sure you right. What's up?"

"Hey I'm working on this case up here in Philly. Nolan "Nob" McCall is my suspect. He's out after 15 years, but he's in the game again."

"Oh yeah?"

"Yeah."

"We believe he's getting his product from your way."

"How's that?"

"We have pictures of two young ladies, a Penny Caldwell and a Ruth Walters. They were here recently and we smell a rat. Their visit was quick, like a drop. They didn't stay long...in and out." "It could be innocent, but to me, it looked suspicious."

"Alright give me the info and we'll put our feelers out and see what's up."

"Cool. "Look, don't be calling me just when you need."

"Go head, Man, you know I got you."

"Yeah, sure."

"Alright, later."

"Later."

CHAPTER FIFTY-FOUR

MR. BLUE HAD several people in his network. Travel agents, Legal types, doctors and even the bank. His runners were safe as long as Mr. Blue paid his cut. Everyone had a price, but no matter how much it was, it wasn't enough to keep the "Force" out of the loop. They had cameras everywhere.

He had it all set up. His cousin on his payroll, worked at TRAMAC railways. They provided bogus train tickets, allowing them to ride free anywhere.

This time they were on their way to New York. It was Ruthie's turn to be put in front of the gun. He felt it was time she got her feet wet. Penny and Mr. Blue had Ruthie down in the bat cave putting the plan in place. The "bat cave" is located in the back of Shags. Even he had his price. He allowed Blue to conduct business as long as it didn't interfere with his business and he got his cut. They were instructing her on how it will work.

"I'll take you and Penny over town Chester and drop you off." "Just like before, catch the "ticky-tock train to 30th Street Station." "This same time, days from now, go downstairs to the TRAMAC station." "Now at TRAMAC, go to the agent at window 12." "Pretend you're paying." "As a matter of fact give her $20. Her name is Brenda. She normally works that window. If it changes, she will let me know. "he will give you the tickets. Go downstairs and wait at track number 4. When the train comes, get on the next to the last car. Sit anywhere and act normal."

Penny, a veteran, tried to ease her tension. "Don't worry Penny, I'll be with you. Just act like a normal passenger." Ruthie was having second thoughts about the whole thing, but she didn't let on. She just listened as they rattled on. Anyway....

With this new found info from the Philly Police Department, the Chester Drug Task Force was heavy on Mr. Blue's case, but could not get nothing on him. They knew for quite a while he was into that life, taking pictures of him and his associates coming in and out "The Wire", one of them being Larry "Feet" Morris, a known low level drug dealer. From the binoculars they could see all type of exchanges. They decided to put a tail on Mr. Blue. They ran his license tags. They found out his real name, but the address was a warehouse on Water Street. They dug a little deeper and found his last known address was 215 Chester Pike, Eddystone, PA. This house was now empty. They decided to go another route. Penny and Ruthie.

While they had the neighborhood under surveillance, they noticed Penny and Ruthie talking with Mr. Blue on occasion. It wasn't all the time, but it was enough to draw their attention. So after getting word they were seen leaving Nolan's crib and now seeing them with Mr. Blue, they knew there was a connection. It was time for some answers. But how? Agent Alan Mitchell had been assigned the case. It was either knock on the door or catch them out an about. He didn't want to do the obvious. He wanted to catch them off guard. Out and about was the answer. He watched their house, gathering information about their schedule. He noticed Ruthie was a homebody kinda of girl with a baby boy. Penny, on the other hand, was always "in the street." He decided she was his target.

A car pulls up in front of their house. A green Chevy. He ducked down. Who's that? He glances at his pictures on the seat. "Oh, that's her boyfriend, Ira." She comes out and gets in the car. They pulled off and after several seconds, he follows. The tail leads him to Avenue of the States in front of Kinney's Shoe Store, across from Weinbergs. Ira kisses her and she gets out. "See you later baby," she says as she closes the door, Ira pulls off.

The agent, thinking to himself, "She's cute and man, look at that booty." He was mesmerized by her walk. Swish Swish. He says out loud to himself, "Damn, If I wasn't on my job." Agent Alan Mitchell, not bad on the eyes at all. Average height, around 6'2, pearly white teeth and a low haircut. He wasn't a pretty boy, but he's that deep dark fine and Penny's panties was on fire and his for the taking. She passes York's clothing store. She stops in Rogers clothing store and spends about 15 min, spending her ill- gotten gains she got from Mr. Blue last night. She leaves the store with their trademark pink bag and heads towards Lee's record shop when Agent Mitchell caught her eye. He pretended he was window shopping and accidently bumped into her. He was smiling at her and she was grinning.

"Hey good looking."

"Hey yourself cutie."

"What's your name?"

"Penny."

"I'm Alan. As fine as you are, what you doing all by yourself?"

"Oh, I'm just doing a little bit of shopping."

"You buy me something?"

Penny was BLUSHING!!!

"How about I buy you something?"

"Buy me something?"

"Yeah, how about having lunch with me?"

"I don't normally do that."

"Liar!" he thought. She looked like the type to give it up on the first date. "Aw come on. I want to get to know you."

She said, "Ok." She didn't see any harm in it. Penny might be 17, thinking she's grown, but she was still naive. So she went.

They walked and talked until they reached the Cambridge restaurant. It was located right across the street from Dial Shoe Store. He opened the door for her. "Ooh," she thought, he's a gentleman." She walked in switching hard and yes, he was looking. Penny just knew he was going to be her man. They ate and exchanged flirts back and forth. In that short length of time he had both her name and address. If he played his cards right he'd have her panties if he wanted them.

When she least expected it he dropped the bomb.

"I got something I want to show you."

"What?"

He slid pictures across the table of her going into Nolans and talking with Mr. Blue. He waited for her response. As soon as she saw the pictures, she clamped her mouth closed like a vice. Her expression told it all. From the look on her face, he could tell she was thrown.

"OMG!! What's going on?" She started to get up, but he caught her hand and held it.

"Penny, I'm Alan Mitchell and I work for the Drug Task Force Division." He showed her his badge. "We have been trying to bring this man, pointing to Mr. Blue's face in the picture, and his associates down.

We have reason to believe that you are involved with this man in some fashion. We need to shut him down and I need your help."

Offended, "Sir, I'm not a snitch."

"That's all fine and good, and you don't have to cooperate, but know if it comes down to it and I don't want this to happen, we can bring you in as an accessory. If that happens you could be charged as a drug smuggler, looking at hard time. I don't have direct proof, but circumstantial evidence can be a mother."

Penny thought about it. "Well......

CHAPTER FIFTY-FIVE

SHEILA'S OLD BOSS informed her the papers to bring Bunchie in for extortion was ready. The phone rings.

"Hello, Legal Counsel, this is Sheila Mathis."

"Hello Sheila, this is Mark Stiles. How are you?"

"Hey Mark. I'm doing fine."

"Well, the ball is rolling. The papers will be served in about a week."

"Good."

"Before I serve them, I have a question."

"Shoot."

"Are you sure there isn't anyone else that could have spilled the beans?"

"I told you she's the only other person that knew unless…. Unless what?"

"Nothing."

"Okay, if you're sure."

"I am." Click. Sheila replaced the receiver. "Carolyn, could you have done this?"

CHAPTER FIFTY-SIX

"AUNT JANE CAN you watch Justin for me?
"Where are going now? You've been going out right regular lately. I'm not running a babysitting service or a nursery Ruthie."

Lying, "I know Aunt Jane. Just this one LAST time. "Michael wants to spend some alone time with me. He's been working every weekend and this is his first weekend off from working at Weavers in Marcus Hook."

"Well, if he ain't seen you, he sho nuff haven't seen that baby either. Now look Ruthie, I'll watch him this time, but this is it. You need to stay home sometime."

"Thanks, Aunt Jane, I promise."

The trip to New York was today, but was put on hold for another week because Brenda, his TRAMAC connection called last night. She told him she would be out on leave. He was pissed, but did not let on. "Okay, get at me when you get back."

"Cool."

When he hung up, he sat in his easy chair, pouting like a big kid. He thought about the money not going in his pocket and he starting kicking and throwing things around. The phone rang, bringing him out his tantrum.

"Hello."

"Beep, Beep, Beep" and the line went dead. Mr. Blue hung up the receiver knowing what was up. The plan is "business as usual", but the drop off would be at Nolan's in Philly. He still planned on Ruthie and Penny making it happen. It'll just be a different destination. Both Penny and Ruthie were unaware of the change in plans and neither did Agent Mitchell know. As far as he knew the New York trip was today and he was going too. Penny kept him aware of the setup, date, time, etc., looking out for her own hide. "I'm too fine to get caught up", but after thinking about Mr. Bullshit Mitchell trying to pull a fast one on her she decided to return the favor by not showing up, leaving him hanging. Penny had a trick up her sleeve, pretend to be sick, pretend vomiting and everything, hopefully postponing the trip.

Without her going, she thought Mr. Blue wouldn't dare send Ruthie by herself. This is payback for Agent Alan for trying to set me up. He'll be just standing there waiting. Wrong!!! Ruthie left Penny to tell Mr. Blue they couldn't make the trip. She walked in. No 'good morning or hey how you doing.' His first words were, "Where's Penny?"

"She's really sick. I think she may have the flu or food poisoning."

"Oh shit…I need her."

He was pacing back and forth. "Let me make a few phone calls." He called several other "employees" but, no deal. He called his contact. "Yo, seasons' change. "We probably should…." Ruthie heard talking, but she couldn't make out everything but she did hear. "It's now or never."

Mr. Blue slammed the phone down and sat in his easy chair. He thought about the money and decided to proceed.

"Ruthie, you're going solo."

"No, Mr. Blue. I'm not ready."

"Come on Ruthie, I need you to make this happen, plus it's just to Philly."

"Philly? I thought I was going to New York."

"You are, but not today. The New York trip has been pushed back. You're all I have. The others are on other jobs. Plus, I'll make it worth your while."

"I don't think so."

He was nearly begging now. He look like he was about to cry.

"Ruthie, you wanted a job and this is it. It's time to put your big girl shoes on. Please!"

Reluctantly, she said "Alright, but I need to tell Penny."

Relieved, he said, "Alright, I'll drive you. The train leaves in 15 minutes."

They hurried to the car and sped to her house. Penny was still playing fake sick just in case Mr. Blue called her on the phone.

When Ruthie burst in the bedroom, she played it to the hilt.

"Penny, you don't feel any better?"

"No."

"Well, real quick, Mr. Blue is sending me by myself."

"He's what?!!!"

"Yeah. The trip to New York has been put on hold so I'm just going to Philly. He's waiting for me so I gotta go."

She turned and ran out the room.

"Ruthie wait!!" Penny screamed.

"See you when I get back," she hollered as she ran down the stairs and out the door in a flash.

"OMG Ruthie!!!"

Penny jumped up and dressed as fast as she could. "I gotta catch her." By the time Penny got down the stairs, the car was rounding the corner. "OMG!!! OMG!!! Ruthie!!" Her plan backfired. Mr. Blue was about that money, any means necessary, so if that means sending Ruthie by herself, so be it.

They made it to the Chester Train Station just in time to see the train pulling into the station. Ruthie jumped out and up the stairs. The train was just about to pull off.

"Wait!!!"

The conductor saw her and held the train. Smiling, "You almost missed it young lady."

She found a seat and sat down so she could catch her breath. Minutes later, the conductor met her at her seat, pulled out his payment pad and she paid the fare. Ruthie was unaware Agent Mitchell was on the ticky-tock train too. He was already seated and noticed Ruthie as she rushed on the train and sat down. He thought, 'Where's Penny?' She set me up!!! Just maybe. He knew what Ruthie looked like, but wasn't really sure she had anything on her. Luck would have it the train car was empty so he decided to change his seat to a window seat right behind her. She went in her purse for a stick of gum, but left a small opening in the zipper. Before she knew it, she had dozed off. With nobody looking, pretending he was stretching, he stood up to see where her purse was. He sat down. He took a pencil and stuck it between the seat and into the opening of her purse. It made the zipper open more. He pushed down on the pencil and it tilted her pocketbook just enough for him to see inside. 'There it is.' With his discovery of the product in her purse, he made sure he stayed close. After about 30 minutes, the conductor shouted "30th Street, 30th Street Station, next stop."

At 30th Street, she didn't get off the train. The agent was puzzled as to why she didn't get off. He was under the impression they were going to New York. His contacts were already on notice. "Oh, I see, he thought. "The plans have changed. Well, I'm flexible."

The announcement, "Temple University next stop," from the conductor jarred her from her sleep. She gathered her things, making sure not to forget anything. She noticed her purse was slightly open. She had a bewildered look on her face. "I thought I closed it," and quickly zipped it. She left the train and made her way through the station and up the stairs to 9th Street. She found her way to the spot - the Red Fox Eatery on 8th Street Before she left, Mr. Blue drew her map of where the place was and he also told her the code: "Excuse me miss, do you have change for the phone?" He also made Nolan aware of what was going on as well as what Ruthie was wearing.

Ruthie enters the restaurant. "Welcome to the Red Fox. "Will you be dining alone this afternoon?"

"Yes."

"Right this way." The hostess showed her to a table with two seats by the window. She sat down.

"Thank you."

"A waiter will be with you shortly."

Minutes later, the waiter shows up and gave her a menu.

"May I get you something to drink while you look at the menu?"

"Yes, please. I would like water with lemon."

"Right away."

Meanwhile, the hostess is showing Alan Mitchell to a table, but she allows him to pick the table of his choice since the restaurant was not crowded. He picks an out of the way table from Ruthie, that gave him a bird's eye view. Nolan strolls in. He walks so smooth, he glides. He didn't bother to wait for the hostess to seat him. He was too cool for that. As a matter of fact, when she up stepped up to him to help him, he slightly pushed her.

"Get out of my way. I'll find my own seat."

She stepped back and looked him up and down, "Well excuse me." Nolan gave off a vibe so strong that the waiter was scared to even ask him anything. He walks over to the hostess stand, "Hmphf, if he wants anything, he'll have to ask me."

Nolan notices Ruthie and sits down at the next table. Moments later, he stood up and started going through his pockets like he was looking for something. He walked over to Ruthie's table and asked, "Excuse me miss, do you have change for the phone?"

She knew who he was and said "Yes." While she looked in her purse, he sat down. Instead of giving him the change, she didn't have any better sense but to pass him the product in full view. He looked around, not with his head, but his eyes.

He thought, "What is she doing?" He wanted to slap her. Instead, he went on with it because it seems no one noticed. Oh but it was noticed, by the Agent's mini camera. Nolan made idle chit chat with her. He was going to have a bite with her so that it wouldn't seem strange, but after she did that, he changed his mind. He was pissed.

He then excused himself. "I'll be right back. I need to use the men's room." After he got out her sight he made a false turn and walked out of the restaurant.

"That girl is crazy as hell pulling a brainiac move like that."

After so long, realizing he wasn't coming back, when the waiter returned to take her order she told him. "I changed my mind. How much do I owe you?"

He handed her the check. She asked, "Where's the payphones?" He sucked his teeth and told her "Find it yourself" and walked away. She walked around until she found a bay of payphones. She picked up the phone and pushed the "O" for the operator.

Nolan left the restaurant and found a payphone on the street. He called Mr. Blue.

"Blue man, don't never send her again. That stupid trick didn't have no better sense but to give me the stuff right out in the open. Is she crazy? You better be glad I didn't go off on her. I wanted to slap the taste out of her mouth."

"Ok, Nolan, I hear you man. Sorry about that. I'm picking her up and I'll have a talk with her."

"You better do something, man. With shit like happening, we'll be in the clink in no time."

Once the exchange was made and Nolan left the restaurant, Alan fast walked his way to the bay of phones in the restaurant. He placed a call to his friend Bernard AKA Benny McKnight.

"Yo, man, remember the guy Nolan you told me about."

"Yeah, what about him."

"Well, I witnessed an exchange made in the "Fox" between him and a suspect I'm interested in."

"Did you see what it was?"

"Yeah, I had a bird eyes view."

"Man, why didn't you put me on earlier?"

"It's a long story, but Blue and his boys pulled a switch on me. I found out last minute."

"Thanks. Me and my boys are on our way." Click!

He returned to the table and saw it was empty. "Damn, she's gone. "Where did she go?" He looked around and saw her on the phone. He eased closer so he could eavesdrop, pretending he was making a phone call.

Right after Mr. Blue hung up with Nolan, the phone rang again "Collect call from Ruthie. Will you accept the call?"

"Yes."

"Ruthie!!!"

"Mr. Blue."

Knowing the answer, he thought he'd ask her anyway.

"How did it go?"

"Okay."

"Just Okay?"

Solemnly, she replied, "It was okay."

"What's wrong?"

"I'll talk to you about it when I get back."

"Okay, what time is the train?"

"The train leaves at 6:30 and I should be at the Chester station by 7:15."

"Okay, I'll meet you."

Ruthie walked away and out of the restaurant.

The agent heard it all. He made a phone call of his own. When the phone was answered, he said, "The train arrives at the Chester station at 7:15." He described Ruthie to a T. "Be there."

The station was surrounded by black sedans. They were already there by the time Mr. Blue arrived. He was too busy finger popping to the sounds coming from his stereo to even notice. "WDAE is jamming" he thought. They were playing "Outstanding" by the Gap band. When he saw Ruthie coming, he started the car. She was walking slowly. Just as she put her hand on the handle of the car door, a dozen headlights came on blinding her. 'What the....?'

More than a dozen Officers came out of the wood work. On the bullhorn "Put your hands in the air!!!" The voice yelled, You, in the car, keep your hands where we can see them." With his eyes all big and his hands gripping the steering wheel, he nearly crapped on himself. Ruthie, with her hands in the air, thought, "Nothing like Friday nights." All shit hits the fan on FRIDAY NIGHT!!!

Around 7:30 p.m., Michael stopped by the house to see Ruthie. No one was there. "I wonder where she is." He left a note on the door letting her know he stopped by and to call when she got in. About an hour or so went by and he hadn't heard from her he made a call to Aunt Jane looking for Ruthie.

"She said she was going out with you!"

"Where could she be?" Michael is thinking she was back out here. She was out there all right...on her way to jail.

Penny was there in the house the whole time. When she heard the knock, she ran to the upstairs window and looked out. It was Michael. She deliberately didn't answer.

"I can't," was all she could say.

Ruthie and Mr. Blue where put in separate cars for two reasons: number 1, she was minor and, number 2, they wanted to make sure they couldn't talk to one another. Instead of Ruthie going to the Police Station in Chester because she is a minor, they drove her straight to Sleighton Farms School for girls in Crum Lynne, PA while Mr. Blue was driven to the Chester Police station on 5th and Welsh.

The phone rang and jarred Penny from the window. She answered "Hello." It was Aunt Jane.

"Penny, where in the hell is Ruthie? Michael is calling looking for her. Have you seen her?"

"No Aunt Jane. I haven't seen her since earlier in the day."

"She said she was going out with Michael and he's calling me asking where she is. When that hussy comes home, tell her to call me."

"Yes ma'am."

Penny wasn't off the phone 5 minutes when it rang again. "Hello."

"This is Sgt Mitchell Beckett." "May I speak with Beatrice Caldwell?"

"That's my Mom." "She's not here right now."

"I am calling to inform her that we had Ruth Walters here in custody and she is being transported, as we speak, to Sleighton Farms in Crum Lynne."

"Custody?"

"Yes, ma'am."

"For what?"

"I do not have the liberty to discuss this, at least on the phone, but what I can say is, the matter involves drugs. Since she's a minor she cannot be released until her guardian can be reached. She will be held there until seen by the magistrate, Natalie Clark. Since this is Friday most likely that will be Monday."

"OMG!!"

"If your Mom has any questions, have her contact this office at 215-876-0000. Again, my name is Sgt Mitchell Beckett. The number to Sleighton Farms is 215-565-0000."

"Thank You. I'll see she gets the message."

Penny hung up and hung her head in shame as the tears freely fell from her eyes.

Bunchie was at the Wire serving as barfly, spilling drinks along the way. Patrons were complaining. She had a lot on her mind. "I could go to jail." She had spoken with her lawyer earlier that day. Her reason for doing it will not do much for softening the fact – extortion. This will not go down the throats of judges too well.

"Bunch!" Diamond Ice, her boss called her. What is wrong with you?"

"Got something on my mind."

"Well, you better get it off. "You costing me money."

"I'm sorry, Ice."

"Don't be sorry, be careful."

Penny rushes in the bar wide eyed, filled with tears. "Mom! Mom!" Bunchie stopped drying glasses when she heard Penny call her name. From the look on her face and the way she called her name, she knew something was deadly wrong. She thought something was wrong with Calvin. She met Penny at the end of the bar.

"What's wrong?"

"I need to talk to you."

They moved to a corner off to the side.

"What is it?"

"Ruthie has been arrested!!"

Bunchie fell back against the wall. "What?! Why?"

"She been arrested for drugs!"

"Are you kidding me?"

"No. The Police Dept. called and she's been arrested and transported to Sleighton Farms."

"OMG," Bunchie whispered and held her hand up to her mouth.

Penny was beside herself. "It's all my fault!"

"Ssh! Penny, come on. Let's go home." She called her co-worker Marlene to the side. "Hey, Marlene."

"What's up Bunchie?"

"I need you to do me a favor. I got an emergency and I need to leave. Can you finish for me?"

"Sure Bunch. Is everything alright?"

"No!"

As she was leaving, Ice asked "Where you think you going?"

"Ice, I got to take care of something. Marlene will finish for me."

He opened his mouth and took in enough air to give her a royal cussing, but she walked out the door before he could get it off the runway.

The bar was only 5 minutes away so they didn't do much talking. They walked in silence. As they reached the house they could see the door was slightly ajar. They could hear the phone ringing off the hook.

"Hello."

"Bunch, this is Jane. Where is Ruthie?"

"She's been arrested."

"What you say?"

"She been arrested."

"I'm on my way!!!" SLAM!!!

Before she left home, Aunt Jane dialled Rusty. Rusty was in bed with Crystal. She wasn't his girlfriend, not yet anyway. She was working on it. She was this female he'd known for a while. They met at Skinny's bar on a '2 for 2' Tuesday. They were in "the middle" but on a break when the phone rang. He leaned over to answer the phone.

"Rusty, this is Aunt Jane. I hope I didn't catch you at a bad time."

He looked at Crystal. "I was sorta in the middle of something."

"Well, Rusty we got an emergency."

"What going on?"

"Ruthie been arrested!"

He sat straight up. "What?" Crystal touched his arm and he gently pushed her arm away.

"She's in the Sleighton Farm Youth Center."

"OMG!! For what?!"

"From what I understand from Bunchie, it's for drugs."

"What the hell?"

He was sitting on the side of the bed now. "I'll call Reese and we'll be on our way." He stood up putting his draws and pants on, not bothering to wash his behind.

"Get dressed."

"What?"

"Get dressed!!! I've got to go."

"Shit, you make me sick you little dick..." He didn't say a word. He just turned and gave her a dirty look and she shut her mouth. He put his shirt on and walked out the bedroom. He left her in there, cussing him out under her breath.

"Little dick...yeah right." She was screaming "Oh, baby" a minute ago. He reached the living room, but stopped abruptly. He really liked her and felt he owed her more than that. Just as he turned to go back to explain, she breezed right by him and walked out the apartment and slammed the door. She didn't bother to say goodbye; she was so pissed. He waved his hand, forget her. He didn't mean that because he was feeling her. He picked up the phone and dialled Reese. "Please Reese be home."

Maurice was home "tasting." Sandy, his girlfriend, was over and she was "doing her thing." He was on the verge of a blast off when the phone rang. Ringgggggggg! She kept going. He was right there, but the phone disturbed his groove. Damn! He stopped her. Erect, he answered. "Speak."

"Hey man, this is Rusty."

"Hey, what's up?"

"Man, Aunt Jane just called and said Ruthie's been arrested!"

"Get out. Are you serious?!!"

"For what?"

"Drugs. I'm on my way to Chester now."

"Come by and pick me up."

"Okay, I'll be there in a few minutes."

"Cool!!"

CHAPTER FIFTY-SEVEN

WITH RUTHIE ON her way to Sleighton Farms, they focused their attention on Mr. Blue. They wanted to try and rattle his cage. They had all the info in the world on him and had him right in front of them, but their case was lukewarm. Mr. Blue was in the back office waiting to be questioned. He was wringing his hands and sweating like a pig. He played hard, but was scared out of his gore. Reginald "Dick Tracy" Carter and Lionel Davidson were watching him through the glass. "Look at him, scared to death." They walked in and Mr. Blue almost jumped out the chair. The two detectives smiled.

"Well, well, look who we have here. Need anything, a hanky, a tissue, a glass of water?"

"No, I don't need nothing."

"Sure you do. You look all wet. Are you nervous?"

"Look, why are you holding me?"

"We ask the questions. You were in the company of a minor that just did a drop for you with one your cohorts, Nolan McCall."

"For me?"

"What's up with you and Nolan?"

"Nolan? Who dat?"

"Don't play with me. We have pictures of you and him in each other's company."

"So what? I could have been asking him for directions or the time."

Reginald Carter was in his face by now. He had enough of Mr. Blue's smart aleck answers.

"You're a smart ass."

He titled his head back, "man, get out my face. You're spitting on me, your breath stinks plus you so ugly, looking at you makes my eyes hurt."

Lionel inched closer. His hands were itching. He wanted to punch him in the mouth. Reginald notices Lionel opening and closing his fists. He was just about to swing when he stepped in between the two.

Mr. Blue puffed his chest out, "Unless you have something on me, I'm out."

"You're out when we say. How do you know her?"

"Who?"

"Don't get funny on me Theodore or Mr. Blue. Isn't that what they call you?"

Silence.

"How do you know Ms. Walters?"

"Man, look. She's from around the way, you and I know her from her Aunt. She was going through something earlier on this year and I gave her my number just in case she got in trouble."

"Oh, really now?"

"Really."

"So you're the Good Samaritan for young girls?"

"Look, I didn't do anything wrong, just give her a ride."

They knew he was right. They didn't find anything on him or in his car and questioning Ruthie was out. She fought us like a cat, clawing and bucking. They didn't have any other choice, but to let him go. As he left their office, they put their heads together and came up with a plan...PENNY!!!

Rusty, Maurice, Aunt Jane, Bunchie, Penny were all gathered at the house discussing the latest crisis.

"Alright, Penny stop all that crying and explain this bull...."

"Reese, hold up," halting his cross examination.

"Well, she started, "I've been working with Mr. Blue."

"Mr. Blue, who's that?"

Penny swallowed hard. "He's a drug dealer."

Knock, Knock Knock. Aunt Jane moved the makeshift curtain back. "It's Michael." She got up and let him in.

"Have you heard from Ruthie?"

"Right on time, Michael!" Reese shouted. "Comp a squat. You've got to hear this."

"Where's Ruthie?" He asked while taking a seat.

"She's in Sleighton Farms."

"What she doing in there?"

"Penny was just about to tell us, weren't you?" Reese was in rare form. "Reese, let up!"

"No. I'm not letting up on this trick."

"Hold up Reese." That's my daughter you talking about."

"I'll talk to you like that. TRICK! She's just like you."

"Wait a minute now Reese. You can get the hell out my house."

"I aint going nowhere and you can't make me."

"Alight, Alright, Alright," Rusty said. This is not getting us nowhere. We need to keep cool heads about this."

Calmly, Rusty says "Alright Penny, you got the floor. Explain."

She got an attitude now. She blew her breath and sucked her teeth. "Well, I've been working, running packages for Mr. Blue for a while. After Ruthie had the baby, she started getting welfare. She was running short all the time and Michael wasn't hardly giving her any money. She got tired of being broke so she asked me about making some money I told her about coming and working with me and that I would talk to Mr. Blue about bringing her on."

"She's only 16!"

"I know! At first, I thought it was a good idea, but after some thinking I decided against it, so I never mentioned it again."

"So during her 'get high' time, Mr. Blue stepped to her himself and offered her a job."

"How you know?"

"She told me."

"How did you get involved with him in the first place?"

Penny got defiant and refused to explain their relationship. "I just did, she said," But Calvin blurted out "I know."

He'd come in just as it was getting heated.

"What you know about it?"

"I use to get on Penny about hanging out with him. I knew he was a horny old man." Calvin was about to spill all the beans, but he stopped when Penny gave him a sideway look.

"What else Calvin?" He could still feel Penny's eyes burning a hole in the side of his head so to cut it off, he said, "I knew he was trying to get at her."

"Oh, so to get close to the panties, he decided to give you a job, huh Penny?" Reese asked.

Bunchie stepped in. "Did you screw this man?"

"NO!"

"Ah huh. Okay."

"So Penny, how did this day come about?"

"Well, Mr. Blue sent us to Philly to this guy name Nolan's house. We made the drop and everything was cool. Little did we know this guy Nolan was being watched. The Philly Drug Task Force took our picture."

"How you know that?"

"Because an agent from Chester approached me one day when I was downtown. I met him on a humble. I was shopping and he approached me. He flirted with me and offered to take me lunch. I thought he was really interested in getting to know me, so I went. We were sitting and talking when he showed me a picture of Ruthie and I in Philly coming out this guy Nolan's house. Right then and there I knew it was a set up and we could be in big trouble. He told me if I didn't cooperate we could be looking at big time as co-conspirators."

"Right then and there you should have told Ruthie."

"I didn't tell her right then because I had a plan." The next drop was to be in New York. The day of, I decided to play sick. I didn't think Mr. Blue would try and send Ruthie by herself since she was new to the game, but, he did."

By this time, Michael heard enough. He jumped up off the couch, "You set her up!!!"

"No, I didn't!!!"

"So you thought by playing sick that would stop him? This man is about money. Why didn't you tell Ruthie about it?"

"I tried!"

"No, you didn't!!! You are so stupid. You were being selfish and thinking of nobody but yourself! Now look!" He stepped to Penny as if he was about to slap her.

Calvin jumped in. "Don't do that man."

Michael hollered, "You make me sick, Penny!!!"

CHAPTER FIFTY-EIGHT

RUSTY ASKED, "HOW long does Ruthie have to stay in this place? What's it called again?"

"Sleighton Farms."

"Yeah Sleighton Farms."

"I think that's the name of it…you think?"

"That's it."

"Before you got here, I called the police station and spoke with Sgt Beckett. He told me they took her straight there. She's has to stay there before she goes before the Judge, usually within 48 hours. It could be as early as Monday or Tuesday. She'll learn what her charges are, and what, if any, her bail is."

"What kind of place is this?"

"It's a reform school for delinquent girls."

"A reform school, delinquent?"

"Wow, if isn't one thing it's another."

Mr. Blue was allowed to walk. As he left, he had a smart aleck smile on his face. SUCKERS he thought to himself. The smile on his face would soon be wiped off his face. Soon!!!

She arrived at Sleighton Farms by way of the Chester Police. She was assigned a room, given a change of clothes, sweat pants and shirt and bedding. She was escorted to her room by the Sargent of Arms, a hard-nosed, short, stocky woman name Daisy Abbott.

"This is your room. "here's your rule book. Follow them to the letter and your stay here will be smooth. Get out of line and …."

As she laid in her bunk, Ruthie thought, "Why didn't I tell the Officers what I knew? Holding back information isn't helping me right now. Looking up towards the sky, she started to pray, "GOD, you got to help me turn my life around. No matter what I do my good turns out bad. I know you love me and I love you. I'm not going to let this get me down LORD. Thank you for your joy, your peace." Amen."

She didn't realize she was praying out loud until she heard a voice, "Shut up that noise in there. Your prayers ain't what got you here in the first place, now was it? Lights out!!!," the counsellor screamed.

Nolan was pissed. He was caught red handed and it was no way to get around it. "That mofo set me up with that trick he sent. I'm going to get him. That punkass. I'm not going down by myself without a fight. He wanted a deal for lesser charges. He was willing to sing. "The next call I make will be to my lawyer."

Its early Monday morning. Ruthie prepared herself for her appearance. She combed her hair the best she could. The night before, she laid her clothes out carefully so they wouldn't be wrinkled. As she changed into her own clothes she thought. After today, I hope I will not have to wear this again.

Everybody was at the house, milling around. Penny's appearance time was 11 a.m. sharp. Bunchie came down the stairs and headed towards the door. "Where are you going? I'm going to see a man about a horse and burst out laughing." She's the only one that laughed."

"That's not funny, Mom."

"Well, it's funny to me."

"Aren't you going to the courthouse with us?"

"No, I got to take care something."

"Mom, Ruthie needs all our support."

"I know. I'll be there. I just got something I need to do first." "See you later."

After Bunchie left her lawyers office on 5th Street, she made another stop.

"Hey Bunchie."

"Hey girl. What can I do for you?"

The courthouse is located on W. Front Street in Media. Ruthie's case is being heard in Courtroom F. Everyone filed in and took their seat in the back. It was empty except for the family.

In the courtroom, there was big screen. Reese asked, "What they gonna do, show movies?" Rusty sniggled and hunched Reese to be quiet.

The bailiff appeared and called "ALL RISE, court is now in session. Judge Carolyn Bagley presiding."

"Good morning ladies in gentleman." "You may be seated."

For Ruthie's first appearance, a video was necessary. The Judge announced, "Case Number CA150159, Pennsylvania vs. Ruth Walters." Ruthie appeared in front of the camera. The family gasped when they saw her.

Aunt Jane said, "She looks so sad," to no one in particular and started to cry softly. Rusty put his arm around her shoulders, hugging to comfort her.

"Ms. Walters, you are being accused of conspiracy to drug trafficking. How do you plead?"

"Not guilty."

Video conferencing was something new to the court so when Ruthie appeared, it was fuzzy and the audio was so bad that everybody had to lean in and strain to her voice.

Reese, mumbling to himself, "I can't hear shit!!" Hunching Rusty – "Hey Russ man what is she saying?"

"Ssh!!'…

"What?! Shit…Ay Ay Judge can we move closer? I can't hear."

"Order!!! She told the bailiff, "Stop the video! Excuse me sir, who are you?"

"I'm her brother."

"If you don't want to join her, I suggest you be quiet."

"But I can't hear."

Aunt Jane looked at Reese. To herself, she said "That's Beulah's child. Loud, wrong and GHETTO!!" The Judge looked at him over her glasses. She took them off and started biting on the end of one of the arms, thinking. She put them back on.

"Okay, I'll give you that one and allow you to move closer, but if you speak out of turn again, I'll hold you in contempt."

The sound of everyone shuffling to move closer for better seats can be heard throughout the courtroom. Once everyone was settled, he stated, "We can proceed." Quietly, Aunt Bunchie eased in and took her seat behind the rest of the family.

"At this time Ms. Walters, until your next hearing in 30 days or less, you are to be released in the hands of your guardian. You will be notified of your court date via mail. Your public defender has requested bail. Since this is your first offense, her request has been approved. Your bail is set at $25,000 and as such, 10% of that, which is $2,500 is due.

Until such is paid, you will be reprimanded to Sleighton Farms. Do you understand?"

"Yes."

"Do you have any questions?"

"No."

"At this time court is adjourned."

The family was breathing a little easier now that the hearing was over. They walked out the courtroom and headed back to Aunt Bunchie's house.

In the parking lot, Rusty asked, "Hey Aunt Jane, how's Barbara and Cece?

"Cece is fine, but I had to get with Ms. Barbara.

Rusty laughs, "What happened?"

"She got a few 'around the way' girlfriends, named Treasure and Secret. They can be a bit much, but I let her see them from time to time. I try not to be strict. A few weeks ago, Barbara sassed the teacher. I tried to talk to her about it and she started hollering at me. Oh wait" I told her. Who in the world are you talking to like that?" "I told her, if you think you are going to talk to me like that you are wrong. By the time I finished laying her soul to rest, she will think twice before coming at me like that. Since she's been hanging with these girls, she's gotten a little too grown for my taste. Don't get me wrong, Treasure and Secret have parents that don't play, but when kids are out of their parent's eyes, especially girls, they can get side-tracked."

Everybody laughed - all except Reese.

"What's wrong with you?"

"I'm still on that bail money. $2,500 bond! Is she crazy?" Reese whined. "Who got that type of money?"

"Well, we will have to come up with the money for Ruthie to come home. How much do you have Rusty?"

"I got about $300."

"Reese?"

"Hmphf, about $300."

"I got $500, Aunt Jane boasted. So that gives us $1,100."

Bunchie walked up on the end of the conversation. "What y'all talking about?"

"We are talking about the bail money."

"Keep your money. I got it!!!"

"You got what Bunch?

"The $2,500. I just paid the court clerk." She waved the receipt in their faces. The court clerk told me it would take about a week for processing. By FRIDAY, Ruthie will be sprung."

"Thank you, Aunt Bunch," Rusty said as he hugged her.

Aunt Jane also hugged her. Reese was still salty over the whole thing.

He said, "Thank you Aunt Bunch, but this don't let you off the hook. If it wasn't for you…"

"Be quiet, Reese."

"No, it don't get me off the hook. As a matter of fact, I'm due in court myself. Are you happy now?"

"For what?"

"That Sheila chick is pressing charges for me "borrowing" $10,000 from her."

"I told you!!! Time to pay the piper." Reese exclaimed. He sorta did a two-step bop. Bunchie rolled her eyes, ignoring Reese and kept talking.

"I received the papers a few weeks ago. When I left the house this morning, I went to see my lawyer. My hearing is in about 3 weeks. I've already decided to plead guilty to avoid a trial so that means I could be going to jail."

"Mom!!!"

"Don't' Mom me. I did it and I'm guilty. My lawyer wants me to go through this long and drawn out thing, but I want it over. It's just a matter of how much time I will get. So for the next three weeks, I will be free."

All their mouths flew open, all except Reese. He had a grin on his face.

DONNA EARL

CHAPTER FIFTY-NINE

BEULAH WAS IN the dayroom talking with her girl Annette. It's still difficult for her being held down, but she is taking it in stride. She missed her kids and now that she has a grandchild, she wished things were different. She hadn't see her girls in a while, a long while. Deep in conversation, neither one saw Roselle Harding approaching.

"Hey Beulah, can I speak with you a minute?"

"I'll see you later, Beulah."

"Okay Annette." She could see Beulah getting upset so she talked fast, looking over her shoulder.

"Don't trip Beulah, but word is that one of your own, Ruthie, has been arrested."

"You say what?"

"I'm not supposed to tell you so don't…" Beulah holds her hand up.

"Don't worry."

"This came from the courthouse in Media. Your daughter was arrested and for now is at Sleighton Farms. I can't give you any more than that."

"My family didn't tell me."

"It just happened Beulah. I think she's seeing the Judge today." "I'll let you know the outcome."

"Thanks, girl."

She went straight to the phone and called Rusty. His phone went to voice mail. "Boy!!! This is your Mom. Get your narrow behind here NOW!!!"

CHAPTER SIXTY

THAT BODY!!! HE tried to keep his mind off her, but he was having a hard time. The thought of her got him feeling some type of way. He could feel Wally nearly breaking free. Wally is his one eye, heat seeking monster, and he wanted some attention. His throbbing told him he wouldn't be denied. To satisfy him, he rubbed his head and the tingly feeling told him he liked it and to don't stop. He rubbed him some more. 'More!!' He screamed. 'Faster!!' He cried. The more he rubbed and the faster he went, he screamed, "I'm almost there!" He kept rubbing then he screamed 'Ah Ah Yeah!!!' Then he slowly relaxed. He was done. Andrew, with his eyes closed, let out a breath of air..." Wow!!"

Since what happened with Ruthie, Mr. Blue has become a phantom. He was nowhere to be found. Penny's funds were starting to grow thin. She still had a few coins, but not many. She knew where he was, but she did not dare go there. Ira, her well, pretty much ran dry after hearing of her extra-curricular activities. She needed some air so she made her way over town to John Doggie's. She just put the last of the hotdog in her mouth, when in he comes. He stopped at her table. Despite how they met, there was an instant spark and they both knew it.
"Hey Penny!!"
She tried to ignore him, but those dimples.
"What do you want?"
"I want you for real."
"You set me up!"
"I was doing my job."
"You do it so well. You normally play people?"
Silence.
"What do you want?"
"I told you."
She looked at him. Those dimples. Lawd!!

It's about three in the afternoon and Rusty gets home after court and goes in the kitchen to get a glass of water. He notices the message button flashing. He has two missed calls. He smiles slightly thinking, it's probably Cynthia calling. He pressed the button and, just as thought, it was her, talking her mess.

"Rusty, this is Cynthia. I need to talk to you."

Talking out loud, "Sure you do, but I thought I had a little..." He listened to the next message and it stopped him in mid-sentence.

"Boy!!!" This is your Mom. Get your narrow behind here now!!"

The sound of his mother's voice sent chills down his spine. He was instantly afraid. She is angry. He called Reese.

"Yo man, didn't I just see you?" he said half-laughing.

"Shut up. Reese. Mom left a message on my answering machine." "She sounds angry."

"Aw man, she just mad because we haven't been there."

"Maybe."

"What you doing tomorrow?"

"Nothing."

"Go with me."

"You scared?"

"As a matter of fact, yeah." They both laughed.

"Alright."

"Okay, I'll be there around 9."

"Alright."

"So Rusty and Reese, what's this I hear?"

"Hear what, Mom?"

"Ruthie's been arrested?"

She is sitting in front of them calm, but they both knew she is mad as hell.

"Don't try and sell me sugar knowing its shit. Bring it down front."

"It's true Mom. She was seen delivering. They have pictures and everything."

Beulah sat back and stared at them with her arms folded over her chest.

"She's been working with this guy name Mr. Blue. Penny introduced them."

"She had my baby peddling drugs?"

"Not directly. She was working for him too."

"Where was Bunchie through all this?"

"It was news to her too. We all found out the same time, when Ruthie was arrested."

"Is she still locked up?"

"Yes and No."

"What you mean?"

"Aunt Bunchie paid her bail. She should be home by Friday."

"How much was it?"

"$2,500."

"$2,500? Where did Bunch get that kind of money from," she said out loud.

"I don't know, Mom," Rusty answered.

"I bet I can guess. It was probably left over money from squeezing my lawyer. Shaking her head, "I'm thankful for her paying Ruthie's bail, but Bunch is going to get hers one day."

"Well, that day may be sooner than we think Mom."

"How so?"

"Your ex-lawyer brought charges of extortion against her. Aunt Bunchie told us the day before yesterday. Her hearing is in about 3 weeks and she's planning to plead guilty. I think she'll get some time."

"For sure."

"When does Ruthie go back to court?"

"I think in thirty days. "It could be sooner."

Friday morning, Aunt Jane pulled up in front of Sleighton Farms. Ruthie was sitting down now in the lobby waiting for her. Just a minute ago, she was looking out the window with her face plastered against the window pane thinking out loud, "Where is she?" She sits down. She couldn't stand it. She walked to the window again and here comes the Calvary.

Ruthie was jumping up and down, "Aunt Jane! Aunt Jane!" Being in here wasn't so bad, but I'm so glad I'm going home, she thought.

Aunt Jane couldn't make it up the steps fast enough. Aunt Bunchie had made phone calls to the Director, Alma Tucker and the court clerk explaining her situation and asked could Ruthie be released to her sister Jane. It was okay, as long as she was driven straight to her house. Aunt Jane signed all the necessary paperwork for Ruthie's release.

"You have everything?"

"Yes."

Ruthie holds up a plastic bag with all her personal toiletries provided by the Farm.

"Okay we're all set. Let's go." Aunt Jane and Ruthie walked out the door to the car.

As they were driving home, Ruthie asked, "Do I have to go back to Aunt Bunchie's?"

"I'm afraid so. You know the deal. It's still the same. You haven't been in this place that long. It's only been a week."

They both laugh. "Have you seen Justin?"

"That Boogie, her pet name for him, is as sweet as ever." Michael and his Mom have been taking good care of him. You better call him, Ruthie. And, just so you know, your Aunt Bunchie paid your bail."

"She did?"

"Yeah."

"Where did she get the money from?"

"We didn't ask. Probably from the money she stole from your Mom's lawyer. Speaking of that, you know that woman is bringing charges against her for extortion and she may be going to jail."

"What you say?!"

"She found out a few weeks ago. Yeah, the same day you were going to court, she went to see her lawyer. He lawyer advised to her fight, but Bunch told us she will go before the Judge and plead guilty. Her hearing is in about 3 weeks."

"OMG, what's going to happen to Penny and Calvin?"

"Penny and Calvin?!!! You better be thinking about yourself. Just because you're out today don't mean this thing is over. Remember you're going to juvenile court in about 30 days or less."

"I know, Aunt Jane and I'm scared."

"You should be."

They arrive home and things were still the same…dirty! She almost wanted to turn around, but where would she go? Where's everybody? It wasn't a soul home. Aunt Jane made sure she was okay and turned to leave.

"Are you okay?"

"Yeah, I guess."

"Call me if you need me."

"Ok."

"Don't forget to call Michael."

"I'm not."

Ruthie picked up the phone. She wondered, what do I say to him? I want to see my son. She dialled the number. After the second ring, "Hello?"

"Michael, its Ruthie."

Silence.

"Michael?"

She could hear Justin crying in the background. Her heart sank.

"Hey, Ruthie."

He sounded like he didn't want to be bothered.

"I'm home."

"And?"

"What do you mean and? I want to see my son."

"Why?"

"Why? I want to see him."

"Now's not a good time."

"I'm his mother!"

Michael snapped. "Were you his mother while you were out dealing drugs?"

"Michael, you don't understand!"

"I understand plenty. You left him to deal drugs. What were you thinking?"

"I made a mistake."

"You don't make mistakes like that."

"You got some nerve, Michael. You've been dipping and dapping, getting high plenty of times and I never once denied you him."

Silence.

"Michael, don't do this to me!! I want to see my son!!" Click! He hung up.

Ruthie looks at the receiver and broke down crying.

CHAPTER SIXTY-ONE

THEY BOTH LAID there from exhaustion. She snuggled up against him. Penny was in la la land and Andrew was just being a man. He didn't really her, but was willing to screw her for as long as it takes to get what he wanted. Yeah, he liked her and she was sexy as hell for a young girl, but she was too loose for him. He was having second thoughts.

He was too quiet so she asked, "What are you thinking about?"

With his hands behind his head, "I'm thinking this was a mistake. This should have never happened."

"Boy, you sure know how to mess up a wet dream!"

She jumped up and went to the bathroom.

He laid there. "I crossed the line."

Penny comes out of the bathroom and sat on the bed and started putting her clothes on. He needed her and he had to think fast.

"Penny wait." He started rubbing her leg "You knew from the beginning what it was and what it is."

"I know. You were pumping me for information."

His hand was traveling farther. She pushed it away.

"I still need it."

His hand got further and he started playing her song.

In between breaths, "What's in it for me?"

He was playing a long winding song. Her head was thrown back and her eyes were closed tight, legs wide open.

"This is too easy," he thought.

"What you want?"

"What's it worth?"

She held his hand there.

"Keep doing that and $1,000 dollars."

"In her dreams," he thought.

The song was getting good to her. "Work it baby!!!"

He think he's getting over. "Yeah he's playing my song and greasing my palm at the same time. I learned from the best. Thanks, Mommmmmm!!!!" her mind screamed as she "jumped that fence."

"Michael, who was that?"

"Ruthie."

"Oh she's home?"

"Yeah. She wants to see Justin and I told her no."

"Why not?"

"Mom, she…"

"She what, made a mistake? Michael, that girl loves that boy and you know that. You know Justin misses his Mommy. Take him to see her."

"Mom."

"Come on Michael. Don't be like that. Now, you know you want to see her too."

"I guess."

"You know I'm right."

"Where have you been?"

"You smell like…did you bother to even wash your behind?"

"Shut up, Ruthie. Glad to see you too."

"Where's everybody?"

"I don't know. It wasn't anybody home when I got here."

"How you been?"

"Girl, don't you know? It's been a nightmare. Have you seen Mr. Blue?"

"No girl. He's been ghost since…."

"Don't remind me, Penny."

"I've seen Shoes, though. He said Mr. Blue's been around and he's alright. I can't believe what happened Ruthie."

"Yeah, Penny it all happened so fast."

"What happened?"

"Well, you know I did the drop at Nolan's, but it was in a restaurant, called The Red Fox. I thought everything went fine except…."

"Except what?"

"I made a dummy move and gave him the package out in the open."

"You did what?!"

"Yeah, but you know, there was this guy I saw in the restaurant that was there when I got arrested. As a matter of fact, I glanced at him when I got on the train in Chester. I think it was all a set up, but I was too stupid to catch on in time. Shits' crazy."

Guilt ridden Penny wasn't saying a thing.

"What's wrong with you Penny?"

"I...."

They were interrupted - Knock Knock Knock. She heard crying, Justin!!! Ruthie rushed to the door. She opened the door and it was Michael and her son. A big smile spread over her face. She snatched Justin out of Michael's arms... She squeezed him and covered his face with kisses.

"Hi, my baby!! I missed you."

She left Michael standing at the door with the diaper bag.

Feeling left out and jealous, "Don't I get a hug?" Ruthie looked at him while taking Justin's coat off. He comes closer and tries to kiss her. She pulled back and turned her face.

"I'm sorry, Ruthie. I was just mad."

"Mad enough to keep my son from me?"

"No, for keeping you from me."

She blushed. She had to admit she missed him too. This time she kissed him. Their kiss was sweet. So sweet that Ruthie licked her lips as if to keep the taste on her tongue.

"So, how are you?"

"I'm doing Michael. I made a big mistake and now I have to pay."

"When do you go back to court?"

"In three weeks. What do you think?"

"I think It'll be a fine, probably probation or community service." A little voice goes off in her head, "Who are you trying to convince?"

"I'm nervous though."

Michael reassures her. "Well, I'm here."

CHAPTER SIXTY-TWO

TIME PASSED SLOWLY, but surely. Penny was going back and forth between Andrew and Mr. Blue. She hadn't 'muled' for Mr. Blue in a while. Reason being he hadn't asked her. He was acting funny, only asking Harlan, Flash and Shoes to do his dirt. With Andrew nickeling and diming her, giving money here and there, Penny has to go to Mr. Blue to keep up her end of the bargain.

"Hey Mr. Blue. Hey y'all," she said greeting Eyes, Harlan and Shoes.

"Hey Penny. What's happening?"

"Ain't nothing."

"Sorry to hear about your cousin," said Harlan.

"Yeah."

"How she doing?"

"Well..."

"Let's talk about something else." Mr. Blue wanting to change the subject. He was feeling guilty.

"Hey Mr. Blue, my funds are kinda tight. You think you can put me on?"

"Put you on?"

"Yeah, I need some money."

"Quiet as its kept Penny, so do I."

"What's going on?"

Lying, "Things have slowed for me. My contact is on low and plus the streets are hot. I need to chill out for a minute."

"I hear you. Let me know when things pick up."

"I'll keep you in mind."

"Alright now. I'll talk to you later."

Penny left Mr. Blue's place through the back door. Just as the door closed, Shoes, his main boy, starts in.

"Something's up with her."

"What you mean?"

"She seems a lot chattier nowadays, always asking questions."

"So, she's always talking."

"More than usual if you ask me, like she's fishing.

Harlan chimed in, "Maybe her mouth has the flucks."

"The flucks?"

"Diariha." They all laughed.

"Seriously though, man. You need to put something in her ear to see if she nibbles."

"You think she's giving up the tapes?"

"There's only one way to find out."

CHAPTER SIXTY-THREE

I TS' CRYING TIME. Aunt Bunchie is upstairs sitting at her vanity smoking cigarette after cigarette. She is nervous as hell. Today is the day…Court. For the first time in a LONG time she's been praying day and night. You can hear her saying sometimes, "Please GOD." She outs the cigarette as Penny walks in the room.

"Mom, are you okay?"

"Yeah, I'm okay."

"Nervous?"

"Yeah, but It'll be alright."

"Who knows?" "You may just get probation and have to pay back the money."

"We'll see. Where's Calvin?"

"I don't know. I haven't seen him this morning. I think he didn't come home."

"Is Ruthie going?"

"No." She said she was going to stay home with Justin." Actually Ruthie didn't want to go. She knew it was a matter of time before it was her turn.

"Ok. Go ahead Penny so I can finish getting dressed."

"Okay Mom, see you downstairs. Aunt Jane is already here."

"I'll be right down."

Calvin stayed the night out with Tracie, his on and off girlfriend. She was about 5 years older and had her own place.

"What time is it?

"8:30."

"Aww man. I need to go. My Mom is due in court by ten."

"Roll me a joint."

He rushed in the bathroom to take a shower. Trina sat up, looked under the bed and grabbed the shoebox top with the reefer and top paper and rolled a big fat joint. She noticed Calvin's wallet on the dresser. She grabbed it real quick and looked inside. "Since he's working at Steel Mill's, I know he got...uh huh. Here it go. Money!!" She snatched $40 dollars out and put the wallet back. Calvin came out the shower with the towel wrapped around his waist.

"Where's the joint?"

"Here."

He lit it and pulled on it so hard it looked like he would smoke the whole thing with one puff. He passed it to her and found his drawers. He dropped the towel and started putting them on. Trina watched him and started licking her lips. He liked it when she did that. He started to get aroused.

"Smiling, don't start Trina."

He looked at the clock, thinking he had time, but he noticed he only had a few minutes to dress and leave so he changed his mind and finished dressing. He grabbed his watch and then his wallet. He opened it and looked straight at her. Trina smiled.

Calvin told her "All you had to do was ask. Where are your car keys?" She got up, showing all her body and gave him her keys. He kissed her lips and palmed her butt. "I'll talk to you later."

He made it to court just in time. He snuck in and sat next to Penny. He whispered, "What I miss?"

"Mom pled guilty and the Judge asked her if she had anything to say before she made her decision."

Aunt Jane told them both to Ssh.

"Your Honor, I am fully aware of what I've done and I take full responsibility for my actions. Your Honor, I did what I did because my son was in danger and I wanted to save his life. I didn't know what else to do."

Calvin jumped up. "Say what?!! You did it because of me?!!!"

The Judge banged her gavel, "Order!!!"

"You stole money because of me?!! Mom, you did what you did for you!! I can't believe you are trying to pin your bullshit on me."

"Order!!" The Judge half-heartedly banged her gavel. In her mind, she was thinking I want to hear this. This is good.

Aunt Bunchie turned and looked at him, "Baby, they were going to kill you!!!"

"Any excuse will do won't it, Mom?"

Penny and Aunt Jane urged Calvin to sit down.

"No! I can't believe what she just said."

"Alright, I've heard enough." Bang Bang Bang!! "Order in the court." Young man, one more word and I'll hold you in contempt!"

Calvin kept talking. "Mom you are a bigger skank than I thought you were," and walked out the courtroom.

Aunt Bunchie burst out crying. When the smoke cleared, the Judge continued. "Ms. Caldwell, as you can see your actions not only affected yourself, but your family as well. I am convinced you believed that what you did, you did out of love. However, a crime has been committed and I must punish accordingly. I am ready to rule. You have entered a plea of guilty and it is hereby accepted." "You are hereby guilty in the eyes of the court and I sentence you to seven years in the Philadelphia Correctional Facility."

Penny had her hand over her mouth and Aunt Jane's eyes were big as saucers.

"You are to surrender and start serving your sentence immediately. "Bailiff take her away."

Aunt Bunchie stood and turned around to be handcuffed. She stared back at her family and mouthed "I love you" as tears fell from her eyes. She also saw a familiar face…Her!!! Sheila was there sitting behind her family. She slipped in unnoticed to watch the whole thing. She had to be there. They made eye contact. She smiled and held her hand up just enough for her to see and wiggled her fingers, waving goodbye. She almost burst out laughing as she watched them take her away. She then got up and quietly left.

CHAPTER SIXTY-FOUR

THEY WERE CRUISING down 7th Street when Harlan yelled, "Yo man, slow up."

"What for?"

"I think I seen something."

"Seen what?"

"That's him!"

"Him who?"

"That's the dude I've seen Penny with a couple of times."

"Where?"

"Right there."

"Who is it?"

Mr. Blue replied, "Oh snap!!" That's the same guy that was there the night I got nabbed with Ruthie over at the station!"

"Oh yeah? He hangs down the Legion on 7th and Pennell. "He's with the Task."

"What she doing with him?"

"Hmmm."

Quiet as it's kept, Harlan had a thing for Penny at one time and still do. Inside Harlan was steaming. "Oh so it's like that...."

The mailman put the mail through the slot in the door. Ruthie was upstairs with the baby waiting for everybody to come home. She wanted to know how everything went. Knock, knock, knock. She left Justin sleeping in his crib and went downstairs to answer the door. It's Michael.

"Hey baby."

"Hey."

"What you doing?"

"Just chilling."

"Oh. Here's the mail."

"Thanks."

"Have you heard anything?"

"No not yet. They haven't come home yet. Want something to drink?"

"Naw, I'm good. Where's Justin?"

"Upstairs."

Justin started crying so Ruthie goes and gets him. She comes down with him in her arms.

"Hey boy." Michael saw how unsteady Ruthie was holding him. "Give him to me before you drop him."

"Are you okay?"

"Yeah."

"Sit down, talk to me."

"Michael, I'm scared to death. I'm scared for Aunt Bunchie and myself. What if I have to go away?"

"Don't say that."

"It could happen."

"When is your court date?"

"Not sure."

He put Justin on the floor and took her in his arms and hugged her real tight.

"Whatever happens, I'm here. We'll get through this together."

Calvin was sitting in the hallway when Penny and Aunt Jane filed out of the courtroom. Calvin got up and approached them.

"What happened?"

"Mom got seven years Calvin!!! Seven years!"

He grabbed Penny and hugged her.

Aunt Jane asked, "Calvin are you alright?" He let Penny go, but kept his arm around her shoulder.

"Yeah man, but I can't believe she said that. It's like she's blaming me for what she did, like it's my fault. In his heart Calvin knew exactly what his mother was talking about 'his life being in danger,' but he had no idea she did all of that.

Penny was scared. "What are we going to do?"

Aunt Jane couldn't and didn't say a thing. With their future uncertain, what could be said?

Penny fell in the door. From the look on her face, both Michael and Ruthie knew instantly, that things didn't go well. Aunt Jane and Calvin followed behind her.

"OMG what happened?"

"Our Mother has been sentenced to prison for seven years!!!"

"What?!!"

"Yes, seven years." Ruthie ran and hugged Penny.

"Calm down Penny," Aunt Jane said.

"Calm down?! How? "What 's going to happen to me; to Calvin?" We can't afford to stay here!!"

"Don't worry, we'll figure out something."

Beulah made her way back to her cell. She sat on her bunk and picked up a magazine and leafed through looking at the pictures. She couldn't concentrate. Her other informant, Correctional Officer, Elyse Renee, (Rozelle Harding was transferred) just told her the latest. Her sister is on the way.

"Just so you know, she will be sharing the same block with you for a short period of the time due to overcrowding. You know it's not normal to have family members sharing the same block."

"I know." Thanks for telling me."

She didn't know how to feel after hearing the news, but the idea of her sister coming here unnerved her. She started pacing back and forth. Her heart softened, "That's my sister." I can't turn my back on her but… her mind drifted to her kids…if it wasn't' for her. I can't do it. I can't get involved. She's on her own."

Bunchie, along with several the other women, arrived at the Philadelphia Detention Center. Enduring the intake procedure, she tried to be brave, but this being her first time, she couldn't control herself. She was visibly shaking. She was striped searched in and out of her body, she was issued prison regulation garb, bedding, toiletries and ordered to follow the CO to her cell. They arrived at her cell and she was told to step in. Her cell mate, Constance, an older woman, was laying on the bottom bunk.

"Connie, you have company." She sat up, stood up, looked Bunchie up and down then walked out.

"What is wrong with her?" Bunchie thought.

Standing in line for food, Beulah saw Bunchie. Her heart sank and her eyes teared up. "My sister." Their eyes locked and Bunchie slightly smiled. Beulah turned her head and kept moving. Neither one let on that there was a connection. It didn't matter. In prison, it's like Peyton Place. They knew who Bunchie was before she came.

There were other eyes on Bunchie as well. Fats, as they called her, was watching. Why they called her Fats one couldn't guess. She was short, skinny and wore her hair in a ponytail. There wasn't anything fat about her, all except for her lips.... real big soup coolers. She hunched Kelly, a fellow inmate, "Who's that?"

"That's Beatrice Caldwell, Connie's new cellie."

"Oh really now?" A smile appeared on her face.

"I heard she's Beulah's sister. She's only here for a short period due to overcrowding. They'll either move Beulah or her sister."

"Well, I guess that means I gotta work faster. I'm going to have some fun tonight."

"Ruthie, phone!

"Who is it?"

"I don't know," and slammed the receiver down on the table. Penny was still in a foul mood.

"Hello."

"Ruth, this is Lillie Brandt."

Ruthie's heart started beating fast. "Hi."

"How are you?"

"I'm good."

"The reason I'm calling is to ask did you get a letter notifying you when you are to appear?"

"Letter?"

"Yes, you should be getting a letter of your upcoming hearing. I didn't hear from you so I thought I'd better call just in case you had any questions."

"Hold on and let me check to see if it came." Ruthie went to the table where she laid the mail. She sifts through it and saw the letter. She tore it open and started reading. She picked the receiver up.

"I got it." She read it aloud on the phone. It's next Friday at 10:00." OMG! After she finished reading, she got quiet.

"Ruthie, are you okay?"

"Yeah, I just didn't know."

"Don't worry, Ruthie." "It'll be okay." "We have the fact that this is your first offense."

"What are my chances?"

"I'm not going to lie and tell you that there wouldn't be a possibility that you may get some time, however, with, like I said, this being your first offense it could be community service, a fine and a stern warning." Just know, I'll be there with you and I'll give it my best."

"Thank You."

"Okay, so I'll see you next Friday, bright and early at 9:30, okay?"

"Okay." After hanging up, Ruthie felt reassured by the calmness in her store bought lawyer's voice. SURPRISE!!

CHAPTER SIXTY-FIVE

BUNCHIE WAS SITTING on her bunk. She and her roommate were exchanging war stories, not going into deep details. Bunchie thought, "She's cool so far, but I know I need to be careful in here. I got seven years, plenty of time to make friends."

All of a sudden, Fats and two other women stopped in front of her cell. The air suddenly became thick. Constance's whole demeanour changed. Bunchie noticed she was scared. Fats was standing there with the look of hunger in her eyes.

"Out!!!" Fats yelled at Constance.

Constance got up and squeezed herself out. Fats wasn't the least bit afraid of Constance telling the CO. She knew better. Bunchie was nervous, but she wasn't about to back down.

"What's your name?" Bunchie just looked at her mentally, preparing herself for a fight.

"You hear me?" Bunchie just looked at them.

"Oh, so you don't talk."

"Let's see if you can scream." They rushed her.

They starting fighting. Bunchie was holding her own, but three women on her at one time, she couldn't win. The held her down on the floor and tore at her pants, pulling them off. With one of them having their hand on her mouth, she couldn't scream. With her tightly secured, Fats went to work.

Penny was desperate. With her mother locked down now, she knew she needed to get money fast if she was to stay off the street. Calvin was so pissed; nobody hadn't seen him since the day of reckoning for Bunchie. She went to see Mr. Blue, but first she met up with Andrew. "You got a couple of coins to spare for a sister?"

"What you got for me?"

"Nothing yet."

"Hey Penny, you know the deal. I've been fronting you money, but the info you've given so far hasn't produced nothing. Dealing with you is like a good fuck gone to waste."

"Come on Andrew, I can't help that. He hasn't given me any jobs. He says he's laying low."

"Well, unless I get something from you, this cash cow is closed."

Desperate, she starting pulling at his clothes. "Come on Andrew, I know you miss me." She still turned him on, but he pushed her back half heartily. He wanted her to 'sing on the mike' but he was playing hard. She saw he was aroused, so she unzipped his pants. "Come on," she whispered softly in his ear. She knew anything sounded sexy if it's moist enough. She put her hand in his pants. "Penny, stop" he said hoarsely. She released him from the confines and commenced to showering him with her kisses. "I got him now. Mission accomplished," she thought.

There she go again man, with that dude. They realized then that they couldn't trust her.

"I know she's getting down with him. I ought to kill her right where she stand, wet panties and all."

Harlan wanted to kill her, but Blue calmed his trigger finger. Despite what they knew, Mr. Blue was sad because he really liked her.

"She's not worth it, man. We'll just disassociate ourselves."

"Yeah, right after we set her stinking ass up."

Beulah heard about it…Bunchie was raped last night. Her heart broke. "Damn, she thought. They sure didn't waste any time. She at least waited to try that shit with me, but I have a cool ass roommate and she told me about Fats, so I was ready. She shook away the memory. I can't" Then she saw her. Her eye was swollen and her spirit broken. This time it was Bunchie who turned away, but not before their eyes met and locked.

Then, she kept moving.

Beulah got instantly nervous. "I need to do something before she kills or be killed." She knew how vindictive Bunchie could be and she knew how her mind works. She also recognized the look Bunchie gave her…she read her mind. It's on…PAYBACK!!!

Before she could get at her, Beulah was transferred to the upper block.

"You have a collect call from inmate Beatrice Caldwell from the Philadelphia Detention Center. Will you accept the call?"

"Yes," Aunt Jane answered.

"Hey, Jane."

"Hey Bunchie. How are you?"

"I'm doing okay."

"No, how are you?" "You don't sound too good."

"I'm okay Jane, just trying to get used to being in here. How's the kids?"

"I don't know. I haven't seen Calvin and it's hard to keep up with Penny. I stopped by the house the other day and she wasn't there. I did see Ruthie. She's nervous as hell because she has her court date next Friday."

"Oh. I don't have much time on the phone so I'll make it quick." "Tell Penny and Calvin that I made arrangements with the landlord to keep the house for them. I paid the rent up until the end of next month with the money I had left."

"Really? When you do that?"

"I did that days before I was to appear in court. I had a feeling I wouldn't be coming home so I wanted to at least do that."

"That's good. I'll tell them."

"You think after that Penny would be able to stay with you?"

"Now, Bunchie, you know the deal. I got Barbara and Cece and my two kids still live here. Maybe she and Calvin can stay there. You know he's working. I guess Penny will have to get a job."

"What about school?"

"Maybe she can get a job after school."

"I don't know Jane."

"Alright Bunchie. We will talk about it later. You talk to Beulah?"

"She's not talking to me in here."

"Are you serious?"

'No. We've seen each other, but we haven't talked."

"I'll talk to her."

"No Jane, its' okay." Bunchie sounded so sad.

CHAPTER SIXTY-SIX

WITH HER NEW found wealth of $200, she thinks, "That's a lot of money," but she knew she needed more. I hate to do this, but...she went to Mr. Blue's bat cave.

"Hey y'all."

"Hey Penny." They all looked at each other sideways. "What's up?

"Aw nothing, except..."

"Except what?"

"I got something I need you to do."

Greedily, she answered, "Oh yeah? What I got to do?"

"I need you to deliver some money to Cy for some "snow."

"Ok. When?"

"As soon I get the word. I got a call in with my boy Cheese and he'll let me know. He's expecting something in a few days, maybe sooner. The plan is to meet him at Wards Grill on 3rd Street."

"How am I going to get there?"

"We'll go with you and drop you off. We'll sit out in the car and wait for you. His partner, Sparks, is going to have it all bagged and ready."

"How much is it?" Mr. Blue started to say, 2...

"It's enough!!" Stein said cutting him off. He said it so hard that Penny jerked her head around at him.

"Golly Stein, I just asked."

"We'll pay you half and the other half when the job is done."

"A'ight."

"So, when it's a go we'll get at you."

"Ok."

Penny couldn't wait to get home. She damn near skipped. She got in the house and did a James Brown slide, chanting, "I'm going to get paid!!! Owww!!!" Out of breath, she flopped down on the couch and grabbed the phone.

"Hello."

"Here is the deal."

CHAPTER SIXTY-SEVEN

THE MORNING OF her hearing, Ruthie is nervous as hell. She is so nervous she couldn't hardly get dressed. She buttoned her blouse all wrong and her hair was a mess. Luckily, she dressed Justin first. He was in his crib sucking on a bottle. She talked to herself. "Get it together and calm down." She couldn't shake the feeling that things would go horribly wrong."

"Penny! Penny!"

"Yeah, Ruthie what's up?"

"I'm so nervous. Can you help me?"

"Sure."

Grabbing the hairbrush while Ruthie fixed her blouse, she tried to encourage her.

"Girl, get it together. You'll be fine."

"I don't know."

"Sure you'll be...what time is it?"

"8:30."

"Where's Michael?"

"He needs to drop his Mom off so he'll meet us there."

"I'm not going."

"What? Why not? Come on Penny. I need you there."

"I really don't...."

"Penny!!"

"Okay, Ruthie."

"Aunt Jane is coming soon so get dressed. Rusty and Reese will be there too." Penny really didn't want to go. The guilt was killing her.

"I'm sorry Ruthie, she whispered. It's all my fault."

Sitting up front with her lawyer, she was schooled on how to act in front of the Judge.

"Now Ruthie, be poised and answer any questions to the best of your ability. Don't be nervous. It'll be okay."

"Promise?"

"No, I can't do that, but…"

"All rise, the bailiff bellows, the Honorable Lucille Granger presiding.

"Good morning. Everyone, please be seated."

CHAPTER SIXTY-EIGHT

CALVIN WAS REFUSING to go back to the house. "Penny and Ruthie have been hounding me to stay." Just last week,' he thought he was the man. He was rolling in the dough, fronting, but that has now changed. LAYOFF!!! He hadn't saved a dime and his girl was threatening to put him out. The only thing saving him from that was his unemployment check. She told him "I like you and your sex is all that, but it's not enough for you to stay here."

With another argument under their belt, leaving Calvin riding the old sofa, he was rethinking his options. 'Maybe it will be good for me to go back. Trina, she a 'right, but she steals from me, she is constantly threatening to put me out and I'm getting tired of her asking me where you going, where you been. Something gotta give before I end up hurting her. I have never hit a woman before, but the next time she slaps me in my face I don't know."

"Ms. Walters, you are hereby in this court, reason being, drug trafficking. How do you plead?"

"Not Guilty."

"Not Guilty, huh? Well, based on the evidence in front of me, you have been seen in the company of a known drug dealer on more than one occasion. To make matters worse, you were arrested with this same person on suspicion of making a delivery to a person you gave the drugs to and who himself was arrested a short time later. I have copies of your school records. Your grades exemplify a good student. Are you still in school?"

"No ma'am."

"Explain to me, Ms. Walters, how did you go from an A-B student to this? Help me understand."

"Your Honor, it was something that just happened. I lost my father to death and my mother is jailed. I was moved to a situation that I had no idea how to handle. I was young and I'm still young. I was trying to fit in. Then I ended up pregnant."

"Pregnant?"

"Yes, your Honor. I have a young son."

"I see."

"I made a huge mistake."

"Indeed." Where is your son now?"

"He's with his father right now, but we both raise him."

"Oh really now? Despite the fact that you have a young child, he played no importance in your decision to get involved in the drug game. I sympathize with your beginnings, but you have shown a lack of maturity and your decisions show that, but how can you know better at the age of 16? Your parental guidance or lack thereof had a profound effect on how to make rational decisions. Now that your guardian herself has been incarcerated, I hardly have any choices. I have the right to enforce probation, foster care or commitment to the Dept. of Juvenile Detention. In all honesty, I can't, in good conscience, send you home under no supervision."

"She has another Aunt and two brothers," her public defender announced.

"That's all well and good Ms. Brandt, but how can I be assured she would get the proper support that she would need? Where were they when all this was going on?"

Aunt Jane almost blurted out, "What you mean by that?" She looked at Reese and Rusty with a puzzled look on her face.

"It's becoming a habit of young people coming in this court, cry a couple of crocodile tears and expect this court to have mercy. "Well, I'm not having it."

"Ms. Walters, you have plenty of book sense, but street sense you have none. I believe you can be easily swayed to be pulled into a bigger life of crime under the best supervision. I find no other choice, but to reprimand you to the Juvenile Detention Center in Lima PA until the age of 18 in which at that time your case will be revisited. It may be possible, based on your behavior in this facility, early dismissal can be recommended. You are…"

Ruthie screamed and all went dark.

Aunt Jane was beside herself. She couldn't believe what she just heard. "Ruthie!!" She cried after hearing what the Judge ordered. Penny didn't say a word, but it showed on her face what she was feeling…guilt. Reese knew better than to say anything and Rusty was bent over with his head in hands, thinking, "What in the world has happened to this family?'

Nolan met with his lawyer in jail earlier. "Finally his dumb ass came to see me," he thought. "He's been putting me off."

His lawyer explained to him, with his previous stint in prison, whatever information he had or may not have may not do him any good in getting him a break. He reminded him that it was him that got caught, not Mr. Blue. This didn't sit well with him. He was so pissed he yelled, "GET OUT!!!"

In honesty, his lawyer was scared of him and gladly left. You should have seen him scrambling to his feet. He made a mental note. "Find yourself another lawyer. I quit."

Facing a long sentence, he planned to nail Blue to the wall by his nuts. "That brother is going to pay, sending that trick with her dumb behind. I knew I smelled a rat when I noticed this guy staring at us, but she had already given me the package. I knew he looked…" Bam!!!

Nolan slammed his hand down on the table.

"Hey man," his fellow inmate, Buddy Rudy yelled. "Don't hurt the table. He didn't do it."

Nolan had to smile.

"What's bothering you?"

Nolan didn't answer. He just stared into space. I got to make a phone call." Walking to the phones, he thought, "Time's up little boy Blue."

CHAPTER SIXTY-NINE

"WHAT?! OMG!" BEULAH just got the word from Elyse that Ruthie, her baby, was sent to Juvey. Just the thought of it made her blood boil. Any thought of trying to help Bunchie went right out the window. "Fats can turn her pussy inside out for all I care."

The van ride from Media was short, but it seemed like the longest ride of her life especially in handcuffs. She sat by herself at the back of the van, listening to the changing of the gears. For where we're going, the other girls had a lot to say, but their chatter didn't distract from her thoughts. Tears flowed down her cheeks, thinking "Why couldn't the Judge see it was all a big mistake? "Why couldn't she see?"

"We're here, ladies," the bus driver announced.

Ruthie noticed two counsellors were standing outside waiting for them. She and the others, told by the driver, had to line up and file off one by one. While the others filed off, she just sat there.

"Come along, Ms. Walters." Ruthie didn't move. They noticed she was still sitting there. They realized she would be difficult. One of the counsellors climbed aboard the van and called Ruthie's name. She did not budge.

Walking along the aisle he said, "Come along now. We don't have time for this."

She didn't budge.

He yanked her out her seat, "Come On!!"

Inside, she and the others were led into the intake area for processing. The handcuffs were removed and were told to stand along the wall until their names were called.

"Ruth Walters."

She was then led to the showering room and told to remove everything, earrings, shoes etc. Soap, towels and shampoo were passed to her through an opening in the door. After showering, she was given sweatpants and sweatshirt, socks, underwear and lace less sneakers.

The whole time, she cried. She wanted to go home so bad. She was given her assigned POD location and cell number. She was then met by The Detention Officer, Della Harvey. "Hello ladies, my name is Della Harvey. I am here to maintain order during your stay here. I'll make your stay easy or hard. The choice is yours. Follow me." The Detention Officer was considered a hard nose, but for some reason she instantly took a liking to Ruthie. She thought "she reminds me so much of my granddaughter." She rushed the others to their room, but she took her sweet time with Ruthie, making her last. As they were walking, she spoke words of encouragement.

"Young lady, I know this is a new experience for you. For some, this is no biggie. You can make it hard or you can get all that you can out of this experience. Take full advantage. There's classes, church, etc. You have your rulebook describing everything."

Smiling, she said, "I'm gonna keep my eyes on you. "Good Luck."

Standing in her doorway next to Ruthie's room, watching the new arrivals in the POD was Sandy Manchester, a white girl from Darby.

"This here is Sandy, our so called resident house mother."

"Hello Sandy."

"Hi, Ms. Harvey."

"I'll leave you two to get acquainted. Take care of her."

As Ms. Harvey walked away, Sandy licked her tongue out. The minute the counsellor was out of earshot, she started talking.

"Don't trip. It's a piece of cake. I've been in and out of juvey since I was 10. My parents don't understand me" …and burst out laughing.

Ruthie thought, "What's wrong with her? This is not funny."

Weeks have gone by and it was lonely in the house without Calvin and now Ruthie is gone. Her girls were still her girls, but they were into their own thing. I hope this deal goes through because I got about two weeks before the rent is due. Thanks to her mother she was allowed to stay this long. Aunt Jane told her what she did.

Knock, Knock. "Who is it?"

"Who it is" the voice said from the other side of the door.

Penny peeked out. Harlan. She opened the door.

"What's up?"

"What's going on girl? You still trying to do that?"

"Do…yeah."

"Well, it's on tonight. Come on."

"Well, I need to do something first. Give me 5 minutes."

"A'ight, I'll wait."

"Naw, that's okay. I'll come over."

Harlan just stood there and stared at her.

"Okay. Meet me at the store."

"Okay."

He hesitated for a second then he turned around and left. Penny felt a chill rush over her body. "He scares me."

Ten minutes later, she walked over to the store and Harlan, just as he promised, was waiting for her. She couldn't shake the bad feeling she felt when she saw him. "This don't feel right she thought," but that didn't stop her. They made their way through until they were in the cave. Squeak and Hershey were there, packing the bag as she walked in.

"Hey Penny!!"

"Hey."

"Where's Mr. Blue?"

"He's out."

Harlan spoke. "A'ight now Penny when you make the delivery, it will look like you're giving clothes to someone." She peeked in the bag and saw several stacks of money and her eyes watered over thinking, "If only all this money was mine. They placed the clothes on top. "Let's get this going. It's almost 7 and I told my boy, Cy, a.k.a. Magilla (a name called behind his back), we'd be there by 7:30."

Nolan had made several phone calls during the course of the week since he's been in the clink. He made arrangements for his boy, "Sir Nose," to pay Blue a visit, always talking in code.

"It's on the water. Pay him a visit. He'll be glad to see you. Tell him I said hello." His boy knew just what he meant and knew of the location.

"Will do."

Quiet as it kept, Mr. Blue was bigger than he let on. He had a stash house in an unlived in, but fully furnished house that sat alone on the waterfront, off 2nd Street. His boys Harlan and Shoes, were the only one who knew where it was, except…. He brought him there one night. He and Nolan were at the Town Bar having drinks. He got word from Joyce aka "Ankie" the barmaid that a prescription needed to be refilled. He made a couple of calls but couldn't get a hold of anybody so he made the delivery himself. He didn't have what was needed on him so he needed to make a stop. He and Nolan go way back so he didn't think nothing of it to take him with him. Bad Move.

Blue was there checking on things when he hears the door open.

"Hey y'all back early. How did it go?" He turns around, but when he sees who it is, his eyes grew big. "Hey, what" …. Boom!!!

Harlan, Squeak and Penny where on their way to the "Grill." Squeak was driving while Harlan sat in the back. WDAE was playing on the radio and Harlan lit up a joint and they laughed and joked on the way. Two cars back was Andrew and his team. As they pulled up, they could hear things were in full swing. The music could be heard as people are filing in and out the doors.

"Okay, Penny. Gilla, I mean Cy, is waiting. Here." He hands her a bag.

She grabs it, but didn't notice it was a different bag. Only thing in that bag was clothes. The original bag was used to sike her ass out, to get her juices going. She grabs it and gets out the car. She walks down the sidewalk and pulls the door open. For the few minutes the door opens, the music grabs Squeak and he turns down the radio and started snapping his fingers and moving his body side to side. They jamming.

Penny spots Cy. A few minutes later the both of them come out and entered a side door that led upstairs. A few minutes later Andrew and his boys had the place on lock. Squeak and Harlan watched the whole thing unfold as Andrew and his team rushed the door. They laughed so hard as they pulled away from the curb, leaving Penny high and dry, holding the bag, literally.

They robbed Blue and beat him until they were tired. They stole his stash, his money leaving high and dry. Their job was done.

Harlan and Squeak pulled up the store to let Mr. Blue know what went on. They were laughing as they went in. They couldn't wait to share what happened.

"Hey, Blue, man it was so funny!"

"He's not here. He's probably over at the Wire." They walked over and ran into Bunchie's old co-worker, Dot.

"Hey Ms. Dot. Have you seen Mr. Blue?"

"Naw, we ain't seen him."

"Ok."

They knew where he was. When they arrived, they saw that the lights were on.

"He's in there."

They knock on the door and it fell open.

"What?" They tiptoed in not knowing what lies ahead.

"Hey, Blue man, guess what? Blue, where you at? "OMG Blue!!" They found him lying there on the floor in a small pool of blood. Squeak ran over to him. He checked his pulse.

"He's breathing."

Mr. Blue groans when Squeak turn him over.

He's screams in his face, "Who did this? They knew better than to call the police or an ambulance. "We got to get him to the hospital." They put him in the car and drove as fast they could to Crozer. While Squeak sat in the car, Harlan rushed in the emergency doors and told the first nurse he saw.

"Hey, we need help!! We found this guy in the street all beat up. Can you help us?"

"Where is he?"

"Right out here."

The nurse and an orderly ran out. Squeak managed to get him out the car and sat him on the bench.

"Get a gurney," the nurse barked to the orderly.

"Do you know who it is?"

"I've seen him around. I think his name is Theodore Brooks."

"Thank you, young man. We'll take it from here."

"You think he'll be okay?"

"I can't say."

"Thank you."

As they walked to the car, "Squeak, man, who would want to do that?"

The drug deal was a bust. Penny was sitting on the couch inside Cy's apartment, patting her feet impatiently, thinking "Hurry up. I got to go." While waiting, Penny got a good look at him. His family nickname was Sweet Tooth. He was Sweet tooth alright. He must have eaten candy morning, noon and night because his teeth were.... wow.

They look like shark teeth, all pointy. He was taking his time, but wasting hers, just talking. All of a sudden, the door burst open and in flies Andrew and his team.

"What the hell?" Cy yells.

"Put your hands up so we can see them."

Cy, with his hands in the air ask, "What's this all about Officer?"

"We have reason to believe there's a drug deal going on."

"Drug deal? I don't know what you're talking about?"

Looking in Penny's direction he asks, "Do you Penny?"

Penny didn't say a thing.

"Look around fellas."

The other task members started tearing through the apartment, turning over things.

"Hey!!!"

"Shut up." Andrew ordered.

Andrew turned to Penny, "Where's the bag?"

"What bag?"

"The bag I saw you come in here with?"

"Over there."

He grabbed the bag and sifts through it. "There's nothing in here, but old clothes."

"Yeah, that's all, Cy squeaked. A friend of mine sent over some old clothes. I'm collecting for the Salvation Army and a friend of mine told me she's sending them over by Penny."

"Penny?"

"I…"

"Let's go fellas. Ain't nothing here."

The Task files out. Before leaving, Andrew stared at Penny.

"I ought to lock your ass up."

"They tricked me."

"Yeah, they did."

Penny couldn't do nothing, but stand there with her mouth open.

"I thought"

"You thought wrong. You're done," and he disappeared.

Cy just looked at Penny and shook his head. "Girl, you crazy. "Harlan and his boys played you just like a fiddle. Now they know fo sho you were living foul. It wouldn't surprise me if they don't rock your damn ass to sleep, permanently."

"You knew all the time this was a setup?"

"Sure did and they did too. What you thought you had a secret?" There's no secrets in Chester as small as this city is. Everybody knows everybody. That's what you get." He pointed his meaty finger towards the door, "Now, get out."

CHAPTER SEVENTY

BUNCHIE HAD ENOUGH. Fats was trying her patience. She tortured her with daily "bullying" or sending her on sick dates she set up. The rule inside was don't be a snitch, but she needed to get her off of her. She came up with a plan. It's either me or her.

Ruthie was making her way in Juvey one day at a time. She decided to make the best of it. She really didn't have a choice. At dinner time, the menu consisted of chicken, rice and mixed vegetables. She got her food and sat at the table alone. Sandy saw she was sitting by herself and invited her to come join her at the table she was sitting. "Hey Ruth come on over and sit with us." She, Addy and Freda were sitting at a table of four. Ruth decided to squash her fears, get over herself and sat with them. Sandy did the honors and introduced her. They all spoke and began to eat. Addy made a face like there was something wrong. Freda asked, "What's wrong with you?"

"Is it me or is this rice not done?" Addy answered

Ruthie spoke up. "I know, it's like I'm eating popcorn."

"I think I just broke a tooth." Freda said.

Sandy chimed in. "Well, if they have a whole lot of trash, I'm sure it's going to be nothing, but rice."

They all laughed and this broke the ice.

Kelly "Bulldog" Wilkins, a Detention Officer, was not standing too far away from them and heard the joke. She laughed too. She had her eyes on Ruthie's dark skin and taunt little body. She thought, "What I would do." Ms. Harvey was across the room watching too. She noticed how Kelly's mouth was watering when she looked at Ruthie. She knew of her previous "work" and kept a watchful eye. She thought, "Better not let me catch you."

Blue was in the hospital with bruised ribs, a busted lip, a few missing teeth and a black eye. He was lucky. Those guy meant business. Blue knew who was behind it and when asked by several of his visitors, he kept his mouth shut. He was scared. "When I get out of here, I'm done. I'm too old for this. No telling what will happen the next time." He picked up the phone and dialled the number. When it was answered, he spoke… "Listen…."

Kelly couldn't stand it. She waited patiently for her chance. While all the others were in the rec, Ruthie decided to take a nap. She got up to leave and Sandy asked, "Ruth where are you going?"

"I'm so tired. I'm going to take a nap."

"Okay. See you in a few."

Kelly watched her leave and kinda' sorta followed her. Ruthie was so tired; she was sleep before her head hit the pillow. Kelly snuck in her room. She stood over her. She couldn't resist. She eased on her bed careful not to shake it. She moved closer. She started lightly touching her. Ruthie rustled. Kelly eased her hand up Ruthie's leg up towards her panic button. Just when she was about to push, she felt cold water fall down over her head. What? Ruthie woke and screamed.

Mrs. Harvey yelled, "Kelly, Get your ass out of here right now. You low down…."

Kelly stood up.

"Buck me, bitch, so I can knock you down." She had a mop handle in her hand. Kelly left, dripping wet.

"Stay here Ruth. I'll be right back." Mrs. Harvey left and went straight to her Commander to report Kelly and have her removed from the area.

Penny is laying low. She's scared of being seen ever since the fake drug deal so she does most of her running in the wee hours of the day. She was coming out of John Bargains Store on 5th and Edgemont when she saw Harlan ride by. She was hoping he didn't see her. Too Late. He saw her and stopped. She saw his reverse lights come on. He backed up to where she was standing, smiled and then showed her his hand in the form of a gun. Then he pulled off. This shook her up so bad she felt like her teeth loosened. She got home as quickly as she could. Since that day, she's been a nervous wreck. Every sound the house makes scares her to death. She's too afraid to sleep upstairs, so Lumpy the sofa is her new bed. She was looking out the window, when Sylvia walked by. She tapped on the window to get her attention. Sylvia heard the noise and turned to see where it was coming from. She saw Penny and walked up to the door. Penny opened the door.

"Hey girl."

"Hey."

"Haven't seen you in a while. Where you been?"

"Here and there."

"Did you hear what happened?"

"No. What?"

"I heard Mr. Blue got beat up two nights ago."

"Get out!!"

"Yeah girl. You didn't know?"

"No. Is he okay?"

"Yeah I think so, but he's beat up pretty bad."

"Wow!!"

She wanted to go and see him, but was scared she'd run into Harlan, Squeak or the rest of his boys. Harlan still wanted to kill her, but Blue made him promise to stay far from her.

"I'd better not catch her..."

"No, leave well enough alone. She's done and she knows it."

The money she had left was running low having to pay to keep the lights on. She didn't have enough to pay the rent and now she found an eviction notice on the door telling her she had to vacate the premises in days. She searched around the house to see if she can find something to pawn at Otis's over town to pay the rent for at least another month. She went in her mother's room and searched through her stuff.

"Mom sure kept a messy room." She smiled at the thought of her. "I miss you Mom." She checked all the coats. All she found was lint. She even looked under the mattress. Nothing. She looked through the jewellery box on her dresser. "All this crap is fake. Oh my goodness, what am I going to do?" She kept looking, searching through papers, thinking it was money in the envelopes that was mixed in. She didn't find money, but she did find a name and number on a piece of paper. "Hmm...." Changing gears, "I got to find a place to stay." Maybe I can stay with Calvin. I gotta go see him, but...." She got bold. "Bunk them.

I'm going out. I ain't scared," but as she turned the knob to leave, she looked both ways. The coast is clear. Luckily she didn't have to go far since he lived right on McIllvain Street. She cold dashed to Calvin's girlfriend's house, walking so fast she walked out her shoes several times. She knocked on the door, looking over her shoulders, making sure nobody snuck up behind her. She heard his voice yell, "Who is it?"

Thank GOD he was home. "It's me, Calvin. She was so happy to see him when he opened the door.

"Hey Calvin."

"Hey Penny." "Come on in."

They hugged.

"What's up?"

"Oh nothing."

"Yes it is. I can hear it in your voice. Tell me."

"Guess what? I found an eviction notice on the door and it says I got a few days to get out."

"What?!!"

"Yeah. I need a place to stay. You think I can stay here?"

"I don't know, Penny."

Eyes all bucked out, she screams, "You don't know? Calvin, I need you! I don't have nowhere to stay!" She started to cry.

"Ok, Ok Penny. Let me run it by Trina and get back to you. What about your girls? What about Carla? Can't you stay with her?"

"I don't know. I was going to stop by her house when I leave here."

"Well, after I speak with Trina, I'll stop by the house and let you know."

As she was leaving, Trina came in the door.

"Hey Penny."

"Hey Trina. Alright Calvin, I'll see you later. Bye, Trina."

"See ya, Penny."

The door hadn't closed fast enough before Trina was asking, "What was she doing here?"

No good time like the present, he thought. "She stopped by to ask a favor."

"What's that?"

"Well, you know the situation. Now the landlord gave Penny a few days and then she's has to move out. You think she can stay here?"

"Stay here?! Are you serious? No!!!"

"Come on, Trina."

"No. You're living here on borrowed time yourself and now you want your sister living here? I don't think so."

"Trina, it'll be just for…"

Holding up her hand to stop him, "Didn't you hear what I said? No. As a matter of fact, Hell No!!!" She shouted as she went into the bedroom and slammed the door.

"Hey Carla!"

"Hey Penny."

"Girl, where you been? I haven't seen you in a minute. You been hiding?"

"No girl."

"Uh huh" … Carla heard about what happened to Mr. Blue and the makeshift deal Penny was involved in.

"What's been going on?"

"Oh, nothing much."

"How's your Mom?"

"She's doing. I'm trying to get up to see her. I think my Aunt Jane is going soon and I'll go with her."

"Okay. How you like living in the house by yourself?"

"It's creepy with nobody there, but me. You know, I gotta move out soon though, in a few days."

"Oh yeah?"

"I just left Calvin's and ask could I stay with him and Trina. I don't think that will happen. Trina's a trip and I'm not sure how long Calvin will be there himself."

"Wow."

"I didn't ask my Aunt Jane because her house is full."

"So, what are you going to do?"

"I don't know."

She looked at Carla. "Do you think your Mom's will let me stay with y'all for a little while?"

Before answering, Carla took on a faraway look thinking, "Well wonders never cease…here this chick always thought she was cute, Miss 500, talking about people like dogs, now look."

"Carla?"

Blinking fast, "Uh, I don't know Penny. I'll have to ask her, but I don't think it'll be a problem. Or so she thought, but…

"No, Carla!"

"Mom, she's needs a place to stay.

"What has that got to do with me?"

"She's my friend and I want to help her."

"They should have thought about that instead of running around with everybody else's man, especially her mother. What happen to all the money her Mom collected from all the men she dated?"

"Mom, Penny's not like that."

"The hell you say! I've seen that girl in action, the way she twists and turns. Penny is one of the biggest…"

"Mom!!" Carla had to bite the inside of her mouth to keep from laughing. She couldn't laugh too hard. She was no better than Penny. Maybe a little. Her mother would hit the ceiling if she knew about her "private" life.

"Penny will be in the street, beside if it was me, she would be there for me." She took a long pause.

"Mom?!!"

"For how long?"

"Until she can get herself together."

"That sounds like forever."

"Come on, Mom."

"Okay Carla, against my better judgement, she can stay, but if I even get an inkling she's up to no good, she's out."

"Thanks, Mom."

She didn't trust Penny from day one. Things were not gelling all that well lately between she and her husband and she didn't need this fast hussy in her house. I feel sorry for her, but I don't want that sizzling hot kitty cat around my house. I should have told Carla no, but I don't want the girl in the street."

Despite how she felt inside, she treated Penny like another daughter. Everything seems harmless at first. Everybody got along good, but as time went by subtle changes could be seen. Before, her husband couldn't wait until they were alone before he was pestering her for sex. This was a major problem in their marriage. She'd become somewhat frigid, uninterested.

"It's not like I don't enjoy it. I just don't enjoy it as much as he does." She didn't want her husband to poke her let alone take him for 'a ride'. The last time I let this man be with me, he beat and banged on my behind until it was so raw I couldn't stand to wash it. All I could do was 'hold it.' The whole time I gritted my teeth, wishing it was over soon. It's like he turns into a different person. Ever since Penny…Now, he doesn't bother me at all. Hmm, what's up with that?"

What don't come out in the wash comes out in the dryer.

Carla and her Mom were going out. They asked Penny to come, but she decided against it.

"Hey Penny, we're going shopping. You want to go?"

"No, I'll wait here." Carla's mother bristled when she heard the answer. Her husband was off from work today and she hadn't quite let go of her trust issues.

"Okay, well we won't be gone too long."

"Ok."

Looking in the mirror, Penny thought to herself while combing her hair, "Carla's Daddy is fine. I know he wants me. How I know? I've caught him watching me. I've played it off time and time again, but wow, he's fine. I can't do that," shaking her head back and forth. "I hope he don't try nothing. On second thought, I should have gone with Carla and her Mom. I think I better leave now and come back later."

Standing in the doorway, he called her name shaking her from her daydream.

"Hey Penny."

"Hey Mr. Sterling."

"Did I scare you?"

"No, not really."

"What are you doing?"

"Oh just getting ready to go out, go over town to browse, get some air."

"Need a ride."

"No that's alright."

"I don't mind."

"No, the air will do me good."

"Suit yourself."

DONNA EARL

He just stood there watching her. Suddenly he got this sheepish look on his face. She didn't like the look he gave her. He walked up behind her and put his arm around her waist.

"Please, Mr. Sterling," pushing his arm away. She turns to walk away he kisses her. She pushed him away and started to run out the door, but he wanted her and grabs her tighter.

"Mr. Sterling please."

"You know you want me."

"Please, Mr. Sterling" she said with urgency and fright in her voice. He forced her down on the bed. She was clawing at him, "Stop!! Stop!!"

Carla and her mother pulled up in front of the house. Her mother was so in a hurry to get home that when she parked the car she almost drove on the sidewalk.

"Mom, why are you rushing? Are you in a hurry?"

"Naw girl, it's the coffee."

Carla got out first on the passenger and rushed towards the front door. Getting out on the driver's side her mother calls her name, "Carla." This stopped her in her path.

"Ma'am?"

"Where are you going? We got bags."

"I know Mom, but I got to use the bathroom."

"Well hurry up and comeback. If Penny's home, tell her to come and help."

Hearing all this noise upstairs when she opens the front door, she races up the stairs. Carla's father was still pulling on Penny, trying to get at her when she walked in. Eyes as big as silver dollars she screamed, "Daddy!!"

"Carla!!"

"What's going on here?"

"It's not what you think baby girl."

"Carla, I'm sorry."

"Penny, I'm your friend. How could you do this?"

"Carla, I didn't do nothing! He came on to me!"

"Penny, you got to go!"

"It's not my fault Carla!"

Carla's Mom comes in the door with a bag of food and hears all this yelling upstairs. She dropped the bag in the floor and took off running up the stairs, taking two at a time. She was not prepared for what she saw.

"What the…" She saw the sheepish look on her husband's face, the look of a deer caught in the headlights look from Penny and the 'I can't believe this' look from Carla.

"I knew it!"

"Baby….!"

"Baby my behind. You've been foaming at the mouth since she's been here. I can't believe this!! In my house!! You stinking…" She went for Penny, grabbing her by the throat, choking her.

"Diane!! Diane, let go!!!"

Her fingers around Penny's throat was like a vice. It took a minute for husband to be able to pry them lose, pinning her arms behind her back.

"Mom!!!"

Jerking away from him, she screamed "Get off me!!!"

"Penny, get your things and get out!!'"

"Mrs. Sterling!!"

"Get out Penny!!!"

She turned to her husband, "As for you Tyrone, you can get out too!!!"

Payback is a bitch!!

Penny grabbed her things and ran out the house. She stopped at the corner and burst out crying.

"I didn't do nothing."

Since Carla lived on 9th and Caldwell Street, right around the corner from where she used to live, she walked back there and sat on the steps. "What do I do now?"

She then walked around to the "Wire" and went inside. Ms. Dot, her mother's co-worker had her back to the door.

"Hey, Ms. Dot."

She turned around to see who called her name. She was shocked to see who it was. It was Penny with bags and tear stain streaks on her face. From the look on her face she looked as if she had been crying.

"Uh oh," Dot thought. What done happened now? "Whatever it is, I'm don't want to know."

"Hey Penny." "How's your Mom?"

"Good."

She was careful not to ask too many questions. She learned if you ask too many questions you end up getting involved or writing a check.

"You okay?"

"Yeah, I'm okay. Can I use the phone?"

Looking around to make sure Ice wasn't around, she put the phone behind the bar on the ledge.

"Go ahead, but make it fast. You know how that bonehead is about using the phone." They both sniggled, at least Dot did, but Penny just smiled. Dot started wiping down the bar, leaving her alone for some privacy.

She dialled the number. The phone answered. "Hello Aunt Jane, its Penny."

"Hey Penny. What's up?"

"I need your help. I was staying with my friend Carla and I got put out."

"How'd that happen?"

"Her father came on to me and her Mom snapped."

"Where are you?"

"I'm at the old house."

"Stay right there. I'm coming to get you."

She hung up the phone and bid Ms. Dot goodbye and walked back to the house. She is sitting on the steps with her run over shoes, her fake raggedy Gucci bag and makeshift suitcase. No money to be fly and no friends. "Nobody wants you when you're down and out" by Bobby Womack is the song playing on the car radio as it drove by.

CHAPTER SEVENTY-ONE

I T HADN'T BEEN all gravy in this place. Sandy, Freda and Abby was cool, but she had an enemy. Francine, Frankie for short, was this one girl that tried her hand at disturbing Ruthie's groove. Since day one, Frankie tried to bully her on the slip tip, but Ruthie wasn't having it. She tried on several occasions to ignore her, but Frankie kept trying her patience. She spoke to her girls about her. They suggested she do like they do… ignore her. "Don't feed into her bullcrap." Ruthie did as they suggested, but at every turn Frankie was always following her and standing around watching her. She tried Ruthie one day in the cafeteria. In line for food, she felt hot breath on her neck. She turned around and… Frankie. Ruthie edged up a bit, and Frankie edged up a bit too. She blew hot air on Ruthie's neck again and that did it. Ruthie turned around and without speaking grabbed Frankie's finger and bend it backwards. She bended it more and more while staring in Frankie's eyes. Not once blinking. "Ow!! Ow!!" "Let go!!" "Let go!" Ruthie kept bending until Pop!! Frankie's finger was out of joint. She started dancing and jumping around holding her finger.

"What's going on here?" the counsellor shouted?

"She broke my finger!!"

"Ruth, you wait in your room while I take her to the infirmary."

Meeting Ruthie in her room, the counsellor asked, "Ruth did you do this?"

"Yes I did. She kept bothering me, following me around. I tried to ignore it, but then she started breathing on my neck in the food line."

"That's no reason for hurting her."

"A person has a breaking point and I tried, but…"

"Well, your privileges are suspended for thirty days and this will go on your record. If there aren't any more infractions, there's a possibility it will be erased. Understand?"

"Yes ma'am."

After that Frankie, stayed as far away from Ruthie as she could. Until...

Despite her beginnings, Ruthie had become a model to the other girls that had it worse. She completed her GED and enrolled in a work program inside. Michael, Justin, now walking up a storm, Aunt Jane, Barbara and Cece visited regularly. Ruthie noticed Cece had "buds." Her "dots" were beginning to shake as she walked. Rusty and Reese came too. Her family noticed a huge change in her, a change that Michael was falling in love with every time he visited. "I love you Ruthie," he would tell her and she would say the same to him.

Sitting in the TV room, the few educational programs she saw, her mind soaked up everything. She wanted to learn more. She read just about everything from the book cart. Sandy would tease her. "You're becoming a regular book worm."

"You should try it sometimes." They both laughed. Church on Sunday in the chapel was something she never missed. Mrs. Harvey even brought her a bible for a present.

"Ruthie, you got mail."

"Maybe it's from my Mom."

She grabbed the envelope. She notices that it does not have a return address. She turns it over and "hmmm, it's nothing on the back either, except a candy cane. "Candy cane" That's odd. I wonder... OMG!! Mr. Blue." She knew it was him. He always kept a dish of soft peppermint in the bat cave. She decides to open it.

"Hey, Ms. Pretty. Just a few words to say hello. I miss seeing your pretty face. I can't wait to continue our journey."

"Is he crazy?"

She didn't need to read another word. She crumbled the letter up and threw it in the trash...game over.

Graduation day is here. Ruthie was so excited, dancing around and around. "I'm leaving. Praise the Lord!!!"

"You're excited?" Sandy asked

"Yes!! Aren't you?"

"I'm excited about leaving, but I'll miss you."

They hug. With tears running down her face, "You have been there for me since day one."

"Don't cry, Ruthie, then you'll have me crying. "We've got to keep in touch."

"We will."

Ruthie was sitting on her bunk when Francine appeared in her doorway.

"What do you want? I'm not for your bull right now."

"Ruth, I want to say I'm sorry."

"Really now?"

"Can I come in?"

Ruthie scoots over as a sign to say it's okay. Francine walks in with her hands behind her back.

"I want to apologize to you."

"Oh yeah?"

"Yes."

"Tell me something. Why did you treat me so bad?"

"I was jealous of you."

"Jealous of me for what?"

"It's something about you. No matter what, you kept an upbeat, positive attitude. You did the time and not let the time do you. Just because you were in here, you were determined to do better. To see your family visit…I don't have much of a family."

"I'm sorry to hear that."

"Don't be. It's cool. You made friends. I went about it the wrong way…bullying. I tried to be like you. When I tried, it didn't work. I guess I stepped on too many toes." Tears fell from her eyes.

Ruthie hugged her. "Look Francine. I never had anything against you. I just didn't like the way you treated me."

"Well, starting today, I'm going to try and treat people differently."

"That's a start."

Francine smiled. Getting up to leave, she said "Good luck to you Ruth."

"Right back at you."

Tears flowed down at the ceremony of completion. Everybody was there. Looking in the crowd, she saw Michael, Justin, Cece, Barbara, Aunt Jane, Rusty and Reese even Uncle Louie and Aunt Evelyn came as a surprise. Calvin's not here. Neither is Penny. Where's she?

CHAPTER SEVENTY-TWO

L IVING DOWNSTAIRS IN the basement, she finally was at peace.

Upon entering her domain, Aunt Jane laid down the laws, "Don't be coming in my house all hours of the night. You do not have a maid service. Put stuff back where you got it. Everything has a home, eat what I cook or don't eat at all," and on and on. She even sang a song about it. "You don't have to eat it, you don't have to eat it, you don't have to eat it now." Penny really didn't mind. She didn't miss her old life, but Mr. Blue frequently popped up in her mind. She wanted to know how he was doing. Graduation day for Ruthie was today, but the guilt of everything, not going to see her in the Center, kept her from going. She didn't want to face her. Since everybody was out she decided to catch the bus over town to the 'Bootery' to get a pair of shoes. Something told her not to go, but she wanted to get out. After she brought them and left the store, she ran smack into Harlan. He was leaving Cody's Record Shop which is right next door to the Bootery. As he walking to his car, he saw her. Penny was visibly scared and he knew it.

"Hey Penny."

Voice shaking, "Hey Harlan."

"Where are you going?"

"Home."

"Want a ride?"

"No."

"Sure you do. Get in the car."

"That's alright."

"GET IN THE CAR!"

She knew he was serious, so she got in the car. He started the car and put it in gear. Then he snatched it back in park and turned it off. He pulled out a gun and started handling it, pointing it at her. She almost peed on herself.

"You know I ought to kill you for what you did. If it wasn't for Mr. Blue, I would have done it long time ago, but. Just so you know, he ain't in the game no more. He left everything to me and Squeak to do what we see fit, so you ain't got him to keep me from leaping on your ass. I'm going to cut you a break this time. I suggest you never let me catch you again. It may be different next time. Now, get out of my car."

She hesitated.

"NOW!!!"

As she was getting out, he palmed her butt and squeezed it hard. The car turned over and sped down the street. "I've got to find me another place to shop," she said as she practically ran home. From now on, I'm going down Delaware to the "Dry" or better yet, find me somewhere else to live."

CHAPTER SEVENTY-THREE

L IFE ON THE outside couldn't be sweeter. Through the program in Juvey and with Ms. Harvey's help, she landed a job as a receptionist at the Cohen and Lawson Law Firm in Chester on 5th Street after working for the Water Company for about 6 months. It's been a year and she kept thinking how life has changed for her. Sitting at her desk, she thought it was ironic that she would get a job at a law firm with a Juvey record. Mrs. Harvey must have had to pull some strings and some more shit. Whatever it was, Thank God. Being with Michael and Justin, who was a busybody now, getting into everything, was like a family. They even talked marriage. "In time Ruthie. In time."

CHAPTER SEVENTY-FOUR

I T'S BEEN A minute but, Judge Andrew Lord is still pissed at
Sheila. He had Beulah's legal jacket in his briefcase. He put in a
request to have the case document sent to him. His lady friend, Juanita,
was head of the department and she was sweet on him. She was more
than willing and able. It didn't take much to sway her, dinner and a
little bit of "grownup."

"Come on Juanita, help me out."

"What you gonna give me?" she asked with a seductive slur in her
voice.

"I got something for you. Hmmm...let me check my pockets. Here
it is."

"You're so silly."

"You like it."

"Well, I'll see what I can do."

At home, with Beulah's case folder in hand, he studied it with a
fine tooth comb. He wanted to see if there was something he could do
to switch this thing around. "There's gotta be something. I got a few
favors coming to me. I need to..." he picked up the phone and dialled
the number.

"Hey, Richard."

"What's up, boy?"

"I need to talk to you and Sherman about something."

"About?"

I got this cold case and I need your advice."

"Ok, but what it's all about?"

"Beulah Walters."

"Oh yeah, I remember you mentioning something about it one time
or another. What's up?"

"I believe her legal counsel threw her rights away with plea bargaining trying to hide the fact she couldn't keep her "business" to herself. I don't want to get into it over the phone. You think you can stop by the crib?"

"When?"

"Tomorrow. I've already checked with Sherman. He's down."

"Cool. A'ight man. "See you tomorrow."

His place is sharp, dining room chair cushions matching the drapes, hardwood floors shining like new money, etc. He kept his place spotless, neat as a pen. He was expecting company so he threw together a little something something to eat. It was simmering on the stove. He has jazz playing, filling the room with soothing sounds by Miles Davis and the like. The file was spread out on the dining room table. Ding dong. He opens the door. Richard was the first person he saw.

"Hey, what's up killer?" greeting him with a soul man handshake.

"Hey Sherman," greeting him with a half hug and fluttering fingertips. "What's up man? Come on in."

"Don't mind if we do."

"Have a sit down. Something to drink?"

"What you got?"

"What you want?"

"Well, Richard says, I'll have Remy on the rocks."

"Sherman, what's your poison?"

"What kind of wine you got?"

"Cuvasion."

"I'll try that."

"Coming right up. Clink clink of the ice cubes and the uncorking of the wine. Here you go fellas."

"Thanks. So what's this all about?"

"Come over here and check this out…"

CHAPTER SEVENTY-FIVE

IN THE REC room, Bunchie was sitting sideways because her "area" was still sore. After her last cigarette paid date, Bunchie had enough. "This is it. I can't take it no more. My cootie pie will never be the same."

Fats and Trish, a potential customer, was over in the corner having an "I wanna get at that" session. Taffy was anticipating her date she had just paid for, rubbing her hands together. "Let's iron out the details."

Bunchie got up to walk back to her cell and Fats noticed her leaving the room. She told Trish, "Hold up. Let me get at Ms. Girl real quick to let her know what's up."

Fats caught up to Bunchie blocking her path. Pointing in her direction, "Trish over there wants to meet up with you later."

Bunchie turned to walk away.

Fats grabbed her arm. "Where you think you going? I said..."

Bunchie snatched her arm away and said, "I'm not doing it."

Mad at the possible loss of her fee, Fats pushed her.

Bunchie pushed back.

Fats reared up, "Oh so it's like that? Let's do this."

"Fine with me."

She went at Bunchie with both hands reaching for her throat. Bunchie swung, but not empty handed. She had a homemade blade tucked in the sleeve her shirt. Her swing left a nice clean, but deep cut on the side of Fats' face. Fats grabbed her face. Trish reached in her socks and pulled out a homemade blade. She never left home without it and threw it to Fats.

"Oh. It's on" she said with blood dripping down her face and on to her shirt.

All the other inmates chanted, "Fight!! Fight!"

The correctional Officers saw what was going on, sounded the alarm and rushed the room like locust. They were a little late because the fight was in full swing.

Bunchie swung again, but this time she missed. Fats swung and caught Bunchie by the throat. Bunchie grabbed her throat and dropped to her knees. She twitched and gurgled as her life spilled out on the floor. Lights out!!

CHAPTER SEVENTY-SIX

"HOW WAS WORK today, baby?"
"It was good, but busy."
"Oh yeah?"
"Yeah. That phone never stops ringing, but you know, it's much better since he's not yelling."
"What do you mean?"
"I never told you, but, when I first started, he would bark orders at me. He would scream at me every day. No matter what I did, file, answer the phone, whatever it was, it wasn't good enough."
"Why didn't you tell me?"
"I'm a big girl Michael. I had to figure it out for myself. I remembered a scripture given to me by Mrs. Harvey, II Thes. 1-6."
"What does it say?"
"It says "GOD will trouble those who trouble you and give you reprieve from what troubles you. That scripture made me forgive him because I realized that GOD had my back as long as I was obedient and let him fight for me."
"Is it better now?"
"Yeah, after we had a talk but it's this other person who I can't figure out. Her name is June."
"Oh? Why's that?"
"She follows me around and I catch her watching me sometimes. "As a matter of fact, it's all the time."
Laughing, "Maybe she like you."
Giving him the sideway look, "Whatever Michael. What's for dinner?"
Cleaning the kitchen after dinner, Penny was washing dishes. Aunt Jane was busying watching TV. It was almost 6:59 p.m. and she herself was writing down the Lottery numbers as they were being called. "Aunt Jane".
"Ssh, the numbers' on."

When the final number was called, she turned to her, "What is it baby?"

"I want to go and see Mom."

"You do?"

"Yeah."

"That's funny, the last time I couldn't get nobody to go with me. I had to end up going by myself. What's the sudden change?"

"I don't know what it is. I just want to see her."

"Okay, well the next time I'm going. Alright now. I'm going to hold you to it. Have you talked to your brother?"

"Yeah. He's working at Ship Ahoy, across from the Upland Shopping Center, where the Thrift Drug's is."

"I know where that is. Good for him."

"You know he's not living with Trina anymore."

"Honey, hush!! So, where's he living?"

"Over by the "High" in those apartment across the street on 9th and Barclay. It's a converted house turned into an apartment building. He's living on the top floor."

"How you find out?"

"He called here last week."

"Oh."

"We've got to go and visit him."

The phone rings…Deda aka Linda, her daughter, called her from the living room. "Mom, telephone!"

"Who is it?"

"I don't know."

"Hello? This is she. OMG!!! OH NO!!"

Sitting in the Commanders' office, Beulah just received the bad news.

"My sister's dead?!!!"

"Yeah Beulah."

"How?"

"There was a fight over in POD F and your sister was killed."

"OMG!! What happened?"

"Her cellmate said she and Fats got into it. Quiet as it kept, she said it was rumored that Fats was pimping her. She said she was not sure about it, but she heard about it."

"Did y'all know this was going on?"

"We hear things, but couldn't find any proof."

"Y'all did not try and stop it?!!!"

"How could we? Beulah, your sister never said anything. Without her talking, our hands were tied."

"My sister," she cried with her head in her hands.

"No! No!" Aunt Jane was screaming. Penny dropped the dishes in the sink and ran in the living room.

"What's wrong Aunt Jane?"

Shedding tears and almost unable to speak – "I've got bad news."

"What?'

"It's your Mom."

"What?"

"She's dead."

"Get out of here. That's got to be a mistake."

"It's not a mistake baby. That was the Pennsylvania Department of Corrections on the phone. She was killed by another inmate."

"Noooooooooo!!" Penny started jumping up and down, screaming, "Mommy!!!" Aunt Jane jumped out of her seat and grabbed her. She pounded on Aunt Jane's back as she held her in an embrace. "She's all I had."

"You have me baby. You have me."

Calvin came home from work, tired and hungry. He took his coat off and sat on the couch to catch his breath. He noticed the answering machine flashing two messages. 'Hmm…I missed 2 calls.' He pushed the play button as he went in the kitchen to get a beer.

"Calvin, baby. It's your Aunt Jane I need you to call me." The next message. "Calvin, it's your Aunt Jane again. Call me, it's important." "What's going on?" He sucks his teeth, "she probably don't want nothing. I'm tired. I'll go down there tomorrow."

"Hey Aunt Jane."

"Hey Michael."

"Is Ruthie there?"

"Yeah, hold on. Ruthie, it's your Aunt. She don't sound too good."

"Hey Aunt Jane. What's up?"

"Ruthie, I got some bad news."

Her heart skipped a beat thinking it's about her Mom. "What's wrong?"

"Your Aunt Bunchie is dead."

"What?!!!"

"We just got the call."

Ruthie was outdone. She had her issues with Aunt Bunchie, but she didn't want her dead.

"What happened?"

"They said she got into a fight with an inmate name Francine and was killed."

"Omigosh NO! How's Penny?"

"A wreck. She's in shock. I made her go upstairs and lay down."

"Does Calvin know?"

"Not yet. I left him two messages. I'm waiting for him to call me back."

"So, how are you?"

"Angry."

"Angry? Why?"

"Because I didn't go see her like I should have."

"Have you heard from Mom?"

"Not yet, but I'm sure I will."

"Well, you get some rest. I'll be there tomorrow."

"Okay Ruthie. Love you."

"Love you too. Goodnight."

Ding Dong. It's Calvin standing on Aunt Jane's porch.

"Get in here boy," she said while hugging him.

Ruthie and Penny both yelled, "Hey Calvin."

"Hey, y'all."

"I've been trying to reach you." He sat down.

"OK, I'm here now. What's wrong?"

"I got bad news."

"What?"

"I got a call from the prison. They called to tell me that your Mom was killed by another inmate."

Calvin blinked. "What happened?"

"The Department of Corrections called. From what I hear, from what they tell me, she got into a fight with this woman name Francine.

Then I talked to your Aunt Beulah. From what she heard, your Mom was being passed around in prison by this woman, something that's been happening since day one. She and this woman got into a knife fight and her throat was slashed."

Calvin stood up. He walks back towards the door like he was leaving. He turned around.

"So they turned her out in prison? Oh well."

"How can you be so cold?"

"No disrespect Aunt Jane, but she tore her clothes with me when she extorted that money and tried to blame it on me. She wasn't nothing but a low down...."

"Calvin!! I am not going to sit here and listen to you talk about your mother, my sister like that."

"Then stand up!!"

"What did you say boy?"

"Aunt Jane, if you lived with her like me, like us, you would understand. All she did was cuss us out and screw men. She was like a bus. All the men had to do is stand and wait, pile on, pay their fare, ride, pull the cord, and pile off. She'd sometimes came home from the bar so tore up she be sandpapering the wall, barely able to stand up. If it wasn't for us she would be...."

"It couldn't have been that bad."

"Yes, it was," Penny confirmed.

Calvin continued talking, screaming by now. "That's how we got sucked into the life of drugs, in the game. How you think we paid the bills? We got involved because that's how we ate!!" He burst out crying. Voice shaking and full of hurt, "I started dealing with Mr. Blue on account of her. I would peddle his drugs, to keep a roof, lights, food, clothes. The kids teased us constantly, calling us dirty girts, nappy head and any other cruel name they could think of. How do you think that made us feel? That woman didn't raise us - we raised ourselves!!" Penny, with tears in her eyes, went over and hugged her brother. Together, they cried in each other's arms...

The money was hard to come by, but they managed to scrape up enough money to have a memorial service for Bunchie. The best they could do was have her cremated. The memorial was held at Lundy's Funeral Home on 10th and Lamokin Streets. There wasn't enough

DONNA EARL

money to put a notice in the local paper, "The Rag" so most of the people who knew of her passing, found out through word of mouth. Diamond Ice and Dot, her co-workers from the "Wire" were in attendance as well as the immediate family. Beulah wanted to come, but the program that allowed prisoners to attend family funerals was terminated due to manpower and funding. The day of the funeral, she stayed to herself, not saying anything to anybody not even her girl Annette.

At the end of the memorial, the urn with Bunchie's ashes was given to her children. The Funeral Director handed the urn to Penny. She refused it. He then handed it to Calvin. He took it and said thank you. He turned it over and over in his hands. His mind told him to throw it in the trash, but his heart wouldn't let him. No matter what, she was still his Mom and he loved her.

At the repast, Ruthie was sitting at the table nursing a headache. Penny walked up to her.

"Hey girl."

Rubbing her temples, "Hey."

"What's wrong, you alright?"

"I'm good, I just got a headache. I took two aspirins." Penny turned to leave, but Ruthie stopped her.

"Where are you going?" She patted the seat next to her. "Come sit down and talk to me. I've been wanting to talk to you anyway."

Penny hesitated and then sat down.

"This is the second, no the third, time I've seen you since I've been out.

"I had a lot on my mind, plus…"

"What's going on, Penny?"

Her eyes fill up, "Ruthie I couldn't come. I couldn't face you because…"

"Because what?"

"It was all my fault."

"What are you talking about?"

"The day you went to Philly."

Ruthie stared at her, listening, in disbelief.

"See, I knew about the "Task Force" on Mr. Blue's case."

"You knew?!!! Why didn't you…"

"Hold up Ruthie and let me explain. I'm sorry Ruthie."

"Sorry? Sorry? Is that all you have to say?"

"I was scared."

"Penny, I did time in Juvey because of that!!! I can't believe…
Ruthie got up from the table and started walking away.

"Ruthie, please forgive me."

"I don't want to hear it."

"Wait!"

"There's more."

"What now?"

"I may have to leave town."

"Oh really? Why is that?"

"I set up a drug bust for Andrew and it fell through. Now, Harlan,
Stein, Squeak, especially Harlan, want me dead."

"Oh my gosh!!"

"Yeah. Mr. Blue is no longer in the game so he can't help me
anymore. Harlan and Squeak are now running things. Harlan told me
if he ever catches me in and around Chester again, he may kill me."

Forgetting her anger, Ruthie felt sorry for her. "Oh Penny!" "Where
are you going to go?"

"Who knows, but it has to be far and out of their reach."

Unless she'd become invisible, they were bound to find out. Chester
ain't but so big.

Keeping their ears to the street, Harlan and Squeak found out where
Penny is staying, at least the area, hoping to get at her. Since finding
out the general area of Penny's whereabouts, they cruised past the house
several times hoping to see her. They parked on the corner of third and
Wilson. Perfect bird's eye view. Penny comes out the house to the car
to get her purse she mistakenly left in Aunt Jane's car.

"There she go, man."

They creep slowly as if to turn down her street, giving Harlan enough
time to get in position. He aimed his gun, get ready get set…. then Cece
runs out the house. Dag!!! Banging his hand on the dashboard. Go!!!
They made an about face and sped down third.

Penny saw them. She was sure of it. She knew the car. She shook so
bad she could hardly catch her breath. Where is that piece of paper with
the number on it? Here it is. She dials the number. It rang three times
before it was answered. "Hello. Hello Daddy, its Penny."

CHAPTER SEVENTY-SEVEN

ANDREW, SHERMAN AND Richard struck up a deal that would allow Beulah a possible early release. They contacted the Prosecutor, as well as the Judge that presided over the case. They were all in agreement. They just needed to speak with Beulah to get a full understanding of what went on that night and other details.

"I know just the right person."

"Beulah Walters, you have a visitor."

She heard her name announced on the PA system.

"Who is it? Maybe it's my kids. I sure would like to see them."

The Correctional Officer met her at her cell and prepared her. She escorted her to the visiting area. When she saw who it was, she turned around.

"Take me back."

"What's wrong?"

"Take me back!!!"

"She refused to see me."

"Do you blame her? Go back. You screwed her. You fix it."

CHAPTER SEVENTY-EIGHT

"Y'ALL NEED TO give the Lord some of your time," Michael's Mom screamed at them. She was dressed and on her way to church. Penny wanted to go, but as she lifted her head off the pillow, it seems like it was too heavy. It felt like her head was full of water. "I can't. What is wrong with me?"

CHAPTER SEVENTY-NINE

"HEY BABY GIRL!!"
"Don't baby girl me, Daddy."
"Look Penny, if you are calling with an attitude, we can hang this phone up right now. Now, what's it going be?"

Silence.

"How are you?"

"Ok, daddy."

"You don't sound good. What's wrong Penny?"

"I don't know. You missed out on so much of my life Daddy. So much has happened."

"Talk to me..."

Ding dong.

"Wait a minute Daddy, there's somebody at the door."

Looking through the curtains, oh, it's a delivery guy from TLC Cutthroat Delivery Service. Hold on."

She laid the receiver down, yelling, "I'm coming." He had his back to her so she couldn't see his face, holding a make believe package.

Penny opens the door.

"Yes?"

He turns to face her with a .357 magnum pointed at her.

"No!!!"

Bang Bang!!!

Her father hears the shots on the phone and he screams her name. "Penny!!!!"

EPILOGUE

WOW, TIME SURE does pass fast. I'm 23 years old now. So many good years were lost trying to be grown. In the 8 1/2 years I been in Chester, I've been a junkie, a drug runner and spent time in juvenile. I never expected, in my wildest dreams, that my life would have this much drama. All is not lost though. On the upside, I went from being a receptionist, to a secretary and now that I have my certificate for a paralegal, I received a promotion on the job. I had another baby, a girl name Julia and now I have my Mom back in my life. When I look back over these times in my life, I know now that GOD was there all the time.

On the downside, I lost my aunt and my cousin. Aunt Bunchie's funeral was short, but Penelope aka Penny's, was packed. I looked around the room and saw all her friends and some enemies, but a familiar face was hiding among them. Mr. Blue! My stomach did a flip flop when I saw him. He still had the power to make me nervous. Seeing him, made the tape in my mind click on and show me the life I left behind. I quickly turned around and faced the front. Moments later, I half turned back around to see if he was still there, but he was gone. To this day, her killer/killers have not been found, but we all got an idea who done it, at least Calvin does. The sad thing is we can't prove it. No proof. Just hearsay. Calvin told me that Penny got in his ear about Harlan threatening her. As her brother, he stepped to him.

"Yo man, what's this I hear about you threatening my sister?"

"What you talking about Calvin?"

"Penny told me that you threatened her over town telling her the next time you see her and all this shit."

"Calvin man, you know what your sister did and there's a street tax that needs to be paid and sometimes money won't do."

"Please man I ain't trying to get into anything with you, but that's my sister. She ain't know."

"Ain't nobody gonna touch your sister man."

"Yeah, A'ight."

"For real, for real Harlan, don't touch my sister."

"I hear you."

Calvin didn't believe a word he said, but what else could he do? As Calvin walked away, Harlan mumbled under his breath, "Rock-a-bye baby."

Now I'm sick again with these headaches, and I don't know why. Early on, I was getting headaches every now and then and then they went away. Now they are back. At first, taking aspirin would do the trick, but now they've become worse, nearly blinding sometimes. Probably from work, the kids and married life. Didn't I tell you? Yes, Michael and I got married! We went to Maryland and got hitched. A sweet ceremony, just the five of us; Michael and me, Justin, who's 8, Julia, who's 4 now and his Mom for a witness. My Mom couldn't go. She can't leave the state. That's part of her release/probation.

My Mom and I, we've gotten closer since she's come home. We see each other often with her living off of the Avenue of the States in the Hillside Rooming House and Michael and I living in the area ebonically called "Holy City" on 8th Street. She loves my kids to pieces. Her eyes light up when she visits with them and especially when Justin and Julia call her Mom-Mom. We talk about everything; about the time Daddy got us lost in DC or the time we went to Cape May and I got stung on the lip by a bee, but when I come anywhere near the night she and Daddy got into it, she skips the subject. I guess the wound is too deep and scab hurts too much to try and pull off. I will not push. When's she ready, I'm ready.

"Ruthie, you need to go to the doctor."

"I'm fine, Michael."

"No you are not!! Look at you. Dark circles under your eyes. Every time I see you, you are moving slow like you're in pain."

"I just have a headache."

"These headaches are coming way too often to be normal."

"I'm okay," downing two more aspirin.

"Whatever you say, Ruthie. You need to see somebody and you are next week."

The look in his eyes said he meant business.

DONNA EARL

"Yes Michael, I'm going next week."

"Damn straight you are."

I woke up screaming. My heart was beating a mile a minute, real fast. It felt as if my heart was about to jump out my chest. It took a minute for me to figure out where I was. When the room came into focus, I breathed a sigh of relief when I realized I was in bed beside Michael, who is staring at me.

"Ruthie what's wrong?"

"I had a bad dream."

"What was it about?"

"My Mom."

"What about her?"

"I dreamed my Mom died."

"She's okay Ruthie. It was a dream."

"I know Michael, but it felt real."

"It's alright. Come on and lay back down."

"Okay, but I'm calling her first thing."

He knew the thing to calm her. Ruthie, scooting closer and kissing her neck, since we're up...giggling, "You are so ignorant. Come on now, stop ...Don't... Stop...Oh Michael."

Ring..........

'Hello."

"May I speak with Ruth Walters?"

"This is she."

"This is Clarice Moore."

"Who?"

"Ms. Moore, your mother's neighbor who lives across the hall from her. I'm calling because they just took your Mom to Taylor Hospital."

"What?!!! What happened?"

Ruthie instantly got dizzy, dropped the phone and nearly fainted. Michael, alarmed, grabbed her and made her sit down.

"Gimme the phone!! Hello this is her husband, Michael. What's going on?"

"This is Ms. Moore and they just carted her mother to the hospital."

"What happened?"

"Well sir. She came to my door beating and banging saying she didn't feel good and she was out of breath. I told her to come in and sit down and try to calm down. She sat, but she couldn't keep still. She said she didn't feel any better. I asked her if she wanted me to call 911 and she said yes. At first, the fire department came, then the ambulance showed up. They put her one of those heart machine and then gave her oxygen. After that they strapped her on one of those wheeling chairs and took her to the waiting ambulance. I walked outside with her and that's when she asked that I call you. Then they took her away."

"Thank you, Ms. Moore. We are on our way." Hanging up the phone, he turned asking, "You okay?"

"Yeah Michael. Just overwhelmed by the phone call."

"Maybe you should rest first before…"

"No. We need to go now!"

"Ok then, lets' go."

"Wait a minute, before we go, I need to call Aunt Jane to let her know." Watching her on the phone, in his mind Michael is thinking, "There is something wrong with Ruthie. Something just ain't right."

In the ICU, it's like another world in there.

"We're here to see Beulah Walters."

"She's resting, but you may go in."

We all started towards Mom's room. Ms. Twala Newson, RN, put a wrench in that plan.

"Hold up. Wait a minute. Only 3 people at a time could see her."

"Please, can we all go in? She would like that."

She thought for a minute. In a hushed voice, she said, "Okay, we'll make an exception this time, but for only 30 minutes."

"Thank you."

We each took our turn visiting with mom, even Cece. With all the noises from the machines she was afraid at first, but after some coaxing from Barbara, she did her part. It was good to see Rusty and Reese. I tell you, Reese looked like he had been "pop skulling" all night. Instead of his eyes being red, they looked orange. He needs to give that liquor a break. To not tire her out, the nurse peeked her head in and told us the visiting hours were just about over.

"Sorry to interrupt, but visiting hours are over in about 5 minutes."

"Thank you."

DONNA EARL

Something we use to do around the dinner table, we held hands to prepare for prayer. Just as Rusty parted his lips to speak, Reese kicked in. "Bow your heads. Heavenly Father. This is the Walters Family. We come to you in the name of your son Jesus Christ. Embrace this family in your peace, strengthen us where we are weak. Bless your daughter, our Mom, in the only way you can." Have your way in this situation. Any way you bless us LORD we are truly satisfied. In Jesus name we pray, AMEN."

We embraced each other and then said out good byes to Mom, telling her 'Love you' as we filed out of her room one by one. I was last to leave and she grabbed my hand and held it tight. She lifted her hand to the mask and lifted it off her face for a split second. With gravel in her throat she said "I love you." "Love you too Mom."

I went to Dr. Trimble's office and I explained to her what I was feeling. She poked and prodded me in every way possible. She noticed my blood pressure was up and warned that I needed to relax. She checked my heart rate and everything was fine. She looked in my eyes and a look of concern crossed her face.

"What's wrong?" I asked.

"I notice your pupils are dilated. How's your vision?"

"Blurred sometimes."

"I am going to send you to get a MRI."

"Ok. I'll make an appointment."

"No, I think I want you to go now."

"What's going on, doctor?"

"Don't be alarmed. I know of some possibilities, but I need the MRI results first. I'll call ahead and let them know you are on your way."

On the 3rd day of Mom's hospital stay, the tide had changed. The minute I stepped in her room, it felt different. What the hell happened? She was just talking and laughing just yesterday. Today, she is quiet, breathing heavy and the look in her eyes said she was slipping away. She didn't have too much to say. She answered what was asked of her, but she didn't hold her side of the conversation. I felt as if I was talking to myself, so I decided to leave.

"Mom, I'm gonna go now."

"No Ruthie stay. I want to tell you something."

"Mom, I'll be back tomorrow."

"No, sit!" pointing at the chair!

"Okay."

She just stared at me.

"Over and over again, you've been asking me about the night your Daddy died. Well, Ruthie I'm ashamed to say it, but to tell you the truth I halfway meant to do it."

My eyes got big, but I didn't stop her from talking. I felt if I interrupted her I wouldn't get the full story, so I kept my mouth closed.

"I had got tired of that man treating me like a piece of gum on the bottom of his shoes. He was running on me, staying out all hours, talking about he had to work late, lying about overtime. His co-workers turned him out, had him in Chester either at the Town Bar, The Bonnets, The Rainbow or out Media at the Blue Magic Inn."

"How you know all that?"

"Your Aunt Bunch told me all about it. She was out there catting around. And…"

"What Mom?"

"It all begin one night when you were, oh, I'd say about 6 or7 years old maybe a little older." "You came to me and told me your Daddy was touching you kinda funny in the area of your "pocketbook. You remember that I always told you to keep your pocketbook closed and never let anybody go in it."

"Yes, I remember. I've squashed that memory of him doing that until now. My mind drifts. I hated to see him coming. I would tense up. When he called himself washing me up I would push his hand away. I would scratch and fight him something terrible. Water would be all over the floor. Mom would come in. "Ruthie, why is this water all over the floor?" It got so bad I hated to be by myself when my Mom would go out. "Ruthie, what is wrong with you?" I couldn't take it anymore so I told. My daydream ended when I heard Mom calling my name….

"Ruthie?"

"Huh?"

"Girl, you didn't hear a word I said."

"What you say?"

"I said how you had the nerve to tell me something like that, floored me. So I asked you to repeat it again and you did with a straight face. I grabbed and hugged you tight, telling you that I believe you. I told you

I would take care of it and Daddy will never do anything like again. I'd already stop giving up the "good goods" long time ago after watching him in action with other women. I didn't trust him anymore. I wasn't about to just lay there and let him give me VD!!! Besides, Peter started spending more times on his knees than standing up, if you get my drift. He couldn't even hop up and say good morning."

Laughing, "Mom you something else!!"

She smiled at me, "Girl, don't play with me. Besides, your Aunt Bunchie would tell me she'd see him out winding and grinding on other women too. The thought occurred to me that she may have been sneaking around with him herself. He had already..."

"Already what Mom?"

"Nah, that's okay. I said enough. It ain't good to talk bad about the dead like that, but seriously, I would never think he was that hard up to start fooling with his daughter. That night, after you told me, I went to your Daddy and calmly asked him about it. He denied it up and down. That girl is lying. I said "Samuel, I'm not gonna say I don't believe it. As a matter of fact, I do. The only thing is I didn't see you do it. He got to ranting and raving and before I knew it, I grabbed that man in his collar and told him, with my teeth gritted, "Let me tell you something. If I ever catch you with my own two eyes, even smell it in the air that you're screwing around with my daughters, your black ass will be dead before the Lord gets the news and that ain't no stage joke. You understand me? He could tell I meant business. He snatched away from me and walked out. "From that day on, I didn't have no problems out of him."

"Why did you stay with him?"

"I stayed for the sake of my kids as dumb as that sounds. He was the breadwinner in the house and he knew I depended on him to keep myself and you kids with a roof. I couldn't do it by myself on a nurse's aide salary."

"But Mom, if that is your reason for what you did, why didn't you defend yourself at trial?"

"Nobody knew what went down between us. I never told a soul. I don't know Ruthie. I guess I felt it was easier on everybody. Ruthie, it nearly ate me alive every time I looked at him, sitting there thinking his feet didn't stink...serving that man's dinner on TV trays...too good to eat with the rest of us at the table."

"I don't blame you Mom. You're a stronger woman than I thought you were."

"Baby, I'm tired now. I'm going to take a nap."

'Alright sleeping beauty. I'm gonna go so you can rest. Thanks for telling me. I love you Mom."

"I love you too baby."

She snuggled down in the bed and pulled the covers up. I looked back at her as I was walking out the door. I waved and she winked. My face smiled and so did my heart.

It had been about a week and the results were finally in.

"Ruth, this is doctor Trimblet. I have your results and I would like to see you in my office. I have an opening on Friday around 11:00. It's important I see you."

This was the message left on the answering machine. After hearing it, my face flushed and my heart skipped a beat. Talking to myself, calm down. It's nothing. I'm not going to tell Michael until after I see the doctor. No need to worry him.

Friday, I HATE FRIDAYS!!!

Mom was released from the hospital and the doctor didn't want her by herself so Michael and I insisted she stay with us. All the family visited at my house including Rusty and Reese. We told stories of back in the day to make her laugh, to lift her spirits including the one about the lie detector test.

"The lie detector test? I never heard that one. Tell it to me."

Reese told the story. "Rusty and I were young bucks at the time. Ronnie, Hardy and Lil Jessie were old heads on the street. They played a trick on us. They had me and Rusty in the garage We wanted to hang out with them so bad. So, they had us sitting on these metal milk crates. One end of the jumper cables was connected to the crates and the other part was in their hands." They threated to electrocute us if we told a lie. We were sitting on the milk crates crying!! We thought we were going to die. They asked us a question and we'd answer. They ran it across something and it didn't do anything. Then they asked again and we told them something that wasn't true. They ran it across again and all these sparks started flying we just knew we were electrocuted. I cried out Mom!!!"

My Mom was laughing so hard she had tears running out her eyes. "That's what you two get, always doing something."

Mom stayed with us for about three (3) weeks. My doctor's appointment is today and I hate to leave her here by herself. I know, I'll ask her to go with me to the doctors. She could really use the fresh air.

"Mom, I'm going to go to my doctor's appt. You want to go with me?"

"Why? Michael not going with you?"

Lying, "He couldn't get off. I told him that was okay. I'll just go by myself and fill him in later."

"No baby. I'll stay here. My stories are about to come on and I don't want to miss nothing. You know Fridays is when it gets good."

"Ok Mom. My appointment shouldn't take long. I'll be back in about an hour."

"Okay. Bring me back a hoagie, a special with everything sweet, oil and vinegar. Also, I want a bag of Herr's plain and an orange soda."

"Is that all?"

"No, bring me back some cat cookies."

Laughing, "Are you sure you should be eating them?"

"No, but I got a taste for one of those bad boys right now. It's been a while."

"Alright see you later."

"Ruth, have a seat. Where's your husband?"

"He couldn't make it."

"Maybe we can schedule it when he can come with you."

"No, I'll tell him when he gets home from work."

"I'd rather tell you and your husband together."

"It's okay."

"Well, I have your results here and I'm afraid I have bad news."

Driving home was a nightmare. Tears falling from my eyes was making it hard for me to see. "What do I do? I know I need to tell Michael. He is going to flip for not telling him about the appointment and lying. It's treatable so she says. OMG, my babies…"

I got home safely despite crying all the way. Thank GOD. Wiping my face…. oh crap. I forgot Mom's hoagie. Oh well, she'll have to do without it today. I can hear the TV through the door. Why is it so loud?

Mom!! Mom, I'm back. Mom!! Walking through the house, where is she? Oh there she is. She's still where I left her, on the couch sleeping. Watching her stories, she says…yeah right. How can she sleep with all that noise? Turning the TV down, shaking her "Mom I'm back. Mom!! OMG MOM!!!!!!!!"

A week later and I still haven't told Michael. Mom's service is 11:00 a.m. and the kids are up and making way too much noise and my head is pounding. I can hear them over the water in the shower. "Dag nabbit. They are going to shut up. I swung that bathroom door open ready for war.

"Can't you keep them QUIET?!!!"

"Ruthie, why are you hollering like that?"

"I'm sorry Michael. I got a lot on my mind with Mom's funeral and with me…. nothing."

"Whoa wait, with you? "What does that mean? Talk to me Ruth." "You heard something?"

Tears filled up in my eyes.

"What's going on?"

"Michael, I…" Knock Knock.

"Come on y'all the cars here."

We stood staring into each other's eyes.

The day was sunny, but a little cloudy. Perfect example of how I was feeling as we rode to the church. As we walked in, I noticed some of Mom's old co-workers, neighbors and some of the neighborhood kids we grew up with. Even Uncle Louie and Aunt Evy were there. So good to see them. Ok, here we go. There she is…Mom. Michael, my hero, had my back. Aunt Jane was right behind me, crying as loud as she could. Her husband, Uncle Frank had to practically drag her in the church. "I'm the only one left," she screamed." I thought Rusty would have to drag Reese inside as well. Look at him, stumbling all over the place. I just know he's not drunk, smelling just like a beer garden, slurred voice and he can't barely keep his eyes open. I can't believe this.

Part of the program, before the service began, the pastor requested the family have one last view of the body before closing the casket. Aunt Jane, Rusty, Reese, Barbara, Cece and I went up. I still felt a little dizzy so I gripped the casket. Rusty asks, "Sis, you okay?"

DONNA EARL

"Yeah. 'm fine."

After a few moments, the staff came to close the casket and Aunt Jane almost jumped in. She screamed both her sisters' names.

"Beulah!! Bunch!! Why did you leave me? Why!?"

Her husband and the two male staff members had to hold her back. Reese also chimed in "Momma!!!"

Emotions were raw. Wasn't a dry eye in the place!!!

The last thing I remembered I was at the repast waiting to eat. When I woke up I was in the hospital hooked up to every machine known to man. Michael was over in the corner with his hands in his head.

"What happened?"

Michael rushed over to my side. "You okay?"

"Yeah, what happened?"

"You were eating and the next thing you know you passed out in your food."

I started laughing.

"That's not funny, Ruthie."

Just as he was about to keep ragging on me, Dr. Trimblet walked in.

"Good Morning."

"Good morning, Doctor."

"How's my patient?"

"I'm okay."

"Doctor what's going on?"

She looked at me like she could kill me.

"Well, your wife has a brain tumor that has attached itself to her spinal cord. That's why she having headaches."

"Ruthie, why....?"

"Now Mr. Campbell, there's no need to play the blame game." We need to get your wife well and being here is the first start."

"What happens now?"

"We will perform a surgery called open biopsy. A part of the skull is removed then a sample of brain tissue is removed and viewed under a microscope by a pathologist. If cancer cells are found, some or all of the tumor may be removed during the same surgery. Tests are done before surgery to find the areas around the tumor that are important for normal brain function."

"When is the surgery?"

"We have scheduled tests and surgery for the morning."

Most of the tumor was removed, but a small portion was left because of its location her speech. To remove it would have left her unable to speak. The doctors felt chemo would erase the remainder of the tumor away. The schedule was 3 days on and 4 days off. The treatment took a toll on her body as well as her spirit. When she looked in the mirror, she saw a withered woman who felt so ugly. In Michael's eyes, her opinion didn't matter. He saw the same Ruthie he met and fell in love with and he told her every day. With the chemo eating away at her body, to hear those words, lifted her.

It's been a year since my Mom's death and my brain tumor. The last doctor visit gave me a clean bill of health. "You will need to visit me every 3 months." If you start having any problems, please let me know immediately. She gave me the okay to go back to work and my boss was so glad to see me."

"Ruth!! Welcome back. I'm so glad to see you."

"It feels so good to finally be back...living."

"I see things haven't change since I been gone."

"I see you haven't changed either...still bossy." We both laughed and hugged each other.

Since Mom died, family became even more important. My sisters and brothers, we either met at my house or Aunt Jane's. It's good times, but the air is never the same. I see the changes in both my brothers. Reese, he just seems to wither away every time I saw him. Rusty, he tries to put on a brave face, but he is suffering in silence.

Now for my sisters, Cece she is so different. No trouble at all, in junior high now and doing well. She tells me she wants to be a teacher. Aunt Jane tell me she is always doing something for Ms. Guy and Ms. Harris down at the church. As for Barbara, I don't know what's wrong with her. She's a little too fast for me. Aunt Jane told me she now has a boyfriend at school and she almost had to put her out.

"Chile, I came home early because Frank, you know he's a HVAC man, called and told me he had a service call and he'll be late. So I left work early. So, I get home and walk in the house and this boy named Steven Erics had Barbara laid back on the couch and he's on top of her. Now, Ruthie, you know I like to have had a heart attack. I grabbed the first thing I could get my hands on...my shoes. I beat that boy all around his head and the whole time I'm screaming "damn your soul." Get the hell out of my house!! He ran out the house leaving the door wide open. Then I went on her. I chased that hussy round and round. I really was pissed when I found out that Deda and Frank Jr. were home upstairs all the time. I whooped everybody that day. Ruthie, I told Barbara get your shit and get the f.... I snapped. By that time Frank came home and he talked me out of actually putting her out. That girl..."

"I know Aunt Jane."

It will go away; I just need rest. Tears are flowing down my face. My headaches have come back. Oh please, not again. I kept telling myself, it'll be okay.

"I heard about you, girl."
"What?" Barbara sassed.
"Don't play dumb."
"I'm not."
"Guess what?"
"What?"
"I got invited to the prom."
"Get out!!"
"Yeah. Aunt Jane is threatening not to let me go."
"Why Barbara. What did you do?"
"It don't matter Ruthie. She is always in my ass..."
"Barbara!!!"
"I'm sorry, but she is getting on my nerves. You know she tried to put me out."
"Yeah, I heard."
I stood up, "You need to..." suddenly sweat started forming on my forehead and I started feeling dizzy. I grabbed the end of the table to steady myself.
"Ruthie!!" Barbara shouted with her eyes bugging. Are you alright?"
My eyes were closed and I barely heard her.

"Ruthie?!!!"

"I'm calling the ambulance," Cece screamed.

"No, please"

"You're sick!"

"I know Barbara. I know. Just gimme a minute." I shuffled over to the sink and turned the cold water on and threw some on my face. Then I grabbed a cup and filled it with water and grabbed two aspirin from the bottle in the kitchen cabinet. Once I took them, it seemed to settle my head.

"Ruthie, you got to go to the hospital!"

"NO!!! Sitting down, I said, Listen Barbara." I got choked up trying to get the words out. "I'm leaving y'all soon."

Barbara and Cece both grabbed me. "Don't say that!!"

"It's true. These headache, they are different this time. I'm just fooling myself. Listen, when it's all said and done, I've written down what I want." I went in my purse on the table and pulled out this piece of paper that had been read at least twenty times and handed it to her. Barbara was listening, but silent tears rolled down her face. She unfolded it and read the title.

"NO!!" She tried to give it back.

I pushed it back. "Read it!!"

Cece sat down next to Barbara as they both read it. When they finished, they looked up at me. Barbara said "Ok" as a tear fell from her eye.

GOD is so good. He kept my headaches at bay so that I can at least celebrate another anniversary and see my kids celebrate their birthdays. What I wouldn't give to have more time, but watching my kids and knowing.... I hated to lie to them.

"Mommy are you okay?"

"Yes Julia, Mommy is fine."

We kiss and hug then she goes about her business. Miss 500, I call her.

So here I am again in the doctor's office. Michael insisted I come back here after finding me lying on the bathroom floor crying.

"Ruth, how long have you been having headaches?"

I hung my head down in shame, "for a while."

"How long is awhile?"

Silence.

"Ruth, you should have come earlier. The tumor has grown in size and in order to attack it we have to act aggressively. Why didn't you come earlier?"

"The headaches, they came and went."

My doctor, practically screaming at me, "I specifically told you at your last visit, if you felt ANYTHING, to come and see me immediately."

"Doctor, I…", and then I broke down.

She jumped up and came from around from her desk with tears in her eyes and hugged me tight.

"We are going to win this okay?"

"Okay." By the time we left her office we all were crying.

The chemo is aggressive and it's making me sick.

"Michael, I am so sick."

"Hang in there baby."

"Michael they have been at this for weeks and I don't feel no better."

"Let us pray."

Tears flowing down their faces, they grab each other by the hands and bow their heads.

"Heavenly Father, Michael starts off, "it's your son and daughter coming to you in name of Jesus. You said in your word that by your stripes one is healed. We are standing on your word that GOD, you will restore my wife's body. She is in so much pain." "Restore her Jesus. I am trying to encourage my wife, but I can't do it all by myself. Walk with her and talk with her. In the name of Jesus, Amen."

"Baby I'll be right back. I need to use the bathroom."

He leaves the room virtually crying. He didn't want her to see him crying. His mother is in the other room and sees him in so much distress. She grabs her son and they both cry and rock each other back and forth. Wiping his eyes, Mom, "I can't stand to see her like this."

"I know son, but you got to be strong for her."

Ruthie has taken over the prayer. She is in a zone that is between her and GOD. "Father God, I am ready whenever you want me." I know your work and it's been all good. Restore me Lord. Restore me in the name of Jesus." Ruthie lays her head back on the pillow, resting in the fact she was heard by the Lord. Moments later, Michael came back in the room and finds her unresponsive. He calls, no, he screams her name. "Ruthie! Ruth! Ruth!!!" She can hear him calling, but it's becoming fainter by the second until she can't hear it anymore.

She hears GOD say, "Close Your Eyes My Child. I am here."

Friday…Grace, hope and mercy. I see the KING!!! Beeeeeeep………………..

Stay tuned for Ms. Earl's next book. "Eyes Wide Open." Here's a sneak peek:

The telephone rings again.

"Hello."

"Hey Aunt Jane. This is Cece."

Hearing her voice raised her spirits from her last call. "Lord have mercy." My goodness it's been a while since I've heard from you, Barbara and…. Girl where have you been? What do I owe the pleasure?"

"When I was little, you know how kids are always snooping through things, in things they have no business and I found something. "I hid it in my things and with so much going on at the time I forgot all about it until one day I was searching for something else and ran across it. I thought maybe if I showed it to you that you would be able to explain it."

"Sure. "What is it?"

"I'm not sure. I thought maybe I'd drop by so you can tell me what it's all about."

"Sure baby, anytime."

"I'll see you in a few."

Knock! Knock!

"Hey Cece baby!!! Come on in here and sit down."

"Hey Aunt Jane."

"Want something to eat?"

"No. I've already eaten. I stopped by Barbara's before I came."

"Oh, how's she doing? She feeling alright?" She's aint still mad about the "golden slipper" days is she?

Laughing, "No, she's stop talking about them FINALLY." She's over them." So am I." "You used to tear our butts up. Anyway, she's hanging in there."

"So Missy, what's this you got to show me?"

She hands me a folder. I open it up and I can't believe my eyes.

"This can't be right Aunt Jane can it?" This is a mistake, RIGHT?!!!"

I stare at her with my Eyes Wide Open. Oh Shit…It's Friday again!!

CPSIA information can be obtained
at www.ICGtesting.com
Printed in the USA
LVOW12s2220290916

506790LV00001B/77/P